THE ROTHSCHILD JEWELS

BY

A. TRAURING

This edition published in 2015 by AT Press, Atlanta, Georgia

ISBN 978-0-9915291-6-2

© 2016 AT Press, Atlanta, Georgia
v 5.2

This is a work of fiction. Names, characters, and incidents are products of the author's dubious imagination; all persons and events depicted are fictional. Any resemblance to actual persons living or dead is an unintended coincidence.

While some places depicted may exist in what some refer to as the real world, they are used fictitiously.

Other books by A. Trauring in the Amy & Paul Saga:

A Different Kind of Twin

The Beaded Necklace

The Wedding Fatality

Available at Amazon.com at
http://www.amazon.com/A.-
Trauring/e/B00JCC9RCO/ref=sr_ntt_srch_lnk_1?qid=1427046154
&sr=1-1

Thanks to Sue Sandell for editorial support. Once again, she has made my work into a better book.

Thanks to Shanae Jellick for fictional inspiration.

Thanks to the EPC Book Club for fellowship, good reading, and wonderful support.

Amy and Paul live at
http://atrauring.weebly.com

✄ 1 ✂

Amy and her friend Florence were in the audience for the Crescent City Haute Couture presentation at the Orleans Parish Art Museum. As an exhibitor, Florence was hyper-alert to everything on the catwalk—the way her creations were shown, how her competitors' pieces looked, and the reaction from the audience of area buyers, big couture house representatives, and assorted fashion junkies. Amy did her best to support her friend, but as she was a tomboyish police detective, the novelty of the show had worn off thirty minutes earlier. Instead, she let her dyad Paul evaluate the dozen or so models strutting up and down the runway.

A stunning blonde made another appearance, this time in a purple mini-dress topped by a khaki hybrid between a motorcycle jacket–double-breasted, long sleeves, zippers everywhere–and a vest, abruptly cinched and stopping at her waist. Most notable, Florence whispered, was her size. All fashion models are petite, with not one in a hundred who can be described as 'plus-sized,' suitable for showing off size 12 clothing. The model was not fat, just big. And, as Paul thought to Amy, she was gorgeous.

The woman didn't walk like the other models, either. Instead of putting one foot exactly in front of the other like a driver walking a straight line for a traffic cop, her steps were parallel. This meant her hips did not sway the way they did for the other models, and it came across as a bit clunky. Like all the women, her face was expressionless, staring into the mid-distance. At the tip of the runway she rocked back on one leg to show off the dress, pausing three or four seconds. When she moved to return down the catwalk, she passed another model on her way to the lip of the runway.

And then she fell.

The audience inhaled loudly at the rare sight. Florence half rose at her seat, professional interest mixing with concern for the model's safety. Amy heard Paul think, *Did you feel that? That was way too much for a girl falling.*

She hadn't noticed anything, but then she felt an abrupt vibration in the floor, followed by a low bass tone.

As the model struggled to her feet, supported by the applause of the audience, Amy stood and walked to the side aisle, against the wall that separated the fashion show from the next gallery. The museum itself was closed for the night, with access limited to the Haute Couture event. She tried knobs at two doors but found them locked. At a third, the knob turned. Quickly, quietly, she let herself in and closed the door behind her.

"Cordite!" Paul said out loud. "Somebody's been shooting." She nodded in agreement, then asked, "What's that other smell? It's like metal."

The lighting was dim, since the gallery was closed to the public for the night. A noise from overhead distracted her for a moment, but she saw no movement. Looking back at the ground, she noticed some piles of clothes off to the right, and things sparkling like broken glass on the marble floor. "What have we here?" Paul said aloud as she walked toward the piles. Pieces of broken Plexiglas crunched under their feet.

"No. No," Amy whispered. She bent down beside the prone museum guard and warily felt his neck, but there was no pulse. She saw blood seeping from the top of his head and the place where his jaw once had been. Still crouching, she sidled a few feet away to find the splattered remains of one of the fashion models. Despite the training she had gotten from her surgeon father, she had to work at fighting the urge to vomit. When Amy stood up, she thought to Paul, *Half of her is inside out.*

What a waste, Paul thought. He remembered seeing the model at work a few minutes earlier–a stunning girl with streaked blonde hair, she had had the temerity to smile while on the catwalk. *The Commander warned you, no such thing as an off-duty detective*, he added.

Amy reached under her skirt to find her cell phone, and made the call to her uniformed mentor. "Patrick, it's Detective Clear.

Yes–uh-huh–no, not a social call. Two dead at the Art Museum. I think–What? Of course I'm sure! Would you like me to send pictures?" Paul was smiling inside as he heard how Amy dealt with the disbelieving officer. "Okay, hang on." She took a photo of the mess that had been a model and pushed 'send.' "Just make sure you're done throwing up before you get here."

A moment later she heard Patrick Kowalski say, "Damn! Oh, no. Who did it?"

"Perp unknown, probably still in the building."

"Secure the crime scene," he barked. "I'll have a squad over there in, what, ten minutes."

She returned the phone to one of the holsters under her skirt. "Crap," she said, looking up, thinking. "Two hundred people at the fashion show having a good time. But no telling who the killer is."

She opened the door to let herself back into the couture show to look for museum security people, and was confronted by a huge man wearing a blue blazer, with a bright blue ascot in the open neck of his yellow dress shirt. There were wire-rimmed glasses on his fat face. "What do you think you're doing?" he hissed, and reached for her arm.

Paul used their left hand to pull Amy's badge case out from under her skirt, and he unfurled it. "NOPD," he said. "Let go of me."

"Not until I know what you're doing," he said, pushing her back into the closed gallery.

Amy broke free and said, "This is a police crime scene. You can't–"

"It's my museum," he said, and pushed past her.

"Stop!" she yelled, but he ignored her.

The man was twice Amy's weight and likely twice her age, so she had no trouble catching up and coming around in front of him. Paul barked, "Damn it, I told you to stop!"

"Get out of my way!" he shouted.

Paul used their left foot to kick the man on the side of his knee, and watched him collapse on the floor. He crouched down, knees against the man, and managed to roll him onto his stomach. Amy led as they sat on his back to hold him down. She got the handcuffs from their holster under her skirt. "You are so under arrest," she said as she closed the cuffs on his wrists. "You have the right to remain–"

"Do you know who I am?" he bellowed as he tried to buck out from under her. Amy grabbed him by one ear and twisted it; she said, "You'd be the easiest eight seconds of my life. Yes, I know who you are. You're the asshole who disobeyed an order from a police officer."

The man stopped thrashing. She released his ear. "You going to behave now?"

"My name is Doctor Bradley Richardson," he said. "I'm the Museum Director."

"How about that," she said as she stood up. "I'm Detective Amy Clear. I'm the one who's going to read you your rights. This is a crime scene, and I can't let you just wander around in it."

"Okay. Let me up."

Amy shook her head, but she heard Paul think, *He's the director? He can help us.*

"Maybe," she replied. Then, looking down at Richardson, she said, "What do you know about this?" She waved one arm toward the bodies.

"Tyrone. What a shame–he's been here three years. But, Detective–" he was trying to sit up "–The Rothschild jewels! You've got to find them!" Amy turned to face him, and he continued, "Nearly thirty-four million dollars' worth of gemstones in gold and platinum settings. Exquisite. We have a two-month display in this gallery."

"Do you now," she mused. She gave a wide berth to the two bodies, and found a gallery program near one of the locked doors. She read aloud, "The Rothschild jewels were assembled by Baron James de Rothschild, founder of the French branch of the international banking family. He had them created in 1826 as a gift for his wife, Betty Salomon Von Rothschild, after French King Louis XVIII refused to receive her at court because she was Jewish."

She looked across the room at the remains of the display case. "What was the case made out of? Saran Wrap?"

"One inch Plexiglas acrylic," he moaned. "I should have ordered one-and-a-half inch."

"That's a lot of jewelry," Amy said, "but I'm a little more concerned about two dead bodies lying on your floor."

Paul thought to Amy, *It'll be easy to keep this gallery secure. But we'll need help with that crowd.*

"You're right," she answered aloud. "Richardson, how do I find your security people?" To Paul she thought, *I want a list of every person in that fashion show–performers, techs, audience, everyone.*

"I'll get them," the director said. "Help me up and I'll call."

"No, no, no," she shook her head. even as she heard Paul think, *What? Why not? He can help us!* "What extension? What room? Tell me where they are."

"I said I'll get them," the director said sharply.

She walked back to where he lay on the floor. Amy attempted to lift him by the shirt collar, but she couldn't move his 260 pounds. Instead she leaned toward him and slapped him, open handed, across the face. "You are still under arrest," she hissed. "You're going to lie here until I get a forklift to move you to a holding cell on Rampart Street." Richardson pouted. She thought to Paul, *Can't show weakness. Establish authority fast and don't let go of it.*

Amy hurried back into the fashion show, trying not to alarm the spectators, and darted back to her seat. "I need your help, Florence," she whispered.

"Not now; I'm up in two and a model got lost."

Paul thought directly to Florence, *No joke, Florence. We need your help. Now.*

Florence Draper turned to stare at her friend. She knew about her dyad, Paul; how his mind was transferred into her body when Amy was a child, and how he shared with Amy the creepy ability to send his thoughts into peoples' heads. It had taken a few years for Florence to accept this truth, although she got to like Paul a lot. She realized whatever was going on had to be important, so she followed her friend to the doorway to the other gallery. "You don't want to go in there," Amy said. "There's been two murders, and a ton of jewelry is missing."

Florence had lived through several episodes of Amy consulting the Parish police on crimes in New Orleans, and she understood that Amy now, at long last, was an honest-to-God detective. "You will owe me big time," Florence said. "What do you need me to do?"

"I've arrested the museum director and he's being a jerk. I need building security here. We need a roster of every person inside for the fashion show. That includes spectators, the models, lighting and sound, and everything. My backup is still about ten minutes away."

Florence nodded and ran toward the back of the fashion show gallery, toward the ticket booth. Surely someone there could find security.

Back in the jewelry gallery, Amy said, "My deputy is getting your security here. Do you have an assistant?"

Richardson turned his face away from her and remained silent. She walked over to him and kicked his foot. "Hey! I'm talking to you, Asshole." He shook his body and turned even farther away from her. *Amy, stop!* Paul thought. *If we let him up he'll help us. We don't have to do this all by ourself.*

She shrugged. *Too late*, she thought back, and retrieved her notebook from its under-skirt pocket.

Amy opened it and began a circular search of the gallery. Shattered Plexiglas was everywhere, so she shuffled her feet to push pieces out of her way rather than walk on them and crush them. When she found a shell casing she stopped.

"Hey, Mister Director," she called, "looks like someone shot your guard with a .380." She heard him groan. Amy drew a quick sketch and estimated the position of the spent cartridge. Then she dragged a chair from against a wall and placed it over the empty shell so it wouldn't be disturbed.

Amy shuffled to the side of the pedestal that had held the jewelry display. A few large hunks of Plexiglas remained on top. Paul pulled out their flashlight and they examined the floor around the display. "What do you think?" Amy asked.

Richardson said something, but she ignored him because it was Paul she was talking to. Business-like he said, "Pieces of Lucite scattered evenly in front of the pedestal. If the person who smashed the case had been standing in front of it, there would be footprint shaped places with no debris. And if they walked up to it afterwards, there would be footprint shaped areas of crushed glass."

Amy nodded. "So they were floating over the case."

"Once you have eliminated the impossible," he quoted Sherlock Holmes, "whatever remains, however improbable, must be the truth."

Amy walked toward something big and round leaning against a wall. "What do you think this is?" she said, crouching by the object. It looked like an automobile oil filter, wrapped in duct tape.

"I once made one of these!" Paul said. "It's an improvised silencer. Look–" and he pointed their left index finger at one end, "–that fitting slips over the barrel, and this side–" now at the other end, "–see that hole? That's where the bullet comes out. The one I made was filled with steel wool."

"How did you learn to do that?" she asked, smiling.

Richardson had been muttering where he lay handcuffed. Finally he shouted, "Who the hell are you talking to?"

Laughing, Paul thought to her, *I wasn't always a pillar of the community.*

She walked to the director, then pressed her skirt between her legs and crouched down beside him. "I'm talking to myself. To the other me. You have never known anyone like me, Doctor," pointing at her head.

"You're crazy," he said, eyes wide.

"Whatever."

What did you just do? Paul screamed in her head. *We don't want to get locked up!*

Nuh-uh, she thought back as she stood up, *I think he's scared of me now.*

The door to the gallery opened, and there stood Florence with three museum guards. Amy's friend said, "It's getting strange out here. Mackenzie is missing and now the show doesn't match the printed program. The producer is freaking out."

Amy carefully walked to the door so she could talk to the guards without letting them invade the crime scene. "I'm Detective Clear with NOPD," she said, holding up her badge. "Director Richardson here says you will cooperate with me." They nodded. "My backup team is on its way, but we have to move fast. There are two dead and the jewels are gone."

"No way!" one guard exclaimed.

"I have to assume the perpetrator is still in the museum," she went on. "I want all doors to the outside locked, and we need to get names and contact information for every person in the building.

Deputy Draper and I can't do it ourselves and also secure the crime scene, so I need your help."

Paul continued, "Besides, you're in uniforms. These people are more likely to pay attention to you than us. No one goes out or in except law enforcement, okay?"

One of the guards turned toward Richardson and called, "Boss? That okay with you?"

Amy said, "Doctor Director will spend the night at *Chez Gaol*. You can see him tomorrow during visiting hours. Any questions?"

Yeah, I've got one, Paul thought. *Why are you being such a jerk about this guy?*

"Boss?" the guard repeated.

"Yes, Bob," Richardson replied in a low voice. "We must help the crazy policewoman."

"Okay, then," Amy smiled. "We're all on the same page." She heard Paul blow a silent raspberry. *Who's side are you on?* she thought.

Bob and the other guards set out to secure the fashion show, and Amy let out a sigh of relief.

"Do you need me to help more?" Florence asked. "Andy, the producer, is being a total drama queen, and I don't think he can keep the show going much longer. I want to help him. And find my dresses, damn it."

"Thanks for getting the cavalry," Amy told her. "You probably can get out of here whenever you're done, since the guards think you're a deputy."

"I'll stay with Andy. Thanks. Call me tomorrow and let me know what is going on."

Paul thought to her, *Thanks, Florence.*

"That's so fucking weird," she muttered as she left the room.

Amy resumed her search of the gallery. She found a black shirt button and two cigarette butts, and dutifully marked them on her sketch. "When was the last a janitor came through here?" she asked Richardson.

Sullen, he said, "Five, maybe five-thirty today. Why?"

"Clues may not be from the perp, but at least we know they aren't from today's paying customers."

After awhile Richardson called, "Let me up. I've got to pee."

"Hold it in, big boy," she said, not looking up from scanning the floor, trying to finish a spiral search for clues. "You're going to have to hose this gallery down with bleach anyway, so a little urine won't make any difference." She tried to resume her silent discussion with Paul about the various possibilities the crime scene presented, but he interrupted, *What kind of power trip are you on?*

What do you want me to do? Say 'I'm sorry' and undo his handcuffs?

Well, yeah! That would be a–

"There you are," she heard Officer Patrick Kowalski say as he entered the gallery. "I was wondering–Whew! This place smells like blood."

A smile popped up on Amy's face and she waved. "Come see why." As he began to walk around the edge of the room, looking for a path to get to Amy, she said, "I'm finished with the spiral search. Did you bring a photographer?"

"No," he said, stepping around particularly large pieces of Plexiglas. "Dr. Jermaine is bringing him." When he was standing next to her he said, "Let's see what you've got."

Amy pointed to the guard. "I found a spent shell casing, 380 or 9mm. Looks like he was shot in the top of the head. Dead right there." Kowalski nodded. "Our inside-out fashion model, on the other hand..." They stood about eight feet from what had been the woman's head, as close as they could get without compromising blood spatter evidence.

"Ach." Kowalski flinched. "That's even worse than the picture you sent."

The officer was just over six feet tall, a powerful two hundred pounds. Short black hair in a professional cut showed under the blue police cap. He was in his early forties, with a dimple in his chin that always made Amy smile. He looked up and counted four floors of railings. "Have you been up there yet?"

She shook her head. "Just now finished the search and sketch. Besides, I didn't want to leave my guest of honor alone." She led Kowalski to the handcuffed director.

"Thank God!" he cried, "an adult. That crazy bitch hit me. She slapped me. She attacked me!"

Kowalski let out a hearty laugh. "You're what, six feet tall?

Two hundred fifty pounds? Detective, how tall are you?"

"Five-six," Amy answered, "one hundred nine pounds before I ate dinner tonight."

Still laughing, the officer said, "I can see how she must have terrorized you. Just wait 'til the citizen review board hears about it. Clear, how did you subdue him?"

Paul said, "Sir, kicked him in the knee, Sir."

"Well done, Detective." Then, to the handcuffed man on the floor, "Who are you and what did you do that my detective saw fit to arrest you?"

"I was trying to protect my museum!"

"I ordered him not to interfere with the crime scene and he ignored me."

"I have a duty to the board!" Richardson shouted.

Kowalski squinted. "Who are you again?"

Fighting anger and desperation, he worked at keeping his voice low and steady. "Bradley Richardson. I am the museum director. This is my museum."

The officer put a hand on Amy's forearm and walked her a few steps away. "Can't you let him go?" he whispered. "He's not going to make any more trouble."

Yeah, she heard Paul agree.

"If I release him, he'll never listen to an officer again. I mean, Pat, he's wearing an ascot, for God's sake."

The officer shook his head, but turned back to the museum official. "Don't leave them lying down," he said sternly. "Every now and then one has apnea or throws up and then suffocates. Prop 'em up against a wall." The director's mouth dropped open.

"He must be twice my weight. I couldn't budge him. You try."

"Hey! HEY!" Richardson yelled when the officer took him by the shirt collar and dragged him to the wall. "I see what you mean," Kowalski told her.

"This isn't just about the guard and the model, Pat." She turned toward Richardson. "You want to tell him about the jewels?"

The director said, "Officer, you have to find them. There was almost thirty-four million dollars in antique jewelry in this gallery. It's gone."

Kowalski whistled. "Insured?"

"Yes," the director said sadly, "but inland marine coverage is like nailing Jello to a wall. The company's going to drive us crazy with an investigation."

"How crazy can they drive you?" Amy interrupted. "Looks like you'll be safe and warm in a twelve by twelve cell."

"Now, now, Detective," Kowalski said. They bent down beside the museum director. "Let me show you something." The uniformed cop pointed to the metal handcuffs on the man's wrists. "If you hold it like this," cradling the cuff's receiver in his left palm, "and you push like this," slamming down on the hinged, toothed arc with his right, "you can get them a lot tighter. Let's go look upstairs." While Richardson shouted in humiliation, the two police officers rose. "Which way to the elevator?" Kowalski asked. The answer was just a moan. Amy said, "Never mind, we'll find it."

"We convinced him you mean business," Kowalski whispered as they stepped away. "Next time, maybe mean a little less business." Paul silently added, *I told you!* Amy pouted inside and thought to Paul, *Five years as a consultant, but this is my first case on the NOPD. Give me some slack, damn it!*

To reach the lobby and elevators, they had to leave the Rothschild jewels gallery and go through the area where the fashion show was taking place. Had been taking place, but now chaos reigned. The house lights had been turned up, and two hundred annoyed people were milling around and shouting. The three museum guards were using clipboards, writing down names and contact information for everyone, and then ordering people to "...stand over there, by the Sergeant." One of Kowalski's uniformed officers was keeping order. Amy waved at Florence and said to Patrick, "I came here with a designer friend, but she's trying to help the producer."

"Let's talk to her. Oh, wait," and he turned toward one of his sergeants. "Mullinax!" He pointed to the unlocked door that led to the crime scene. "Make sure the guy in custody doesn't pull a Houdini."

Florence was hugging the show producer, Andy. Between sobs he was crying, "Why do you hate me, God? What did I ever do to you?"

"Uh, how's it going?" Amy asked.

"Don't ask," Florence replied. "Andy's losing it, the sponsors want their money back, the missing model's roommate is freaking out, the lighting people want to get paid–" she looked up. "Typical fashion show. And you?"

Amy introduced her to Kowalski. "The missing model," Amy asked, "who is she?"

"Mackenzie Slaton," Florence said. "Her roomie is the big girl that fell, Savannah Walsh. What happened?"

"I'm not sure, but your–what's her name? Mackenzie? She's dead."

Andy stopped in mid breath. "Did you say–dead?"

Out came the notebook. "I'll find you upstairs later," Amy told the officer, then began asking Andy for his contact information. "When did Mackenzie disappear?"

"Who knows?" Andy cried. "We didn't notice she was gone until she was up next and wasn't at her mark."

"What time was that?"

"I don't know!" he shouted, and began sobbing again. Florence said to her, "Easy, he's kind of melting down."

Amy nodded. "Sorry to have to pester him at a time like this, but it's police business. Look, Florence. You get me the contact information for Mackenzie and her roommate."

"I don't know where their place is," Andy said. "I guess Savannah is still here somewhere, the assholes in blue aren't letting anyone leave. Uh, excuse me."

"Yes, that's us," Amy smiled. Then, to Florence, she said, "Find the roommate and get an address. I'll visit her tomorrow."

When Amy got to the elevator, Kowalski was in front of it, talking to several of his squad and the head of museum security. He was giving the police instructions on how to release the fashion show people when everyone's contact information had been recorded. "Then we start on museum staff. Volunteers, too."

A sergeant nodded, and the group dispersed.

"Did you find anything up there?" Amy asked.

"Fontenot and them grabbed me before I could go. Uh, Detective Clear, this is Logan Spong, he's in charge of museum security." He was a thin, wirey young man in black pants and a plaid flannel shirt, and with the hint of a goatee. They shook hands.

"I hope you can help us," Amy said.

While the elevator took them up, it was Paul who asked, "What usually happens on the fourth floor?"

"Nothing," Spong answered, "especially after hours. Sometimes an exhibit will be so large we'll go up there, but that's rare. We have some overflow offices up there. Huh—we don't hardly use them, either."

The car went 'ding!' and the door opened to the fourth floor. There was a walkway about seven feet wide that went around three sides of the building. The carpet was a mottled rust and yellow. The railing was made of three wide round tubes.

Amy stepped to the railing and looked down four flights to the two bodies spread on the marble. Medical Examiner Jermaine Tallant was working on what was left of Mackenzie Slaton, while the photographer was documenting the guard's body *in situ*, and working on framing pictures. Paul asked, "How long would it have taken her to fall?"

"Thirty-two feet per second per second," Spong said. "We're sixty feet up." He shrugged. "Less than two seconds."

Paul responded, "I'll bet that felt like forever." He heard Amy think back, *Not nearly long enough.*

They walked to the section from where it seemed Mackenzie Slaton had fallen, where the walkway dead-ended into a wall. Sitting neatly by a stainless steel trash canister were a cell phone and a small black purse. When Spong leaned toward them, Amy grabbed his arm and said, "No. We need pictures first." Turning to the officer, she said, "Is that Lawson down there with the doctor?" Kowalski took out his phone and turned away.

"What's above this?" Amy asked Spong, looking up at the dim ceiling.

"The usual. Duct work, insulation. We have a flat roof; that's where the air conditioning is."

She continued to look up while Spong spoke. Paul had turned on their flashlight. Finally she looked at the security chief and said, "Are those skylights?"

"Lawson'll be up in a few minutes," Kowalski said, closing his phone. To Spong he explained, "He's the photographer. We try not to touch anything until we've got pictures."

He nodded, then turned back to Amy. "Yes, skylights. They make a huge difference during the day. We save a lot on our power bills."

Paul pursued the thought. "Do they open? Easily?"

"I know they open, but I don't know how easy. I've never tried."

Paul pointed to a door marked 'Janitorial.' "Ladder?"

Spong went to unlock the door, but found it wasn't fastened. There was a ten foot painter's ladder against one wall.

"I knew it!" Amy said. "We want prints from this." Kowalski scribbled in his notebook, nodding. "And if someone opened that skylight, who did they let in? How did they get there? Spong, how do we get up to the roof?"

The photographer, Lawson, joined them, following Spong up the emergency stairway.

Amy and Paul looked at the New Orleans sky. The multi-colored lights of the Central Business District and the Vieux Carré cast soft blue and yellow and red against some low clouds, diffused by summer humidity. "Smells good," Paul offered, "like trees." He felt the skin on their arms relax in the warmth after the goose-bump air conditioning inside the museum. He heard Amy think, *It looks so normal out here. I like normal.*

The security head cautioned, "Keep to the parapet path or the stepping stones. Otherwise you'll tear the roof membrane."

"Lawson, let's see that klieg light." She took the portable flood from him and aimed it at the top of the skylight that was above the landing where Mackenzie had left her purse.

"We got handprints," Kowalski said, leaning toward the closed glass. "I'll dust it." After he laid out his fingerprint supplies he leaned over the skylight. "Hey!" he exclaimed, "It's not locked."

Amy gave the light back to the photographer, then used Paul's flashlight to examine the inside of the parapet. There were scrape marks a few inches below the top of the wall.

What have we here? Paul thought, while Amy turned the light to both sides to see if there were other anomalies. "Why would a snake be up here?" Amy asked aloud. She heard the officer laugh, but Paul leaned forward to take a closer look, moving the flashlight this way and that. *What?* he thought to her. *That thing? That's not a snake.*

Amy stood straight and called, "We got something!" Lawson and the security director began to turn, trying to see it, when Kowalski barked, "Hold the damn light! I'm almost done." Spong came over and sniffed, "Small thing." Amy slapped his hand when he reached for the object, and said, "Pictures first." He looked down but backed away.

When Kowalski finished lifting the skylight prints, he came to view Amy's find. "Looks like a giant fish hook," he said. He knelt closer, careful not to touch it. "I think, maybe, this was part of a grappling hook. This fluke broke off." The officer took the portable spotlight so Lawson could take pictures of the discarded tool.

"Let me think," Paul said out loud. "The scrapes on the parapet–they'd be from the claw the perp used to get up here from the street. Then–" Paul was looking up, drumming their fingers on their chin as he thought "–more marks by the skylight; that must be how he got down. And then this guy here," pointing at the broken tool, "it must have broken off when the killer was leaving."

"Okay," Kowalski offered, tentatively.

"But the broken hook," Amy said. "Maybe when it snapped, that's how Mackenzie fell?"

"Even so–" the officer began.

"Nah, couldn't be," Paul interrupted. "It's by the parapet, so it broke when he left. Any signs where he put stuff down? He would have had the gun he used to shoot the guard. And a zillion dollars worth of jewelry. I'd say his hands were full."

"May I?" Kowalski asked. Amy turned to look at him. She thought to Paul, *Let him talk*, then nodded at the officer. "What you say is plausible, Detective. But just because it's the first thing you thought of doesn't mean it's the right answer. And don't make the mistake of assuming our murdering thief is a man. Maybe—but maybe not."

Amy smiled. "Wise counsel, Officer. Thank you." She paused and added softly, "I'm glad you're here."

Kowalski was shocked at the compliment. Police investigation, even when the team included women, tended to be adversarial and competitive. He didn't remember the last time a co-worker told him something so supportive. He had worked with Amy in the years when she was a consultant, but this was the first job they had shared since she had been sworn in. It occurred to Kowalski that he just might be ready to walk through walls for her. A bit embarrassed, the officer nodded and looked down.

"Lawson, you got those pictures?" Amy called. He grunted in agreement. She stretched out a latex glove and pulled it over her right hand. Careful not to disturb any evidence that might be on it, she lifted the discarded hook. "I think we're done up here," she announced. "Spong, get us back to earth."

On the elevator ride down, Amy asked, "Isn't there an alarm system?"

"Sure," Spong said. "As soon as the doors are locked, we turn it on."

Kowalski said, "So, since the museum was open for the fashion show..."

"That's right. The alarm wasn't on."

The elevator dinged as they passed another floor. Paul asked Spong, "How about video surveillance?"

"Ten zones, each with two to five cameras," he said. "In each zone, the view rotates through all the cameras. Maybe fifteen or twenty seconds per camera. And it's all captured on computer hard drives."

Paul heard Amy think, *Oh, I get it.* She took the lead to add, "How many cameras cover the gallery where the jewels are? Uh, were."

"Two or three, I think."

"And how about the fourth floor where we found the purse?"

"Two."

"Great. Let's look at them."

Spong glanced at his watch; it was 2:15 AM. He grimaced and said, "There's a fair amount of setup I need to do. The files are kept at a secure remote site." Desperation and exhaustion showed in his face. "Can it wait until noon?"

"Sure!" she said. "We'll meet you here at eleven." As they got off the elevator, she heard Paul and Kowalski laugh, and she thought she saw Spong roll his eyes.

Amy led them all into the main gallery to see if Jermaine was still working on the bodies. He was gone, as were the corpses, although the blood, not entirely dry, remained. Kowalski muttered, "This place is going to stink by tomorrow."

"Hey! Hey you, detective bitch!"

They all looked around to see Bradley Richardson in handcuffs, leaning against the wall, in the remains of a yellow puddle. She thought to Paul, *Oh no! I forgot about him!*

This is going to be trouble, he thought back. *Better charge him with something.*

"Yes, that's me," she said. She took Kowalski by the elbow and led him to the fuming museum director. "Come on, let's get you cleaned up. You've got a date with the night court judge." She helped the officer lift him up.

"For what?" he shouted.

"For disobeying police orders," she stuck out the index finger of their right hand. "For interfering with a crime scene," their middle finger now extended. Their ring finger joined the count as she added, "And for being a jerk. Officer, did I leave anything out?"

"Public urination?" he grinned. "Let me turn him over to the sergeant. Come on, big fellah, this way," and he led the man out of the room.

Amy dismissed the photographer, then told Spong she wanted one last look at the jewelry gallery before she left. "I'll see you at eleven," he said, and left her alone.

She leaned against the back wall, opposite the pedestal where the jewelry had been on display. Halfway between them was the drying dark red sea of blood that had been Mackenzie Slaton's life force. "All those years dad took me to his emergency room," she whispered to Paul. "All those dying and dead people. Nothing prepared me for this."

She felt Paul nod. After a few moments, he thought to her, *We can always go back to doing market research, like before the police hired you.*

Amy shook her head. "No way. This matters too much."

They stood silently, the two people in the one body. Amy slowly rubbed her right hand up and down their left arm—by their convention, Paul's arm. "Was it awful?" she asked him.

"No!" he said quickly. "I've always hated cops, been scared of police. But this—the thinking, the brain work. And whoever did this cannot be allowed to live unpunished. I hope I've run my last Z-score."

"Who are you talking to?" Kowalski asked as he came looking for Amy. "And what's a Z-score?"

"I talk to myself a lot," she smiled. "And I answer me, too, so don't freak out about it."

He nodded blandly. "So, now what are you going to do?"

"Me, I'm going to get in my car, roll up the windows, and scream. You?"

"I was thinking more along the lines of a beer and dinner," he said.

Amy inhaled sharply, which caught her by surprise. But she shook her head and said, "I was here for two hours before I called you. I'm wiped out, and I'll be busy tomorrow with that Spong guy and the girl's roommate."

They stood awkwardly for a moment. Then Amy looked up at the officer, pain on her face. "That woman was the only model who smiled during the fashion show. She was skinnier than me, she was prettier than me, and she acted like she owned the place. And, and then–" she stopped and swallowed "and then she was a puddle in here." She shook her head and said, "I really have some screaming to do tonight. I'll see you tomorrow, Pat. Thanks again for your help."

The officer nodded, and quietly walked with Amy through the nearly empty gallery. Some technicians with tattoos and long hair were disassembling what was left of the fashion show catwalk, while a uniformed sergeant was talking to the three museum guards. He held open the only unlocked door, and Amy began to make her way home through the New Orleans night.

❡ 2 ❦

In the morning Amy called her friend Florence.

"What a disaster," the woman said. "Andy cried all night. He's convinced his reputation is ruined."

"Why would anyone hold it against him that somebody broke into the museum to steal from an exhibit?"

"Ah, you're being sensible. He's not. But he's my friend and he needs some more hand-holding."

Amy heard Paul think, *She's a good friend.* Then Amy got down to business: "Did you talk to the big girl?"

Florence dictated the address, a loft in the Central Business District. "Savannah is a nice girl," she volunteered, "but she's not exactly Stephen Hawking. She's afraid whoever killed Mackenzie will come for her next."

"Huh! That will be an interesting line of inquiry. I'm going to be busy for a few days. Let's have dinner next week, okay?"

Once they were in Amy's old blue sedan, on the way to the museum, Paul said, "I want to call Christine."

"Okay. I'll drive, you talk."

"Paulette! You're alright!"

"You bet, sweetie."

"It was all over the news when I got home," Christine said. "I even saw you in the background a few times. Is Amy okay?"

"I'm just peachy," Amy answered.

Christine was Paul's girlfriend. His lesbian girlfriend, who knew he was a man, but still referred to him as Paulette. Although medication now kept her stable, she was schizophrenic and used to hearing voices. This seemed to be the reason she was so calm about Amy and Paul's dyad existence. Amy had learned to tolerate the physical part of their relationship, and had grown quite fond of the woman herself. Paul–still a man, even after fifteen years encased in Amy's female body–was crazy about Christine.

"I'm so glad you're okay," the woman said. "I didn't call. I figured Amy would be busy, so I called Gina and made her talk to me for an hour until I calmed down."

"It's good you two stayed friends," Paul said about Christine's former girlfriend. "Look, we're on our way back to the museum, Amy's got to look at surveillance tapes, and then we're going to interview the dead girl's roommate. Amy, any guess when we can get together with Christine?"

There was a pause while Amy tried to imagine her schedule. It was Friday. Jermaine wouldn't complete the forensics testing until next week, but there was all that laundry... Finally she said, "Christine? It's Amy. How–"

"Hi, Amy. Solve the case yet?" It always was a pleasant surprise to both of them that Christine was never unsettled by the way they changed places.

"Not yet, but soon, I hope. Can we visit on Sunday? I know what Paul's like if he doesn't get his minimum daily requirement of Christine."

"That'll be great! There's a neighborhood festival near me; we can go. I'll make dinner?"

"It's Paul. You had me at 'hello.' See you around noon then?"

There was a noise behind Christine's voice. "Uh oh, phone ringing, I gotta go. See you Sunday. I love you, Paulette!"

By the time Paul said, "I love you, too," the line was dead.

"Thanks," he said out loud in the safety of the car. "We'll have a good time."

"Yes, we will. You know, I had my doubts about her when you met her–"

Paul laughed inside. "I know. You had to get drunk before I could sleep with her."

"She's a delight," Amy said with a smile. "She's the big sister I never had."

As they drove closer to the museum, Amy said, "I have to call the roommate. What's her name, Charleston? Augusta? Metairie?"

"Savannah," Paul corrected. "Great stage name for a model. I wonder what her parents call her."

When they were parked in the museum deck, Amy called the woman. She heard a tired "hello" and introduced herself. "I'd like to visit you this afternoon and ask you about last night."

"Bring a bottle of bourbon," she said.

"Uh, I'll be on duty."

"I won't."

They set three o'clock to meet, and went over parking advice.

As Amy went through the stairways and elevators to the museum, Paul thought, *What do you think? Grief? Or alcoholic?*

A shrug of indifference. "Both, maybe." It was not her problem. "Now, let's see what the surveillance videos have to say."

Logan Spong and Officer Kowalski were waiting in the museum lobby. In the jewelry gallery, a service company was cleaning and disinfecting the leftovers of the night before. She glanced at her watch and saw they all were early; no need to apologize even though she was the last to arrive. "Good morning," she said. Then, to Spong, "Coffee?"

"Half a pot left in Security. Come on."

As they walked to the security suite, Amy asked Kowalski, "What happened to Doctor Director?"

"Judge accepted interfering with a crime scene investigation, but let him out on personal recognizance."

Spong volunteered, "He called to say he wouldn't be in today, and I should, uh, tell you, Detective, that he's sending his dry cleaning bill to NOPD."

"Oh, come on, tell me what he called me." She was smiling.

"Uh, okay. He called you 'that crazy queen bitch from hell.'"

"Not bad," Amy said, "somewhat creative and fairly accurate. Good. Where's the coffee?"

Holding the Styrofoam cup Spong gave her, Amy sat beside him at the seventeen-inch computer monitor, while Kowalski rolled a chair to sit behind them. His notebook was open to a blank page.

"Let's start with the jewels," Amy said. Spong went through some menus, and brought up an image of the Rothschild jewels in the Plexiglas display case. Although she had seen the photo that was part of the gallery program, she was not prepared for the comprehensive video unfolding from the security hard drive.

Behind the insufficient Plexiglas casing were half a dozen tiaras, each with matching earrings and extravagant necklaces and brooches. Every piece glittered with faceted diamonds and emeralds and rubies, punctuated with pearls, lapis, and sapphires. The program had said the ornate settings were a mixture of silver, gold, and platinum. Thirty four million dollars worth of luxury.

After fifteen seconds the image changed to a different angle, with the jewels still in the center of the screen. Then they saw a large shape fall into and out of the picture. "Wait!" she called. "Back that up and go slow."

The security man clicked away at the keyboard. Now they saw a slow motion replay of a body–they knew it had to be Mackenzie Slaton's–falling into the top of the frame. The figure was mostly face up, head a little lower than the rest. Every time Spong pressed an arrow key the image changed slightly, the body moving down, through the main part of the screen, and finally out the bottom of the image. The last thing they saw of Mackenzie was a finger from her left hand.

"Time stamp!" Amy called. The image rewound until Mackenzie first appeared, and Spong said, "Eight thirty-six and twenty-three seconds." Kowalski wrote it down.

The security chief restored the normal playback speed. About ten seconds later they saw feet appear at the top of the screen. Someone was rappelling down a nylon rope, gradually revealing a pistol in an outstretched right hand—and then an abrupt burst of flame from its muzzle; what looked like a tin can flew off the gun and out of the frame. The figure was clothed in black; when the head was revealed, it was covered with a ski mask.

The view changed to the other camera. The figure holstered the pistol while swaying slightly on the rope. It seemed to twist, turning its back to the camera as it faced the jewelry display. They saw black gloved hands touch the Plexiglas display. The right hand disappeared, hidden by the torso.

Another shift in view. The right hand was holding a collapsible baton. A flick of the wrist and it was extended. The person on the rope pushed itself away from the display, then made two rapid strikes on it with the baton. The display was obscured by a sudden cloud of Lucite dust.

The other camera picked up and showed the remains of the Plexiglas on the pedestal. The body obscured the hands, which Amy guessed were stuffing jewels into pockets. The body still swayed on the rope; the person's feet had never touched the ground. They saw the figure begin to rise, and the switch in camera angle showed a few seconds of legs and feet disappearing out of the top of the frame.

It was Paul who said, "I hope Jermaine took some of the Plexi pieces to examine. Looks like the case was made out of window glass."

"You'd be surprised how much force you can generate with an extended baton," Kowalski said. "That's why police got rid of night sticks."

"Okay," Amy offered, "we see Mackenzie fall, and a few seconds later the person I will hereby label as the killer descends. We see him, her, or it fire a pistol, I assume at the guard, and in less than a minute he, she, or it is leaving with almost thirty-four million dollars in jewelry." She heard Paul think, *Sweet!*

She turned to Spong, "Can we look at the fourth-floor cameras now?"

He worked his keyboard, and they watched a graphic of a big hourglass with the legend "Loading..." He said, "We'll start at eight twenty-five, okay?" A dim picture emerged of Mackenzie Slaton leaning against the wall where they found her purse and phone. Her cell phone was pressed against her ear. They could see her mouth moving.

"Do you have sound on this system?" Amy asked.

Spong shook his head. "Does any CCTV system have sound? You'd need microphones."

"Damn! I wish I knew what she was saying. And who she was saying it to."

Paul thought, *To whom she was saying it. She was so pretty, what a waste.* He was taken by the long blonde hair that needed brushing, the tiny nose, and the loooong body.

"Jermaine's got the phone. He'll find out who she was talking to," said Kowalski.

The camera angle changed but still showed Mackenzie on the phone. She was smiling as she talked, and laughing. Several camera cuts showed the ongoing conversation, so Amy got up and refilled her coffee. She ran back to the monitor when Kowalski called, "Here we go!"

The woman closed her phone, bent over, then reappeared with her hands free. She walked to the janitorial closet and pulled out the painter's ladder they had seen last night. She looked up, then opened the ladder and started up.

The next camera angle displayed her from the knees down, standing near the top rung. Shadows were flickering as if something was moving above her. "I wish we could hear!" Amy hissed. They watched the model step back down the ladder, then fold it away in the closet.

The point of view shifted again. A person slowly dropped into the picture as Mackenzie looked up, smiling. "What's the time stamp?" Paul asked. Spong looked at a tiny window in the corner of the screen and said "Eight thirty-four and change." Amy thought that the model was two minutes away from her death.

The figure on the rope swayed slightly. The ski mask kept them from knowing if the person was talking, but they could see Mackenzie was smiling and seemed to be talking. When their heads were level, the woman threw her arms around the person. Their conversation went on long enough for the camera to shift once more.

Slowly the figure on the rope began to sink, rappelling down. Mackenzie kept her hold on the masked person, and as the figure disappeared out of the bottom of the picture, her legs came up and she slid over the railing. The camera view changed again and displayed an empty area.

"Eight thirty-six eighteen," Spong volunteered.

They sat in silence for three minutes and 42 seconds, until the top of the ski mask crept into the bottom of the image on the computer monitor. Amy used her right index finger to poke the security chief in the back of his hand and said, "Stop. Time check?"

"Eight forty exactly."

As the playback resumed, the perpetrator slowly climbed upward. They could see the pistol in its holster. The figure stopped when it was even with the fourth floor railing, resting both hands on the top metal tube and sliding them to the right. "Wait!" Paul called,

"Stop!" Kowalski sat up, dropping his pen to the floor. "The hands," Paul said, sounding like Amy, "can you zoom in on them?"

"You watch too much TV," Spong said. "I can make the picture a little bigger, but we'll lose resolution."

"Do it."

As the image was magnified, the officer asked, "What is it?"

"Something about the left hand," Paul said. "Look–" pointing to the screen "–the ring finger. The tip is fatter than the rest of it." Then, to the security man, "Go forward, but slow." He heard Amy think, *I don't see anything,* and he thought back silently, *Let's see.*

A few frames later Paul barked, "Stop!" He peered into the monitor. "Pat, do your fingers bend like that?"

The officer leaned forward. The end knuckle of the left ring finger was bent backwards. "Not without a lot of pain," he said. "Maybe the hand isn't all the way in the glove."

"Possible," Paul responded, "but look–the part that's bent, it looks fat. Full of something."

After a few seconds it was Amy who said, "Ah, but not full of finger. Let's look at some more."

Spong advanced the video frame by frame while all six eyes in the room watched the glove. The intruder moved its hands along the railing, and the bent fingertip never collapsed. After resting a moment, the figure resumed its upward motion. As the last view of its black shoes reached the top of the image, Amy asked for another time stamp.

"Eight forty-two and seven seconds."

Amy slapped her thighs and stood up. "Burn me a DVD, maybe I can see more on the PD equipment. You know, when I went into the gallery last night I thought I heard something overhead, but I didn't see anything. Maybe it was our killer closing the skylight when he was done. Or she," she added when she saw Kowalski prepare to speak.

He smiled at her consideration of the point he'd raised the night before. "What do you think is the deal with the finger?"

"I don't know," Amy said honestly. "It's just—it's just wrong."

While Spong attended the computer, Amy and Patrick discussed a time line. "I'll call Jermaine this afternoon to see what he's got today," Amy said, "and what he thinks he'll get to on

Monday. God, I want to know who she was on the phone with up there–it just may be our killer."

Nodding, the officer said, "After seeing the video, we don't need prints from the ladder. It might be worth our while to go over the top of the rail up there."

"You've got a kit in the prowler, right? Dust it. Just promise me you won't fall over the railing."

Paul picked up the conversation. "We're going to interview the roommate in a little while. I have to stop at Walgreen's and get some bourbon."

"Are those two things related?"

"Actually, yes. We called her to make an appointment, and she told us to bring bourbon."

Kowalski tilted his head and squinted. "Permission to speak freely?"

Amy took the lead. "What are you talking about, Kowalski? We're both Officer IIIs. What?"

He looked around, as if to make sure no one would overhear him. "'We'? 'Us?'"

Paul! she shouted silently. *Please stop doing that.* Out loud she said, "We. Us. You and me, Pat, you and me."

"I've got other things on my plate today, so it's just you," he responded. Then, "Getting suspects or informants drunk is not considered a professional way to get information."

"Oh!" Amy said, surprised. "No, that's not—I mean, it's not to get information. The booze is the price of admission."

He squinted at her again, not sure if she was being honest.

"Here's your DVD," Spong said as he handed her the disc in a paper sleeve.

"Great. Do me a favor, don't erase last night from your hard drive. Just in case we need to see more."

Amy and Patrick walked to the parking deck together, still discussing plans for dealing with the forensics they would get the following week. "Do you get a weekend?" he asked. She felt her pulse quicken.

"Of course. Laundry, and spending time with a buddy and his girl friend. You?"

"My weekend is Tuesday and Wednesday," he said. They

walked to Amy's blue sedan. "You know I can get called on other cases."

"Me too," she said, thinking of the multiple jobs the detective who began training her sometimes handled. "Maybe Ramirez will think two dead and almost thirty-four million dollars gone deserve a dedicated team." She unlocked the driver's door. "I'll see you at the station house on Monday."

He nodded. He stood there until Amy had started her engine and began to drive off, then headed for his black-and-white.

✆ 3 ✇

"Why can't you damn Cajuns talk American?"

Beau Sonnier replied, in carefully annunciated syllables, "Just call me George Fucking Washington. What the hell you want, hey?"

"I need you two to return a favor. You know how I sell those car parts you 'find'? I got something I need you to sell for me."

"I dunno, do we have the contacts for it? Why don't you sell it, man."

"I can't, you got to."

Beau Sonnier sighed. He was on the phone with a professional associate, someone he met while he and his brother were serving three years at Angola for car theft. Usually the man was an agreeable enough colleague, although Beau heard stories about drunken tirades from the man's daughter. The daughter who had returned the attention of Beau's younger brother. "What you got, then?"

"I found a pistol."

"No way!" Beau shouted. "Darius and me keep a low profile. Just touching a gun puts us back in Angola."

"I need you to sell this gun."

"Shit. We don't know no one what wants a gun."

"Find someone. Otherwise your brother doesn't get into my Belle anymore."

It wasn't the first time Beau thought that his associate just might be a little bit insane. The daughter was eighteen now, out of school, working, and living in the Sonier's second bedroom with Beau's younger brother Darius. But the affair had begun two years earlier, and this associate, who was Belle's father, sometimes forgot time had marched on. "Yah," Beau protested, "Like when she still lived at home and you told her she couldn't see him no more?"

"Just sell the fucking gun. Get as much as you can for it. And you better clean it first."

"Clean it? What you do with it?"

"You don't want to know, coon-ass. Just sell it." And the associate hung up.

Beau Sonnier put the phone back in his pocket and looked across his back yard in Marrero. He and his brother took advantage of the job training in prison and learned to stay under law enforcement radar. They were succeeding in fitting in with the normal people, keeping their extracurricular petty thefts hidden from their neighbors. The brothers were tent-masters for a traveling circus that was due to leave for Tulsa on Wednesday. Sell a gun, what a perfect job for a two-time felon. But Beau knew that his brother Darius was attached to the sad-eyed girl with messy hair and full lips. They'd sell the damn gun. They'd find someone in Tulsa who wanted it.

❧ 4 ❧

Amy made a stop at the Walgreens near where Rampart crossed Tulane Avenue. *It never ceases to amaze me,* Paul thought to her, *that you can buy liquor from a drugstore. We had ABC stores in West Virginia when I learned to drink.*

As she walked to the section for alcohol, she thought, *What's a decent brand of bourbon?*

Hirsch. Four Roses. Stagg.

She found them and blanched at the price. "Hey, this is an admission ticket, not a tithe," she said aloud. "How about, uh... Early Times? We can afford it."

He looked at the label. *Kentucky Whisky, that's bourbon. 80 proof? We're good.*

Paul led to drive from the City Park area into the warehouse district where Savannah Walsh lived. Driving was one of the activities he missed most from the days when he had his own body and led his own life. It was common for them to talk out loud in the privacy of the car. "How do we give her the bourbon?" she asked.

"Tell her you want to talk a bit and then you'll give it to her. Florence said the girl's not too bright. We don't need her to get smashed while we're pumping her for information."

The model lived in a converted loft on Notre Dame at Tchoupitoulas, with its own convenient parking lot. Amy walked up a flight of stairs to the building atrium, holding her notebook and a small brown bag with the required 750 milliliter tribute. The atrium extended three floors to a glassed-over dome. There were several abstract sculptures in childlike bright yellow and red.

S, S, S... hey, no Slaton, Paul thought. Amy looked at the directory and spotted Walsh, Vanna, C-201. She mashed the button.

When the vestibule door buzzed, she went inside to the elevator lobby.

Vanna? Paul mused. *Her parents liked 'Wheel of Fortune'?*

"I don't understand," Amy said as they got off on the third floor and found the right apartment. "I thought it was bad to depend on luck."

Paul was saying "What?" out loud as Savannah Walsh opened the door with a big smile on her face.

"You're the detective," she said, before Amy could identify herself. "I saw you last night; you were with that hunk of a policeman. Come in, please." She stepped back so Amy could enter.

Paul was captivated. Savannah was an inch shorter than he–Amy–was, and weighed fifteen or twenty pounds more. She was blonde, with heavy eye makeup. Now that she wasn't on a runway, Paul saw the most striking thing about her was her broad smile, white teeth, and large blue eyes. *If I didn't love you,* he thought to Amy, *If I didn't love Christine, I would fall down on my knees and pledge eternal fealty to this animal.*

Amy flinched at the thought.

They walked down a long hallway to a brightly lit living room. When they reached it, Amy saw the light was from four floor-to-ceiling windows that opened on the startling sight of the Riverwalk, and Algiers across the Mississippi River. "That's quite a view," Amy offered. Silently she thought to Paul, *This place must be three grand a month.*

"Did you bring it?" the woman said.

Amy sat without asking permission, facing a side wall so she would not be blinded by the lighted window. "Sure, but first let's talk some." She patted the table next to where she sat.

Savannah came around to sit opposite. *Damn,* Paul thought. He turned sideways in the chair to offset the unfortunate confrontational seating arrangement.

"Have you caught the guy yet?" Savannah asked. "He's coming for me next, you know."

"You say that like you know who did it. Why—"

"Hunter," she said emphatically. "He's Mac's friend from back home. He's jealous."

Amy opened her notebook on the table, thinking, *Hot damn!*

Let's wrap this case up right now.

But Paul jumped to the lead and said, "We'll come back to that in a minute. First I want to find out about you. I think you are stunning, but you don't look like a typical anorexic fashion model." Silently Amy shouted, *No!* "How did you become a model? What work do you do?" *Oh, for crying out loud! Paul, let me talk!*

He thought back, *In the words of Amy Clear, shush! I'm busy.*

It's not just law enforcement who stoke a person's vanity in order to get them to do what all people want to do, which is to talk about themselves.

"My mother was Miss South Texas before she got married," the model began. "She put me in a contest when I was sixteen. I won a scholarship to an acting and modeling school, and a contract with Select in Houston." Her eyes were wide and so was her smile. "So I dropped out of high school, I left my boyfriend, and Mom and I moved to be near the agency. I filled out pretty fast—not just on top, but everywhere. Next thing I knew, I was at shoots three days a week for catalog jobs. You probably saw me if you shop at Nordstrom or Macy's or TJ Maxx. I was in their print ads."

"Made decent money?" Paul asked.

"I made tons of money!" she squealed. "Those jobs pay great. And there aren't a lot of women as big as me competing."

Amy took notes with their right hand while she let Paul continue his line of questioning, silently muttering, *You'd better solve this, dammit.* Savannah squinted momentarily, wondering how Amy could write and talk at the same time, but she quickly was distracted by the next question. "When did you come to NOLA? And why?"

"It's so silly, I know. I had all the work I could handle and more money than I ever hoped for, but–" she shrugged "–it's fashion work that counts. I'd talk to other models and they'd laugh at me when I told them I did a big spread for Target."

"So...?" Amy prompted.

"So two years ago I came to New Orleans. Select made a deal with Doll Face. I still get a lot of catalog work, but Doll Face got me some couture jobs."

"So that's how you were at the museum yesterday. Are you doing better now? I mean, after that, uh, that fall."

"Yeah. Well, yeah, I'm fine. I landed on my ass; plenty of padding there."

"People clapped when you got up."

"Like I say, I'm fine now."

Curious, Amy took advantage of Paul's pause and asked, "Why weren't you fine then?"

Savannah put her elbows on the table and hid her face in her hands. "I get nervous in front of people. And there's all this stuff you have to remember–how to walk, stop at the tip of the catwalk, don't bump the next girl when you walk back, and all this timing stuff—you're always counting." She let her eyes peek out between her fingers. "It all confuses me. So I had a few drinks, you know, to get past the stage fright. My first walk went great, and I took another drink, and the second walk was even better." She lowered her hands and went on, "And I took another drink and on the third walk I ruined my fashion career."

"Ruined?" Amy asked, "One fall is really enough that you won't get more runway work?"

"Ah. Let's just say this wasn't my first fall."

Paul, infatuated with the woman's looks and simplicity, put their left hand on Savannah's right hand and said, "Oh. I'm so sorry."

A shrug. "It was fun while it lasted. The catalog stuff is easy, 'cause when I screw up we just take another picture. There's no audience."

You're going to get me in trouble. Amy took the lead. She put their hands in their pockets and asked, "How did you meet Mackenzie Slaton?"

"What a doll! I'd been in town three or four months and I was on a fashion job and Mac was there. She was looking for a roommate, and I'd just broken up with some bozo, so I said yeah." She smiled and turned toward the window view. "Not bad, huh?"

Amy phrased it as an open-ended question: "Tell me about Mackenzie."

"She's a lot of fun," a smile spread across Savannah's face. "She's good enough that she breaks the rules and gets away with it. She smiles on the runway, she makes eye contact. We're not supposed to do that, but she does and everyone loves her."

Amy heard Paul think, *She's talking about Mackenzie in present tense. I think she's in denial.*

"Where's her family?" *Hmmm. Yes. You're right.*

"Somewhere in Mississippi. They talk every week, too." In her notebook Amy wrote a reminder to talk to NOPD Communications to make sure someone notified the woman's family. She was relieved she wasn't the one who had to place that phone call.

"Does–I mean, did she date?"

"There are two guys she sees. I really like Skyler. He's an older guy, but he's real good-looking, and he's mysterious, and he treats her good."

It was Paul who asked, "What's 'older' mean? Mackenzie was just twenty."

"Yeah, I tease her a lot about it. Would you believe, the guy is in his forties? He's a hunk, though." She smiled wistfully.

"Did you, uh, you ever, you know, mess around with him?"

"What? No!" Even though she was sitting she held her hands on her hips. "I may be a blonde, and I may drink, but I'm not that kind of girl."

Amy played her get-out-of-jail-free card: "Sorry. Police have to ask these awkward questions. What about the man you mentioned earlier, the jealous one?"

"Hunter," she said. "Mac says they've been buddies since middle school. They still sleep together sometimes. I think he's jealous about Skyler."

"The older man?"

"Yeah. That's Skyler."

"He lives here now?"

"Oh, I don't know where Skyler lives."

"No, the old friend. Hunter? Where does he live?"

"Oh, him," she snorted. "I thought you meant Skyler. Hunter's out in Kenner, near the airport."

Finally Amy got to ask the question she'd been holding since Savannah first claimed it: "So, why do you think he wants to kill you?"

Savannah stopped, then said, "I'm sorry, what is your name again? Can we open that bourbon?"

"I'm Detective Amy Clear," and she reached under her skirt to pull out her badge case.

The model examined the ID, then looked up at her. "You know, you're using the wrong shade of foundation."

Amy couldn't help it. She burst out laughing. "That's great," she managed to say, "I'm here to talk about a murder and you're giving me make-up advice. Thanks." Savannah began to laugh, too.

Amy handed the bag and bourbon to the woman. When the model lifted the bottle up, she crinkled her little nose and said, "Hey, this isn't Hirsch. Early Times? This is rotgut."

"And it's what's on the menu. Do you have any mint?"

Savannah went into the kitchen, talking over her shoulder to Amy. "I've got some spearmint extract. Let me get some glasses, and–wait, I thought you were on duty."

Amy looked at their watch; it was 4:15. *Close enough,* she thought to Paul, then shouted, "Quitting time."

Let me drink, Paul thought. *That way you stay sober.*

"Absolutely," she whispered aloud, "but let me have a couple of sips." Savannah walked back into the living room, holding a tray with glasses and supplies, just in time to see Amy and Paul shake hands.

"What are you doing?" she asked. She was unloading things from the tray.

"Shaking hands with myself. Don't you ever do that?"

She set the tray down on the table, and stared down at her hands. Carefully, tentatively, Savannah tried to make her right hand and left hand shake. After a couple of moments she looked up and said, "My thumbs are in the wrong place."

Paul thought to Amy, *The Not-Einstein theorem at work.*

"Uh, I wouldn't worry about it. Actually, I think your thumbs are exactly where they belong."

Puzzled, the model said, "You think so? Oh, okay." She finished emptying the tray, then sat down.

As the woman opened the bourbon, Amy said, "You were telling me why Mackenzie's young friend hurt her. And he wants to kill you?"

Nodding, Savannah said, "Hunter. He's jealous. He's been Mac's squeeze since high school, and he doesn't like Skyler and that she's been sleeping with him." She measured bourbon into a shot glass and splashed it into one highball glass, then the other.

Paul thought, *If he was jealous, wouldn't he take it out on Skyler? Why would he hurt his friend?*

Happens all the time, Amy thought back as she wrote in her notebook. "Why do you think he's going to kill you next?"

She used tongs to move cubes from an ice bucket to each glass. "I know too much. I'll bet he's afraid I'm talking to you right now." Savannah unscrewed the top of a two-liter bottle of Big Shot Twist soda and half-filled both glasses.

Amy rubbed their cheek, thinking. "Do you have problems with this man? What's his name, Hunter?"

"No, not at all." She smiled. "Sometimes he comes to see Mac and she's out? We sit and talk and stuff." She opened a bottle of Tasty spearmint and sniffed; her eyes opened wide and she jerked her head back. "How much mint do you like?"

Uh, how much mint do you like? she thought to Paul.

He said, "Make mine like yours. It'll be okay."

Savannah nodded and splashed spearmint into one glass, and then the other. "Sugar?"

"Let me taste it first."

The model took two heaping teaspoonfuls from a yellow ceramic sugar bowl, and stirred them into one glass. She passed the other one to Amy. "There! I finished off my last bottle this morning. It's not Hirsch, but I'm glad you brought this."

"So, Hunter," Amy offered. "I want to talk to him. What's his story?"

Savannah's face lit up. "Mac says Hunter and her have been best buddies for ten years, since they were just kids. They had a thing once, and I told you they still sleep together. That's why he's jealous."

"What's your opinion of him?"

"I like him. We get along, like I said. He's good-looking; he's got hair down to his shoulders like one of those, those, those zombies."

Paul squinted. "Uh, hippies?"

"That's it, like a hippie. Great bod, he's a rock climber." Savannah took a sip of her drink and frowned. "Does yours need sugar?"

Amy thought, *First sip for you.* Paul came to the lead and took a very long swallow. *A bit sour. Whoo!*

"Yes, please," Amy wheezed, and held their glass out.

While Savannah doctored their drink, Amy said, "So, he's a rock climber." She hid her excitement at the news and asked, "You can do that for a living?"

"He works at a place where you can climb walls. He all the time goes up to Arkansas to climb real places," the model went on as she sipped her drink, then added still more sugar. "He's a real hunk, and Mac has a good time with him. But he disapproves of Skyler. He says it's because the guy is twice her age, but I think he wants her all for himself."

"How can I get ahold of Hunter?" Amy asked, turning a page in the notebook. "What's his last name?"

"Stringfellow," and the model laughed. "Give me a sec, let me look." She took her phone and swiped through her contacts until she found Hunter's entry, and she dictated the number.

Amy dropped her pen when she was done, then took a tiny sip of her corrected concoction. It was much easier to swallow. *Let me know when you want more.*

Immediately Paul jumped to the lead and took another long mouthful. "Oh, much better!" he said. "You make a dynamite bartender, you know that?"

The model smiled at the compliment but said, "Nah, I'd drink up the profits."

"Excuse me a minute," Amy said, and stood up. "Powder room?" Savannah pointed down the hallway.

As soon as she was inside the little room, she stood in front of the mirror and whispered, "You cannot make a pass at her. Do you hear me?"

It's just fun.

"This is serious. I'm a detective now. I can't get away with sleeping with the suspects anymore. You just be a good dyad and enjoy getting drunk. When we get home you and I can play in bed. But Savannah is off limits."

Awww.

"Paul. Let me hear you say it. Savannah is off limits."

Dammit, no, I won't–

"I'll tell Christine."

Paul paused. *You wouldn't dare.*

She stared in the mirror. All she saw was her own reflection, but she knew her eyes were boring into Paul's mind. "Savannah is off limits."

Amy felt him sigh. *Okay. Savannah is off limits.*

When she got back to the living room, she found the model had topped off her drink. There was not a lot remaining in the bottle Amy had brought.

"Much better," Amy said as she sat back down. "So this Hunter. Did he have a confrontation with the older guy?"

"They haven't met. Mac says she knows it would be a disaster, so she makes sure they're never here at the same time."

Drink! Amy let Paul lead to have more of their jury-rigged mint julep.

"Did she date anyone else?"

Savannah shook her head. "Mac is happy with them. She's got lots of friends with the models on the circuit, and the photographers and all, but since she met Skyler, she's happy."

"When was that? That she met Skyler."

"I was there, thank you very much." She took another sip, then reached for the sugar bowl. "When the producer announced last night's show, there was a press conference at the museum. Must have been, oh, three months ago. There was a luncheon, and all of us were invited."

Amy thought a moment, then asked, "So why was Skyler there?"

A shrug. "Mac got up and yelled, 'Does anyone have a God damned cigarette?' and he came over with a box of Marlboros. That's what Mac is like."

"Did she have any plans for last night? Was she going to meet anyone at the show?"

"Nope," shaking her head. "We were going to stop for a pizza and bring it back here."

Paul thought, *Drink!* When Amy let him lead, he said, "How about you? Who are you seeing?" He took his swallow of bourbon while Amy hissed silently at him.

"Nobody," she said, looking down. "I used to go out a lot, I know I'm pretty and guys want me..." The model looked up at Amy and said, "You're a woman, I can tell you this. When I was younger, it was a lot of fun to sleep my way through all of them. But one day I woke up and I didn't know where I was, or who the guy was, and then he was mean to me and told me I had to get lost before his girlfriend came over. It made me feel bad."

Amy thought to Paul, *No, you will NOT hold her hand. Repeat after me...* and she heard him think, unsteadily, *Savannah is off limits.*

"So I decided to do what my mom told me. You know, the stuff your mom told you, about not giving it up so easy." There was an awkward pause.

"Is it better now?" Amy asked.

"At least I know where I am in the morning." She laughed, then shook her head and became serious. "When you're pretty and men know you're a model, they're scared of you. Well, the good ones are. Lots of guys make passes, but—" she turned her head and looked out the window at the incredible view "—nothing serious. I don't think any of them care." She took a long swallow and drained her glass. "So no, I'm not seeing anyone."

Amy nodded. "What are you going to do now?"

"Call my agent, see if she's got any work for me for next week."

Drink! While Paul gulped, Amy thought to him, *Do dumb people know they're dumb?*

Then aloud, "No, I mean—well, now that Mackenzie is, you know..."

"She signed a lease with me. It goes for another three months."

Amy rubbed her temples, trying to think of a kind way of asking her question. Nothing came to her, so she bulled ahead. "Mackenzie is dead. She won't be paying any more rent. Are you going to stay here?"

Savannah poured the last of the bourbon in her glass and didn't bother with sugar or mint. "It isn't real yet. Mac is younger than me. I can't believe she's, she's, she's passed away." A few tears made her heavy mascara drip, growing a dark streak on her cheeks. "I don't know. She's my friend. I'm going to miss her." She took a cocktail napkin and dabbed at her eyes. "Maybe I'll finally get a dog. Mac is allergic."

"I've got one more question for you. Your name. The tag on the buzzer downstairs–"

"Yeah. Vanna. That's my real name. My parents were ga-ga about some actress back when I was born. I've seen her picture, she was real pretty. But people always gave me crap about the name. So I changed it professionally to Savannah. People think it's okay. I like it."

Paul took the lead for a last drink. "Pretty name for a pretty woman," he slurred as he stood up, knocking their chair over backwards.

The model peered at them. "Are you okay to drive?"

Amy jumped back to the lead, and her speech went back to normal. "Oh, I'm sorry. Yes, I'm fine. Thank you." She picked up the chair and silently swore at Paul.

As Savannah walked her down the hall to the front door of the loft, Amy thanked her for her cooperation. "If you think of anything that might be useful to us in tracking down Mackenzie's killer," and she handed over her business card.

"Don't let Hunter kill me next." she said.

"Why do you think he–"

"Because I know too much."

"Ah, so you said." Amy closed her notebook and nodded. "I'll look out for you." At the threshold Amy stuck out her right hand.

She was not prepared for the woman to hug her tightly and whisper, "Thank you. I needed to talk about Mac." She gave another squeeze before releasing Amy.

Paul thought, *I've died and gone to heaven.*

As she walked down the hall, Amy whispered to Paul, "You're sleeping on the couch tonight."

"That's an odd thing for a person to say to herself," the model said, before she closed her door and went to call her agent.

✶ 5 ✶

By the time Amy got to the police station on Rampart Street she and Paul were laughing together. She didn't see him drunk very often, and he was funny–he would stop in mid-sentence and say, "What was I talking about?" He was praising her looks, her intelligence, her taste in dyads, her wonderful ancient blue sedan, even her decision to leave their previous career of market research behind to become a detective.

"I'm going to look for Jermaine and Kowalski," she said as she parked in the police lot. "Behave, okay? They'll fire me if they think I'm drunk."

Oh, boy! We're going to see the wizard. Mister Wizard!

She flashed her badge to get past reception, then headed to the lab section. The medical examiner was closing one of the temporary morgue lockers after finishing an examination. "And a gracious good afternoon to you, Miss," the courtly doctor said. Jermaine was in his mid-fifties, with a thinning crop of white hair. He was wearing blue scrubs with various stains.

"Good to see you again, Doctor Tallant," she called to him. "You look like you're finishing up for the day."

I'm glad to see him, too. Can I tell him? Please? Pleeeeze?

Hush, you, she thought back.

"I'm meeting my son and his wife," he said, "we're going to Mobile for the weekend."

"What, no grandson?"

"Ah. That's my daughter's child. My son has not yet given me that for which every father longs."

What? His kid hasn't given him a two hundred piece socket wrench set? We should get him one for Christmas.

Amy didn't let her giggle cross their face, although she thought to Paul, *I don't think that's what he means.* To the medical examiner she said, "Have a great time. Do you have anything for me to work on this weekend?"

He pulled the scrubs off and stuffed them in a shiny silver trash cylinder. "I finally finished with the model. In case you were waiting for official word, she seems to be dead."

"Alert the media!" She sat on one of the short, wheeled stools in the office.

"Cause of death was exsanguination, method of death is uncertain, but could be accidental. Or suicide, come to think of it."

Paul blurted, "You should have seen her in the fashion show, Doc. She was so pretty and so sexy, I wanted to tell her lies and give her presents."

"That's not a very police-y attitude," Jermaine responded, head tilted and eyebrow cocked. "Where was I? Oh, yes. The woman had a broken neck, massive head injury, extensive hemorrhaging—I'd say internal bleeding, but most of her internal was external."

"Yes, I thought I noticed that. How about the guard?"

He took a seat so he could remove the scrub booties and trash them. "Also dead. As you told me, a single gunshot to the head. Incontrovertibly homicide."

Do you think those are his teeth? They're too straight. Not cute like our front tooth.

This time the smile worked its way to their face.

"I'm glad you find humor in unlikely places," Jermaine said, "but I feel obliged to tell you that if I didn't know you I would find it unsettling. Even, dare I say, creepy."

Amy kicked their right leg to spin the stool. When she faced the doctor again she said, "We found some other things. Cigarette butts, shell casing, and the grappling hook. And what about the big hunks of plastic?"

Don't forget the silencer. I want a Doc Jermaine gold star because I made one, too. Oh, I made one, too. One, two. I crack me up! and he laughed silently

"I haven't gotten to all of them. Well, hardly any of them. I did examine the Plexiglas, those large pieces we found on the display pedestal. No fingerprints, but I did lift impressions from someone's gloves." Amy nodded. "Eight spots, no thumbs. And one of the spots was anomalous."

Huh? I don't talk Forensics-eese. "In English," she asked

"Without thumb prints I can't tell which is the left hand or the right hand. But there's something peculiar about one index finger or ring finger."

Drunk though he was, Paul thought, *I told you!* Amy said aloud, "And what might that be?"

He stood up and straightened his necktie. "Much heavier impression than any of the other fingers."

Amy said, "Like maybe there was something big stuffed inside the glove there?"

He stared at her. "That's one possible explanation. There could be others."

Amy handed him the DVD of the museum security camera pictures. "Kowalski and I spent a few hours with the museum security chief this morning. I noticed something like that."

The doctor raised his eyebrows as he took the disc in its paper sleeve. "Monday morning, okay?"

"See you at eight-thirty," she smiled. "And when will you have the cell phone numbers for us?"

He laughed as he turned off the overhead lights. "Ah. That'll be first thing Monday morning."

They parted company when Jermaine went down the corridor toward the parking lot. As Amy walked up the stairs to the uniformed bullpen, Paul thought, *I like him. He's all formal and stiff and old-fashioned, but he's great. Hey! Let's go to Mobile with him this weekend.*

I'm fond of him, too, she replied silently, *but I don't want to spend a weekend with him. And Mobile? Haven't you ever been to Mobile?*

In the work room, half a dozen men and two women were busy in cubicles. Some were writing case notes, one was transcribing court dates into a calendar. One was playing World of Warcraft on her iPhone. "Anyone seen Kowalski?" she called out.

There was a murmur of 'no's. So Amy went to the dispatcher's window and greeted Shanika. "Where's Patrick?" she asked.

How does she work a keyboard with those talons? Think she cuts her nails with pruning shears or tin snips? Ooo, ooh, with a chain saw!

Amy thought back, *I hear she keeps them razor sharp with a grinding wheel.*

"He got sent out around two-thirty," Shanika read from the monitor. "Smash and grab in the Quarter."

"So much for updating him. Thanks. Have a good weekend."

Amy heard *I, uh, I'm not feeling so good.*

That's strange, she thought back, *I feel great. I'm going for a run when we get home.*

Amy took an unoccupied cubicle and began typing a message for Kowalski:

Pat

Interviewed the dead model's roommate. Seems Mackenzie had two boyfriends—hometown honey who followed her here from Mississippi, and some guy twice her age who wears gloves all the time. Roommate says it's the hometown man who killed the model out of jealousy, and will try to kill her next.

Can you make sure the Comm unit notified the model's family what happened? Glad we don't have to make that phone call.

Jermaine says he'll have phone numbers on Monday. Have a good not-your weekend.

–Amy

"See you, guys," Amy called as she left the bullpen. She waved at Detective Veronica when they passed in the hall. As she unlocked her car she thought to Paul, *Are you hungry?*

"No!" he moaned aloud.

"Ah. I'll roll down the window. Let's go home, big guy."

❧ 6 ❧

When Amy got to Christine's double on Sunday (in New Orleans a 'duplex' is called a 'double'), Paul's lover was jumping up and down on her porch. "Paulette!" she shouted, and ran up the driveway to intercept Amy and embrace Paul.

Christine and Paul had met one night at a lesbian bar. He had convinced Amy, after one of her unsatisfactory affairs, that it was his turn to lead and have a good time. Despite the years he had spent inside Amy's body–he finally had learned how to sit in a skirt, and to head for the ladies room–he still felt like a man to himself. Christine had approached him in the bar, thinking he was a woman named Paulette. Even after their affair began, even after Paul had introduced Amy and explained the bizarre events that led to him living inside Amy's head, Christine continued to think of him as female. The three people in two bodies had become close friends. Christine was honest about the schizophrenic voices that had plagued her before medication stabilized her condition, while Amy and Paul were open about their dyadic life.

"Oh, you honey!" Paul said as he hugged her back, then kissed her deeply. His lover was an inch or two taller than Amy, with a childlike smile that showed off her turned front tooth—which mirrored Amy's own.

Christine took him by the hand, but said, "Hi, Amy. How are you doing?"

"I'm glad to be here," Amy answered, with the same voice as Paul–uh, Paulette. "If I were home, I'd be thinking about work."

"Don't do that!" Christine teased, and hugged Amy sideways. "You'll solve it, you always do. Come on in. That festival doesn't start until two."

The double was tidy and sparsely furnished with wood floors, their varnish worn. The landlady green walls were punctuated by an Australian tourism poster featuring a brown kangaroo staring into the living room. In the bedroom Christine had a queen size mattress on the floor, with overturned milk crates serving as night stands. There was a small bookcase near the bed with a jewelry box, an incense burner, and a handful of paperback novels; across the room was a four drawer bureau. The only decoration was a framed color photo of her Paulette on the wall.

By two o'clock Christine and Paul were recovering in the bedroom, with tired smiles on their faces. "We were together on Wednesday," he nuzzled her ear, "but I missed you."

She giggled when he tickled her ear, then turned to face him. "Me, too." Then, "Amy? Are you doing okay?"

"I have a crush on Kowalski," she blurted out. In stereo she heard Christine and Paul say, "What?"

Amy sat up on the queen mattress that lay on Christine's floor. She was holding the woman's hand. "You know I love you," she began, "you're my other sister. You're so good for Paul, and I can be myself with you." She sighed. "But even though you make my body feel good, you know I'm straight. It's just–"

Softly, Christine whispered "Uh-oh."

"While you and Paul were making love, I was thinking about Patrick. I was pretending he made me feel those things."

There was silence. Finally, Christine asked, "So–what does that mean? Paulette, what does this mean?"

I don't know, he thought directly to his lover. *This is the first I've heard of it.*

Amy tugged at Christine to pull her into a sitting position and hugged her. She petted Christine's multi-hued, multi-length hair; she rubbed her shoulders and back. Amy was feeling an overwhelming affection, a sisterly love for the woman who had turned Paul's life around. Even though she hadn't heard them, she mostly repeated Paul's words: "I don't know. I just now realized it."

"Paulette?" she whispered, looking up at Amy's face.

He said, "I'm here." Christine hugged him tightly. He thought to her, *I love you. It's going to be okay.*

Amy smiled wistfully at Christine. "Can I take a shower? Then we can go to the festival and talk. I need your help figuring this out."

"My help?" Christine asked

"Of course," Amy said. "You're my best friend. I trust you. Will you help me?"

Christine kissed Amy on the shoulder and nodded. Amy went into the bathroom and closed the door.

I know what you're going to say, Amy thought to Paul as she turned on the shower.

"That's good," he said, "because I don't. Look, as long as I still spend time with Christine, I'm all for you having a love life."

"Oh," she stuck her hand into the stream of water to check the temperature. "That's not what I thought you would say." She stepped inside the shower.

Kowalski's a good guy, Paul thought to her. *Savannah called him a hunk. You think he's good looking?*

"Oh, my!"

Okay then. He's mature but not too old, that's good. But–

"Damn you and your damn 'buts'" she laughed.

I thought he was married. And you know what they say about dipping the quill in company ink.

"No, I don't know. What do they say about dipping the quill in company ink?"

Aloud, he answered, "They say 'Don't.'"

She pouted, "Get 'they' on the phone. I want to talk to 'they' about it. I mean, what does 'they' know?"

That'll be an interesting conversation.

Amy rinsed and turned the water off.

"Two things I'm concerned about," Paul said as she took a towel to her hair. "First, please don't let it interfere with me and Christine." He felt Amy nod. "And–can you let him know about me? Us? That we're a dyad."

"I don't know," she said honestly. "I'm afraid to."

"Think about it. We are so comfortable with Christine because she knows. We don't have to hide anything. She's your friend, and that couldn't happen if she didn't know about you."

When Amy opened the bathroom door, Christine was holding some of her clothes. "These'll fit you. No need to get back into sweaty stuff."

Amy took the woman's hand. "It's going to be okay, Christine. Paul laid down the law: he insists that he still gets to spend lots of time with you." Christine pulled her close for a hug. Then she stepped back to hand Amy the clothing, and wore a big smile that showed off her own crooked front tooth.

"That's what I needed to hear," she said. "I love you, Amy. See you in a bit, Paulette," and she went to bathe.

When Amy was dressed she sat on the floor, leaning back against a wall. Paul started to say something, but she stilled him, saying, "Let me think for a minute."

What she thought about was the comfort of their relationship with Christine: how the woman somehow always knew which of them was leading, and made the effort not to be sexually forward with Amy like she was with Paul; how Christine really did love her as the sister she never had; how Christine understood Amy's refusal to move in with her; how peaceful it was to be with Christine, who knew Amy and knew Paul and was comfortable with both of them. The comfort of the intimacy that came from honesty. She felt a glow of peace and possibility as she considered it.

"You're right," she said to Paul. "It would be best if Patrick knew about you."

"Good!"

"I just don't know how to do it."

She felt Paul smiling inside. *Maybe first go out with him. It's always possible that he smells bad or something.*

"Patrick?" she said in mock indignation, "Never!"

And what about the company ink?

"Yah. Crap on the company ink."

Christine returned to the bedroom in time to hear Paul say, "I suppose we can always get a job in Jefferson Parish."

"You're changing jobs?"

"Paul is making a plan B in case things don't work with Patrick."

She took a towel to her hair, standing naked in the bedroom. "Even I used to wait for a first date before I started planning the wedding."

Finally they were ready to go to the neighborhood festival in

London Park. As Christine was locking the door behind them, Amy said, "A woman told me I'm using the wrong foundation. What do you think?"

"I think she should mind her own beeswax."

ᘓ 7 ᘖ

In their morning shower Christine said, "My favorite was that ottoman. It was a fake elephant foot, and each toenail was a different color."

Paul said, "I have never put a dish on a wall, but those cartoon cat plates were so funny." He was soaping his body, which was also Amy's. "What did she call him? Aristo-cat? Funny."

"How about you, Amy," Christine asked. "What did you like at the festival?"

"Two photographers had some sentimental pictures. They made me think of Kowalski." There was silence for a moment, until she added, "Everything makes me think of Kowalski. How old am I? When did I turn sixteen again?"

Christine turned Amy so she could start scrubbing their back with a washrag. "You're crushing on the boy, enjoy it! I want you to tell me everything about that officer you like. Well, almost everything." They all laughed, even Amy. The moment was a reminder of the relaxed fit they had with Christine. Would she be able to create it with Patrick? Would she be able to create ANYTHING with him?

Under the low overcast and drizzle Amy hugged her friend, and then Paul held his lover tighter for a kiss. Christine drove off to her job at a real estate office, while Amy climbed into her blue sedan and headed for the Rampart Street station.

The uniformed officers' bullpen was a large, cluttered room in the cinderbrick building. The walls were a faded and peeling landlady green, obscured by taped up memos, wanted posters, shopping lists, and police morale placards. The overhead fluorescents cast a harsh blue light on everything, except for the one bulb with the infuriating flicker. Two long tables filled the center of the room, with open laptops, lunch bags, case notes, and a copy of the Daily Racing Form. Sixteen men and three women in blue uniforms, from Reserves and Officer Ones up to Lieutenants, talked quietly among themselves while the duty officer took roll. Captain Grant called a name, listened to the officer's plans for the day, and moved on to the next name on his clipboard.

Amy, as a detective, caused no notice when she snuck into the room during muster. She heard Kowalski's name called, and listened to his report on the store robbery he had worked on Sunday. Before he let the captain move on, he said, "Today I'll be working with Detective Clear on the museum case." The leader nodded, made a note on his clipboard, and called the next officer.

When the muster was over, Kowalski came to Amy. "Good morning, Detective," he said. She imagined his dimple, his square, freshly shaved face against hers. Then she heard Paul thinking, *Earth to Amy!* She was flustered, shook her head, forced a smile to her face. "Morning, Pat," she managed to say. She pushed the pleasant image from her mind, "Jermaine says he'll have phone numbers and names for us this morning. Let's go see him."

When they reached the medical examiner's lab, Doctor Jermaine greeted them with, "What'll it be today? How to turn off the nuclear reactor in your bathtub without frying the neighbors?"

Amy said, "We did that last week, Mister Wizard. Today I need to know why the porridge bird lays its eggs in the air."

Kowalski swiveled his gaze from Jermaine to Amy and back. "What did I miss? Was there a memo or something?"

"We're just playing," she said, and patted his hand. "Doc, we need phone numbers and clues."

Paul added, "But not just any phone numbers and clues. No, we need the phone numbers and clues that will break this case wide open."

"Is she okay?" the officer mouthed to Jermaine from behind Amy.

"Excellent question, Officer, something I've begun to wonder myself. Are you okay, Miss?"

"Peachy. Thrilled to be young and alive, I guess. Have you gotten into Mackenzie's phone yet?"

He leaned over his desk and pulled a clipboard out of a cubbyhole. "As a matter of fact." He stood between Amy and Kowalski and let them see as he scrolled through the transcribed phonebook. "Thirty-five entries, numbers with names." Pointing here and there, he went over the contacts that accounted for the most calls and most minutes, incoming and outgoing. Her hometown friend Hunter Stringfellow was first in all categories. Second was Skyler Blunt, the quadragenarian boyfriend.

"Any wild cards in the last week? You know, unidentified numbers?"

Jermaine nodded and pointed again. "See here, four numbers we don't have names for."

She heard Paul think, *For which we don't have names,* and she whispered "Hush."

"I'll get them from AT&T," Kowalski volunteered.

"We can get them without a warrant?" It was Paul, whose memory of an eroded Fourth Amendment went back fifty years. Patrick laughed and said, "Where have you been, Clear?" He copied the four numbers onto a blank sheet of paper and snapped it from the tablet, then left for the bullpen to do the searches.

"The last call," Amy said. "Who was it? And was it incoming or outgoing?"

The medical examiner laid down the clipboard and picked up the model's phone, safe in a zip-lock baggie. He called up the history. "Eight twenty-one she called Hunter. At eight thirty-one a call came in from Blunt. She put Hunter on hold, then went back and terminated the call. She was connected to Blunt until eight thirty-three." He looked up at her.

Amy nodded and thought to Paul, "Two calls, two suspects." She glanced at the clipboard again and asked, "What about this one? It shows up every Wednesday evening."

"It seems our inside-out supermodel was a good little girl who called mom and dad every week. That's the name on that number, 'mom and dad.'"

Amy pressed the medical examiner about when he'd process the buttons, the cigarette butts, and the improvised gun silencer. He tried to assure her that the museum case was of such a high profile that it was at the top of his list, "Right after I help the mayor get his nephew off on a stolen car charge."

Paul shuddered and said, "I don't want to know." Grimly, Jermaine said, "Neither do I."

"Got 'em!" Kowalski shouted as he returned to the lab, waving the paper with the strange phone numbers over his head. "Every single one is from a modeling agency–two local, and two in Houston."

I wonder, Paul thought to Amy, *would an agency have a reason to kill Mackenzie?*

Amy snorted, which startled Kowalski, then she silently answered Paul, *Oh, sure. And stealing almost thirty-four million dollars in jewels was just seizing an opportunity?*

He frowned and thought, *'No' would have been sufficient.*

"You okay?" the officer asked.

"Peachy. I warned you, I answer when I talk to myself. Sometimes I don't do it out loud, but the conversation–" she pointed to her head "–is always going on."

The doctor said, "Please don't ever give me the opportunity to perform an autopsy on you, Miss. Your brain must be fascinating."

She laughed, "You'll have to wait in line. My pediatrician said the same thing when I was eleven. Patrick, why don't you talk to Mackenzie's buddy, and I'll interview the boyfriend."

"With all due respect, Detective, no. We're talking about murder suspects. Let's both go to see these people."

Amy stared at the officer for a moment, thinking to Paul, *Damn, this is not cute.* Aloud she said, "Are you really suggesting that as a woman I can't handle an interview with a male by myself?" Jermaine rolled his eyes and went to his desk to pretend to do work while he eavesdropped.

"No. I am suggesting that police always double-team when visiting people suspected of violent crime." He crossed his arms in front of his chest. "You're new to the force. Ever notice that you never see one cop in a squad car? We're in twos, always, even big burly. manly men. It's considered a sensible precaution."

Amy felt her face beginning to burn. What a great way to impress a man she thought she might be getting to like-like. "Oh," she finally said, looking at her shoes.

The officer let her stew in a few more seconds of silence before he said, "It's okay. But you might want to consider the possibility your co-workers aren't total assholes."

"As opposed to me," she whimpered. "I hear you, Pat."

He nodded and dropped his arms to his side. "So, boss, where do we go first? Friend or lover?"

Amy's pulse raced in the moment she misunderstood Kowalski's question, but she managed to reply, "What does loverboy do? He's a tree surgeon, and it's raining. We should be able to catch him at home. I think Skyler Blunt needs to discover that we know he exists."

The officers split up to gather material they needed for the interviews, then met in the parking lot. "I'll drive," Kowalski said. "Something about the sight of a cop car that makes guilty people sweat."

As the officer backed out of his parking place, Amy looked at her notes for Blunt. "He lives in Lafitte," she said.

"Damn, that must be 30 miles of bad road. It's easier to get there by boat."

Amy untied her shoes and put her feet up on the cruiser's dashboard. "I'll navigate," she said, and tilted the GPS readout to her new position. She filled the officer in on Savannah's interview, including her story of the way Mackenzie met Blunt. They talked strategy: if a 'good cop/bad cop' approach was needed, Kowalski convinced her that it would be more unsettling to someone like Blunt if the female officer was the 'bad cop'.

I want to talk to HIM, Amy thought to Paul. *How do I get him off of police business?* A moment later she felt Paul open their mouth and say out loud, "Seen any good movies lately?" She winced and silently groaned, *That's so lame!*

"Yeah," Kowalski said. "Last week I caught a matinee of that new cartoon thing with all the cars."

Amy's heart sank. "How old are your kids?" she asked.

"None for me, thanks," he laughed. "But I like animation. The stuff Pixar and Marvel are putting out is incredible."

Amy heard Paul think, *Ooh! Ooh! A tooner! Let me talk to him, please?* She shook her head but let him lead.

"I love Aardman's claymation," Paul said. "Do you remember Wallace and Gromit?"

"Vaguely," he said. "That was with the dog that drank tea but didn't have a mouth?"

For the next half hour Paul and Kowalski had a lively conversation about changing animation styles and old favorites. The officer admitted he liked anime, largely because it could be so sexually graphic. Paul as Amy waxed poetic about Bugs Bunny and Pinky and the Brain and what he knew was Amy's favorite, SpongeBob Squarepants.

During a lull, Paul thought, *That's a start. At the worst he'll take you to a kids' movie that I'll love. Ask him about books. Sports. Anything. If he likes you that way, it doesn't matter what you talk about. And if he doesn't like you that way–well, it still doesn't matter what you talk about.*

"Are you okay?" Kowalski asked, stealing a look at Amy. "Your face is all red. Are you allergic to something?"

"I'm embarrassed!" she said. "I was a kid the last time I told anyone how much I like SpongeBob."

"My reason is much simpler for Panty and Nino–lust."

"We'll keep this our secret, right?"

He glanced at her, a smile creasing his face. "Right."

They drove farther south, the intermittent rain getting heavier. As Amy looked out the cruiser's passenger window she thought the trees and brush and swamp that went to the horizon were a combination of beautiful and desolate. "There's nothing out here!" she commented.

"Not much. A bunch of fishing, a little citrus, and a whole lot of oil and gas."

"It's pretty, but it's creepy, too."

"People die out here, Detective," Kowalski said. "Mother Nature can be unforgiving."

As they neared the little town of Lafitte, the officer said "It's one of these dirt roads away from the bayou. Better put your shoes on, we'll be there in a couple of minutes."

Amy read the numbers on the mailboxes as they slowed down on Route 45, and looked at her notes again. "Over there!" she called. "Left at the equipment rental place, then keep going." They came upon a house after a half mile, and Amy said, "Keep going."

Another three-quarters of a mile along, they saw a double-wide trailer set on cinder bricks. Two vehicles were in the gravel yard: a dirty, dented red pickup truck and a late model gray sedan. When they opened the cruiser doors they could hear dogs barking. Kowalski straightened the weapons and tools hanging on his belt as he stood by the car; his uniform hat kept the drizzle off his face. Amy had dressed in slacks and opted for the same display of police paraphernalia. "Break a leg," she muttered as she led the way to the trailer's front door. There was a small clay pot with a sorry geranium by the door on the pathetic excuse for a porch, the sole effort at making things look homey.

"Get out your badge case," Kowalski said. "It's easier to establish authority and dominance from the get-go."

"Like I did with the museum director, right?"

"Dominance doesn't have to include handcuffs or a beat-down." He opened his badge case, letting the ID documents accordion into view. "Besides, this guy hasn't done anything wrong yet."

"That we know of," Paul said aloud.

When he saw she was ready, the officer hammered on the door. They heard the dogs resume their barking. A male voice shouted "Shut up!" They heard a thud, and one of the barks turned into a series of whimpers.

The door opened as far as the security chain would let it. "Yeah? What the fuck you want?" The voice was sharp, filled with annoyance and anger.

"Good morning, Mister Blunt," Amy said. "We're NOPD police and we'd like to talk to you. May we come in?"

"No!" he barked. Amy and Kowalski exchanged looks as the door closed, but then it reopened with the chain undone. Skyler Blunt let his two dogs out, then he followed. Ostentatiously he turned his back on the police and used a key to lock the deadbolt behind him.

When he faced them, Kowalski and Amy were holding their police IDs at eye level. "Just a few questions, Mister Blunt," Amy said. "I'm Detective Clear, this is Officer Kowalski. We'd like your opinion on a few things."

The Rottweiler was barking sharply every few seconds, standing between Amy and his master.

Skyler Blunt was five–eight – taller than Amy, but shorter than Kowalski. He weighed 180 and appeared to be thick but not fat; strong. His wavy black hair showed some salt, but had not retreated from forehead or pate. His brown eyes were wide-set, with distinctive eyebrows that peaked near the sides of his tanned face. Three features were arresting, among them extremely white teeth and a nasty scar on his chin.

Amy addressed the third feature. "What's with the gloves?" He was wearing clean white cotton gloves, the kind a drill sergeant wears for inspections.

The Rottweiler alternated between low-pitched growls and short, loud snarls. Its companion quietly padded around the front step, sniffing the officer and detective.

"You caught me cleaning my rifle," he said, and folded his arms, tucking his hands into his armpits. Paul in Amy leaned forward and took a deep sniff, then thought to her, *Bullshit. The gloves were clean and I don't smell gun solvent.*

Kowalski crouched down to get a better look at the dogs. The larger was a black-and-tan Rottweiler, easily more than one hundred pounds. When the officer held his hand out to it, the dog lowered itself on all fours and growled deep in the back of its throat. Amy bent over toward the other, a Bluetick hound about 65 pounds, and it came to her, licking her hand. *What a sweetie,* Amy thought to Paul.

"Heel!" Skyler cried and stamped his foot on the porch. Both dogs sidled closer to their master. Then, "I asked you what the fuck you want?"

Amy straightened up and walked to within a pace of Blunt. "What did you talk to Mackenzie Slaton about Thursday night?" Her hands were on her hips; the left was on the butt of her holstered 9mm.

"Who?"

"Skinny blonde girl, twenty years old, so high, and dead."

"Dead?"

"As in no longer alive. As in fell four stories to a marble floor. As in what did you talk to her about?"

"She was stalking me. She called me a dozen times a day."

Kowalski glanced down at his notebook. "AT&T says you

called her Thursday night."

"Oh," Blunt turned his head to look at the officer, "they blur together. I called to tell her to leave me alone, not to call me anymore. Crazy bitch."

Amy thought to Kowalski, *No. Let him bluster. We'll trip him up later.* Then she realized what she had done and muttered "Shit," frowning. She heard Paul laugh silently.

The officer's head swiveled to look at Amy, a question mark across his face. Amy smiled, then continued with Blunt. "Let me get this straight," she said. "Twenty-year-old fashion model. Skinny and gorgeous. Making great money. And she was... stalking? You?" She smiled.

"That's right," defiant. Paul thought, *Savannah said he visited all the time. Nobody stalking anyone.* Amy nodded and answered silently, *This is an interview. Like I stupidly thought to Pat–let them lie all they want, we bust their chops when we interrogate them.*

"How did you and Mackenzie become acquainted?"

Blunt looked up and to his right. "I saved her dog. It was in traffic. I pulled over and grabbed it and she was there."

Paul thought, *But Savannah said –*

"What kind of dog?"

"Little. A chick's dog."

Amy smiled thinly. "You have these two dogs, you know dogs. What breed was Mackenzie's dog that you saved like the hero we all know you are?"

"Next question."

"Beg pardon?"

"I said 'next question.'"

Amy nodded. "Officer Kowalski, did you get that in your notes? That Mister Blunt doesn't know the breed of Mackenzie Slaton's little chick's dog that he saved from certain death on an unnamed street?"

"Aye, aye," he said with a big smile.

Amy went on. "Where were you Thursday night?"

"Let's see..." holding his chin in his gloved right hand, "...I was home with my loving wife. You can ask her."

"I will. When did you learn Mackenzie was dead?"

"About two minutes ago. You told me."

Despite herself, she smiled. "Any thoughts?"

"Yeah. Maybe now my wife will get off my back about the phone calls."

"Maybe. I'd like to ask her. May we come in and talk to her?"

He glared at Amy, and at Kowalski. "I'll get her," he muttered. He unlocked the door to enter, but left the dogs outside. They heard the lock click.

"Hey, pooch," Kowalski said, hunkering down and reaching out to the Rottweiler. The dog lowered itself and held its ears back, a low growl coming from deep in its throat. When the officer slowly moved his hand to the animal's head, it stepped back and barked twice; the growl resumed, louder.

Meanwhile the Bluetick came up to Amy and lay down across her feet. When she laughed, Kowalski looked over. "A woman's dog," he opined. "Must be the wife's."

"You keep Skyler busy," Amy said as she bent to pet the hound. "I want to talk to the wife. She must know something."

"Hey, what happened back there?" the officer asked. "I could have sworn I heard you say something."

"Tsk, tsk. Sounds like a guilty conscience to me. Actually, I'm a ventriloquist." Paul thought to her, *Careful! It's not too late for us to end up at Mandeville.*

The front door opened, and a tired, short woman timidly stepped onto the porch. Skyler locked the door behind them. When he turned and saw his dogs, he stamped his foot and shouted "Heel!" The Rottweiler continued to growl as it backed toward its master. The hound on Amy's shoes lazily looked around, then finally lifted itself and padded back behind Skyler.

"Mrs. Blunt, I'm Detective Clear and this is Officer Kowalski, we're with New Orleans Police." The woman looked up nervously at her husband. "Would you walk with me?" She held her hand out to the woman to lead her away.

"No!" barked Skyler. "She stays here."

Kowalski stepped up to the man and said, "Show me the rest of your property. If you don't mind."

"C'mon," Amy said, and the wife followed her as they walked to the gravel driveway, and stood on the far side of her car. Amy positioned the woman so her back was to the house where her husband still stood, to keep him from overhearing anything his wife said. Amy would try to keep the woman between her and Skyler, just in case he was a lip reader. "Call me Amy," she offered. "What's your name?"

"I'm Crystal. Please tell me, what has Skyler done?" The woman was no more than forty years old, but in the drizzle she looked older, harried and worn. Her print dress was faded, her shoulders sloped, her hair was in some disarray. Amy noticed that the woman had hastily applied makeup to cover a bruise on the left side of her face.

"As far as I know, he hasn't done anything. I'm just trying to rule out possible suspects. Tell me, Crystal, where was Skyler on Thursday night?"

"He was here with me," she said, "he always is. He doesn't go out much." She reached into a torn pocket and pulled up a pack of Newports. She squeezed it to spread the opening wider, and peered inside; finally she spilled a bent half-cigarette into her free hand. "What happened Thursday night?" A cheap butane lighter, and she lit her half smoke. Paul inhaled and thought to Amy, *Damn. It's tobacco.*

"Something in Orleans Parish," she replied. "What time does Skyler usually get home from work?"

"Depends where the last job is." She exhaled a long blue plume from her nostrils. "Sometimes he's home right after five, sometimes it's seven."

"Any particular day of the week that he's always late?"

She could see Crystal Blunt considering the question, maybe for the first time. "Uh...I don't think so. No."

"Mackenzie Slaton. What do you know about her?"

The drizzle was sticking the woman's hair to her skull, making her look smaller. "Yeah. Skyler says she's stalking him." Amy let the silence build until the woman added, "I don't know why he has to go into town to tell her to leave him alone."

"Tell me about Skyler," Amy asked, trying to sound kind. "You asked what he did. Has he been in trouble before?"

A sigh. "Before we married, before I knew him, he spent three years in Angola. I think he tried to hold up a liquor store. But he learned his lesson, really he did."

"How is the family fixed for money? Is he in debt? Anyone shady?"

"Sure, money is tight," and she tossed the butt of her half-cigarette into the grass. "But it's tight for you, too, right? So I work part time at Walgreen's; I'm a cashier."

"Does Skyler drink, or do drugs?"

"Yeah, he drinks some. More than I like. Sometimes–" and Crystal stopped herself, as if she had been on the verge of giving away a secret. "Anyway."

"Do you have kids?" Amy asked.

A smile came across the woman's face. "Bella. She's eighteen now." The smile flitted away, "She got a place three or four months ago. We, uh, we had some trouble controlling her."

"Uh-oh. Did she get in any trouble?"

"Only in school, they kept sending her home with notes. She was disrespectful in class, smoked in the bathrooms, that sort of thing. Plus, we didn't like her boyfriend. He was too old. Somebody Skyler knows. We said she couldn't see him anymore, but now that she's eighteen, she went to live with him."

Amy reached her hand out toward the barely hidden bruise on the woman's face, and Crystal flinched away. "I'm sorry," Amy said, "but I know how to use makeup, too. Does he hit you a lot?"

"What are you talking about?" she said, standing straight for the first time. "Skyler loves me. He'd never hurt me."

She shook her head, then handed Crystal a business card. "If you think of anything we ought to know about Skyler, call me. And if you decide–well, you know. You can call me."

The woman examined the card closely, then slipped it into the torn pocket of her dress. As they walked back to the front door, she volunteered, "It's a hard life out here. I've got some rich relatives, but they don't much like Skyler. We do what we can. All we have is each other. You know?" Her face was a plea. Paul thought, *If this weren't police business I'd say give her a hug.* Amy nodded, then touched her on the upper arm anyway.

As they closed on the front porch, Amy saw Kowalski had his right hand on his holstered mace canister. The Rottweiler was standing in front of him, barking every few seconds. Skyler had a smug smile on his face. "My property, boy scout," the man said, "and I want you and that bitch off it."

"Problem, Mister Blunt?" Amy asked. The Bluetick came to her and licked her hand. She heard Paul think, *Looks like an old fashioned pissing contest.*

"I didn't do nothing. I don't want to talk to you. And I don't want you talking to my wife. Get off my property."

She smiled and turned to Kowalski. "I guess we're not wanted here, Officer. Put that in the 'suspicious' column." Then Amy thought to Paul, *Go ahead, I know you want to do this.*

Paul said, "If I have to come back here with a warrant, I will make you my bitch. You understand me?"

Blunt blinked. He muttered, "And you can suck my dick."

It was Amy who said, "Don't give me a chance to bite it off," and turned to leave with Kowalski.

"Nice day for a drive," Amy said to the officer as they walked in the drizzle back to the cruiser.

In the safety of the car, she asked, softly, "What happened?"

"Son of a bitch was going to sic that dog on me. I was this close to macing them both." He started the engine and backed up to turn around. "We were right, you being bad cop threw him off."

"YOU were right, Pat," she corrected. "Tell me what you found out before it turned into dueling dicks."

He aimed the car toward the highway for their long trip to their next stop in Kenner. "He dodged or refused most things I asked. I did learn he joined the army out of high school and somehow got an honorable discharge after eighteen months–I didn't think that was possible. And he cuts trees for a residential company in Westwego. The list of things he wouldn't answer is a lot longer."

She laughed out loud. "What a piece of work. Sure is behaving like he's got something to hide."

"Yep." Then Kowalski added, "But maybe not murder and jewel theft."

"You're right, of course. So, what wouldn't he tell you?"

The officer ran down the unanswered questions: how long has he lived there in Lafitte, how long has he been married, does he have kids, what are the dogs' names, what kind of rifle was he cleaning, what's with the gloves, has he ever been arrested... "Hell, he wouldn't tell me if he's been to a Zephyrs game this season."

Amy shared what the wife had told him, about their daughter and her boyfriend, and about Skyler's jail time. "She all but said she knows Skyler was having an affair with Mackenzie. Plus I'm pretty sure he beats her. Did you see the bruise on her face?"

He turned right onto highway 45 and headed toward New Orleans. "What bruise? I must have been keeping my eye on the husband. I just don't trust him."

"She had makeup over it, but it was obvious to me. She said he doesn't hit her, just like too many battered women do." Amy felt Paul come forward, and he said, "You ever hit a woman, Pat?"

He laughed but kept his eyes on the road. "Twice. First time, I was maybe nine; it was my big sister. She knocked me into next week. Second time was a couple of years ago when a female perp objected to being apprehended." He glanced at Amy, "When's the last time you hit a man?"

"Last week," Paul answered, smiling. "The museum guy. I forgot to thank you for showing me that trick about getting the cuffs tighter." He heard Amy think, *Okay, he's not a batterer. I wonder what's going on with his wife?*

"Yeah," Kowalski began, then cleared his throat, "about that. Why were you such–no, why did you think you had to be such a hard-ass with him?"

"Establish dominance from the get-go," she answered, without much confidence. The things the officer and Paul had said to her at the Haute Couture Cares event made her know she had over-reacted, but she didn't yet understand how she had done so.

"Like I said, Detective, dominance doesn't have to include cuffs and abuse."

Amy felt a tinge of pink start at their neck and work its way up their face. She sighed. "I'm still learning. You know I didn't go to the Police Academy." She looked out the passenger window at the gray drizzle, trying to avoid the look of reproach she expected from Kowalski.

They drove on in silence for a minute or two. Finally Paul said, "If I can ask–you can shut me up if I'm out of line, but what's up at home? I've heard some things." Silently, in their head, Amy screamed *NO!*

His grip tightened on the steering wheel, and his eyes

remained fixed on the road. "No, it's okay. I know it'll be better if I talk to someone about it, but I just don't trust the employee assistance counselor at work. Like he's really not going to tell the commander."

Amy took back the lead. She turned in the passenger seat and said, "What is it, Pat?"

He took a deep breath. "We're married eight years in March. No kids, neither of us really wants 'em. Her folks are okay, she gets on all right with mine. Everything should be great, right?" Amy nodded, paying close attention to the man's profile. "Then three months ago she tells me to sleep in the guest bedroom. I ask why— am I snoring or something? She says, 'I don't think I love you anymore.' I mean, what the fuck?" He turned his head for a moment, long enough to see Amy's eyes fixed on him, concern all over her face.

He drove in silence for another mile. Amy said, "Three months. Any change?"

A silent head shake. "I'm still sleeping in the guest room. We cross paths maybe twice a week."

"No explanation?" Amy asked. He shook his head. "Nothing?"

A grim smile. "Nothing is exactly what I've got."

A few miles on, Amy pointed to an upcoming Spur station. "Can we stop? I need to, uh, to freshen up. Can I get you a coffee or something?"

He flicked the turn signal and pulled up to the food mart building. "Thanks," she said," and went in. Paul thought, *We need to pee?*

She thought back, *No, but you taught me that rule of rock and roll travel–eat, sleep, and pee any chance you get.*

I hate it when you quote Paul to me.

What I really want is to find some dinky little nothing for Pat. He really opened up to me. I want to let him know I appreciate it and that his secret is safe with me. But I don't want to seem pushy. I don't know.

She hung her belt on the coat hook inside the stall and sat looking at her gun, her cuffs, and her baton. She heard Paul think, *If you were a guy, you could just treat him to a whorehouse.*

Guys do that?

She felt him shrug. *I don't know. Guys always brag and lie about that kind of thing. I talked a good game when I was a man. Uh, I mean, when I had my man's body.*

"Yes. I know." She smiled. "So, what do you think?" She flushed and began reassembling her arsenal.

I seem to remember Amy Clear once telling me, 'Feed me liquor, I'll be alright.' Tell me I get to see Christine tomorrow and I'm fine if you two stain the back seat of the cruiser.

She was laughing as she muttered, "Trash mouth."

Browsing in the little store, Amy's eyes lit up at a display of cheap pocket knives. *This is a guy thing, right?* she thought.

Yup. These are kind of crappy though, I don't–oh, there you go! He pointed at a display of budget multi-tools. *Those are better than knives. Everyone loves them. Look–*Amy took it off the display and examined it–*Phillips and slot head screw drivers, pliers, can opener, tweezers–and what's that round thing?* She twisted a knurled knob and a light came on in its center. *A flashlight!* Paul finished, *Too much!*

Grinning, Amy put the tool on the counter. She took a Barq's and a Diet Coke from the cooler by the cash register, and opened her wallet.

Pat was in the cruiser, hands still locked on the steering wheel. "Got some supplies," she said as she let herself in. "You like root beer, right?" He nodded and took the bottle of Barq's. He was starting to say thank you when Amy said, "And I saw this and it had your name on it. What do you think?" She held the multi-tool in her palm. It was three and a half inches long, dull black.

The officer peered at it. "What is it?" When she smiled without answering, he picked it up gingerly. Suddenly he recognized it. "These things are great. How did you know I lost mine?" Amy thought his smile was that of a happy little boy.

"That little voice inside me," she said. "C'mon, we have to get moving. I want to see Mackenzie's BFF today."

As they motored north, Paul thought, *That worked.*

Yes indeedy, she answered silently. *Thanks for the advice.*

You were smart to tell him to get back on the road. Kept things from getting awkward or emotional.

She snickered aloud. *Are those synonyms to men? 'Awkward' and 'emotional'?*

"What's so funny?" the officer asked. Through his words she heard Paul answer, *Yes.*

"Talking to myself again," she said. "I assume you do it, everybody does–" he nodded "–but sometimes I have to say, 'What were we talking about?' If I didn't laugh I'd be worried about having Amyheimers."

Playfully, he asked, "Just how crazy are you, detective?"

"I'm as crazy as everyone on the force. At least I'm housebroken." She glanced at her clipboard, then said "The buddy is in Kenner." Then she looked up at him and thought his dimple was deeper than before. "You can call me Amy."

Gradually the drizzle stopped and a band of blue opened in the west. As they neared the Mississippi River the rural landscape morphed to suburban and then city. It took almost an hour to get to the strip shopping center in Kenner where RockWallUSA was located. The anchor store was the Mister Mudbug Catering office. "Crawfish for lunch?" Amy asked as they got out of the cruiser.

"Only if they have beer," Kowalski replied.

When they entered the gym where Hunter Stringfellow worked, they were assaulted by loud music. A forty-foot artificial rock wall was at the far end, with three or four people in harnesses working their way up or down. "Can I help you?" a young man shouted from a desk just inside the door.

"What?" Kowalski shouted back.

"I said, "Can I help you?"

"What?"

"I said–wait," the man ducked behind the counter and lowered the music to merely earsplitting. "I said, 'can I help you?' I can offer a group rate if your precinct wants training."

Amy smiled when Paul thought, *Good salesman.* She introduced herself and the officer. "We're looking for Hunter Stringfellow. Is he here?"

The young man turned pale. "Uh, that's–" his voice broke "–uh, that's me. W-w-what is it?"

"Relax, son," Kowalski said, which seemed to increase the man's nervousness.

"Y-y-you mean I'm n-n-not relaxed? I-I-I think I'm relaxed. W-what can I d-d-do for you?"

Amy said, "I'm sorry about your friend Mackenzie, but I need to talk to you about her. Is there somewhere quiet we can talk? Somewhere private?"

"Let me g-g-get Bill from in b-b-back. We c-c-can't leave the c-c-climbers unat-unat-unat-tended." He began to walk toward a door beside the climbing wall.

"Wait, Hunter," Amy called as she trotted after him. "Let me come with you." She thought to Paul, *No way I'm letting this guy slip out the bathroom window.*

Hunter led her to a small, cluttered office where an older man was going through adding machine tapes. Amy cleared her throat and the man looked up. "Bill, I'm detective Amy Clear. Officer Kowalski is in the main room. We need to talk with Hunter here about some police business."

The man looked from his clerk to Amy and back again. "What have you done now, Stringfellow?" he barked. Paul thought, *What a jerk!*

"Mister Stringfellow's best friend was murdered last week," Amy told the man. "We hope he can help us find the woman's killer. Is that all right?"

Bill stood up with a loud sigh and came out from behind his desk. "Okay, I'll watch the floor." To Amy he said, "Don't keep him too long." Then he reached over and ruffled Hunter's hair.

Outside in the parking lot, Amy and Kowalski talked with Hunter. "That Bill guy seems like he thinks you're family," Amy offered. "How long have you worked here?"

"Two years, I think. He hired me a few weeks after I moved from Meridian. Sometimes he likes to think he's my dad."

"How so? Will you be grounded because of this?"

"Nah. He g-g-gives me advice about everything. Some of it's been g-g-good."

Amy nodded. "I have to ask you some uncomfortable questions," she began her interview. "Police ask everybody these things. I'm not trying to judge you, I'm asking for information. Okay?" When he nodded, she asked, "Have you ever been arrested?" He shook his head. "Do you have a problem with alcohol? Drugs? Gambling?" He smiled and said, "N-n-nope, n-nope, and n-n-n-nope. Next?"

"Are you in debt for anything except a car payment or a mortgage?"

"I've got an Op-p-p-ptimo card, but I p-p-pay it off each month."

"Are you friends with anyone convicted of a felony? Related?"

Another head shake, "N-n-not that I kn-kn-know of."

Why did I bother? Amy thought to Paul. *I don't know a damn thing more now that when I started.* She changed gears: "Tell me about the funeral. How are the Slatons holding up?"

He sighed. "Luh-Luh-Lorena just cried and cried and cried. Muh-Muh-Mac's dad was like a z-z-zombie, he was stu-stu-stunned. And her sister, I f-felt so sorry for her." He looked up at Amy. "Brittney idolized Mac."

"I am sorry for your loss," she said. With her memory of the model splattered on the museum floor, her words were not mere police boilerplate. "I was at the fashion show that night. She impressed me."

The man nodded, then said, "I'm going back to Mi-Mi-Mississippi day after tuh-tuh-tomorrow. The funeral was just family and old friends. I want to go to the memorial service. Mac was a b-b-big deal in Meridian."

Amy asked, "What did you talk to Mackenzie about on the phone Thursday night?"

"Th-Th-Thursday? I'm nu-nu-not sure."

Kowalski spoke up. "Unless you can talk to the dead, it was the last time you spoke to her."

"Oh. We tuh-tuh-talked every day. I wi-wi-wishhhhed her luck on the runway show, and we made puh-puh-plans to go upriver for Suh-Suh-Saturday. We hiked a lot."

She took a good look at Stringfellow. Five-nine, thin, maybe twenty-two years old. Extraordinary biceps busting from his T-shirt sleeves. He had dark shoulder-length hair, vaguely parted in the center. She nodded, and said, "Tell me about Mackenzie. You and her."

He took a deep breath. "I love her. She's my b-b-best friend."

He paused to control himself. "We've buh-buh-been friends from mu-mu-middle school. We've been lovers for what, s-s-six or s-s-seven years. She moved here after high school and I fu-fu-followed her."

"So, you were her boyfriend?" Amy asked, frowning.

"Sort of. Wu-wu-one of them."

"What about the other guy you mentioned. Was he her boyfriend?"

"Wu-wu-one of them." He looked sad.

"Didn't that–" she stopped and began again with more neutral wording, "Did that bother you?"

"Mac all the time told muh-muh-me to g-g-get used to it. You saw her, you saw how b-b-beautiful she was. She was twenty, she wasn't going to be a wu-wu-one-man woman." Hunter scratched at his left cheek. "But wh-wh-whatever her love life was, it neh-neh, uh, neh-neh-never got in the way of me and her. Us. I was the cuh-cuh-constant in her life. But this Blu-Blu-Blunt-guy," shaking his head, "he b-b-bothered me." Amy and Kowalski raised eyebrows, and the man went on, "I never met him. Mac th-th-thought it would b-b-be a dis-dis- a disaster. B-b-but everything she told me ab-ab-about him, he was so creepy. He was, like, twu-twu-twice her age. He talked ugly. And she said he always wu-wu-wore gloves."

"Gloves?" from Amy and Kowalski.

"Isn't that wuh-wuh-weird? I asked her if he wuh-wore them to bed. She said he d-d-did."

Amy asked, "Why?"

"She never said," he shrugged. "It buh-buh-bothered me a lot more than it buh-bothered her."

So much for Blunt cleaning a gun, Amy heard Paul. *We should have asked his wife about the gloves.*

"Were you jealous of Skyler?"

Instantly he cried, "No!' and shook his head. "I t-t-told you, the other m-m-men in her life didn't g-g-get in our way."

"Do you have a girlfriend? I mean, other than Mackenzie?"

"I see some guh-guh-girls, yeah. I like them, but they're not Mac." He paused as if a new realization were working its way into his brain. "Oh, shit."

"Tell me about Savannah Walsh."

"Mac's room-mu-mu-mate? N-N-Not much to tell. She's a looker. She's kind of du-du-dumb. And she's really a nuh-nuh- a nice girl."

"Was she at the funeral?"

He shook his head. "I ought to t-t-tell her about the memorial service. She m-m-might want to go to that."

"You get along with her?"

"Sure. Whu-why?"

Paul was about to explain her question when Amy took the lead. "Just checking," she said. "Where do you live?"

"About a m-m-mile from here. A crummy apartment complex."

Amy asked, "I did some checking, Hunter. I have an idea of what you earn. I have an idea of what you spend. Can you help me make the math work?"

"Y-y-you know all th-th-that?"

"We know everything," Kowalski offered. It took Hunter eight seconds to get past the first letter and finally say the word "Shit."

Amy said, "All I care about is who killed your friend and who stole a bunch of jewelry. Whatever you've done, it doesn't match two dead and $34 million of stolen jewelry." She shifted her weight to her right leg. "Since I'm sure I don't care what you think you've done, just relax. Don't let yourself get upset."

"Ups-suh-suh-set? I dih-dih-don't know whu-whu-what you muh-muh-mean."

Paul thought, *It's funny when Porky Pig stutters, but this is painful.* The man had no idea why Amy nodded, but she said, "Sounds to me like your speech, you have trouble when you're nervous. You can tell me what's bothering you, Hunter. It's okay." She smiled to encourage him.

Hunter looked back and forth between Kowalski's impassive face and Amy. "I duh-duh-don't want to guh-guh-get in tttttt-trouble."

"What is it? A ticket you haven't paid? Get a girl pregnant and run out on her? It's okay, you can tell me."

"But I don't trust hi-hi-him," he jerked his thumb at Kowalski.

"Trust who?" Amy smiled. "It's just you and me, Hunter, just you and me." Kowalski lowered his pen and notebook, and turned his back on the detective and suspect.

Stringfellow leaned back against a car in the parking lot. His shoulders slumped, he looked down at the butts and debris around his feet. With eyes closed, he began, "Yi-yi-you know I don't muh-muh-make much. Every muh-muh-month I t-t-take some p-p-people to Arkansas and lead a rap-p-p-pelling tour." He took a deep breath. "I charge sixty buh-buh-bucks a person and I've never put it on muh-muh-my taxes." He opened his eyes, as if looking for Amy's judgment.

Amy heard Paul silently laughing. *Taxes!* and more laughter.

"That's very enterprising," she said, trying to sound enthusiastic for Hunter's benefit and also not to laugh out loud. "How many people do you guide?"

"Fuh-fuh-five or six," finally allowing himself a smile. "On a good mu-mu-month I might get ten."

She nodded, "That makes the math work."

Paul thought, *What? You ran a background check on him? You don't know...*

You're right, she thought back, *I don't know. Just a bluff. You know me, all talk.*

It took a moment before Amy returned her attention to Hunter Stringfellow. "What do you do about insurance? I mean, what happens if someone falls or gets hurt?"

The smile had turned into a grin. "It's in Muh-Muh-Mount Mu-Magazine State Park, I hope that means they've got an infuh-infuh - inffffirmary or something. I tell everyone I'll help if I cuh-cuh if I cuh-can, but climbing can be dangerous."

Paul laughed out loud and said, "Caveat emptor."

Amy took back the lead and said to Kowalski, "Officer, there's no reason to put any of that in your notes." Kowalski turned to face Amy.

To Hunter, Amy said, "You really ought to get insurance. It might cut into your profit margin, but it can save your butt. I'm just saying. Where did you learn to do this climbing and rappelling?"

"Started on trees in the buh-buh-back yard. I guess I taught muh-muh-myself, and I'm pretty good at it. I used to think–" his smile was wistful "–that Mac and me would muh-muh-move to Denver and I'd li-li-lead big tour groups. You can make a good living duh-duh-doing this out west."

"I had no idea." Then, "Pat, any questions?"

Kowalski cleared his throat. "Did Mackenzie have any enemies? People who made threats, or might have had a reason to harm her?"

"You didn't nu-nu-know her. Mac was fearless. She handled herself with everyone f-f-from CEOs to creeps ogling her on the street." He shook his head, "I duh-duh-don't think she ever felt th-th-threatened."

"Professional jealousy, maybe? Did she beat someone out for a job?"

"She said it was a com-com- a comppppetitive life. She had to audition for mu-mu-most jobs, so sometimes she tuh-took a job from sum-sum-someone else, and sum-sometimes she luh-luh-lost out." He paused, then added, "Do people make threats over that kind of thing?" It seemed to be a genuine question.

"People kill for a lot less," Amy replied. "Look, we're just starting our inquiries. I'll want to talk to you again–When will you get back from the memorial service?"

"Uh, uh, I guh-guh-guess – Thu-Thu-Thu-Thursd-duh-day or Fuh-Fuh-Fuh-Friday."

She handed him one of her business cards. "If anything occurs to you that might help us find Mackenzie's killer, call me. I'll be in touch." Hunter examined the card carefully while Amy and Kowalski left for the squad car.

When they were in the privacy of the police cruiser Amy asked, "Did you hear him at the end?"

"His stuttering got even worse," Kowalski said. "Sounds like he's not planning on coming back," Kowalski offered.

Paul said, "Muh-muh-Mount Muh-Magazine. If he tries to disappear, he'll go to that park. Do you think Hunter was telling the truth about not being jealous?"

Pat said, "Jealousy and money, the two biggest motives there are." He started the engine and began the long drive downtown.

As they drove, they discussed the interviews Amy had conducted. "Everything about Blunt says 'bastard,'" Kowalski said, nodding for emphasis, "but that doesn't mean he's a killer."

"Agreed. And everything about Hunter says 'scared kid,' but that doesn't mean he's innocent."

It was Paul who offered, "They both have money problems. Did you see Blunt's wife smoking half a cigarette? And both these men have the ability to rappel from the roof to the crime scene."

Kowalski joined, "And they both had relationships with Mackenzie. We know Blunt lied about how they met, maybe he was as jealous of the Stringfellow kid as we're thinking he was of Blunt."

Amy looked out the window at the urban commercial district along Airline Highway and thought. Paul thought to her, *The daughter.*

"Daughter?" Amy said out loud.

Kowalski said, "Hmmm?"

"Blunt's daughter," said Paul. "She's not under his direct control anymore. I want to hear what she thinks about the warm glow of her nuclear family circle."

"Jermaine may have more analysis for us," Kowalski mused. "If we're lucky–if the killer is stone dumb–we'll get a match on that spent cartridge case."

"Yup," she said, putting her feet up on the dashboard, "time to go see the wizard."

During the long drive back to the Rampart Street station, Amy asked the officer about his plans for his weekend, which would start in a few hours. "Tomorrow night I'll cook a nice dinner and wait for Roxy to get home," he answered. "If we can talk like adults, I'll do the same thing Wednesday night."

"Before she got–I mean, like, last year, what did you two do on a weekend?"

The pause was so long that Amy was about to apologize for her question before Kowalski answered, "I don't know. I can't remember." There was another silence. "Maybe that's the problem." He glanced at Amy, then put his eyes back on the road. "I just didn't pay enough attention to her. I–I don't know."

Softly, she said, "I'm sorry, Pat."

"You're a good listener, Detec–Amy. Thanks." His tone became more upbeat as he added, "How about you? Weekends with your honey?"

She cringed, and Paul's silent laugh made her feel worse. "I spend a lot of time with my buddy and his girlfriend. We cook, climb a tree, watch a video, that sort of thing." She wondered what it would be like to shoehorn Kowalski into her life with Paul and Christine.

"When I got married," Kowalski said, "it was like I lost all my single friends. They still wanted to party crazy. Now, after our married friends found out about Roxy and me, it's like they don't want to talk to me anymore." He flicked on the lights and siren to run a red light on Airline Highway. "Like they're afraid whatever happened might be catching."

Paul said, "Or it reminds them of all their issues that we don't know about."

"Well I guess. So how do you hang out with a guy and his girlfriend and not get in the way? A single woman friends with a couple?"

"Impossible to explain," Amy answered. "But they are my best friends, both of them." Paul thought to her, *Christine would hate him because she hates all men except me, and she doesn't like cops because she does drugs.*

Hey! she thought back, *"I'm a cop. She likes me fine.*

Ah. But she knew you before you were a cop. Makes all the difference in the world.

Changing the subject, Amy asked out loud, "What's for dinner?" Kowalski spent twenty minutes describing an elaborate roast, a wild rice pilaf, sautéed mushrooms, and home baked bread. When he was done, Amy said, "You cook like that and she doesn't know if she likes you? She's crazy!"

There was a long, uncomfortable silence. "Pat, I'm sorry," she finally said. "I was out of line. Please–crap, I'm sorry."

"It's okay," he said. Then, "If she doesn't come home, can I call you for a late supper? It would be a treat to cook for someone who says 'thank you'."

She heard Paul bellow in her head, *Christine on Thursday night!* Her face was burning hot, bright red. Hurriedly she thought back, *He's talking Tuesday or Wednesday. I want to say yes but I don't want to be a homewrecker.*

"You okay?" the detective asked, taking a quick look at her.

Paul thought to her, *Sounds like that home was wrecked months ago.*

"Sure," Amy said, firmly. "That would be great. But don't, you know–" and she stopped.

Kowalski raised an eyebrow.

"I mean, if you're having trouble with your wife, is it really such a good idea to have a woman over?"

She smiled as she silently shouted *Trash mouth!* when Paul thought, *You want to have him over, under, sideways, down.*

"No, it's not," he nodded, then faced her with a grin. "But if you're up for it, so am I."

For the remainder of the drive to the station house Paul heard Amy think over and over, *I'm in trouble now.*

At the station house, Amy had to talk Kowalski into delaying the start of his weekend long enough to hear what the medical examiner had to tell them. "Yo, doc!" the officer called as they entered his room.

Jermaine laid down his scalpel, turned off the light over his autopsy table, and began peeling off his gloves. He left Jane Doe #0134-2026 with her abdomen open, then thought to toss a sheet over her.

"Officer, Miss," the courtly doctor said.

"There are days when I'm thrilled to learn that the milk of human kindness still flows through the veins of humanity," Amy said. "And there are days it hurts to be reminded that some of my fellow humans rank in the neighborhood of pond scum and dung beetles. Today was both of them." She gave a huge, false smile.

"Oh, dear. What is she going on about, Patrick?" He finally got his lab coat off.

"Two interviews. One was a USDA prime asshole; I nearly maced him. The other one was a scared kid who still might be our perp."

"Not him," Amy said. "His boss, the older guy in the back room. You were on the gym floor so you didn't see him muss Hunter's hair. It was nice to see genuine affection while we're looking for a murderer."

Paul rushed to business. "Did you get to the buttons and shell casing?"

"Yes, I did. We have some tantalizing possibilities, and some dead ends."

Paul said, "Let's get the bad news out of the way."

"No, I'm saving that for last because it will involve a little field trip." He moved to his desk and took up two non-static plastic evidence bags. "This was on the floor," he said, waving one bag holding a button. Then lifting the other bag, "This was clasped so tightly in Miss Slaton's right hand that I had to break two fingers to remove it."

Amy and Kowalski stepped closer to the medical examiner.

"They are matching. Black plastic, two hole buttons, traces of black thread on the one in her hand. I cannot associate them with a particular brand of clothing, or retail outlet. No street address of our killer. But both buttons have residue of dog dander."

Amy rolled her eyes and said to the officer, "I was an idiot and didn't ask Stringfellow if he had a dog."

"Half right," he smiled. "No idiots here, but no, we didn't find out if he has a dog." The officer turned to Jermaine and said, "The asshole has two dogs."

Amy turned back to Jermaine and said, "Mackenzie Slaton was allergic to dogs. Can you tell what breed?"

"No," he said, shaking his head, "Despite the advanced state of forensic technology, the most I might be able to determine is big dog or little dog."

He went on, "Our killer, if he is an exceptionally stupid specimen of criminal behavior, is in possession of a black shirt missing two buttons. If he has half a brain, he is in possession of a handful of ashes of what at one time had been a black shirt missing two buttons. And if he has three quarters of a brain, he has disposed of the ashes to make all evidence disappear."

Amy mused aloud, "How stupid is a perp likely to be if he can rappel down a rope and make off with almost thirty-four million dollars' worth of jewels?"

"Stupid?" Kowalski blurted out. "I'll settle for careless. We need to ask about the clothing we saw in the museum surveillance video." Then, "Doc, what about the cigarette butt? Or the silencer? Or–"

"I'm getting there!" Jermaine barked, exasperated. "Let me develop this for you both in a reasonable, logical way."

Amy heard Paul think, *Mister Wizard got up on the wrong side of bed,* and she smirked.

"Something to share with the class?" Jermaine asked.

"With all due respect, Doctor Tallant, did you have a bad weekend?"

"As a matter of fact, Miss, yes I did. The Mayor seems to have an inexhaustible supply of cousins and nephews who have been falsely accused of car theft based on the flimsiest of evidence that nonetheless confirms their inescapable guilt. I had to turn off my phone to enjoy any time with my son and his wife. Now, where was I? Oh, yes. The cigarette butt contained DNA traces, presumably from saliva. It doesn't match anything in the database, but we can compare it to samples you take during the investigation."

Paul said, "So we'll be able to convict for smoking in a smoke-free building."

"I do not appreciate your tone, Miss, but you make an important point. We do not know that the cigarette came from our perpetrator, only that it came from someone who was in that room after housekeeping finished its job that day."

Hush! Amy thought to Paul. *Jermaine's on edge, I like him, let's go easy on him. And I thought you like him.*

I do, he thought back. *I'll behave.*

Jermaine went on. "The improvised silencer is clean of prints inside and out. Even the yards and yards of duct tape on it have no fingerprint or glove impressions." He lifted the device, in its non-static plastic bag. "It is based on an old design from *Popular Mechanics* magazine in the 1950s. Merely creating this was a federal felony, let alone using it to commit a crime. It didn't require any special tools or skills, but it would take a certain mechanical aptitude to think of it and carry it off with no evidence adhering. I feel obliged to say I am impressed."

"So, it's a dead end," Kowalski observed.

"As you say. For our last piece of forensics, I need you two to accompany me." He opened a desk drawer and pulled out two copper clad .45 cartridges. "Miss, if you would take one," he handed it to Amy, "And you, Officer." He reached in the drawer again and this time came up with an ancient .45 revolver. Opening the cylinder, he said, "Officer, if you would secure this, let us go downstairs to the range. I have to show you something important."

As they filed into the hallway, Paul said, "But the guard was killed with a .380 or a 9mm slug."

"The caliber is not germane," Jermaine replied.

The medical examiner checked them in at the pistol range. "Eyes and ears, everyone!" he sang, as each of them picked up ear muff sound blockers and goggles. He took a push broom to the area at the head of their lane, sweeping spent brass out of the way. Finally, at the firing line bench, he said, "Officer, if you would please load your bullet in the cylinder and fire it downrange."

"But there's no target!" Kowalski protested.

"Pretend there's one. The cartridge is the point of this exercise."

Kowalski shrugged. He stood in an isosceles stance and pulled the trigger. Six inches of flame belched from the gun's muzzle, while only their hearing protection kept their cochleae safe.

Jermaine instructed him to open the cylinder and give the spent cartridge casing to Amy. He handed her a Sharpie pen and asked, "Would you be so kind as to mark the side of the shell with a '1'?" When she had done so, he said, "Now, put that in a pocket and don't lose it."

Kowalski handed the empty pistol back to the doctor. He placed it on the bench and said, "Detective, let me see you field strip the weapon."

Amy heard Paul think, *Oh, let me.* To the medical examiner he said, "It's a revolver. It doesn't field strip. Give me a screwdriver and I'll dismantle it, but–wait, was this a trick question?"

"Hmm, I must give you credit, Miss. Yes, it indeed was a trick question." Jermaine took a small rat-tail file from his pocket. "Gather around, I want to show you something." With Kowalski looking over his shoulder, he handed the unloaded revolver to Amy and said, "Show me the firing pin." She swung open the cylinder and pointed to the hole where the pin rested. "Make it come out," he ordered, so she pulled and held the trigger. The short, thin pin popped up.

"Keep holding it," he said. "With this little dime-store file I will scrape the face of the pin, just a little. There. You may release the trigger, miss." A few bright scrapings of metal fell to the bench.

He handed the gun to Amy and said, "The bullet I gave you.

Would you put it in the wheel and then fire downrange?"

Amy and Paul smiled inside, they both enjoyed the Zen of target practice. "Too bad it's only one shot," she murmured as she sent the copper clad lead down range to the backstop.

"If you would, Detective, give the officer the empty shell." Then, "Officer, here's a marker, put a '2' on it. Good. Now let us all go back to my office. I want to show you something."

Back in his office, Jermaine pulled the plastic dust cover off his comparison microscope. He blew on the lens to remove some dust, then pulled the Leica to the front of the countertop. "The bullet that killed the guard began to fragment as it pulverized the man's jaw, and it disintegrated completely when it hit the marble floor. Although we recovered enough lead and copper to conclude the man was killed with a 124 grain load, we found nothing of forensics value from the projectile. All we have is the shell casing, and now I will demonstrate why that is most likely another dead end."

He turned to Amy. "May I have the cartridge case from the officer's shot?" She fumbled in her shirt pocket, then pulled out the brass cylinder with her '1' marked on it. He said, "Thank you," as he positioned it, primer up, on the left side of the dual microscope. Then, "Officer, I believe you have the shell marked '2'?" The doctor oriented it the same way on the right side. He peered into the dual optical scope and spoke as he twirled knobs to bring the two pieces of brass in focus and alignment. "What I am about to show you would hold true if we had been able to recover an intact bullet, too. You are professionals, you know about the striations that a gun's rifling leave on the bullet as goes down the barrel. The shell casing has characteristic marks by the firing pin and the ejector." He stood up when he had the images prepared in the comparison microscope. "You both fired the same gun. You used identical ammunition. Now I want you to see how the brass looks."

Amy leaned over the microscope. She blinked twice before she saw the two fired cartridges side by side. The firing pin marks in the primer were obviously not a match. Paul thought to her, *The file.*

Amy stood back and let Kowalski peer into the machine. "That's not possible," he said, still looking at the images. "They look like they came from different guns, but I know we fired the same weapon."

As the policeman stood up, Jermaine broke into a big smile. "Now you see why that big fancy database that Louisiana is pouring money into is a complete waste. It will catch the occasional amateur and moron. But a professional with even a room temperature IQ knows to use a little file like I showed you, and *voila*! his weapon is unidentifiable. It takes a little more work to do this with a semi-automatic pistol, but the principle is identical. And now you see why our museum evidence is not likely to help us find our perpetrator."

Amy dropped her jaw. "You really are Mister Wizard," she said.

"Thank you, Miss. Now, class dismissed. Jane Doe over here is waiting for me to poke around inside her abdomen."

In the hallway, Kowalski said, "I really wish he'd just spit it out."

"Nuh-uh!" Amy said. "The theatre is impressive. This is a lesson I will never forget." Then, "I know you want to get on your weekend. Tomorrow I will find the daughter. I want her view of her loving father. Maybe she can tell me who her rich relatives are. And maybe she knows if daddy dearest has a black shirt."

"Okay. Look, uh, what we talked about in the car?"

"Yes?"

"Is it okay if I call?"

Paul was startled by how broad her smile was. She said, "Yes. Yes, it's okay if you call." As she stood looking up at him, Paul added aloud, "I hope things work out for you, Pat."

He nodded, then flashed a smile and walked to the uniformed division. As soon as he was out of sight–not that she had to wait for that–she thought to Paul, *Why did you say that? It's not true. I hope his wife chokes on a chicken bone! What? Did you just chuckle?*

"Yes I did," Paul whispered. Silently he added, *It's just polite to wish people well with their marriage. Or did you want to say 'I hope she stiffs you and you call me'?*

She smiled as she considered it. "I would love that. But I see your point. Besides, I don't want to come across as too eager." Her smile collapsed and she thought, *Am I really that easy?*

No, you're not 'easy,' so don't worry. You like the guy. And I've been with Christine long enough that I think I'm ready to survive you having an affair with a man. I think I am.

"Wish me luck giving you the chance to test-drive that. Hey, I'm thinking crawfish and corn for dinner."

❦ 8 ❦

That night, Paul and Amy talked on the phone for an hour with Christine. She was full of news for her Paulette, about a favorite song she heard on the radio, an article she read at lunch, an odd customer at the real estate agency where she worked. Paul told her about the day's investigations.

Amy finally said, "I need to talk to my best friend."

"I didn't want to be pushy," Christine answered. "Tell me about your officer."

"I think he likes me. I mean, likes me that way. And Paul has been helpful, when I get tongue-tied he asks the right question." The two women went over what Amy called her progress, and Paul made the occasional point.

They were sitting at the computer desk, the one with above-and-below monitors that let each of them look at different screens at the same time. "It's Paul. Amy, you finally picked a worthwhile man instead of those pathetic bad boys. And Christine showed me how to survive when you're with a naked man. I've got high hopes for you."

"I don't know," Christine offered. "It's all academic to me, since I don't understand how any sane girl wants to be with a boy. But he's married? And he might invite you over while he's still living with her? It's your life and all, but – really, Amy, you're smarter than that."

Stunned, defensive, Amy blurted, "What a terrible thing to say!"

Paul felt caught in the middle, between his lover Christine and the woman whose body he shared, Amy. "Terrible to say you're smarter than that?"

"Can't you be happy for me? I promise, this won't take away from you and Paul." To Paul but out loud, "I thought she liked me!"

"I do like you, I love you," Christine said. "That's why I'm telling you this. I don't want you to get hurt and be all unhappy. The boy isn't available."

Amy started to explain again how Pat had demonstrated his vulnerability and openness, but Christine interrupted. "That's not what I mean. If he's married, if he's living with his wife, he can't be much of a partner for you. What's going to happen at Christmas? He'll spend it with her, not you."

Amy was quiet, fighting Christine's words but also hearing the truth in them. After a few seconds, Paul said, "That's something to think about. You really are a good friend for Amy. I don't think she's happy with what you said, but only a friend risks pissing someone off to tell them something unpleasant."

"I guess," Christine said. "I hate to make Amy sad. But I love her because she's part of you, Paulette. I want her to be happy. Like you are. Like you and me."

"It's Amy," she said slowly. "So, if he calls me tomorrow and asks me over for the dinner that he cooked for his wife but that she's not home to eat, you think—you think I shouldn't go?"

She heard Christine say "Don't go" as Paul thought, *Go for it.* "What if she comes home while you're eating? Or while you're still there after dinner?" Christine usually avoided conflict, but Paulette–and by extension Amy–was the most important person in her life. "There'll be a big scene. There'll be guilt. Shame. Blame. How's that going to help you and this boy?"

When she was finished, Amy said, "Paul? What do you think?"

"Uh... As long as you keep your clothes on, the wife can't bitch much. Sure."

"Oh, Paulette!" Christine cried. "That's just wishful thinking. The wife can bitch as much as she wants; she's not limited by your expectations, or your fantasies. People get mad when they find a partner is unfaithful, even if it's not physical. I know. I've been there."

"Oh, crap," Amy said. "I wish you didn't make so much sense."

"It's Paul. You've been there?"

"I thought I told you. My girlfriend that cut my hair way back when? I came home and found the, uh, the bottom half of a mutual friend sticking out from under her skirt. I had to buy new dishes at the thrift store because I smashed every single plate we had."

"Over-reaction?" Amy asked, hopefully.

"Maybe to them. Not to me, it wasn't."

"Well, crap. Let me think about this some more. Crap, crap, crap."

"Please don't be mad, Amy. I want you to be happy. I love you, I really do."

"And that's the only reason I didn't hang up five minutes ago. I don't know what I'm going to do, but thank you for caring so much about me and Paul."

"It's Paul," he said cheerfully. "We're still good for Thursday, right? Meet you at the club for dinner?"

"You bet! Can you stay over?"

Christine always could tell which one of them was leading, so she knew it was Amy who went on, "You'll recognize us, we'll be the black-and-blue woman on crutches or in a wheel chair."

"I'll bring band-aids. See you Thursday. I love you Paulette. Love you, Amy."

They sat at the computer desk for a few seconds. "That didn't go exactly the way you expected," Paul spoke.

"Not hardly. I wish your girlfriend wasn't so smart. Damn."

"So what'll you do if Kowalski calls?"

"I. Don't. Know. I really don't. Double crap."

9

Amy stopped at the station long enough to get Bella Blunt's contact information from the police sources. Paul thought, *I remember when you needed a search warrant to find an unlisted phone number. What happened?*

"Living in a police state isn't so bad if you're the police."

For some reason that gives me no comfort.

"I don't make the Supreme Court decisions, I just try to make them work for me." She pulled a page off the printer. "Bella lives with Darius and Beau Sonnier across the river in Marrero." She reached for the phone in the detectives' bullpen. As they heard Bella's phone ring, Paul thought, *Let's get the captain to paint this room yellow.*

"Anything is better than this gross green," she mumbled aloud. Then a male voice said, "Hello?"

"Good morning. This is Detective Amy Clear with New Orleans Police. I am looking for Bella Blunt. May I speak with her?"

"Christ, what's she done?"

"May I speak with her?"

"Yeah, yeah, hold your horses." Off microphone she heard the man shout, "Bella! Phone!"

It took a few moments before Amy heard a sleepy, "What? This is Bella, who's this?"

Amy introduced herself and explained she had met the girl's mother the day before, but she chose not to mention Skyler. "I need to talk to you in person," she said. "Can I meet you where you are?"

"What time is it? Uh, yeah, I guess so. I don't have to be at work until two."

She confirmed the address with the woman. "See you in an hour, okay?"

"Yeah. Whatever."

I think she was sleeping in, Paul thought. *Do we know where she works?*

"Some manufacturing plant on the west bank, I'll bet. She's probably an assembly line drone." Amy gathered up her clipboard and files. "Let's see what Marrero is like," she said, walking down the maze of hallways toward the parking lot and her old blue sedan.

Amy let Paul lead to drive. She mused, "Is Christine going to be pissed at me now?"

"I doubt it," he answered out loud. "Disappointed, maybe, but she cares about you. She doesn't want to see you get hurt. Neither do I, but I guess the three of us have different risk thresholds."

"I don't know what I'm going to do."

"Maybe he won't call you. That'll solve some problems."

No! She thought, then added out loud, "Solve some, create another. I want him to like me."

He obeyed a stop sign, then turned left and headed for the Pontchartrain Expressway bridge. "What's the plan for Blunt's daughter?

Amy said, "I want her to spill the beans on her father. Maybe she knows if he has a black ski mask."

The expressway passed through Marrero. Paul got off at Ames and turned right. "Wrong way," Amy said. "Let me drive, I'll get us there."

Marrero was an industrial town on the south side–nonetheless referred to locally as the west bank–of the Mississippi River. The area between the expressway and the river was entirely industrial, with a big electrical contractor and several metal fabricators. There were dozens of huge storage tanks for oil and natural gas. South of the expressway were old houses, built before World War II. For every two with mowed lawns, there was another in need of paint, or with a blue tarp hanging from a section of damaged roof. The main north-south streets hosted a little development, while the rest of the town looked more and more suburban as one traveled away from the river. Marrero was a step toward respectability for those with ambition, or another stop on a downward spiral for those who had run out of drive or luck.

Amy pulled up outside a small gray house on a side street, one of the ones desperate for paint. The siding was obsolete asbestos planking. The yard, unfenced, was a mottled mixture of dirt and weeds. She saw a sedan and a pickup truck in the driveway. Under the carport was a 14-foot boat on a trailer. "What do you think?" she asked Paul as she locked the car.

"I think this place could use a tree. The whole town could. Why are there no trees here?"

"Huh, I hadn't noticed. I'm guessing floods. Maybe I'll ask."

Amy went up the walkway and knocked on the front door. She was holding up her badge case when a short young woman in a bathrobe opened the door. "Hello, Officer," she said with a half-smile, "I'm Bella. Come in."

"Detective," Amy corrected, while Paul thought, *She's more polite than her father.*

She led Amy into a beige living room with a sofa, a TV, and an end table with lamp. The curtains were closed, leaving the room in dim light. *At least a motel has a picture on the wall,* Paul thought. Amy agreed that the arrangement looked impersonal and temporary.

"Have my parents sent you?" the woman asked. She tugged at the lapel of her bathrobe.

"Not hardly. I think your father's head would explode if he knew I was here." The woman laughed bitterly. Soberly, Amy went on, "Skyler Blunt is a person of interest in a crime that took place last week in NOLA. I've interviewed him and your mother, and I have some questions that you might be able to answer."

"Me? Hah!" She reached to the coffee table for a pack of cigarettes and pulled one out. She motioned toward Amy, but the detective shook her head. The woman lit her smoke with adisposable yellow butane lighter.

"Tell me about your father."

Bella shivered. "He's a bully and a drunk and a crook. I hate him. He's why I moved out. Well, him and my sweetie, Darius."

"Tell me about your father being a bully."

She flicked ash onto the table top. "It's got to be his way. Everything. Otherwise he yells and screams. He hits Mom all the time. He used to threaten me. I never knew if it would be quiet at home or if he'd be shouting."

"You say he threatened you. Did he abuse you?"

"Abuse? And how! But he didn't hit me. I mean, he did when I was little, but when I started growing these –" she used her hands to heft her breasts through the bathrobe "– he never touched me again. He never tried anything, you know, sexual. No, he just would yell that I was ugly and useless and stupid." For a moment her eyes looked sad. "All the fucking time."

"But your mother..."

"I love Mom, but I hate her, too. She's such a sheep. Dad beats her once or twice a week. If I were her, I'd kill him. Or at least have some self-respect and move out. I tell her, 'Leave, Mom!' But she says, 'I love him; someday you'll understand.' Hah!"

It was Paul who said, "So, do you understand yet?"

A vigorous head shake, "Not hardly. I'm sure I would hate getting hit."

Amy led again. "Your mother said you were uncontrollable and that they disapproved of your boyfriend. Was that–who?"

"Darius," Bella helped. "Yeah, him. That's so funny, considering Dad gave me to him." More ash on the table.

"Gave you to him? What does that mean?"

"One night, I was sixteen, I was in my room talking to a friend on the phone, and dad came in. He hung up the phone and pushed me into the living room. Mom and a couple of men were there. It turned out to be Darius and his brother. Dad said, "I don't have the money, so, here!" and he pushed me toward Darius. As it turned out, I thought he was a fox, so it was okay with me, but yeah, dad pimped me out. I was payment for some debt."

Paul thought to Amy, *Close our mouth.* She blinked and retracted her slack jaw. "W-what kind of debt?"

"Darius told me later. Dad did some jail time before I was born, and so did Darius and Beau, and that's where they met." Bella went to the front door, opened it, and flicked her cigarette butt into the front yard. "They still do some, uh, midnight requisitions, and they fence stuff for each other. Dad sold some car parts or something, but he spent the money. Beau was going to beat up Dad, and he could, too. So I was valuable consideration." She smiled. "Not bad for the girl he always said was worthless."

Amy held up her hand. "Wait. Are you saying your boyfriend and your dad are currently involved in criminal activity?"

The smile fled from Bella's face. "I will deny I ever said it. Look, I'm trying to be helpful by explaining this stuff. Don't punish Darius for it." She reached for the cigarette packet and lit another.

"Okay, I hear you. Do you know if your father has a black ski mask?"

Head shake. "Not that I know of. Of course, he has his midnight creeper outfit." When Amy raised an eyebrow, she went on, "For those things I'll swear I never talked to you about. Black jeans, a heavy, long-sleeve black shirt. I'd laugh at him when I saw him in it."

Paul asked, "That shirt—is it a pullover or does it button up?"

The woman considered. "Button up, I think. I didn't pay that much attention."

Amy took back the lead to ask, "Any idea if he was home Thursday night?"

She made a funny noise, blowing out through closed lips. "I haven't been home in weeks."

"So you wouldn't know if he's come into some money?" Bella shook her head.

Paul asked, "What's with the gloves that–"

"Oh, it'll piss him off so bad when I tell you! It was, ummm, maybe seven or eight years ago, I think I was ten. He was in an accident at work and he lost the tip of his left ring finger." Her face was animated and her eyes were smiling as she recounted it. "He couldn't do much for a couple of weeks, I think it still hurts. But he's ashamed of it. He must have a hundred different pairs of gloves, I hardly ever saw him without them."

"How interesting," Paul said, sincerely. Amy took the lead and said, "What do you know about his girlfriend?"

"Dad? A girlfriend? You have got to be kidding!" She flicked ashes in the vague direction of a black plastic ashtray.

"He was seeing a twenty-year-old model named Mackenzie Slaton. Your mother knows, but she's pretending it wasn't an affair."

"I moved out the day after I turned eighteen. I've been here for six-and-a-half months. I don't know about this." She laughed, blowing smoke out of her mouth. "Dad? A twenty-year-old? A MODEL?" She shook her head.

"He's not a bad-looking man," Amy offered. "Can he be charming when he's sober?" She heard Paul think, *What? Don't defend the guy, let the woman talk.* She cringed.

"Maybe. He just never bothered to try at home."

"You said your father owed money to, to Darius. Did he owe a lot of money? Was money tight at home?"

"Yeah. I'm pretty sure he owed everyone. And Aunt Holly and Uncle Brad wouldn't help out. Uncle Brad and Dad hate each other."

"Ah, your mother said you had rich relatives. Who are they?"

"Aunt Holly is mom's sister. She's kind of stiff, but she's okay. Uncle Brad is a horror. Big guy, another bully. If it weren't for Aunt Holly and my cousin Larry I'd swear he was gay. He runs one of the art museums in town."

"Bradley Richardson?" Amy said, amazed. "Your Uncle Brad is Bradley Richardson?"

"You sound like you've had the pleasure of his company."

Amy laughed, "Sort of. I arrested him last week."

"Oh, too much. Kick him in the balls for me, will you? He and Aunt Holly have money out the wazoo and they won't help mom."

Amy heard Paul think, *Is this why he was such a prick when you went into the other gallery that night? We may need to pay him a visit.*

"No kidding," Amy said softly, startling Bella Blunt. "Oh, I'm sorry, I'm talking to myself. One thing I need to know—what is your mother's maiden name? Aunt Holly's maiden name?"

"Oswald. Why?"

"Just in case Uncle Brad gives me all the crap I expect from him."

Amy took out her card case and held a business card out to Bella. "If you think of anything that might help us with our inquiries. If you remember a black ski mask, or if you find out about his affair, anything. Okay?"

"You're going to leave? I was just about to pull out some pot and offer you a joint."

"Don't push your luck, Bella." Then Paul added, "Maybe next

time."

In the car, Amy thought, *That was a mixed message you sent her.*

Yup. Sometimes I wish you weren't such a boy scout.

"Too bad, hippie," she said aloud. "You geezer."

"No need to get personal," he laughed as he started the engine. "Next stop, Uncle Brad's office?" He turned the car around and headed back to the Westbank Expressway.

"Yes," she mused, aloud. "We can't call him that; it would tell him who we talked to. I want to hear what lies he has to say about his wife's family." More firmly she said, "Maybe he's not as rich as Bella thinks."

Amy was not in uniform, but wore a police belt with gun, cuffs, and baton over her dark slacks. When she entered the museum director's outer office, a young man in excruciatingly correct business attire stood and asked, "Can I help you?"

"Good afternoon. I'm looking for Doctor Richardson. Is he in?"

"Do you have an appointment?" he asked, with what looked to Amy to be a sneer.

"No, but he'll see me."

"Who should I tell him is here?"

"Tell him it's the crazy queen bitch from hell."

The aide snorted, "You don't look like Holly Richardson."

It was Paul who smiled at the man. "Tell him it's the other crazy queen bitch from hell. He'll see me." He displayed Amy's badge case.

A snort. "I doubt it. Doctor Richardson is a very busy man. He doesn't have time to talk to walk-ins."

"If he can't talk to me here, he'll talk to me at the police station on Rampart Street. Tell him I have a nice warm set of handcuffs with his name on them." When the man stared back, Paul barked, "Tell him. Now!"

Amy thought, *So why was it bad for me to talk tough to the director if it's okay for you to intimidate his flunky?*

The aide sat down and punched the intercom button. "Doctor Richardson, a police woman is here to see you."

"Don't tell me that crazy bitch is back!" they heard.

Amy leaned over the desk and pressed the transmit button.

"Yup, I'm baaaack. Will you see me here or do I have to drag you out of your cave?"

They heard a lot of room noise, a chair falling, the ding of a cell phone, and finally the words, "Shit. Give me a minute, then bring the detective in. I'll need you to stay, Lance. I want a witness."

Amy smiled to the aide. She heard Paul think, *It's so tempting!*

She straightened up, thinking of what issues she wanted to cover with Richardson. The aide, clearly nervous, kept rearranging the stapler and tape dispenser on his desk. Finally the intercom buzzed and the museum director said, "Okay, bring the detective in."

Lance took a legal pad and stood. "If you would follow me," and he pushed open the heavy wooden door to Bradley Richardson's inner sanctum. Amy held her notebook in her right hand, hoping to avoid having to shake the man's hand. Richardson had abandoned his tidy desk and was seated at a round, plain blonde conference table. Amy sat at a 135-degree angle to minimize psychological confrontation for the interview. Unconsciously Lance sat at the same point on the other side of the table.

"How can I help you, Officer?" Richardson began.

"It's 'Detective Clear,'" she corrected. "Tell me when you knew there was an intruder here on Thursday."

"When I saw you letting yourself out of the gallery that had contained the Rothschild jewels. Of course, I mistakenly thought you were the intruder."

Paul scribbled in the notebook with their left hand. "Is your insurance carrier cooperating?"

"Yes, actually. I am surprised and relieved."

"Tell me about your family, Doctor Richardson. Your wife?"

"I don't understand why my family is any of your concern."

Amy stood up and slipped the handcuffs out of their case. "Let's go downtown to finish the interview." Fear registered on the man's face, while Lance looked panic struck. After she took one step toward him, he pushed his chair back from the table and blurted, "My wife is Holly Oswald Richardson. We married in 1996."

"Thank you," Amy said. She heard Paul think, *I know it's wrong, but that worked well.*

Amy sat back down, but left the handcuffs on the table. "Children?"

"Laertes – uh, he calls himself Larry. He's at UC Berkley, working on his MFA. We had a daughter, but we lost her as an infant."

"So, it's just you and Holly at home now?" He nodded.

"Tell me about your sister-in-law and brother-in-law."

"Which ones?"

"How about..." she rolled her eyes to the ceiling, then leaned forward to stare at the man, "How about Crystal and Skyler Blunt."

"Oh." He reached down for something that had fallen to the carpet. "I thought you meant Holly's brother and his wife."

"Crystal and Skyler Blunt," Amy repeated, still staring.

"Yes, well. We're not particularly close. Crystal is a sad case. And that Skyler–" he shuddered "–do you know he's been in jail?"

"And there's always the chance he's going back there. If that happens, Doctor Richardson, will he take you with him?"

"What? What are you talking about?"

"Two people died here Thursday night. Your brother-in-law was on the phone with the model about three minutes before she fell."

"Are you suggesting I had anything to do with her death?"

Amy smiled. "I don't know. That's why I'm here, to find out."

"I don't appreciate your tone, detective."

Another smile, "Duly noted. Tell me about your relationship with the Blunts."

"You're not taking me seriously!" He stood up, shaking.

"I believe you that you 'don't appreciate' my tone. I just don't care. Now, sit down and answer my questions or grab a toothbrush and we'll go downtown."

They stared at one another for a long moment. Amy held out her right hand, palm down, and motioned for the man to sit. Eventually he did.

"The Blunts," she prompted.

"My brother-in-law is an ass. He's a convicted felon. I'm pretty sure he beats his wife. I find him exceedingly unpleasant company. We ceased to share Thanksgiving and Christmas with him many years ago."

"How about the wife, Holly's sister?"

"She's a bland enough person. Nowhere near as smart as Holly. But the fact that she has put up with that boor for so many years," he shook his head, "it's hard to have much sympathy for her."

"Their daughter?"

"They have a child?"

Paul thought, *I guess he really doesn't pay attention to the Blunts.*

"Doctor, do you know how Skyler Blunt met the model who died here last week?"

"I'm still absorbing your news that they were acquainted at all."

Paul thought, *Savannah said they met at the publicity dinner for the fashion show. Uncle Brad is the only way Skyler would have been invited.*

This is an interview, Amy thought back. *I let a person of interest lie like a rug. If I have to interrogate him later I'll bust his chops. Maybe Bella will get her wish.*

Paul was puzzled for a moment, but when he remembered Bella's instructions to kick Richardson in the balls, he laughed out loud.

Amy regained their composure and went on. "Your home, Doctor Richardson. Forgive me for some direct questions, but it's my job to ask everyone these things. Are you having any financial difficulties? Do you owe anyone money?"

"Of course not," he answered. "I am remunerated quite well at the Orleans Parish Art Museum. My mortgage is not small, but it is not a problem."

"Alcohol? Gambling? Drugs?"

He shook his head.

"One last question," Amy said. "Why were you so unreasonable Thursday night?"

"Unreasonable? Detective, I might ask you the same question. Why–"

"Unreasonable," Amy repeated, cutting him off. "You were a jerk. Why?"

He paused a moment, then turned to his aide and said, "Lance, would you please bring me some water?" As soon as the man left the room, Richardson said, "I felt threatened. I'm supposed to know everything at my museum, and I had no idea what was going on. And then to see the Rothschild Jewels were gone! I may have been in shock."

"How much of the museum's support is from donations and membership?"

"Forty-three-point-seven percent," he said quickly. "The rest comes from the city, the parish, and some federal grants."

"I guess news about the theft and deaths can hurt funding."

"Yes, it certainly can," he said sadly. "I've been talking to a new public relations firm that thinks these can be spun into a compelling appeal for support, though. No decision has been made yet."

Paul? Any questions? she thought.

Lance returned with a ewer and glasses on a silver tray, and sat it down near his boss. "Thank you," Richardson said, and patted the man's hand. He poured himself a glass of water and drained it.

It was Paul who asked, "You live uptown, right?"

Richardson nodded and said, "In the Garden District."

Paul went on, "What does Holly do?"

"She doesn't have a job, if that's what you mean. But she's on several boards, she does a lot of volunteer work at Touro Hospital and some education non-profits."

"Who handles the family finances, you or her?"

"I do. We have a law firm that handles the family trust, but I take care of the household money. Why?"

"So, if, let's say, you were having some financial issues, your wife might not be aware of it."

"That's cold, detective."

"I take that as a 'yes,'" Paul replied. Amy stood and said, "Thank you for your time, Doctor Richardson. I can't promise I'll have an appointment next time, but I expect we will be back in touch. And good luck with the insurance company."

Richardson, and Lance, stood up. "Uh, yes. Well, have a good day. Lance, can you show the detective out?"

"This way, Detective," he said, and led Amy from the room.

Once they were in the anteroom, Amy said, "Lance? I need some things from you. Can I get your business card, and Doctor

Richardson's?"

"As you wish," he said, and plucked them from their holders for her.

Amy turned the director's over on the desk and held her pen. "What is Bradley's inside line? His business cell phone?"

"I don't know if I should be giving that out."

Amy used the smile that still worked on her father. "It's police business, Lance. What are the numbers?" She wrote them on the card, then thanked him. "I remember the way out," she said.

Instead of going to the parking garage, Amy crossed the museum rotunda and let herself into the gallery that had housed the Rothschild Jewels. It was vacant, closed to the public, and still smelled just a little like bleach.

She walked to the divot in the marble floor where the bullet that ended the guard's life struck, and looked where she remembered Mackenzie Slaton had fallen. Not even a tinge of red remained, but the after-image in Amy's brain was vivid. Softly, she said out loud, "Do you think she fell? Or was she pushed?"

The video didn't look like the perp was trying to throw her over, Paul thought back. *But a death in the commission of a felony is murder.*

She sat cross-legged on the marble, next to where the girl's body had been, and pressed their palms against the cold, clean marble. "Who do we have? Blunt? Stringfellow?" A pause, and she heard Paul's silent answer, *Those jewels are worthless unless they are turned into money. How do we monitor jewel fences?*

She felt her pulse quicken as she said the name, "Pat might know how to do that."

Another pause. Paul said, "Don't call him about it. Let it wait until Thursday, or ask someone else at the station house."

I see why you give Uncle Brad so much shit, Paul went on. *There's something about the creep that just begs for abuse.*

I guess. I really don't understand what I did wrong, but between you and Pat I understand I did something out of line. She paused. *Maybe I should have gone to the academy. I guess they teach cops this kind of thing.*

Their palms still pressed to the marble, Amy stared at the place where Mackenzie had died. "I wonder if I'd have liked her," she mused. "She was too damn skinny, but on the runway she was irresistible."

"Oh, Amy. We'll never know, so I've decided she'd have been one of our best friends."

She sat for another four minutes. Finally she stood, "What are we doing here? We've got notes to write up." Paul drove them back to Rampart Street.

❦ 10 ❧

Everyone there knew him as Jake, really his middle name. The regulars, the floozies, the dealers and the croupiers, they all smiled and waved and called his name when they saw him. He was comfortable at the Big Easy Casino.

Jake stopped at the cage to buy one thousand dollars' worth of chips. Big Easy provided little cardboard boxes for regulars like him, people who liked to jump from game to game instead of settling in for the evening at one particular table. Smiling, excited, he walked slowly through the crowded casino. True, the tourists were there in blue jeans and "Geaux Saints" T-shirts, but the regulars, the well-to-do New Orleanians, they were turned out in fine suits with sharp silk ties; the women wore stunning black dresses that showed off diamonds and strings of pearls. Jake felt like he was surrounded by family. His people. He felt at home.

The large room was brightly lighted. The walls were paneled in dark wood, punctuated by colorful prints of old sporting lithographs. People said polite "Excuse me"s when they bumped him as he walked. It was all so tasteful, the exact opposite of life in the common streets of the city. Jake held his box of chips close and felt his excitement build as he worked his way to the craps table.

A realtor he knew was rolling the dice against the table wall. They bounced back, one spun, and came up a nine. The boxman called, "Pass line nina, pay the man," and the stickman first pulled the dice away, then pushed some chips toward the player.

"Well done, Shane, well done!" Jake said. The realtor looked up with a smile. "Let's see how the next one rolls," he said, and picked the dice up again. He said to the stickman–an extremely attractive blonde woman in her twenties–"Fifty dollar come bet."

She slid his chips to that section of the green felt table. The realtor shook the dice vigorously in his right hand, then bounced them off the far table wall. "Easy seven," the stickman called, "pay the man."

Shane glanced at his Rolex. "Damn, and I'm on a roll. Here, Jake," and he handed the dice to him. "Keep it going." The realtor gathered his winnings and headed toward the cage.

Jake felt his heart speed up, just feeling the cool cubes. His excitement rose when the boxman said, "May I have the dice, Mister Jake?" The boxman dropped them in his bin, then placed two new ones on the felt in front of Jake.

He was dizzy from excitement. Jake put one hundred dollars in chips on the pass line, and threw a three.

"Ace-Deuce, crap out," the stickman said as she scraped Jake's chips to the bank, and pushed the dice to the next player. Jake didn't know him, but he felt reassured by the cut of the three-piece suit, the French cuffs, the buffed shoes, the trimmed gray hair. The new man threw an eight, and Jake dropped chips on the pass line. One does not have to touch the dice to make a bet.

There were three other players and the dice went around twice. When Jake realized he had lost half his night's stake, he put his chips back in the cardboard box and said "Good evening," then tossed a five-dollar chip to the stickman as a tip.

Jake threaded his way down the large room to the blackjack table. He thought the evening's players seemed a little less than top drawer—men without neckties or even jackets, wearing their fedoras indoors; the women in flat shoes and flimsy crop-tops, some even wearing shorts. He frowned, and continued to push his way through the crowded floor until he spotted the Roulette table

"Good evening, Mister Jake," said Claude, the croupier. Wearing his usual tuxedo, the young black man nodded at Jake, then returned to his patter, "Place your bets, place your bets, ladies and gentlemen!" He gave the big red-and-black wheel a mighty spin and shouted, *"rien ne va plus!"* Even though he was not yet participating, Jake's pulse pounded in his ears. The 'clack-clack-clack' noise of the ball bouncing past the pockets thrilled him, the possibility of wealth and success going around and around and around. He never felt as alive as he did at the casino.

Twenty minutes later he said to Claude, "May I sign a chit?"

He had lost his night's thousand dollars, but he did not want to stop.

"Give me a minute," said the croupier, smiling, while he began the next round of betting. Jake did not see him make a hand signal to the pit boss. He was still standing by the table, waiting for the croupier to present the IOU card he signed so often, when a heavy-set man in an ill-fitting tuxedo said, "Mister Jake, do you have a few minutes? Mister Alphonse wants to discuss something with you."

The words startled him, and some of his excitement began to turn into fear. "Mister Alphonse?—" Alphonse Perez was the manager of Big Easy Casino "–Uh, of course." He followed the burly man down the length of the gaming floor, past the blackjack area, past the craps tables, and through a pocket door hidden in the far wall. The hubbub of the casino disappeared as the door closed behind him, and Jake felt his fear increase. He had met Mister Alphonse once, three years earlier, when he had been noticed as a high roller at the casino. The manager had invited him to his private office for drinks; they had talked easily about financial trends, gaming preferences, and their backgrounds. Actually, it was only Jake who talked about those things–Mister Alphonse had asked pointed questions, and had given only polite, bland answers. Now what? Did this summons have something to do with his request for a chit, for his account balance?

The pit boss put his palm on Jake's back and walked beside him down a dim hallway to the manager's office. It was as Jake remembered: dark paneled wood walls, leather chairs, a huge desk, and rich, red curtains against the wall. Two other men in tuxedos, big and young, were seated while the manager was writing at the desk.

The manager looked up and smiled. "Mister Jake, how good of you to visit us. Please, have a seat," and he waved at the occupied chairs. One of the other men stood up to free a chair, then stood by the door, arms folded in front of his chest.

"How have you been, Mister Alphonse?" Jake asked. "It's a pleasure to see you."

"Would you like a drink? I believe you prefer whiskey neat? Mister Harry, would you..." The other man got up to the bar trolley and prepared the drink.

"How has business been?" Jake asked, swirling his drink. The bits of fear had turned back to excitement, that the man who ran the casino requested his company and even remembered his drink preference.

"Not so good, Mister Jake." Alphonse came around to sit on the edge of his desk. "We love your loyalty and your business, but there is a matter of your account. Perhaps you have lost sight of your balance being–" he glanced at the paper in his hand "–forty two thousand, one hundred and eighteen dollars." Jake began to speak but Alphonse held up his free hand and continued, "And aside from your cage purchases, you have not made a payment in three months."

The fear returned. Jake swallowed, then began fumbling for his blazer pockets. "I have my check book, let me–"

"I'd like to see ten percent," Alphonse interrupted. "That is–" looking back at the slip of paper "–Four thousand, two hundred and twelve dollars. Can I stamp the check for you?"

Numbly, he opened his check book. "Ah, well, I–" another swallow "–uh, how about two thousand dollars?"

"For now?" He sighed. "We have to work out a payment plan, Mister Jake, and we have to stick to it."

There was a knock at the door. One of the big young men opened it, and another employee stuck his head in. "Mister Alphonse? We're ready for you."

"I'll be there in a moment," he replied. Then to Jake he said, "Please excuse me for a few minutes. We'll continue our little talk when I get back." He whispered something to Mister Harry at the door, then left the room with the rest of his staff.

Jake was afraid. He had no idea his bill at the casino had gotten so high. It would take a year or more to pay it down without his wife finding out, but only if he could force himself to stay away from his beloved roulette wheel. Maybe twenty-five hundred a month, and a visit to the bank, or–

"The boss said you can help yourself," the helper said, motioning to the beverage cart. He walked to the curtained wall and opened the luxurious red draperies. But instead of a view of the courtyard, the window showed an adjoining room. Three big young men in tuxedos were standing with hands clasped in front of them, all staring at an uncomfortable gentleman seated in a plain wood chair. The room was outfitted like Mister Alphonse's, except for one thing: instead of carpet, the floor was concrete, with a big drain opening in the center.

They saw Alphonse and his two staffers enter the room. The helper with Jake pushed a button, and they could hear Alphonse apologize for being delayed. He went to the seated man and touched his face. "Marcel, Marcel, I thought we had made arrangements."

The man was seated with his back to the window, so all Jake could be sure of was the man's gray hair and his tan business suit. And a sweat stain spreading across the back.

"I'm so sorry, Mister Alphonse, I have every intention of paying the casino. But last month Becky needed some dental work and–"

Alphonse slapped the man across the face and hissed, "You might need some dental work of your own." He straightened up and resumed his pleasant tone to say, "I am sorry to hear of your wife's difficulty, but I don't believe that is my problem." He turned and looked at the men standing around the room, watching. "Am I right? Gentlemen? Is this really our problem?"

A few men shook their heads, the others remained expressionless and silent.

He turned back to Marcel. "See? Not my problem. No, my problem is that you owe Big Easy Casino sixty-one thousand some-odd dollars. That is my problem." Again he turned to look at his staffers. "Am I right? Is that what our problem really is?" This time each of the men nodded, and two said, "Yeah, boss."

Jake looked for Mister Harry. Out of the corner of his eyes he saw him about ten feet away, between him and the door, holding a highball glass and calmly watching the exhibition in the next room. Silently Jake wished for a toilet.

Alphonse continued. "It was three months ago that you and I shared a drink and came up with a financial plan." One of his helpers handed him a manila file folder. "This plan. You signed it, Marcel." He shook his head, "And now, three months later, no money, no note, not even a phone call. This cannot continue."

Marcel began to sputter, but Alphonse held up his hand to silence the man. "We've already talked about this." He turned and nodded to one of the helpers.

Two of the men rushed to Marcel and grasped his left arm, then held it down on the table in front of him. Another one of the young, big men picked up an aluminum baseball bat and smashed it down on Marcel's hand.

Jake shut his eyes at the impact, and winced to hear Marcel's screams.

"I expect your next payment in ten days," Alphonse said. "Is that understood?"

The goon in the room with Jake closed the scarlet curtains and turned off the sound. "The boss will be back in a minute," he said, then took a position by the closed door to the hallway.

He was tugging at his shirt cuffs as he came back into his office. "I'm so sorry," Alphonse said, "but I had to attend to some urgent business. Where were we? Oh, yes. You were writing a check, and then we'll set up a financial arrangement." He pulled his tuxedo jacket down at the waist, then went to his desk.

Jake began scribbling in his checkbook. He made the draft for three thousand dollars, then leaned forward and held it out to Alphonse. "Ah, much better," the manager said, and motioned to one of his goons to take the check. Then he stared at Jake and said, "I want the same amount every thirty days until your account and interest are cleared." He picked up a file folder and examined some printout. "Three thousand dollars a month, at three percent interest per month, you will have paid me everything you owe in eighteen months. If you pay me early, it will reduce your interest charges, which will be considerable."

"Considerable?" Jake managed to say. "That's thirty-six percent interest a year. It's extortion!"

Mister Harry moved to stand beside and behind Jake's chair. Alphonse smiled and shook his head. "Actually, it comes out to forty-two and a half percent. Mister Jake, what I've outlined is your path to financial independence and physical health. What you saw in the next room– ummm, that's extortion." He clucked, "Such an ugly word for helping a weak person live up to his promises."

The excitement Jake had been feeling on the gaming floor had turned to fear. Where would he get that money? And what they did to the man in the next room! His scratched at his neck where it itched under his ascot.

One of Alphonse's goons brought the file folder to Jake and handed him a pen.

Jake swallowed hard but his mouth was bone dry. He felt dizzy. He was frightened. He signed the agreement.

Alphonse Perez looked over the completed document. "Here are the rules," he said. "If you wish to pay me in person, ask for me at the front door. Otherwise you are forbidden from entering Big Easy Casino until your account is entirely paid off. And I will know if you patronize any other casino, so I beg you not to." He leaned down toward Jake. "Any questions?"

When he found he couldn't make any sound come out of his mouth, Jake shook his head and began to get up. Alphonse and Mister Harry helped him stand, then walked him to the office door. "Please remember everything about your visit tonight," the manager called before his goon escorted him to the gaming floor and the front door.

"You're home early," Holly said when he opened the front door of their Garden District home. "I thought that development meeting would still be going on."

He smiled thinly, then let himself drop onto the sofa. He stared at his feet and said, "It didn't work out." Jake considered telling his wife how much trouble he was in, how much money he owed, and what the people he owed it to would do to him. It was one of those rare moments when he wished his wife were his friend and partner.

"I'm sorry, dear," she said. She was standing by the doorway to the kitchen, unfastening her earrings. "I'm sure you'll think of something. You always do."

He looked up to watch her leave the room. "I always do," he thought to himself, and he shivered.

❦ 11 ❧

Bradley Richardson was gloating over the schedule on his desk. What a coup, to be the only southeast venue to display the Rothschild jewels! Almost thirty-four million dollars of countless gems in exquisite platinum and gold settings, created in 1826 to make a woman feel better about being snubbed by the King of France. The Rothschild Family Group began planning a tour of the fabulous jewels in 2023, and, with the help of the Mayor, the Orleans Parish Art Museum was one of the American sites put forward as a host. Between insurance issues and concern about the city's notorious humidity, there was a fierce battle between New Orleans and Atlanta for the honor of display. Three weeks earlier Bradley had hosted the Rothschild site selection team that included two people with that illustrious surname. A tour of the museum, a stroll down Bourbon Street, and a wonderful dinner at Commander's Palace had won the commission. The final contracts had arrived by FedEx that morning.

The mailer also included ad slicks for marketing purposes. The pictures made the jewels as mouth-watering as TV ads do hamburgers–the colors so deep, with light glinting off gem facets and silver settings. Thirty-three-point-seven million dollars' worth. And suddenly Doctor Bradley Richardson was thinking how just one of those emeralds or sapphires would free him from the tyranny of the Big Easy Casino. He stared longingly at the photograph for a long time before he picked up his office phone and called his wife.

"Holly, can I get your sister's phone number? No, nothing like that. I, uh, actually I want to talk to her husband. Yes, that's right, that worthless toad. Thanks." He wrote down the number and immediately called his sister-in-law.

The conversation was awkward. There was no love lost between Bradley and his in-laws; he thought Crystal Blunt was a foolish woman, and he thought Skyler was–well, a worthless toad. But he just might turn out to be useful toad. Crystal Blunt was happy to get a call from her sister's husband, always ready to value whatever crumbs of human notice he gave her. She dictated her husband's cell phone to the man. But when she attempted to turn the conversation to family, Bradley made an excuse to hang up. "Her daughter moved out?" he thought, "I didn't know she had a daughter."

One more phone call. After the introductory hello, he said, "Skyler, this is Bradley Richardson. I want to discuss a business matter with you."

℘ 12 ঽ

Two days after Bradley Richardson telephoned his brother-in-law for the first time in a dozen years, he placed a second call to him. "The museum is going to host a charity fashion show in July. I think it will be worth our while for you to come to the announcement dinner next week."

"What's in it for me, Brad?" asked Skyler Blunt, deliberately using the diminutive he knew Richardson hated.

"Free dinner, and all the fashion models you can charm. Maybe one of them will help you with the project we discussed."

"I'll have to check my calendar," Blunt said. "I may be in Majorca. Or is it Istanbul? They all blur together."

The museum director bit his tongue. It was painful to endure this low-life's excuse for a sense of humor, but he needed the man's help.

"It's Wednesday night at six. Tell them you're with the *haute couture* dinner, if you think you can pronounce it. There'll be a badge waiting for you. And please don't talk to me."

"If I feel like it," Skyler said.

Rather than risk saying another word to his infuriating relative, Richardson hung up. He knew Skyler Blunt wouldn't turn down a free meal, a pretty face, or the kind of payday they had discussed earlier.

The promotional dinner to announce the fashion show had been finalized that morning. It just fell into place. A week ago the director's receptionist buzzed his intercom and said, "A man I know is on line two. He wants to hold a charity event at the museum. Would you talk to him? I think this could be good."

Richardson rolled his eyes, but he thanked Lance and took the call. It was Andy Chastain, a local small-time promoter who was looking for a venue for a charity fashion show. "It's a benefit called 'Couture Cares,'" Chastain said. "Do you have any idea how many people in southwest Louisiana are still displaced from Hurricane Rodrigo? Eighteen months later, people are still in tents in Plaquemines and Jefferson and LaFourche."

The director smiled at the man's enthusiasm. "Tell me what you're planning."

Andy explained he wanted to stage a full runway show to highlight local models, local designers, and local couture cottages. "We'll charge admission to cover fixed costs like lights and sound system, but I hope to give maybe seventy percent of the gate to The Salvation Army or Catholic Charities–they do great work with low overhead."

"The museum will have to charge you a rental fee," Richardson said, "And our box office is used to handling cash and credit card transactions. What else?"

"I want to use your pouring permit. Even if all the alcohol sales go to the museum, I think we'll get better attendance if I can advertise liquor."

Richardson was thinking of lunch. He was wondering where he could get a fake passport to run out on Alphonse Perez's casino. Absently, he agreed to the alcohol sales.

"I'd like to stage this in the middle of July," the promoter said, and abruptly Richardson was attentive. It would be toward the end of the Rothschild jewels exhibition!

"It will have to be a Thursday night." Richardson said, "That's the only evening we're equipped to stay open after hours for an outside client. May I suggest–" he leafed through the pages of his desk calendar "–oh, the 23rd. Our schedule is open that night." That would be the day before the Rothschild exhibit ended.

"I was hoping for something earlier in the month –"

Richardson interrupted, "Not possible. The 23rd is our only window in July." He held his breath until Chastain replied, "Then it'll be the 23rd. Can you host a press announcement? Next week?"

"Will this just be a press conference, or will it include your participants?"

"What a great idea!" Chastain cried. "Yes, the designers, the models, everyone! Can we cater a dinner?"

He was grinning over the gift that blind luck had just dropped in his lap. "I don't see why not. Let me switch you back to Lance Peters; he'll book the dates and get the contract ready."

After he turned the call over to his receptionist, Bradley Richardson sat behind his large desk and smiled. The events would be good for the museum, they might provide a point of entry for his repulsive brother-in-law, and they would be such a useful distraction. That's when he called Skyler Blunt again.

☙ 13 ❧

Mackenzie Slaton was high. She had slipped away to the ladies' room with two of the other models to smoke a couple of joints, and since then she'd downed two daiquiris at the cash bar. The twenty-year-old runway star was happy–hired for a great gig, the Couture Cares event; a free dinner; plans for Hunter to stay over that night; and buzzing along on her intoxicants of choice. All that was missing, she decided, was a cigarette.

Andy Chastain was addressing the group and the press with a hand-held microphone. Ignoring him, Mackenzie struggled to her feet and screamed, "Does anyone have a God-damned cigarette?" There were titters of nervous laughter from the dining room. Savannah Walsh held her palm against the woman's head and giggled, "Shush! You're embarrassing us."

Suddenly a box of Marlboros hit her on the arm and fell to the table, just missing the remains of her salmon and mashed potatoes. Her eyes lit up and she cried, "Thank God!" as she slid one smoke out. When she looked around for a lighter she saw a handsome stranger standing by her chair, holding a blue Bic in gloved hands. "May I?" he asked. Mackenzie smiled as she cupped his hand and lit her cigarette.

"You're a life saver." She exhaled a long plume of blue smoke. The man was about five-eight, around forty, and extremely good-looking; she particularly liked the way his eyebrows peaked towards the sides of his face. "Hey! Sit down," she said and pushed the model next to her out of her chair.

The stranger ignored the other woman's protests. He kept his eyes fastened on Mackenzie's as he sat. The woman was incredibly, astoundingly, phenomenally beautiful–skinny as a pencil, big blue eyes, a tiny nose, and a little mouth that never quite closed. Her long blonde hair was in every man's favorite style, slept-with. She looked like a vulnerable waif.

"My name is Skyler," he said with a smile. "Who is my cigarette-smoking friend?"

A laugh. "Mackenzie. I'm part of the Couture Cares fashion show. What do you do?"

Slowly, he said, "I do all sorts of things. Amazing things." His eyes sparkled. "My job is to make your dreams come true."

"That sounds handy. Can you get me more gigs like this? Runway work is so much fun, and it pays like a rock star."

"I have no doubt. I'll make phone calls tomorrow. Do you have a specialty?"

"I keep my clothes on," she said; after a pause she whispered, "when I work." She watched him light his own cigarette, then asked, "What do you do?"

"I told you. Give me half a chance and I'll demonstrate." Skyler looked around, then said, "We've eaten. Let's get out of here."

The smile didn't match the shake of her head. "I have plans tonight. Call me tomorrow." She took his gloved hand and pushed his shirt sleeve back, exposing the bare inside of his wrist. Then she grabbed a ballpoint out of his shirt pocket and printed "MAC" and her phone number on his arm.

"Let me return the favor," he said. She handed him the pen and held out both her bare arms. He wrote his number on her right arm, then his name on her left. After a moment he added the word 'Yes' and underlined it twice.

For the next hour Mackenzie and Skyler whispered to each other, laughing in their own world. She, in her intoxicated state, thought he was charming. He thought she was sexy and beautiful and an easy way to a big payday.

"What's with the gloves?" she teased.

"I don't know you well enough yet to show you."

She made a mock frown, "You don't have leprosy or anything, do you?"

"Happiness is the only thing you will catch from me."

The woman's roommate, Savannah, quickly gave up trying to

participate in their conversation, and instead went back to listening to Andy and the museum director tell reporters what a wonderful thing the Couture Cares charity fashion event would be. Savannah was happy to be included. She was a stunning woman but 'big boned'–a size 12. She did a lot of catalog work, but despite being "plus-sized" she wanted to make inroads in runway work. It paid as well as the catalog modeling, but was so much classier. She felt bad when the other models at her agency made fun of her for working a catalog job for Target or Cato.

After an hour Skyler asked again if Mackenzie was ready to leave. When she demurred again, he promised he'd call her the next day and began to walk out of the museum gallery. He winked at Bradley Richardson as he left, but made no effort to talk to him.

"Who was that?" Savannah asked her roommate on the drive home.

She looked at her arm. "Skyler. His name is Skyler. Isn't that cool?"

"What do you know about him?"

Mackenzie smiled slyly. "Not a thing. That's what's so neat. And he's hot!"

At a stoplight Savannah asked, "Gym or home?"

"Home. Hunter's coming over soon."

✍ 14 ࿏

Amy felt uncomfortable when she got up on Wednesday. She hadn't heard from Patrick the night before. Would he call that night?

"Today's going to be so boring!" she said to Paul as she showered. "Comparing lists of phone numbers. Ugh!"

"Let me start," he said back. "I actually like that kind of dumb detail work."

"How can you stand it?" She was soaping their legs.

"It's kind of mechanical. Not a lot of brain power involved, but it's satisfying because it has to be done. And sometimes you find answers."

"No wonder you were better at market research than me."

This time he thought to her, *You did fine at research. You just didn't much care for it.*

"We have a winner," she muttered as she rinsed and stepped out of the tub.

She stood through the detective morning muster, then commandeered a desk to work on the printout. She held detailed phone records that covered the last two weeks for Bradley Richardson, Hunter Stringfellow, Mackenzie Slaton, Skyler Blunt, and Bella Blunt–land lines and cell phones, home and work. When Amy sat in front of all the material, she felt her inside eyes roll back. She thought to Paul, *I want to go home.*

Go where you want, as long as we sit here. He grabbed a pen with their left hand and explained aloud as he wrote, "These are the numbers we're looking for. Cell and home, personal and work, for the people we care about." He tapped the back of the pen against their chin. "The only other numbers that matter are any that crop up a lot, and I mean A LOT."

Amy daydreamed about Patrick Kowalski while Paul methodically plowed through the phone use data. With a yellow hi-lighter he marked the target numbers as he encountered them. He worked steadily for an hour and a half before he stopped and stretched. *Coffee*, he thought, *we need coffee.* She let him lead to walk upstairs to the break room: a dirty, bleak room with a cluster of half-empty vending machines and an overworked coffee pot.

What did you discover? she thought.

I don't know yet. I can't even tell you which phone record I was working on. I just mark the target numbers. Later I'll go back and figure out who was talking to whom.

"Whom?" she said, out loud.

Did you sleep through English class?

"Uh, yes. Not always, but sometimes."

"Whom," out loud.

"Everything all right?" Veronica Meek, an older detective, stopped nearby, holding a cup of steaming coffee. She had short dark hair and deep worry lines, and was wearing her trademark black below-the-knee skirt. On Amy's first day on the force, it was Veronica who demonstrated how a woman can use thigh holsters for her sidearm, handcuffs, badge case, and baton. Amy still shivered at the memory of the woman lifting her skirt, but Paul salivated.

"Hey, Ronnie. Just reminding myself of the rules of grammar."

She looked puzzled. "We're cops. We don't need no stinkin' grammar."

"I agree, but Sister Agnetha at Saint Giles Academy had a different opinion."

"Her paddle can't reach you now." Veronica smiled and walked on.

When Paul led them back to the detectives' area, he thought, *What are you doing while I'm working?*

"Don't give me any crap. I'm thinking about Pat."

He smiled and thought back, *I'm on your side. It's Christine who might give you some crap.*

"You actually disagree with your girlfriend. I am amazed."

I love Christine, but I am part of you.

Amy took the lead and stopped walking. "Say that again," she whispered.

He moved their left hand–'his' hand–and held their right arm. *I love Christine,* he thought to her, slowly, *but I am part of you.*

Amy let the reassurance wash over her for a long moment. Then, "Let's get back to work," and she continued their walk back to the piles of computer printout.

It was after lunch when Paul wrote up his findings on the legal pad, and went over them with Amy.

"Uncle Brad," he began. "Home phone has calls to Skyler's home number twice a week. I'm guessing that's Holly calling her sister. No calls to Skyler's cell phone. One call to Bella's cell." Amy nodded, looking at the notes Paul had written up. "Richardson's cell phone has a bunch of calls home, and five calls to Skyler Blunt's cell phone. In particular, two of them are on the day of the museum murders, and one is the next day. His work extension shows almost daily calls to Skyler's cell, and so does his work cell phone."

"I thought they hated each other," Amy offered.

"Exactly," Paul said aloud. He flipped a page on the pad and went on, "Mackenzie Slaton. All she had was her cell phone. Weekly calls home. Daily calls to and from Hunter Stringfellow, the last one about twenty minutes before she died. One call to Skyler Blunt's cell. Daily calls from Skyler's cell, including about five minutes before her death."

Amy thought, "That matches what Jermaine got out of her phone registry. What else?"

"Stringfellow. Cell phone only. Daily calls to and from Mackenzie. No other overlap."

"Bella Blunt, cell phone only. One call from home. I'm guessing it was mama."

That leaves mister glove man, Amy thought.

"A-yup. One call to his home phone from Uncle Brad's home phone–can we assume that was the sisters talking? As for the cell, one call from Mackenzie, lots and lots of calls to her. Pretty much daily calls to and from Richardson, either his personal or work cell or his work number. And a couple of calls that made me do a lookup."

In a sing-song, Amy thought, *Okay, Paul, what did you find when you did a lookup?*

"Well, Amy," he responded in kind, "when we did a lookup we found two calls to a cell number belonging to Beau Sonnier. That's the brother of Bella Blunt's boyfriend. They all live together in Marrero."

"Oho!" Amy said aloud. "Bella said they're still fencing things. Do you think they can handle almost thirty-four million dollars in jewels?"

Paul considered it for a moment and said, "They don't have to sell it all at once. And they can break the settings, just sell the gems, maybe melt down the gold and platinum."

"I guess only an insane collector would care enough to want all the jewels to be intact," she mused.

Later Amy walked back to Jermaine's lab. He was at his autopsy table with what looked like a dismembered German Shepherd. "Hey, Doctor Tallant. Torturing animals again, I see." She smiled broadly.

He looked up at her, peering over the magnifiers clipped to his glasses. His hand was in mid-air, holding a scalpel. "Good afternoon, Miss," he finally said. "Later you can help me pull wings off of flies." He was not smiling.

"Touchy, touchy. Working on a doggie Frankenstein?"

Jermaine put the scalpel down. "Mistress and dog found dead, no apparent cause of death. If I can determine what killed Rin Tin Tin here, I may solve this."

"Truce," she said, holding both hands up, palms forward. "I forgot to ask you, did you find anything from the broken hook from the roof? Or the prints Kowalski lifted?"

She watched his face change mental gears. "Glove prints from the skylight, just like from the pieces of the jewel display case. There was something odd about a ring finger impression, but nothing definitive. And the isolated fluke was clean. Well, except for where the museum security man grabbed it. Do you think he was involved?"

"Logan Spong?" she laughed. "Anything's possible–but, no, I don't."

"'Forensics Today', over and out," he said, and picked up the scalpel. "Come here, Fido, I got a little something for you."

"Uh, see you later, Jermaine. Thanks." She didn't want to see what the medical examiner was really doing to the dog's carcass.

Amy was restless on the drive home. With the work day over, her mind was free again to fantasize about the officer. "I hope he calls," she muttered. Paul, beginning to have second thoughts about her possible tryst, held his tongue. "I said," Amy said louder, "I hope he calls."

"I want my wonderful dyad to be happy," he finally replied. No reason to go beyond the basic truth.

When they got home, Paul persuaded Amy to call Christine. The three of them exchanged news about the day. "Anything from that boy you like?" she finally asked.

"He didn't call last night. Paul says I should be happy for him if he salvages his marriage."

"And my Paulette is right," Christine responded. "I worry about you, I really do."

"I think he's starting to agree with you, that I shouldn't get involved with Patrick." Neither Paul nor Christine said anything. "Oh..." and she bit her lip, "I shouldn't do this, should I?"

Softly, Christine said, "You should do exactly what you want to do. What you think will make you happy tomorrow and next month, not just right now." She paused. "And no, you shouldn't do this."

While Amy gathered her thoughts, Paul spoke up and changed the subject to their plans to meet Christine the following night. "Seven o'clock at the club?"

"Gina says she and Shawna will drop by, but she's got some deal early Friday so they won't stay long."

"Always nice to see them," he said, "but I'm glad we'll have alone time."

There was a beep on the phone. "Oh shit, that's Patrick!" Amy shouted. "Christine, hold on, let me take this–"

"It's okay, I'll see you tomorrow. Good luck, Amy. I love you Paulette!" and she was gone.

Amy pressed the answer button, already thinking to Paul, *If it's a junk call I'll go postal.*

"Detective! Amy!" Kowalski said, dispensing with 'hello.' "Have you eaten dinner yet?"

"Why, Patrick Kowalski, whatever do you mean?" They both laughed.

"Leftovers," he said, "if you ignore that nobody ate anything last night. I don't think Roxy's coming home. I don't want this roast to go to waste."

Paul considered everything that was wrong with that statement: Kowalski still considered his home to be Roxy's home, and his concern was for the food, not about being with Amy. He'd mention it later, but now she was already waist deep in saying yes to the invitation, taking down directions to his house in mid-city, off Carrollton near Bayou St. John.

Paul could feel her excitement as she took a fast shower and put on a blue mans' tailored shirt and a long grey skirt. When she reached for one of her thigh holsters, Paul said, "You're going armed to have dinner at a policeman's house?"

"The Commander says a detective is never off duty. Gotta be prepared."

"You just want an excuse not to wear underwear."

Amy finished adjusting the holster. "That too," she finally admitted. "Is there a problem?"

"Not about that." Amy stood in front of the bathroom mirror to work on her makeup, so Paul had to think to her instead of speak out loud. *Kowalski said he didn't expect his wife to be coming home, right?*

She was contorting her face, working on foundation. "Yes, so...?"

So he still considers her his wife, and he still considers her home to be where he lives. Where does Amy fit in that?

"Stop it!" she shouted out loud. Then silently, *Let me fit in at all, I'll make a place for me. But I have to start somewhere.*

Paul took a deep breath but said nothing. He had lived inside Amy Clear since she was eleven. Help was more important that blame; time and again he had seen that work. If he told Amy she was making a mistake, she would withdraw from him, leaving him helpless and with even less influence over their life. Generally he stated his concerns, then forced himself to be as supportive as he could for Amy's plans. If she succeeded, he would praise her and apologize for having doubted her; if she failed, he merely helped her pick herself back up. He had learned early on that "I told you so" were words she didn't like, and that she made him regret.

When she finished her makeup she was ready to leave, but Paul said, "Wait," and took the lead. He stood in front of the mirror, examining their–Amy's–face. Gray eyes, a small nose, heavy eyebrows, a thin, tan jaw. Their hair was shoulder length, a generic brown, with natural streaks of lighter and darker shades.

Well? he heard Amy think, *Is there spinach in my teeth or what?* He smiled, exposing the crooked front tooth that he adored.

"No. No, we're good. We look at different things in the mirror. When I was a man, all I saw was the patch in front of the razor, and you just make sure that you look presentable. But I still see you the way I've always looked at women. If Kowalski has a soul, he will melt for you."

It was Amy fueling the small smile. "Thanks." She took back the lead, scooped up her keys, and left the house.

Amy insisted on driving, even though Paul usually got to do that. She wanted to pay attention to every element of this first social meeting with Patrick, she hoped at the end she would want to remember every detail. Glancing at the directions the officer had dictated, she made a right onto Delgado. Forty or fifty yards down she saw Kowalski's cruiser parked on the street, facing the other way. She turned when she could, and let Paul parallel park her car behind the black-and-white.

The address was a large white house that had been carved into a quadruple, if not an octuple. The next street over fronted on the Bayou St. John, and there was bridge access to the neighborhood on the other side with the racetrack, the St. Louis Cemetery, and the looming dome of the Holy Rosary Academy. Kowalski's street was not a particularly bad or dangerous one, but fifty years earlier it had been a more prosperous one.

"Unit four," she said aloud as she got out of the car, and she popped one last breath mint. There still was full daylight, but the sun was getting low over City Park to the west.

She walked up a steep outdoor metal staircase that went from the alley behind the building up to the second floor. A big number four greeted her, so she rang the bell. Almost instantly the door swung open, and Patrick Kowalski stood, wearing a burgundy satin smoking jacket over what she thought were pajamas. She had never seen him in anything but his police uniform before. Amy heard Paul say, *Woof!*

"Dinner's ready," he said, holding out a hand to usher her in.

She wasn't ready to hug the man, so she held out the bottle of Shiraz. She said, "A little something to make it go down easier." She dropped her purse by the door and followed the officer into the dining room.

The apartment was comfortable. They passed family pictures on the walls of the foyer. She got a quick look into the living room, with its huge TV screen and dark upholstered furniture. The dining room table was the right size for four people, now set for two. Everything was sparkling clean, and the bright yellow placemats looked happy. "Can I help?" she offered.

"Everything's done," he replied, "I'll just get it all. Sit, sit!"

"Bring a corkscrew!" she shouted after him.

He made several trips to bring the carved roast (and corkscrew), wild rice and mushrooms, and broccoli in mustard sauce. While she opened the wine, she remarked on how inviting the food looked and smelled. She heard Paul think, *I wasn't hungry before, but I sure am now.* "Yes," she whispered back.

A full glass of wine was waiting when Patrick sat down across from Amy. "A toast!" he called, lifting the glass. "To good food and good people," he said, "Amen." they clinked glasses and sipped the wine. Paul thought, *Uh oh, I hope dinner is better than this swill.*

Smiling at Patrick, she thought back, *This swill is what I could afford. God, you're right.*

Amy took two slices of roast beef, then helped herself to the side dishes. In a long silence Paul took the lead and asked, "So, what happened?" He began to cut the meat.

"Do we have to talk about that?"

Paul put down the tableware. "I'm here, so yes, we do." He stared at the man, but Kowalski would not meet their gaze. He heard Amy think, *No! Don't do this! I want–Back to your cage.*

As he was pushed back by Amy, he thought, *You need to know.*

"I'm sorry, Pat," she stammered, "I don't know what I was thinking."

"Yeah, well," and he put his own utensils down. "I had

everything ready last night. Roxy called every thirty minutes to say she was on her way. Then she got home around nine-thirty and said she wasn't hungry."

"Any explanation?" He shook his head. "Any conversation at all?"

"That she thinks I'm a crappy cook so she got a fish sandwich on her way home."

"That's brutal," she said. "I'm so sorry, Pat. I'm–I'm–" and she fell silent.

He forced a smile. "More for us," he said as he took a forkful of rice.

Amy finished cutting a piece of beef and put it in her mouth. *My God!* she thought to Paul, *he must have used the entire salt shaker on this.* As she chewed she heard Paul think, *Kind of well done. Over-well done. Let's see if the wine helps"*

Indeed, the wine did add some moisture to their mouth. Compared to the salty beef, the wine now tasted sweet, if thin. Amy took a fork of broccoli and tried not to let her eyes bug out at the overpowering heat of the mustard.

Kowalski smiled at her struggle and offered, "My own recipe. I used some cayenne powder to boost the mustard. Good, huh?"

She smiled while Paul screamed in her head, *More wine!*

When she recovered, Amy gingerly poked her fork at the wild rice and mushrooms. She cautiously took a small amount, and was genuinely surprised at how good it was. "This is great," she said, reaching for more.

"Oh, it's alright I guess. It's just the recipe on the box. That's not cooking."

Paul thought, *I'm glad he's a better cop than cook.*

The silence around the meal made Amy uncomfortable, so she began telling Kowalski about her investigation in his absence. "I interviewed Bella, the daughter of the glove man. She says he gave her to a fence because he didn't have cash. And I renewed my acquaintance with Doctor Bradley Richardson. You will never guess who his brother-in-law is, so I'll save time and tell you: Skyler Blunt."

Kowalski was more animated as they discussed the case. By the time the wine bottle was empty he didn't seem to notice that all

Amy had eaten was rice. "You think the museum director may be involved?" he asked.

"I know he wasn't the killer we saw in the surveillance video, but all those calls between him and Blunt make me wonder. They each said they didn't like the other."

When she saw him stand to clear the table, Amy got up to help. "No, no, I'll take care of this. You go into the living room. I've got some more wine."

Amy sat in a corner of a sectional sofa with a brown-and-gray pattern. *I'll need a forklift to get out of this. Comfy!* she thought to Paul.

He thought, *Are you alright with how Kowalski's acting?*

"You bet," she said aloud. Then, *That wine I brought turned out okay.* And then, again out loud, "Oh, right, I was the one drinking. Poor boy, do you even have a buzz?" Alcohol's impact was normal on whichever one of them was leading, but almost nothing on the other.

"Who are you talking to?" Kowalski asked as he brought a newly opened bottle of something vinous and red. He filled a glass and handed it to Amy, then poured one for himself.

"Ah, you caught me talking to myself. I do that a lot." Paul jumped to the lead for a swallow.

"How's that work for you?" He sat in the center of the sofa, close to her. "Do the answers ever surprise you?"

"All the time," she laughed, the wine emphasizing her amusement. "One day I discovered I have two favorite colors."

"Mine is blue. Only one, unless you count different shades."

"I've always loved yellow," Amy told him, "it's such a happy color. Then one day I was talking to myself and I discovered the rest of me likes blue, too."

"The rest of you?" She heard Paul in her head and Patrick in her ears.

"Sure. The part of me that's not Amy." She took another swallow of wine and smiled serenely.

Paul thought to her, excited, *You are going to tell him about me. Hosanna!* They had talked about how peaceful their time was with Christine because she knew the truth of Amy and Paulette's dyad existence, and how they'd like to recreate that with whatever man Amy got close to.

Kowalski put his glass on the beige carpet in front of the sofa and said, "I want to know the part that is Amy."

Her smile got bigger as the man leaned towards her and kissed her softly. If she weren't still holding her wine glass she'd have leapt on him. Instead, she closed her eyes and kissed him again, and thought to him, *What do I do with the wine?*

He leaned back and took the glass from her, and placed it next to his on the carpet. As he turned back to her his expression changed from a smile to confusion. "How did you do that? Oh, you're a ventriloquist."

"Yes," she said out loud, then she planted her lips on his. *I'm a ventriloquist.*

Her shirt was unbuttoned, and his smoking jacket was lying on the floor, hiding the stain the spilled wine was making in the carpet. They were kissing. Paul knew to be silent. In the past he had agonized through Amy's romantic encounters, being revulsed by proximity to naked, amorous men; but his ongoing relationship with Christine–and Amy's tolerance of its physical side–had calmed him down. Would he ever choose to kiss a man? No. But it didn't freak him out anymore.

Instead, Paul could enjoy feeling Amy's excitement and anticipation, and when it came, he would enjoy the physical sensations of her intimacy. He was happy for her, genuinely. He no longer worried that some other man would steal her affection from him.

"What the hell?" Kowalski said.

Amy nuzzled him. "I'm glad to see you. No, that's my service gun." She was rubbing the back of his neck, trying to pull his mouth back to hers.

Gingerly he pulled her skirt up until he saw the holster and pistol. Relieved, he whispered "Mine's bigger" and resumed kissing her.

Amy was breathing rapidly, ready to surrender to the hands that were inside her shirt, the lips that were grazing her neck and shoulders. She rubbed his chest; she got one hand around to his back to pull him closer.

And the front door opened.

Roxy Kowalski stood in the foyer, looking right at her half-naked husband and a disheveled Amy. Patrick was turned away and did not see her, but Amy saw the hatred and disgust in the woman's face.

In a burst of desperation, Paul said, "I was just warming him up for you." Kowalski leaned back in disbelief, then followed Amy's eyes to his front door. And his wife.

Roxy was a square-faced woman, five six, about one hundred thirty pounds. Her flat auburn hair fell to just below her shoulders in stringy, wiry strands. Amy imagined she was Patrick's age, but she looked much older. She looked tired. And she looked angry. "You WHAT?" she screamed, and walked into the living room.

Amy pulled her shirt closed and tried to tug her skirt down, but it caught on the butt of her pistol. Silently she said, *Oh my God, omygod, omygod* over and over. The excitement had instantly been transformed into fear and shame.

Roxy stood over Amy for a moment with a look of contempt. "Huh!" she said, then turned to her husband with closed fists. "You bastard! You mother-fucking bastard! You had to bring your whore to our home!" Patrick held his crossed arms in front of his face so his wife's blows couldn't harm him, and instead she banged away on his chest. "How could you! You two-faced son of a bitch!"

We need to get out of here, Paul thought. *Where are our shoes?*

She saw Roxy harmlessly punching at the officer. "Not yet," she said aloud. Roxy shouted back, "Oh yes, yet. Get lost, bitch, there's nothing here for you. This—" she punched him with both fists "—is mine."

Patrick took advantage of Roxy's distraction to step forward and embrace his wife. He nodded at Amy to go. So she stepped back, and was astounded to see the Kowalskis hugging each other tightly, weeping, whispering. Softly now, slowly, Roxy banged her fists against Patrick's arms and shoulders. "I hate you," she moaned, "I love you, I hate you..."

Amy finished buttoning her shirt. She stepped into her shoes and mouthed silently to the man, "See you tomorrow." As quietly as she could she went to the front door, grabbed her purse, and escaped down the stairs. For some reason, she was surprised to see it was dark out.

In the car, Amy locked the doors and screamed. She beat on the steering wheel, she stamped on the floorboards. After a minute she sat back, breathing heavily and holding the wheel in a death grip. Finally she said aloud, "What just happened?"

"We got caught."

"Caught? We didn't get to do anything!"

"Roxy Kowalski thinks we did."

She leaned forward to rest their head on the steering wheel, while Paul wrapped their arms around themself to comfort Amy. "I don't understand," she whispered. "I just want to spend some time with a man. A man who likes me. Why is this so hard?"

Silently, Paul made cooing noises in their head and slowly rocked their body.

"And you said this was a good one. Finally, you were on my side." She sniffed, trying but failing to keep a wad of snot from sliding over her lips and onto her wrinkled skirt. "I don't–I don't understand." Paul was still rocking when she shouted, "I fucking don't understand!"

It's okay, he thought to her. *You're safe. You're with me. It's okay, I've got you.*

At which point she blubbered and sobbed while he continued to rock them and make "Sssh" sounds to her.

It took a few minutes to get enough sadness and frustration out of her system. She sat up, wiping her nose on her shirt sleeve. Paul said, "I'll drive, okay? Hey, we can stop for ice cream."

It made her smile just a little, but she shook her head. "Home, Jeeves," she thought. "I want to go to bed with you and not wake up."

He turned the ignition key and navigated out of the parking space. "I'm sorry, Amy."

"Yes."

"Wait, wait, wait!" he cried. "I can't drive if you close our eyes."

Her smile was broader this time. "Okay, you big meanie. But just for you."

Paul kept up a running pep talk as he drove them home. He could feel Amy relaxing, but periodically she would mutter, "Crap and a half!" When he parked, Amy said, "I'm glad you're with me.

Thanks for trying to help. But I think I'm going to be sad for awhile."

"Yeah," He retreated to allow her to lock the car and let them in their house. He was relieved he didn't have to deal with a naked Pat Kowalski, but he was sorry that Amy was unhappy. Life could be so messy.

She took off the thigh holster, then brushed her teeth and lay down on top of the bedspread. Between the residual wine and the brief spurt of crying, her head was beginning to hurt. "I don't want to get up tomorrow," she said. Her lower lip was extended, she was pouting.

I have an idea, Paul thought to her. With their left hand–'his' hand–he began to rub their arm, their neck, their breasts. He felt Amy relax a little more, so he continued to touch themself. When she retreated he used both hands to relax and then excite themself. He thought that it was easier without a four-inch barrel strapped to her leg.

When the spasms passed, and then a few minutes of quiet had gone by, Amy said out loud, "I needed that." Then she thought, *Maybe a house will land on Roxy Kowalski tomorrow.*

When the alarm clock went off, Amy moaned, "Make it stop!" But Paul poked at her internally. "The sooner we face this, the sooner it'll be over," he soothed.

She sat up and rubbed their face. "Coffee," she said.

"Without caffeine, western civilization would grind to a halt."

"I'm voting for whoever wants to ban it. Don't make me get up."

"Up!" he laughed. "Come on, a nice warm shower, some chicory, a thawed out waffle–life is good."

She finally got out of bed, muttering, "If this day sucks I will never forgive you."

✄ 15 ✃

Amy walked up the stairs to the uniformed police area and found Kowalski working at a long table. There was a huge purple bruise on the side of his face. He was surrounded by credit card slips and reimbursement chits. "Whoa! You have an expense account?"

He looked up at her and snorted. "Yeah. My monthly limit is $5.98."

"Next time we can meet at the Krystal."

She was disappointed by the sad look that lingered on his face. "I'm sorry, Patrick," she said, her hands fluttering. "I–I didn't mean to–you know."

"Yeah," nodding, "I know." He laid down his pencil and said, "Look, I'm sorry about everything."

"No, no, I'm sorry. I shouldn't have–I don't know what, but I shouldn't have."

Paul went on, with Amy's voice. "Is Roxy okay?"

He shook his head with an odd smile on his face. "I do not pretend to understand women."

Amy stood there awkwardly, and finally said, "We're going to have to talk about this, but not now. We're at work. Look, I want to visit Hunter Stringfellow again. He should be back from Mackenzie's memorial service, and I want to find out if he has a dog. Or a black ski mask."

Kowalski reviewed the piles of receipts on the desk. "I didn't want to do this," he muttered, and he scooped everything into a file folder. "Let's go."

Amy was uncomfortable as they walked down the hallway and out to the parking area. She thought to Paul, *If I have to look at him for an hour while we drive to Kenner, I don't know if I'll cry or punch him.*

When they got to the squad car, it was Paul who said, "Can I drive? I promise I won't turn on the siren unless you tell me to." The officer tossed his keys to her and went around to the passenger side. Paul thought to Amy, *This is great! I don't much like cops, but what little boy doesn't have the fantasy of driving a cop car? Let's go!*

"What's so funny?" Kowalski asked as Amy cranked the ignition.

"A part of me has always wanted to do this, drive a cop car."

"Yeah? Which part of you?"

It was Paul who answered, "Favorite color blue."

Once they were on Airline Highway, Kowalski began to talk about the after-dinner events. "I was–you really turned me on. I couldn't believe Roxy picked that moment to come home. And why did you say you were warming me up for her?"

"Panic," Paul said; then he concentrated on driving and let Amy deal with the officer. "You're a good looking man, Pat. But she did come back, and you use the word 'home' to describe what it is for her. Whatever is going on with you two, I don't think you're on the verge of a divorce." She glanced at him and added, "And tempting though it is, I won't get involved with a married man. Not a *married* married man."

"When I called you, and when you came over, and when we were sitting on the sofa, I really thought Roxy hated me. She had frozen me out for months. I wasn't trying to lead you on. Well, not exactly."

She raised one eyebrow as Paul drove.

"I thought my marriage was over. It still might be, I don't know." He looked out the passenger window for a long time. "After you left, Roxy was different. We made love for the first time in months. She was angry, but she was scared. We talked all night."

"Looks like I did warm you up for her," Amy said with a smile. "That thing on your face looks like you did more than talk."

"Yeah. Well. It took awhile."

"Part of me is glad to hear all this–" "What?" "–Yes, the blue part. The yellow part, maybe not so much."

"Permission to speak freely?" he asked.

"Come on, Kowalski, we're both Officer IIIs."

"Yeah, but I–I still need permission."

"Okay, permission granted."

He nodded. "You're a very attractive woman, Amy. You, uh, you turn me on. I do not apologize for it. Only for the circumstances."

Paul kept their head facing forward, but Amy nodded. "All right. So what do you want to happen?"

"Still permission?" Amy rolled her eyes while Paul shouted silently, *Hey! Don't do that!*

Kowalski said, "I still want to sleep with you."

Flushing, Amy forced herself to ask, "And what about Roxy? Are you leaving her?"

"I don't know. I suppose it depends on what she wants."

Amy stewed for half a mile, then said, "No, Pat. It depends on what you want. When you make up your mind, we can talk again, but I don't promise what my answer will be by then. In the meantime, we have to be able to work together."

The officer was looking down at his shoes.

Anxiety bubbling through her body, Amy said, "These are the rules: except for saving each other's lives, we don't touch each other. There won't be any kissing or hugging or pet names. You've got one chance right now to respond, and then permission is withdrawn. Any questions?" She stole a fast look at Kowalski; he looked smaller and lighter than usual.

"I didn't mean to cause problems. I'm not really a bad man."

"I never thought you were. This is about me, not you. I will not put up with sloppy boundaries. Make up your mind and there's something to talk about. Until then, there's not."

"Christ. I feel desire for you, is that a bad thing?"

"Permission denied!"

They drove on silently, with Paul thinking high-fives to Amy. *I hate that*, she thought back. *I get all itchy when I have to stand up to someone. But I had to do it.*

You came across very strong. You know, courage is not the absence of fear. Courage is doing what you have to do even though you're scared.

Like when I was a kid and dad told me to pretend I wasn't scared. They both smiled at the shared memory.

Paul drove in to the shopping center lot and parked near the RockWallUSA gym where Hunter Stringfellow worked. Silently they emerged from the black-and-white, and each adjusted their gear–Kowalski straightening the way his baton hung from his belt, and Amy sliding her thigh holster so the bobbed hammer of her 9mm wasn't rubbing her right leg anymore. Paul said, "Hey!" and when the officer looked up, he flipped the cruiser's keys to the man. "Thanks for letting me drive. I can cross that off my bucket list now."

Amy was surprised at how quiet the gym was when they entered. Some kind of music was playing, but it was soft music at a low level. Hunter's boss was at the desk by the door. Amy said, "Bill, is it?" When he responded, she went on, "I'm Detective Clear; we met last week. Do you remember Officer Kowalski? I need to speak to Hunter Stringfellow."

"So do I," he said, clearly annoyed. "He was off a few days for a memorial service, and he didn't come back this morning like he said he would." The man scanned the room, looking to see if any of the ten or twelve customers needed help, or maybe scolding. "I should be in the back room with the safe and the adding machine, but now I'm stuck out here all day."

"Does Hunter do this sort of thing very often?"

"No, never. I'm a little worried about him. And a little angry. Actually, a lot angry."

Amy handed him her business card. "Please call me when you see Hunter again, okay? And tell him to call me, too, but it's important that you call to let me know when he's back."

Back in the squad car, Amy typed something into the onboard computer and pulled up her contact information on Stringfellow. "How about you call his parents in Meridian. I'll call his cell phone."

Each of them turned toward their door and dialed. After two rings, Amy heard the common intercept that the number she had dialed, Hunter's cellphone, was not available. At the beep she said, "Hunter, this is Detective Amy Clear. I'm not the only person worried about you. Your boss is frantic. He really cares about you,

you know? Anyway, I need to ask you a few more questions, and I'd like to hear how things went at Mackenzie's memorial. Please call me," and she left her number.

When she closed her phone, she began to pay attention to Kowalski's side of his conversation with one of Hunter's parents. She heard him ask, "When did he leave? Did he say where he was going?"

Amy thought to him, *Ask if Hunter took any camping gear when he left.* Kowalski pivoted in his seat, phone to one ear and hand to the other, and stared slack-jawed at a smiling Amy. She mouthed "Ventriloquist."

"I'm sorry, Mister Stringfellow, can you say that again?" he went on, and then he relayed Amy's question. "Really? An old tent? Do you know where he liked to camp out?"

She heard Paul muse, *Sometimes I wish we could hear what other people think, like we can make them hear us. I'd love to know what Hunter's parents are saying.*

I'd waste all my time eavesdropping on men, she thought back. *And I probably wouldn't like what I heard.*

"Thank you for your help. Whenever you hear from Hunter, please ask him to call me or Detective Clear," and he dictated their phone numbers.

When he closed his phone, Amy asked, "Whatcha got?"

"There was no memorial service," Kowalski was pulling out his notebook to write up the conversation. "The Stringfellows had been to the funeral last week. I was talking to the father. He said the whole family was close to the Slatons. He was surprised but glad to see Hunter out of the blue on Tuesday. He left yesterday afternoon. They assumed he was going back to Kenner. Why did you–how did–"

"Ventriloquist," she interrupted. "If he left Meridian with camping gear, I think I know where he is. Do you know anyone on the Arkansas State Patrol?"

"Arkansas?"

"The state park where he takes rock climbers. I bet he knows the place backwards and forwards. It would be easy for him to hide out there."

"Hide out," Kowalski muttered, shaking his head. "Not exactly the behavior of an innocent person. The Commander probably knows somebody over there."

The officer drove the prowler back to the station. It was a quiet and uncomfortable trip. After a while, Amy and Paul played a few silent rounds of 'Twenty Questions' to pass the time. They preferred 'Rock Paper Scissors,' but they had learned the hard way not to play that where people could see them.

When they got back to Rampart Street, they went to the uniformed dispatch waiting room. "Shanika!" Amy called to the officer behind the desk. "Any cop contacts in Arkansas?"

"Arc and saw what?" the woman deadpanned. It was Paul, lover of puns, who laughed, but the woman assumed it was Amy who appreciated her throwaway humor. She pressed buttons on the keyboard, miraculously preserving her two-inch fingernails. "What part of the state?"

"Mount Magazine State Park. West-central, I don't know what towns are near it. Whatcha got?"

Shanika worked like a demon, rolling through screens and searches. Finally she said, "Looks like Western division, Company D in Fort Smith. Yeah, we know Lieutenant Clyde Washington."

Amy rested her elbows on the ledge of the window that separated Shanika's office from the bullpen, and leaned toward the woman. "Can I get a phone number?"

"I can do better than that, Detective. As soon as I get him on the line, you pick up line three out there."

Kowalski raised his eyebrows, "That's fast."

"She's good."

"Detective! Line three!"

Amy introduced herself to Sergeant Baker. "There's a person of interest from a murder and robbery in New Orleans, and I have reason to believe he's hiding out at Mount Magazine Park. He's not a suspect–well, not yet, anyway. Is there any way I can talk you into locating him?"

"Is this an extradition request?"

"No. More like a missing persons report." She gave Hunter's description to the sergeant, and told him about the man's skill at rock climbing and rappelling. "He strikes me as a kind of Boy Scout," she added. "My first stop would be at the Ranger's office to see if he registered for a camp site."

She heard the man laugh. "What do you want me to do with him if I find him?"

She paused; she realized she had no idea what an appropriate request was. In the silence, Paul spoke: "Put a 'forever' stamp on his nose and mail him to me?"

Another laugh. "If he hasn't been charged with anything, we really can't take him into custody. The most we could do is see if he's there, but even that would be low priority. Detective, under the circumstances you'll have to come to Fort Smith and collect him yourself."

She thanked the sergeant and hung up, frowning. Turning to Kowalski she said, "They won't do anything without an arrest warrant. Can we pool our expense accounts to go fetch Hunter?"

Seriously, he answered, "You can get a mileage reimbursement, but you really want to put in a chit for a squad car. Unless you want to sit next to a possible killer on the drive back."

Paul thought, *Why did Ramirez think we were ready for this job?*

Amy frowned and thought back, *Hush! I am ready. There just are some things I don't know yet.*

She went back to the detective's communal office and pulled up the website for Mount Magazine State Park. She called the posted phone number, but it took three people before she finally was put through to the park ranger's office. Did they require or accept registration for wilderness camping? The woman in the office replied that tent campers could be on their own, but since the park was in black bear country, they encouraged registrations.

"Did a man named Hunter Stringfellow register yesterday or today?"

"Oh, Hunter. Yes, he came back yesterday. He's usually here once or twice a month." Amy heard the woman giggle. "He's a cutie, isn't he?" the woman added. Paul silently thought to Amy, *For a possible murderer, yeah.*

MapQuest told her it would be a ten-hour drive each way. It was after lunch; she decided there was no point in leaving now. Paul thought, *Good. We still get to see Christine tonight, and we can head out in the morning.*

"I wish I could levitate there right now. Or that transporter thing from *Star Trek*."

"How come they never materialized with Kirk's head on McCoy's body?"

"Kirk? McCoy? Who are they?"

Paul laughed out loud and whispered, "I forget, to you it's Captain Janeway."

"Archer," she said, reaching for the phone, "he's dreamy." She dialed the requisitions extension and reserved a black-and-white for the next morning's drive to Arkansas.

Back in the uniformed section, she found Kowalski again sitting at a table with chits and receipts. She knocked at the door jamb to get his attention, then said, "Thanks for the advice. The park ranger's office says Hunter is there, so I reserved a cruiser for tomorrow."

He nodded, pencil in hand. "Put him in the back seat," he said, "he may be a killer."

She looked around, feeling awkward. "Tomorrow's going to be a long day, so I'm knocking off. I may get to wave at you in the morning, or else I'll see you Monday."

"We good?"

Finally, Amy smiled. "Yes. We good."

As she walked out to the parking lot, Paul thought, *Are we good? Really?*

"I guess," she muttered. "Being not good isn't going to help. Isn't Roxy the kind of name strippers use? Like Bambi or Porsche?"

Amy took a nap until it was time for Paulette to meet his girlfriend at Sappho Rising, the lesbian club where Christine had been a regular for years.

Amy was anxious about the coming day. She remembered Kowalski's warning that law enforcement paired up when dealing with suspected murderers, but she would be on her own with Hunter Stringfellow. It finally occurred to her that she would have to stay overnight in Arkansas, since the idea of driving twenty hours in a day was a non-starter. It was June, but would it be cold in the park? Should she pack her sleeping bag? While Paul led to drive to the club, they talked over preparation. Paul suggested a car tarp so Hunter wouldn't notice a NOPD car parked near his campsite. She mentioned candy bars. And bullets.

It was a lively night at Sappho Rising. The parking lot was almost full, and Paul couldn't get their old blue sedan near Christine's SmartCar. There was a line at the door to pay the cover charge. Most of the tiny tables in the club were overflowing. It was extremely noisy.

Christine was in her usual spot near the back. When she saw Amy–Paulette–she stood up and waved both her hands overhead.

Paul took the lead and tried to rush through the clots of women in the club. When he finally reached Christine he hugged her tightly. "Paulette," she murmured to him, and rested her head against their shoulder.

"Let me look at you," Paul said, gently pushing her to arm's length. He liked the bright red blouse and sunny yellow skirt, such cartoony colors. He liked her multi-colored, multi-length blonde hair. And best of all was the smiling face, with the crooked front tooth that he adored, just like the one in Amy's–and his–mouth.

Amidst the noise, Paul explained that Amy had to drive to Arkansas the next day to locate one of their persons of interest. "Will she be back by Saturday? We were going to a movie."

"It's Amy. I'm sorry, I just don't know when I'll get home. Can we move it to Sunday?

"Hey, Amy," Christine replied. "This is because of your new job, right?" Amy hung her head and nodded. "I understand. But bring my Paulette back. We'll have fun on Sunday."

"Let me tell you about the officer." Paul rolled their eyes and said, "What a disaster."

"No! Are you alright, Amy?"

"Paul's right. Disaster. Debacle. Calamity. It was even a fiasco." She described dinner with Kowalski, and his wife's unexpected return.

Christine put her hand on one of Amy's, "I'm so sorry. And–don't you have to work with him? Now what?"

"Excellent question, and I don't know the answer. Today was a bit uncomfortable."

"Paulette, don't let her make this mistake again."

"It's still Amy. I'll damn well make this mistake again and again." She took a gulp of beer. Paul said, "Ooh, can I have some?"

"Sure." She let Paul lead to have his own taste.

Christine went on, "I want you to be happy, Amy. How can you be happy with someone who's married?"

"You're right, I know. Paul's saying the same thing. I can't help who I like, can I?"

"But you can control how you behave. You must. If you ate as much as Paul says he wants, you'd be fat. But you control yourself." Amy heard Paul, *Damn right*.

Amy clenched their eyes shut, rubbing their temples. "I know! You're right, you both are!" She held the glass up and rolled it across their forehead. "Can we talk about Sunday instead? Please?"

Paul thought to Christine, *I think she heard us.* His lover replied, out loud, "Make sure, okay? I love her, too." Amy had an idea of what was happening. She tried to tell herself that Paul and Christine both cared for her, that's why they were looking out for her. She was fantasizing about what would have happened if Roxy Kowalski hadn't come back when Christine said, "There's an eastern European grocery that opened in Kenner. It'll be fun to look at all their strange stuff."

"Oh, sure," Amy said, half-heartedly, "we'll find something to bring back and turn into dinner."

Later, back at her double, Christine rubbed a hand up and down Paulette's breastbone and said, "Amy? Are you mad at us? At me?"

"No, I'm not. Well, maybe a little at Paul—yes, you, you traitor!" She was glad to hear him laugh inside. "I know you're both trying to help. I appreciate the love, even if I hate being told what to do."

Christine hugged her on the bed. "We do love you. You're part of Paulette so I'd love you just for that. But you know," she wiggled against the mattress, "you're like the sister I never had."

"I don't know," Amy said. "I have a sister, and believe me, we never did these things. But you make Paul very happy. And you've turned into my best friend."

"Can I say something?" Paul added. Christine smiled and lifted herself up to look down on their face. Before he could say a word she lowered her mouth to theirs and kissed her Paulette. The only boy who would ever touch her, her Paulette.

In the morning, Paul hugged a sleepy Christine and set out for the station house at seven AM. Although she stuck her head in the uniformed officer's room, Amy was relieved that she didn't see Kowalski. She picked up the keys from motor pool, moved some personal gear from her own car, and hit the road for Paris, Arkansas.

Amy let Paul lead to drive. They listened to the radio, each of them singing aloud with the songs they knew. They talked about Christine, and Amy again refused to consider living with the woman: "My love life isn't much, but it would be non-existent if I lived with your girlfriend." They compared their different memories of a family vacation to Arizona and old Mexico ten years earlier. The two friends, in the one body, enjoyed the relaxed time together, and the privacy that let each of them speak out loud. It was seven-thirty in the evening when Paul parked the cruiser in front of the interpretive center of Mount Magazine State Park. "Show time," he said, and retreated to let Amy take control of their body.

"You got us all stiff," she thought to him as she stood by the squad car and stretched. She did some twists, swinging her elbows left and then right, and then lifted each leg in an exaggerated way. After she re-arranged the gear hanging from her belt she went up the walkway and knocked on the door.

A short, bearded, grizzled man in jeans and a work shirt opened the door. "I'm sorry, Miss, the welcome center is closed."

She smiled and held up her open badge case. "Ranger LaFerry? I'm Detective Clear, New Orleans PD. We talked yesterday."

"Lafferry," he corrected her, "none of those fancy Louisiana names up here. And it's just officer, same as you. Have you found your man yet?"

"I just got here. How long until sunset? Do I have time to look for Stringfellow now?"

He stepped out onto the small concrete stoop and closed the door behind him. He was in bare feet. "If I were you, I'd stay at the lodge and start out in the morning. Geneva gets in at eight o'clock."

She heard Paul think, *I guess we didn't have to leave Christine so early. Damn.*

"Anything I need to know about the area?"

"Bears and catamounts. Uh, that 9mm won't faze a black bear, so be careful."

He pointed her to the lodge and waved goodbye. Amy heard

Paul begin to think something and she said aloud, "Don't even say it. We're here and that's that. Let's find dinner and a shower."

Driving up from the ranger's residence, the tri-level lodge came into view. It was huge–boxy and bulky, with repeating roof peaks and valley facing the front. The main section was four stories of red and white stone. It was at the ridge of one of the mountains, dominating the dimming horizon. Paul said, "It looks like someone just dropped it there. Not really ugly, just...inappropriate." She responded, "All I care about is a hot meal and a clean bed."

The lobby was a cross between a hunting lodge, with log walls and supports, and a modern urban hotel, with a two-story atrium and bright lights. The park was in the middle of nowhere, maybe one hundred miles from Fort Smith, but the lodge felt like Canal Street or the Airline Highway was just outside the door.

When the clerk took her credit card, Amy showed her badge and asked for a law enforcement discount. She felt Paul laugh inside when the clerk marked down the room rent a grand total of seven dollars. "That'll be $175 for the night," he said. He gave back her Optium card, and handed her a room key card.

Amy brought a valise and some of her gear up to the room. It was snug, with two queen sized beds. The view was stunning, of the sun going down on hundreds of acres of woods, rivers, lakes, cliffs and chasms. "I could get used to this view," she whispered, staring to take it all in.

"We have to cover the cop car," he said. She went downstairs to the parking lot and stretched the green tarp over the vehicle. If Hunter Stringfellow was walking around, he wouldn't be tipped off that she was looking for him.

By the time they got to the restaurant in the lodge, the sun was down and the sky outside the two stories of windowed wall was a deep dark blue. The interior was as well-lit as the lobby, and the architecture was the same: hickory furniture, log walls, and peeled log supports for the roof. She blanched at the right hand column of the menu, and placed an order for a bowl of beef stew and a garden salad. Even so, the tab was thirteen dollars.

The stew was hearty, and the salad was filling. Silently, Amy and Paul planned for the morning hunt for Stringfellow. He thought, *Kowalski said no cop should approach a suspected murderer alone.*

Funny, I don't remember him volunteering to keep me company.

We've done stupid and dangerous things before. We'll do one more. Hey, Hunter may not be the killer.

She took another forkful of salad. *Sometimes I wish you could trot out your old body. You were six-one?*

And two hundred thirty pounds. But if it still existed it would be seventy three years old. I think our odds are better this way.

After dinner, Amy pulled on a "Geaux Saints" sweatshirt and walked outside the lodge. A portion of the ridge-top had been leveled to hold the complex. Despite the June calendar, the night air at 2700 feet was quite nippy. When she looked away from the lodge, she could see thousands more stars than ever cut through the haze and light in New Orleans. Paul pointed into the distance and whispered, "I think that's the Milky Way." Both of them stared.

Later they stumbled on the service entrances and employee parking at the back of the lodge. "What's that big green thing?" Amy asked, walking toward a hickory tree. As they neared it, she squealed, "It's moving! What is it?" She covered their head with their hands as if protecting their hair from a bat.

"That's a Luna moth," Paul said, awestruck. "I haven't seen one since I lived in West Virginia. They're spooky, but they're fascinating. Uh, I don't think they bite or anything."

It slowly fanned its wings as Amy examined it closely. The wingspan was about five inches when it laid them flat against the tree trunk. "Those look like eyes, don't they?" she whispered, pointing at the four spots on the wings. The wings were a pale green, with veins like a leaf, and with twin green tails.

Better than the zoo, Paul thought to her.

Amy gently touched a wing with her index finger, and the moth flew off, landing higher up and out of reach in the hickory tree. "It's going to bed," she laughed. "We should, too."

Upstairs, Amy took in the room. "Great, each of us gets a big bed," she joked. Immediately she felt Paul's reaction. "Did I say something wrong?"

In the safety of their room, Paul answered aloud, "That was a surprise. I felt, oooh, abandoned."

"It was just a joke!" she said, defensive.

"I know. But part of me didn't for a second. It's what, fifteen years? I'm used to being a dyad with you. I don't know how I'd cope if I were by myself again."

Amy smiled and wrapped their arms around themself. "Paul Dominic Owens, I swear I will never leave you."

Silently he thought back, *Yeah. Thanks.*

As they existed in one body, they both slept in the same bed.

In the morning Amy put on jeans and a heavy denim shirt, and assembled their gear. Flashlight, gun, cell phone, badge, binoculars, cuffs, baton, and metal water jug, all hanging from her service belt. Paul argued for the fanny pack for some additional supplies, but she vetoed him with "This won't take long," They stopped in the lobby long enough to drink coffee and eat two complementary fruit buns. The view out the two story windows was of exciting cliffs and endless trees, under an overcast sky.

Amy was the first customer of the day at the interpretive center where Geneva worked. She confirmed that Hunter Stringfellow had not checked out from his climbing visit. "Where would he camp? And where would he be rappelling?" Amy asked.

Geneva handed her a brochure map, but they looked at the oversized park map under glass on the counter top. "A lot of wilderness campers like to stay in this area," she pointed, "there are slabs and power outlets, but only a few RVs are registered. Of course, a serious wilderness camper can be just about anywhere. Bears or no bears."

"Okay. And where is the rappelling area?"

"Here and here," she pointed again. "It's against the law for a visitor to put in bolts or pitons in the park, so this is where they all go. Sometimes we get an advanced one who uses cams and nuts, they'd be on the east face. But nobody like that is registered now."

Got that? she thought to Paul as she looked from the big map to her brochure map.

"Thanks for your help, Geneva. I have to ask you not to tell Hunter I'm here or looking for him. This is a law enforcement issue."

The woman's eyes widened. "Oh no, he's such a nice man. Is he in trouble?"

Amy gave the standard answer: "We need his help with our

inquiries."

The brisk walk to the camping area left Amy sweating. She found four pitched tents. She poked her flashlight in each one but found no people, and she had no idea which one, if any, was Hunter's. She heard Paul think, *I guess we go to the rappelling cliff.* They followed the map but missed a fork in the path. When they reached high ground, Amy realized they were on the pristine east face, where only specialized rappelling was permitted. Across the heavily wooded chasm she could see the west face, where a few clots of people already were going up or down on ropes. The breeze was stronger on the exposed top of the cliff, and Amy slapped their hands on their arms to warm up.

"There's a boulder," Paul said, turning to look around. "We can hunker down there and get out of this wind. Please?"

"You had me at 'boulder'," and she settled them down. "Hey, we're concealed now. Let's see if Hunter is over there." She unloosed the little binoculars from her belt and began to observe the rappellers on the opposite cliff face.

Paul said, "That looks like fun, but I think I'd be terrified." They watched a couple on adjoining ropes, using figure eights to lower themselves. Off to the left two men were top-rope climbing back up the cliff face.

Almost directly in front of them they could see twinned ropes hanging over the cliff, anchored to some device in the mesa top. The ropes vibrated, Paul thought from wind. Eventually, though, through the binoculars they saw a lone figure slowly climbing the rope, bouncing its legs against the cliff face as it rose. *That's our man,* Amy thought to Paul. She watched Hunter slowly but steadily work his way up the cliff and pull himself up on the plateau. Even in the chilly wind she could see he was sweating in his T-shirt. They saw him check his ropes, then attach his harness to the rope and rappel his way back down, and out of their sight.

He makes it look easy, Amy thought. *I think he's good at it.*

Paul answered silently, *Okay, let's do it sometime. Not today! But sometime.*

She laughed, "We both drove a cop car; we have to replace that on our bucket list."

They brainstormed a way to pick Hunter up and drive back to

Louisiana. Amy thought the path back to the bluff where the climbers were was so long that they risked losing their prey before they reached the west plateau. She was pretty sure one of the tents they'd seen earlier was Hunter's, and planned to meet him there after he finished his workout.

By noon the cloud cover had gotten thicker and lower, chasing away the other groups. Hunter Stringfellow managed a few more descents and climbs before getting back on top of the cliff and undoing his harness. They saw him reach into a backpack and come up with a sandwich or a block of cheese–they couldn't tell at that distance, or with the slight fog that had developed.

Still peering through the binoculars, they saw Hunter notice something and stand up, food in hand. He chewed slowly, apparently watching something closely. "Damn," Amy muttered, "I think he sees me." She remained hunkered for a few more minutes, but Hunter barely blinked, let alone looked away.

So she stood up.

"What the hell?" Paul said. Hunter was thrashing his arms as if he were conducting an invisible orchestra. Amy tilted their head, puzzled, and brought the binoculars back up to their eyes.

Hunter looked away long enough to reach for something next to his backpack. It took a moment for Paul to shout into the wind, "A rifle! He's aiming at us!" They saw the muzzle flash, then heard the whiz of a bullet passing nearby, and finally the report of the gunfire. Amy ducked down and slipped on the gravel that seemed to be everywhere on top of the east cliff. They heard two more shots and some animal howl as they slid toward the edge of the bluff; there was a sensation of fire in their right thigh. Amy waved their arms wildly, grasping for anything, still reaching as they went over the edge.

✍ 16 ✎

Paul was cold. He opened their eyes and saw clouds all around them. *I guess heaven is real,* he mused. Everything hurt, every part of Amy's body, especially their back near their right hip and their shoulder. Turning their head, he saw the cliff face. It alarmed him, until he noticed it wasn't moving. At least they weren't on their way to the canyon floor. But where were they?

Amy? he thought.

Nothing came back.

He called her name out loud, then again, and finally yelled it. On rare occasions, often fueled by alcohol, Amy would remain asleep after Paul awoke, but this was different. He felt their heart racing with fear and he tried to talk himself down–he was okay, so Amy was okay, she'd come around soon enough, take a deep breath...

He rolled their body forward and the pain in their back relaxed. They had been leaning against a tree that somehow, miraculously, was rooted near the edge of a small ledge and kept them from falling to oblivion. He wasn't ready to risk standing up, so he scooted their body to the center of the ledge. At the most it was twenty five square feet of flat rock sticking out of the cliff face. He found Amy's cell phone and saw zero bars–so much for calling for help. He pivoted to look at the cliff face straight on. They had fallen maybe twenty feet from the top, and now they would have to reverse gravity to get back up there.

He wished they had a grappling hook. A rope. A ham sandwich. A blanket. The sun had moved and the ledge was in cold shadow. A blanket would be especially nice. And Amy waking up would be even better. Every thirty seconds or so he tried to think to her, their common way of communication, but got no response. He tried internally poking and pushing, but with no better results. Paul was fighting panic. He'd spent fifteen years inside this female body, he had learned how to use it, but Amy's absence was a huge sucking hole in his mind. He made himself take more deep breaths.

Finally he sidled on their knees to the cliff face and used it as a support as he got to their feet. Close up, he could see the striations that millennia of sedimentation had left behind. If some layers were softer stone, he could dig finger and toe holds with their knife. They did have their knife, right? He patted their jeans pockets and found a ballpoint pen. It would have to be enough.

He realized he needed to urinate. He rejected a fleeting concern for modesty; if anyone could see them it would mean rescue. He lowered their jeans and underwear, and backed as close to the edge of the outcropping as he dared. He relaxed their muscles and felt relief for a second–until he felt warm liquid soaking their shoes. Damn, after all these years he still was used to being able to aim. Before he was done, their wet feet were turning cold from the chilly breeze and fog.

As he pulled up their pants rain began to fall. Visibility shrank to nothing, the world now was only that ledge and tree, and the cliff face; everything else was hidden by grey clouds. Between the rain and wet shoes, their teeth were chattering. He clasped their arms around their body, holding themself, slapping their shoulders and their thighs, anything to keep from surrendering to the growing cold. As he paced the little outcropping, much of the stiffness in their legs dissipated; only their right thigh continued to hurt.

"Amy, wake up, please wake up," he mumbled over and over. Paul did not want to die on this ledge, and he did not want to be alone. "Please, please wake up."

The rain was heavier for a few minutes, when he felt Amy's inside eyes jerk open. "Are we inside a marshmallow?" she asked. "Can I have some? I'm hungry."

"There you are," Paul said, a wave of relief feeding false bravado. "You okay?"

"Umm–hungry. Ouch, my leg hurts. And I'm cold. What happened? And where are we?" The pitch in her voice rose through her answer.

He explained their predicament. Even so, Amy opened her cell phone to confirm the bad news: no bars. She hoisted themself up to their knees, leaning to the left because of the pain in the other thigh. Pocket check: keys to the squad car, ballpoint pen, nail clippers, and sixty-three cents in coins. Her holsters were empty, the pistol and baton probably eighty feet below them on the ravine floor. She sat back on her bent legs and softly swore. "Any ideas?" she asked out loud. She tucked their cold hands into their armpits.

"I've had a little while to consider this. If we stay on this ledge we're going to die. If we fall, we're going to die. That means we have nothing to lose by climbing back to the top."

Slowly she raised their eyes to survey the cliff face looming above them. "Don't we need one of Hunter's ropes?"

"Sure. And I need a hot meal and dry clothes, but they're on top of this bluff. I say let's go get 'em."

"Won't they notice we haven't come back?" Amy asked. "The cruiser is tarped, we talked to that Geneva woman this morning. They'll look for us, right?" She was pleading.

He wiggled the fingers of their left hand, jammed into their right armpit. "Basing your survival on someone else's actions is a lousy way to die. We have to save ourself."

Give me a minute, she thought to Paul. *I need to pretend I'm not scared.* She took a deep breath. *Wait.*

He couldn't tell if the rain was tapering off and getting warmer, or if their body was getting numb to the wet cold. While he waited for Amy to work up her courage, he concentrated on the task before them: somehow gouge out finger- and toe-holds, and climb twenty-five feet to safety. There were alternatives, but none was satisfactory.

"Okay," she announced and limped to the cliff face. First she knelt, and they used the pen to scrape toe holds every six inches or so. Then they stood up, leaning on their left leg, and continued scraping and gouging as far up as they could reach. Done, she stepped back. *That cliff is twice as high as I can reach,* she thought to Paul. *What happens up there?*

"We find more holds," he said grimly, "or we fall. I vote for finding more. You ready?"

"How do we do this? You work the hands and I do the feet?"

"It's okay with me. We need to let each other know when we're going to move, though."

A nod, and Amy faced the cliff. Paul reached up for finger holds they had made, and when he told her he was locked in, she found toe holds and started up the cliff.

The rock face was wet from the rain, and they had some trouble coordinating hands and feet. They had gotten eighteen inches up the cliff when Paul lost his grip and they fell backwards. It was Amy who screamed, more out of fear than pain. Laying on their back in the middle of the ledge, Paul panted, "What the fuck is in our back pocket?"

"Car keys."

"They hurt!"

"They're fine. We hurt."

Paul sputtered, then laughed. He felt Amy laughing inside. It seemed to release some of the fear and tension. To himself he thought, *If I'm going to die, let me die while I'm laughing.*

They went back to the cliff face. "I'd better work hands and feet," she said, "otherwise we'll slip again. You can enjoy the climb, okay?" Before he could respond Amy attacked the cliff anew.

She was four or five feet up when she ran out of the holds they had made. Hugging the rock face, she twisted their head up to scan for a next move. She grasped a rock that was sticking out, then lifted one leg and then the other. There was an indentation up and to the right, she glanced down to see where she had to move her foot. When she shifted her weight the hand-hold gave way. "Paul!" she shouted as they fell back and bounced. She turned her head to see the edge of their outcropping getting closer and closer and closer.

She felt a jerk that arrested their fall. It took a moment to realize Paul had thrown out their arms and grasped the tree that had kept them on the ledge at the outset. Now their body was dangling over the lip of the outcrop. *I got it,* Paul thought to her, even though he could barely feel their arms and hands for the cold. "Come on, let me breathe," he said, which made Amy aware she was holding her breath. She complied.

He started to pull themself up. He got their elbows on top of the ledge, then rested. *Left leg,* he though to Amy, and they both worked to lift their knee and foot up to safety. He hoped his grip around the tree was secure, but he no longer could feel their fingers. "I'm getting it," she gasped back, "just a little more."

Once she had gotten their leg onto what they momentarily thought of as solid ground, Paul found a burst of energy to pull them up farther against the tree and swing their painful right leg.

They lay on their back, panting. They had made it back to the ledge.

I don't want to die, Amy thought to him. *I'm twenty six and I've never been to Paris.*

It made him smile. *Me neither. Let's catch our breath and try again.*

Out loud she said the word "Groan."

"There's some water in the bottle," he offered.

"Not for long!" He could feel her working their hand at their gear belt to free the canteen.

The rain had stopped, although the ravine was still filled with cold fog that made the west face invisible. "Come on, you," Amy said, struggling to their feet. "I'm hungry and I don't want to die here, so let's get climbing. Maybe it'll warm me up to move."

This time, when she had used all the artificial indentations, she decided to look for protrusions. A rock sticking out to their left, she kept their weight on their feet as she tested the stability of the potential hand hold. Only when she was satisfied it was solid did she shift their weight. A look down for a place to put her foot, again keeping her weight where it was secure while she tested the new touch point. Looking up, she could see the top of the cliff face only two feet above her. *Whatever you do,* she thought, *don't look down.*

She heard Paul think back, *I'm not looking at anything, I've got my eyes closed.*

She tested another bulge, but this fell out of the bluff and disappeared below her vision. Because she hadn't moved her weight from her feet, they didn't fall. Paul thought, *What you're doing, it's working. Keep at it.*

Her eyes darted, looking for another rock extension, but there were none. She was panting from the exertion and anxiety, sweat was dripping from their hair and face, she did not feel cold anymore. Out loud, Paul said in bursts, "There," pant. "to the," pant, "right." Pant, pant. "A groove?"

She saw it, an indentation halfway between their head and the top of the mesa. She reached their right hand to it, trying to keep her weight on the secure footholds beneath her. The groove was wet, and she felt dirt and small bits of gravel spill out from under their fingers and drop on their head and face, She had to lower their head and spit soil from their mouth. Then she went back to pulling more debris from what she needed to be the last handhold.

Paul could feel their calves getting numb from the unforgiving position they were in. The fingers on their left hand, locked on a small rock, were beginning to cramp. Amy brushed more dirt out of the prospective slot in the rock and thought to Paul, *We're about to get out of here or die.* As she shifted their weight to the new handhold she heard him think back, *Getting out would be fine, if that's all right with you.*

Some remaining gravel moved under her fingers, but the grip was good enough for Amy to leverage the rest of the way up the cliff. She rested, elbows on top of the bluff, even as their legs dangled over the edge. A wave of warmth and exhilaration came over her. Out loud she gasped, "I think we're going to make it."

When the needles and pins finally left their legs, Amy hoisted themself up further and grasped for a flange of rock on the top of the cliff. She pulled, she tugged, she dragged their body up until she could throw their left leg up and on top of the mesa.

Amy rolled forward, away from the edge of the cliff, and lay on their left side. She was gulping at air, suddenly she was dizzy, and their legs felt like rubber bands. *Are you okay?* she thought to Paul, as they both hyperventilated to unconsciousness.

When they woke up, they were cold. Their clothes were wet from rain and sweat, and the wind over the east face bluff was biting. It no longer was raining and the fog had lifted, but the sky over the bluffs remained grey and low. To the west an orange sun peeked between the horizon and the cloud bank. Amy said, "Roll call! Paul?"

"Here, boss," he said aloud, then added, "Amy?"

"Yes. Oh God, I'm so cold!" Even so she felt euphoric at having survived. "We have to get back to the lodge," and she struggled to lean forward on all fours, and then stand. Their right leg hurt from thigh to calf, and both legs felt like overcooked noodles. *We have to make it,* she thought to Paul. *We survived everything else, I refuse to die here.*

While each of them could have different attitudes and amounts of enthusiasm, the strength of Amy's body was always the same for each of them. *Come on,* she thought, *we don't have much daylight left.* Woodenly, she lurched from leg to leg, barely bending knees or ankles. Everything hurt.

"Down that way," Paul said softly, "then make a left. I think that takes us back to the road." She continued to reel side to side as she made their way. *Why did Hunter shoot at us?* she thought.

Paul answered silently, *Not the action of an innocent man. I hope he's still in the park.*

"Tomorrow," she said aloud, then went on silently, *I'm too whipped to nab him tonight. I'll get him in the morning. Bastard.*

"At least he missed."

Amy was exhausted by the time they made it back to the paved road. When she saw headlights approaching, she held up her badge in one hand and waved the other. A Ford pickup stopped, and the driver rolled down his window to shout, "What the fuck?"

Amy staggered to the driver's side, still holding her badge up. "Police, I need your help to get to the lodge."

The driver was a man in his thirties, dark hair and clean shaven. "Shit. Okay, get in." He leaned across the bench to open the passenger's door.

Amy hauled herself in. "Thank you," she mumbled. "I was hurt on a stakeout. I have to get to the lodge."

The driver stared and left his truck in park. "Don't bleed on my seat," he hissed.

It was Paul who said, "I'm bleeding? Where?" Amy's badge was still in their hand.

"Your leg!" he barked. "I'll get you to the lodge, let me turn around." He did a three point turn and headed west.

"Thank you," Paul mumbled, as Amy slumped against the passenger door.

"Come on, lady," the driver said, poking her. "We're at the lodge." He leaned across her and opened the passenger door. "I'm supposed to be in Waveland half an hour ago."

Paul roused himself to let themself out, gingerly, and mumbled something he hoped was a thank-you. The moment the door was closed the driver gunned his engine to turn back toward his original destination.

Paul stumbled across the drive to the lodge entrance, and found a chair in the lobby where he could collapse. *I will not pass out,* he said to himself. Internally he poked at Amy to wake her, while he examined their right leg. Their jeans were ripped, and a fair amount of dried blood was soaked into the denim.

"I'm warm!" Amy said out loud, then covered their mouth with their hands. *I mean, I'm not freezing anymore. Are we dead yet?*

Not yet, he thought back, *but hungry and tired are competing. You want to eat or just crash?*

If I sleep in this chair, will they refund my room rent?

They might charge double for frightening the tourists, he thought, but silence came from Amy. He decided to stagger to their room and join her in sleep. They'd worry about Hunter and their leg and food in the morning.

℘ 17 ℞

It was noon when Amy and Paul woke up. They were ravenous. Paul considered leading and running in Amy's naked body to the continental breakfast, but she insisted on dressing first, which meant showering. After their cliff-top adventure the day before, the warm water in the bathroom was a glimpse of heaven. She was reminded by the sting of soap that something had happened to her right leg; so Amy, daughter of an emergency room surgeon, explored. After she gently washed away the dried blood, she saw her wound–a round hole in the outside of her thigh, four inches above her knee, just above the part of her leg that would be flush against a chair when she sat. Paul thought, *Why does it sting on the inside of that leg? Take another look,* so she spread her legs to complete the examination. She found another hole, this one still seeping fluid. A wave of fear washed over her but dissipated as she explained to Paul, out loud, things she had learned from her father. "The first one we found is lateral posterior, outside and back of the leg. The other one is medial posterior, and it looks angry."

"I'd be angry, too, if I had a bullet go through me. In fact, I am angry."

"You think that's what happened?" Amy asked. "I thought gunshots hurt a lot worse than this." She stood up to resume washing themself. *Iodine,* she thought to Paul, *merthiolate, peroxide, something. We'll see if the gift shop has anything.*

"What about Hunter?" he said aloud.

"I wanted to get him in his tent early this morning, but I was so wiped out from yesterday–" She turned to rinse her hair in the shower stream, then stepped out onto the bath mat. "This time we take the right path and get him on the west face."

Amy stopped in the lodge restaurant and ordered a ham and Swiss sandwich with strips of bacon, no mayo, just a bit of mustard, and lettuce and tomato. When the waitress brought it, she thought to Paul, *Isn't this beautiful? Food. One of my favorite things.*

He thought back, *I'll like it even better after we can't see it anymore.*

She laughed and dug in. Chewing slowly, she thought, *Does this taste wonderful or what? God, I am a happy woman.*

Absolutely, he thought. *Of course, I wouldn't say no to more bacon.*

Amy was sore everywhere, as well as hurting where she had been shot in the thigh, so dessert was three aspirin. She bought a grossly overpriced bottle of iodine in the gift shop, then applied it in the lobby ladies room. "Oh, that stings!" she cried aloud, waiting for the red disinfectant to dry.

Paul thought, *We haven't seen your dad in a while. A trip to his office just might be in order.* James Clear was an emergency room surgeon, and he had a side practice with a close friend in a medical clinic that refused to accept insurance. *You're probably still covered by the daddy plan.*

"I'll let you tell him I was stupid enough to get shot, I'd be too embarrassed."

When the iodine was dry and Amy was properly clothed, she removed the tarp from the squad car. She opened the trunk to look at her options. Paul thought, *Pretty shotguns.*

That might be overkill, she thought. She took the spare pistol and baton and slid them into the empty holsters on her belt. When she saw the machete her eyes lit up. *I'm thinking this is the right tool for the job.*

"Mister Natural would be impressed," Paul said aloud.

"Who?" She attached the scabbard to her belt. "Hmm, I'll have to take the shotguns out if I want to put Hunter back here." She slammed the trunk shut. "Mister who?"

No, Paul thought back. *Doctor Who. Mister Natural. He was a cartoon hippie guru I liked.*

"So what you're saying is you were never normal," she replied.

The odometer said it was six miles from the lodge to the overlook at the west face of Mount Magazine. "Do you remember anything about that guy who gave us a ride last night?" Amy asked aloud. "I want to send him a fruit basket."

She straightened her gear, then walked the short distance to the top of the rappelling bluff. The day was warm, with plenty of sun and just a few scattered clouds. She saw three clots of people there to climb and rappel, none of which included Hunter Stringfellow. Then she noticed the blue backpack sitting near two ropes that went over the edge of the cliff. Amy walked to the lip of the bluff and saw someone–she assumed it was Hunter–slowly rappelling toward the ravine floor. "What goes down must come up," she murmured. She emptied the tubular magazine on his .22 rifle and cleared its breech, then sat cross-legged in front of the ropes with the machete across her lap.

When Hunter's head appeared above the cliff, Amy was holding the machete, slowly slapping the flat of the blade against her free palm. "Nice to see you again, Mister Stringfellow," she said. She noticed his eyes dart sideways as he hesitated. She held the machete straight out and said, "If you try to rappel back down I will cut your ropes." She was sore and stiff from the workout she got the day before, but she was able to hold her position until the man began to stutter and haul himself onto the mesa top.

When he was on solid ground Amy sheathed the machete, and instead pulled her handcuffs and her pistol. "Lay down, face down," she commanded, "arms at your sides. Do it! Now!"

The man was still struggling to speak. "Wh- wh- wh- wh--"

"I'll explain," she said as she knelt, her knees on the small of his back. "You are under arrest–" she holstered her 9mm and quickly clasped the metal handcuffs on his right wrist "–for attempted murder of a police officer, and–" he began to struggle, so she shifted more of her weight onto her knees "–for the murder of Tyrone Hutton and Mackenzie Slaton." Remembering Kowalski's demonstration, she hammered the cuff tightly on his left wrist. When she stood up she drew her pistol again and ordered, "Stand up, please."

Dutifully the man struggled to his feet. He was still stammering, he had yet to get a complete word out.

Amy was reciting the Miranda warning when she realized several other climbers had gathered to watch the excitement. She turned her attention and announced, "I am Detective Clear with the New Orleans Police Department. This man is under arrest for murder and attempted murder. Do any of you have any information that can help law enforcement?"

The people drifted away, back to their own exercises.

Amy tried to sound neutral as she said, "Please relax, Hunter. I know your speech is difficult when you're excited. Please take it easy so you can talk. Okay?"

He closed his eyes tightly, attempting to concentrate, and took a few deep breaths. Then he tried again. "Whu- whu- whu- what have I du- du- du- done?"

Before Amy could stop him, Paul slammed the side of her pistol into the man's face and screamed, "You shot me, you fucker!" Hunter fell back two steps, blood dripping from his mouth.

Stuck on the first letter of "No," Hunter shook his head vigorously. Paul held up the man's rifle. "You shot me yesterday when I was on the east face."

He continued stuttering and shaking his head. Amy froze her muscles and thought, *Paul! Stop! We can't do this. You can't rough up a civilian even if you're pissed at him.*

I'm not a cop, and yes I'm pissed at him.

I'm probably in trouble for making an arrest out of my jurisdiction, she thought back. *Don't make it worse for me.* She felt Paul relax a little, then retreat. She heard him think, *Only for you. God, I want to pound that guy's head to goo.* She murmured, "Maybe the Governor will let you throw the switch at his execution." Hunter's eyes bugged out.

"Sorry, talking to myself," she said to him. "Pick up your backpack, we're going to see the park ranger."

"Bu-bu-bu-but all muh-muh-my stu-stu-stu-stuff!"

She pushed him along the path. "I'm sure Officer Lafferry will take good care of it."

She helped the man into the back seat of the cruiser, then drove back to the lodge. "I have to check out, I'll be back in a few minutes." Paul added, "Don't go anywhere."

You're just being mean, she laughed silently on the way back to her room.

Yup. Can we shoot him while he's trying to escape?

Amy threw her loose things into her suitcase. "He's locked in the back of a cop car with a grill and no door handles on the inside. Unless he's Harry Houdini, he's not escaping."

"You missed my point," he pouted. "We can always say he was trying to escape."

Through her smile she said, "It's a good thing I love you. You are such a bad boy!"

She paid her bill, then returned to the cruiser. She could see Hunter in the back seat, sitting up but shaking as if he were suffering convulsions. She threw open the driver's door and yelled, "What's going on?"

The young man stopped shaking, but he did not try to meet Amy's eyes. "P-p-p-please. I ha-ha-ha-have to p-p-p-pee."

"Well, I'm not going to stand you up out here to whiz in a bush," she said as she fastened her seatbelt. "Let's visit the ranger."

She left Hunter in the squad car when she knocked on the ranger's door. The grim faced man, again in bare feet, opened the door and after a moment said, "Yes, Detective?"

"I have a present for you, Officer. I've arrested a man for shooting me, he's in my back seat," she motioned to the car. "Can I transfer him to your supervision?"

"I've got no place to put him. You'll have to take him to Fort Smith."

"Can you at least help me? I have to rearrange his handcuffs, and he needs a bathroom."

He grinned unexpectedly and walked with her to the car. Amy opened the back door and said, "Hunter Stringfellow, may I introduce you to Officer Lafferrey?"

"Good God, son, what did you get yourself into?" Lafferrey said when he saw Hunter's split lip.

"W-w-walked into a d-d-d-doorway," he replied.

Amy released the tight left cuff, and immediately reapplied it with his hands in front.

"Come on," the ranger said, and opened his door. "Let's get you cleaned up a bit. Detective?" and he waved Amy to a chair in the kitchen.

Paul thought, *All this time I thought we'd have to drive him back to New Orleans. This is a relief.*

Should go okay, she thought back. *I talked to the officer in Fort Smith on the phone Friday. Maybe he'll remember me.*

The kitchen was small and warm. There was an old four-burner gas stove, a small round-top refrigerator, and a white porcelain sink; Amy noticed there was no dishwasher. The room was painted a cheerful yellow, setting off a water stained sampler that read "As for me and my house, we will serve the Lord." Mentally comparing it to her own messy kitchen made her start to itch. "This place is too tidy," she muttered.

Hunter's face was clean when Lafferrey guided him back. "I'll take care of your gear," he said, continuing a conversation, "and we're always on the lookout for bears. I'm sure you'll be back for your car as soon as this is all cleared up." Amy put Hunter back in the cruiser, then returned to thank Lafferrey for his help. "Mister Stringfellow comes here a lot," she offered. "Do you know him? Anything I should know?"

"I recognize his name, that's all. On the other hand, that means he's never caused any trouble here."

"Thank you again, Officer."

Amy belted herself in, then thought, *You want to do the honors?*

Out loud Paul said, "Hell yeah!" and he took the lead to drive. Silently he added, *Please can I use the siren to run a red light somewhere? Please oh please oh pleeeeeze?*

"Only if you behave," she teased.

They had gotten out of the state park and made it to the state highway. When Paul headed west, Amy announced to Hunter, "We're an hour from Fort Smith. I'm sure they'll take good care of you."

Her attention wandered when he began to stammer a reply. *Weren't we supposed to do something today?* she thought to Paul.

"Christine!" he cried, "We're supposed to see Christine today!"

Amy glanced at her phone while she ignored Hunter's stammering from in back. "Four bars, let's call her." She turned on the blue tooth and put it in her right ear.

They heard two rings, then, "Paulette! I was so worried! Where are you?"

"I love you too, Honey," he said. "We're somewhere in

Arkansas, taking a prisoner to a lockup. Amy expects we'll get in around two A-M."

"I was afraid you–oh, you know, that you changed your mind." He could hear her sniffling.

"No! Oh, no, Honey, never. Wait until I see you, I'll tell you the whole story. I'll even show you our bullet hole."

"Paulette, are you okay?"

Amy took the lead to say, "We're fine, Christine. We've been kind of busy, and there was no phone reception for part of the time. I'm sorry about today. Can we make it up to you? How about tomorrow night? I think I'm taking off work on Tuesday."

"Okay," they could hear a smile return to the woman. "I wanted to see that movie with you, we can go another time."

"Yes, Honey," Paul said, "Another time. And I'll be thinking about you and I'll see you tomorrow night. I love you."

"Oh, Paulette. I love you, too. And I love you, Amy. We'll have a good time tomorrow."

"Yes we will, Sweetie. 'Til tomorrow!"

Amy removed the blue tooth and sighed. From the back they heard Hunter say, "What was that? Who were you talking to? That didn't muh-muh-make any sense."

"None of your beeswax, my dear prisoner."

"Are you a le-le-le-lesbian?"

Paul laughed, "Nope. But if I were, I'd be the lesbian with a gun who's holding you prisoner. Got a problem with that?"

"Nuh-nuh-nuh-no, ma'am." In the rearview mirror, Amy could see the man was confused. "Is there someone else in the cu-cu-car?"

Paul's laugh was silent, but it made Amy giggle. "There's a strait jacket in the trunk. Do I need to get that out for you?" Hunter shook his head.

Amy thought to Paul, *I'm still whipped from yesterday. I have to take a nap. Will you be okay? Wake me when we get to the state police office.*

Yeah, he thought, *That'll work. What do I do with our hostage?*

Ignore him. If you cuh-cuh-cuh-cuh-can.

A few minutes later Paul glanced back at the passenger. "Can you hear me okay back there?" He heard Hunter stammer something, so he went on. "I have a few questions. First, what's your dog's name?"

"I d-d-d-don't have a d-d-dog. Mac wuh-wuh-was al-al-allergic."

"Hmmm. Okay. Do you have a ski mask?"

"Yeah. Tuh-tuh-two of them. It gets cuh-cuh-cold on the muh-muh-mountain."

"Is one of them black?" Paul glanced up at the rear view mirror to see Hunter's face as he replied, "Actually, buh-buh-both of them."

"I know about your rifle. Do you have a handgun?"

"It's in my b-backpuh-puh-pack, the ruh-ruh-ranger's got it."

"What is it?" Paul went on, "A .45? A .38? 9mm?"

"Nah. It's just for s-s-s-snakes and things. I think it's a .25. Is that a guh-guh-gun size?

Paul winced. "Promise me you won't shoot at a bear with it. You'll just piss him off." Then, "Why did you lie to me about the memorial service?"

He became more nervous, and it took him almost three minutes to stammer out, "I'm afraid I'll get ar-ar-arrrrrested for not paying tuh-tax on the climbing trips."

"For real? I've got two dead bodies, and almost thirty-four million dollars in jewels are missing, and you're worried about some piddling taxes?"

"Juh-juh-juh-jewels? Whu-what juh-juh-juh-jewels?

Paul thought the man sounded surprised. "The Rothschild Jewels. Somebody killed a guard, they were there when Mackenzie died, and that same somebody stole a ton of diamonds and rubies. And they did it by rappelling from a skylight. Am I jogging your memory?"

He was surprised that someone who stammered so badly could let out a low whistle of astonishment. "I hu-hu-had no id-id-idea. Wow." Cynical though Paul was, he thought Stringfellow sounded completely sincere.

"One other question. Why did you shoot at me?"

"Whu-whu-what are you t-t-talking ab-ab-bout? I di-di-di I didn't."

"Yesterday. Maybe noontime. I was on the east face, I was tracking you in binoculars. You had just finished a series of drops and climbs, you were eating a sandwich or something. I stood up and you shot your rifle."

"I di-di-didn't see you th-th-there. I shot at a b-b-b-bear."

He still sounded genuine to Paul. "You didn't see me? I was fucking waving."

"If you're worried about a b-b-bear you duh-duh-don't notice the puh-puh-pretty girl."

After a long pause, Paul muttered, "Well. Fuck, fuck, damn." He shook his head and turned on the cruiser radio. The oldies station was playing "Paperback Writer."

They were still shy of Fort Smith when Paul pulled the squad car into a welcome station. "You want to use the bathroom?" he asked Hunter. "Candy bar? My treat."

"Th-th-thank you." Paul opened the back door, then grasped him by the upper arm and led him inside. They went to the desk, where Paul presented Amy's badge to the uniformed woman on duty. "Prisoner needs to, uh, relieve himself. Can you watch the door at one of the rest rooms so we don't scare any of your customers?"

"I'd be glad to," she said. Paul and Hunter stood outside the men's room while the officer opened the door and bellowed, "Anyone in here?" A couple of voices called back. The woman said, "Hurry up, we gotta close it down for a few minutes." After two men straggled out, the officer held the door open and said, "I'll make sure there's no interruption."

Paul in Amy moved to touch the hat he wasn't wearing, then pushed Hunter to a urinal.

"A luh-luh-little pr-pr-privacy?" he asked.

"I promise I won't look," Paul snickered.

Hunter struggled with cuffed hands but was able to unzip and urinate. Over the sound of running water he said, "Do lesbians even cuh-care about men?"

The question made Paul angry: he was offended that Hunter thought Amy might be gay, and he was sensitive that his own girlfriend was. "Sure, if the man is man enough," he said, cruelly.

"I thought you wuh-wuh-wuh-weren't going to lu-lu-look."

"I've seen better, I've seen worse. I'm sure your cellmate will think you're great."

As Hunter zipped up he said, "Whu-why are you so muh-muh-mean?"

Paul shoved him against the wall face first. "You shot me," he hissed in the man's ear. "You fucking shot me. Do you expect a medal?"

"I didn't," he said, his voice distorted by the way his face was pressed sideways against the paper towel dispenser. "It was a buh-buh-bear."

Paul stepped back to unhand the man. "A bear. A bear shot me?"

"Nuh-nuh-nuh-no. I'm telling you, I shu-shu- I shot at a bear."

Hunter held his cuffed hands in front of his face, as if he were afraid Paul was going to hit him like he had done at the state park. Paul shook his head and took the man by the arm again. "Come on, let's find a Snickers bar."

He bought three candy bars from a vending machine, then led his prisoner back to the police cruiser. After Hunter thanked him for the candy, Paul said, "Wait here. It's my turn," and he went back to the welcome station for the ladies room.

Once he was in the state police parking lot Paul closed his eyes and thought to Amy, *Wakey-wakey, Detective!* It took a few passes and pokes before she said out loud, "What time is it? Where are we?"

"Ummm?" came from the back seat, as Stringfellow worked on his snack.

Paul thought, *Shh, we've got company. We're in Fort Smith. You need to talk to the troopers.*

Oh, okay, sure, she thought to him. *Give me a minute to finish waking up. Any developments?*

We made a bathroom break and he called us a lesbian, so I slammed him against the wall. I didn't hit him, though. And he said he was shooting a bear and he didn't see us.

Arkansas bears have guns? Amy began walking up the cement steps to the state patrol office.

I said the same thing. He swears he shot at a bear.

With a .22? Is he trying to win a Darwin award?

At the security desk Amy held up her badge case. "I'm out of my jurisdiction, but I arrested an assailant at Mount Magazine Park and I want to press charges."

"Louisiana?" the officer said, actually reading her ID card. "That must have been one hell of a pursuit to end up here."

"Look for the slow-speed chase on the news tonight," she laughed. "I was here to question him about a New Orleans case, but then he shot me. I want to press charges."

The officer squinted at her. "For someone who's just been shot, you seem pretty, uh, lively."

"He shot me yesterday, I couldn't catch up to him until today." The officer was staring. "Look, if you've got a matron here, can I show her my wound?"

"Uh, no, it's okay, I believe you," he answered, embarrassed. "What did you do with the perp?"

"Locked him in the truck of the squad car–"

"Jesus, we keep shotguns in our trunks!"

A laugh. "We do, too. He's in the back seat. I'll get him." She turned to do so, but the sergeant stopped her. "Before you bring him in–why did you come all the way to Fort Smith to interview the guy?"

"He's one of the suspects in a murder and theft case I'm working. I don't know if he did it. But there's a hole in my leg because of his .22."

Hunter was quiet and clearly frightened during his processing. He cooperated with being fingerprinted, but kept his answers as short as possible. When the man was distracted, Amy whispered to the sergeant, "He stammers when he's nervous. Shhh."

Another officer came to lead Stringfellow away to the holding cell where he'd spend the night. "Wait," she told the policeman, then said, "Hunter, I'll call your parents. I talked to them on Friday, they were worried about you. And your boss, Bill." He nodded and let the officer lead him away.

"The arraignment will be tomorrow morning," said the sergeant. "You're welcome to stay for it, but since this is a felony charge you don't have to be here to make the complaint."

She slumped in the chair and said, "Thank God. I've got eleven hours to drive before I sleep in my own bed. And I've been going at a dead run all weekend." She thought to Paul, *I hurt everywhere, my leg is throbbing, and I'm wiped out. You want to drive?* When he thought back, *Only if I can turn on the siren,* she laughed aloud.

Paul drove to Vicksburg while Amy slept. It was a rare but not unprecedented occurrence, where he had their mind and body all to himself. He had gotten used to the constant sharing and companionship over the years, and now there was a tension between the relief at being alone, and the fear of solitude. He made use of Amy's spectacular voice, singing along with the True Oldies Channel on the squad car radio. As he approached the Mississippi state line he poked her mentally and shook her awake. He swerved when she stretched their arms and yawned, then pulled the steering wheel back in line. "Where are we?" she asked. "Are you hungry?"

"Yes, I am," he laughed. "We're coming up on a Cracker Barrel in Vicksburg. You've been out for six hours."

She shook their head and said, "I needed it. You can zonk out after we eat."

"Sleep well?"

"Like the dead. Damn, my leg still hurts."

"What do you want? We got shot. With a bullet."

Amy and Paul compromised over the restaurant menu: meat loaf with turnip greens and cucumber salad. When the meal came they had to take turns leading to eat, although anyone watching would think they were looking at a woman sitting alone, smiling, and oddly moving the fork from right hand to left after each bite. True, all the food ended up in the one stomach in Amy's body, but the taste was diminished for whichever of them was in the background; only the person leading got to feel any slaking of hunger. Once they had figured this quirk out, years earlier, it became a joke to them.

I hope I make it through tomorrow, she thought. *I'm still so tired, but there's so much to do!*

"Including visiting Christine tomorrow night."

Amy had learned her lesson. Except for work emergencies, like driving to Arkansas to find Hunter Stringfellow, Paul's time with his girlfriend was non-negotiable. Fortunately Amy liked Christine a lot, but there were occasions when Amy slept through Paul's date. He usually made up entertaining lies to tell her what she missed.

I have to tell Kowalski about Stringellow, she thought. *I told Hunter I'd call his parents and his boss. And I want to check on phone calls between Skyler and Uncle Brad and maybe Bella's boyfriend.* She paused to savor a forkful of tart cucumber salad. *And it just may be time to grill Skyler about some of the lies he told me.*

Amy led for the rest of the drive back to the NOPD station. Paul kept her company for an hour or so, then fell asleep in mid-sentence. She wondered if she and Paul could take turns sleeping and keep her body going 24 hours a day. Maybe between them they'd be able to get everything done.

℘ 18 ☙

Amy hit the snooze button on the alarm clock twice, and Paul pressed it once. "Why am I still so tired?" she whined. "I slept while you drove, I got what–" she looked at the clock, "–five hours just now. I should be bright eyed and bushy tailed."

When she fell back on the bed Paul said, "Red eyed and bushy tailed is more like it. We hurt. Our leg really hurts."

"I guess," she said and poked the bullet exit wound in her thigh. It hurt. It felt bad to her finger. "I'm going to see Dad about it. I hope the Commander doesn't think I'll use the workers' comp doctors for this."

"Nah, you were off duty."

She sat up and bent her leg to get a good look. The wound was small but it was oozing a foul discharge, and a large area around it was an angry red. "Great," Amy moaned, "it's infected." She fell back on the bed. "This is Monday, right? I have to go in, Kowalski won't be there tomorrow to go over the case."

Paul rolled them over and got up to start their shower.

Muster was long over by the time Amy got to the station. When she found Kowalski in the uniform division he said, "Where have you been? It's–shit! Are you okay?"

"Nothing penicillin and ice cream won't cure," she said. "I've got stories to tell."

"You've got one hell of a sunburn. Did you fall off a mountain or something?"

She walked them into an interview room, saying, "Aw, who told you? It was going to be a surprise."

"You–you fell off a mountain?" he asked, a look of concern on his face.

"Maybe twenty-five feet. I landed on a ledge. Took forever to get back on top. It was windy, maybe that's where the burn came from." Amy explained her encounter with Hunter Stringfellow, how he shot her but tried to blame it on a bear, and how he was in a lockup in Fort Smith, Arkansas.

"I should have been with you," Kowalski said softly. "Never deal with a murder suspect on your own."

Paul took the lead, and Amy's smile disappeared. With hands on hips he hissed, "I don't remember you volunteering to come with me."

Silently, he hung his head.

Don't, Amy thought to Paul. *I still have to work with him.*

He's busting our chops for something he could have fixed. That's bullshit.

Yes, she thought to him, then took back the lead. "It's okay, Pat," she said aloud. "We do what we can. We do what we have to. I'm okay."

"I'll do better," he said, still looking at his shoes.

"Stringfellow's behavior is hardly that of an innocent man, but I want to talk to Blunt, the guy with the dogs. And maybe the creep from the museum. When will you be available?"

"Tomorrow is fine. The–"

"Isn't your weekend Tuesday and Wednesday?" she interrupted.

Kowalski said, "The captain told me the Commander told him that he wants to see more progress. I don't get weekends until we make an arrest."

"I'm right with you," she smiled. "I didn't have a weekend this weekend." She kneed the door to the interview room closed and sat at the interrogation table, and the officer sat across from her. "I'm still exhausted from mountain climbing, I'm going to the doctor to get this bullet hole treated–I'm leaving as soon as I can. Let's go over a plan." Kowalski nodded and leaned forward. "I'm going to call Skyler Blunt to make an appointment to visit again, I've heard too many things that contradict his story. I want to talk to his boss at that tree surgery place. And we need to look at the latest phone logs, maybe there's been some change. Can you do the phone analysis?"

"Yeah," he grunted. "I hate that stuff, but I understand we need it. What should I look for?"

Paul thought to Amy, *I'll explain, okay?* Kowalski didn't know why the woman nodded, but then Paul as Amy said, "Any change in patterns of our persons of interest calling anyone else. Are there complementary changes, anything in common?" Quickly, he described to the officer how he could do the comparisons.

"I never—where—that's great. Where did you learn to do it that way?"

Amy felt Paul's burst of pride at the complement. "We used to do market research," he answered.

"We?"

Paul thought, *Aw, crap. I did it again.* Then to Kowalski he said, "Royal 'we'. Bad habit, sorry."

Amy took the lead and said, "Let me call Blunt and his boss, We—I'm sorry, I'll report back before I go to the clinic." When she stood up, the officer stood also and opened the door for her. "I'm going downstairs to the detective lair. See you."

As they walked away, Paul thought, *I'm so sorry! I don't want to give us away, but I always think of us as you and me—we.*

She smiled and shook her head. *It's fine,* she answered silently. *I don't worry about it like I used to. At the worst people think I'm crazy.* She stuck out her tongue and blew, "Pttthhhhhh!" much to the surprise of a beat patrolman who was walking toward her.

"Did I do something wrong, Detective?" he asked.

"Not at all, Sergeant. Your behavior is exemplary and you're doing one hell of a job. I'm sure your family is quite proud of you."

"So...–" Paul thought the officer was trying to turn the encounter into a social conversation "–the, uh, the raspberry...–"

"Exercise," Amy said, walking past him. "Making sure the lips and tongue and lungs are working in proper synch. Besides, I like the sound." Without turning back to the man, she repeated "Pttthhhhhh!"

Back in the detective bullpen, Amy opened her file and dialed the phone. When she heard a grunt she said, "Good morning, Mister Blunt. This is Detective Clear with NOPD."

"Huh! What the fuck you want?"

In anger, Paul jumped to the front and said, "I the fuck want you, bitch. Time for us to talk again. When will you be home tomorrow?"

"Let me look at my daytimer, I'm–"

"You'll be home at one o'clock tomorrow. If you're not, I'll issue a warrant for your arrest. Any questions?"

Blunt asked, "You bringing your chaperone, little girl?"

"You misunderstand," Amy replied. "He's my pet gorilla. No matter how much I feed him, he's always hungry."

There was no response, so Amy said, "One PM tomorrow." It was creepy to hear him breathing down the line, so she hung up.

Smooth, Amy thought. *I like how you ignore the carrot and jump straight to the stick.*

While she was looking for the phone number of the place where Blunt worked, Paul thought back, *Got to out-badass them. Show him who's boss.*

"Establish dominance quickly," Amy said. "You didn't like it so much when I did that with Uncle Brad."

Ouch. Touché.

Into the phone she said, "Yes, this is Detective Clear with Orleans Parish Police. I need to speak to the office manager or the owner."

"What is this about?" the receptionist asked.

"A capital criminal case. I need their help in our inquiries."

There were clicks on the line, and a badly recorded message about how important Amy's call was to Westwego Tree And Stump. The disembodied voice was asking when she had last examined the health of the trees on her property when there was a loud 'clunk' and a real voice came on, "This is Larry Proctor, can I help you?"

"Yes, thank you. My name is Detective Clear, I'm with New Orleans police. There is a person of interest in a felony case, and they work for you. I'd like to visit you tomorrow to look at your employee records."

"One of my people?" incredulous. "Who is it?"

"It's an active case, Mister Proctor, I cannot tell you that."

There was a pause before Proctor said, "This sounds like a fishing expedition. What branch of the police department are you with?"

"I'm investigating grand theft and murder. If necessary, I

investigate interference in a police investigation. Shall we say around nine tomorrow morning?"

"You'll bring a warrant with you?"

"I'll have everything I need. See you in the morning," and she hung up.

Warrant? Paul thought to her. She said aloud, "Why do people always think I need a warrant?"

Used to be, Paul thought back.

Amy blew a little raspberry. Then, "Let me get this out of the way." She dialed the number for RockWallUSA.

There was no background noise when a mature voice answered. "Is this Bill?" she asked.

"Unfortunately," the voice answered. "Can I help you?"

Amy pulled her chair closer to the table as she introduced herself. "I want to let you know about Hunter Stringfellow. He's been arrested in Arkansas. I told him I'd contact you."

"Oh great," the gym owner said, "I'll never get the deposits done if I'm sitting out here."

"I'll, uh, I'll let you know it there are any developments. I know you care about him, and he seems very loyal to you."

"Yeah. He's always been a good kid, this is the first time he's ever gone AWOL." She heard him making some clucking noises, as if he were moving his tongue while thinking. "Do you think he's in serious trouble? I mean, should I get a temp in here, or look for a replacement?"

"I don't know, Bill," Amy said. "I'll probably hear from Little Rock PD in the next week. Like I said, I'll call when they contact me."

"That poor kid. First his girl friend, now this. Look, I appreciate you calling me. I just don't know what I'm going to do."

When Amy finished the call Paul observed, "I notice you didn't tell him that Stringfellow SHOT you."

"There's such a thing as too much truth."

She picked up the phone again, and this time placed a call to Hunter's parents in Meridian. "Mister Stringfellow, this is Detective Amy Clear with New Orleans PD. My colleague Officer Kowalski talked to you recently?"

"Yeah. You're the one who arrested him, right?"

"I'm sorry? What?"

With an angry voice the man said, "Hunter called home yesterday. He said he's in jail in Arkansas, and that the woman cop hunted him down."

"Mister Stringfellow, Hunter shot me. You bet I arrested him."

There was a short silence before the man said, "He didn't tell me that." His voice was softer.

"I suppose not. Look, the wound isn't serious, I'll be back at work tomorrow. I called because I promised him I'd let his family know."

"I didn't know police did that."

"Your son seems to be a good kid. He said he was shooting at a bear. Maybe that's all this is about."

"Loretta drove up there this morning, she's going to bail him out."

"They granted bail? Good. Anyway, I just wanted to let you know what's going on."

The man did not say 'thank you' or 'go to hell;' he just hung up.

Paul thought, *Awkward. He didn't know if he was pissed or grateful.*

Amy held their head in their hands. "Me neither. I really like Hunter, but he shot me." She gathered up the file and glanced at her watch. "I have to brief Kowalski. Then I go see Dad. Damn, my leg is sore."

She walked up the single flight of stairs and found the officer in the uniformed police work room. He had three sets of fanfold computer printout on the desk.

"Any progress?" she asked.

He looked up, startled, then nodded. "Something weird happened." Kowalski pushed out the chair next to his. "This is the log of calls by Doctor Richardson. His last call to Skyler Blunt was on Friday evening–" He pointed at a page of printout "–and then nothing. It's like his phone broke or something."

"Hmmm," Paul as Amy mused. "What about Sklyer's log?"

The detective moved to the second set of printout. "Friday night he got a call from a new number, and for the next day there are only a few calls–one to a car repair shop, one to his home, and a couple to a chicken restaurant on the west bank. Any by Saturday afternoon–" pointing to a highlighted row "–nothing. Again, like the phone broke."

Paul heard Amy think, *Maybe that new number relayed a 'cool it' message.* Silently, he agreed. "The Soniers?" he asked.

"Sunday morning, a new number to Beau and to Darius. I don't see any change in Darius' log after that, but Beau hasn't used his phone since."

Amy led to ask, "What does AT&T say about the new numbers?"

"I knew you'd ask," the officer said with a smile. "They say they aren't their numbers."

Amy thought a moment. "Not theirs? Whose are they?"

"AT&T says they are cell phone numbers, but they are off the registry. The man says they're probably pre-paid cell phones, maybe one of the Latino providers. No credit card information, no address, no user name."

Paul said, "I'll find out," and reached for the desk phone. He dialed the new number that appeared on the Soniers' logs on Sunday. The voice that grunted on the other end of the line was a familiar one. "Hey, Skyler, just updating my phone book."

"What?" They could hear steam coming out of the man's ears. "How the fuck did you get this number?"

"NOPD," Paul answered, "we know everything. We're still on for tomorrow at one."

"Actually, something has come up and–"

"I wasn't asking, I was telling. You will be home at one o'clock, or I'll get a fugitive warrant. See you tomorrow," and they hung up.

"That. Was. AWESOME!" Kowalski bellowed. "I never would have thought of that!"

Amy led to say, "Just another trick in the toolbox. And my guess is that the new number on Blunt's call log belongs to our favorite museum director."

"I'll call him!" the officer said, excited, reaching for the phone.

"Don't bother," Amy said. "I'll bet Blunt's already talking to him."

"Oh. Yeah, I guess," and he put the handset back in the phone cradle, disappointed.

"Nice work on these phone logs," Amy offered. "Those new numbers are important. Not what you'd expect from innocent men." She stood up, holding on to the back of a chair until the pain in her leg subsided. "Tomorrow morning, come with me to see Blunt's boss, I want to look at his employee records. And you heard, one o'clock at Blunt's plantation. And check to see if anyone has been trying to call Hunter Stringfellow."

Between Amy's complement and his sincere admiration of her quick decision to dial the new number, all Kowalski could say was, "It's a pleasure working with you, Detective."

"Back at you. Now, if you'll excuse me, I have to get my leg amputated. See you in the morning."

It took thirty five minutes to drive to the Jefferson Parish Medical Center where Amy's father was an emergency room surgeon and shared a private practice with his best friend from medical school, Amy's 'Uncle' Charlie Eberhardt. Amy rapped at the glass window of the nurse's booth and told Susan, the long-time office aide, that she was there to see her father; then she took a seat as far away as possible from a harried woman with two small crying, sniffling children. She heard Paul think, *A doctor's office is where you go to catch what everyone in the waiting room has.* She stared at the woman–thin, hair escaping from a barrette, a mixture of exhaustion and fear on her face, wearing a utilitarian grey and blue shift. The children, boys about one and two years old, acted bored and ill, with intermittent cries. *If I ever get pregnant, shoot me,* she thought back. *God, I despise children.*

Even Kaylee's kids? Your nephew?

Amy held her hand in front of her mouth so no one could see her lips move when she whispered, "The only reason I haven't smothered him in his crib is that she named him Paul."

Does her husband–you know–does–

She shook her head. "No way! His head would explode." After a moment, she added, "If I ever want to break up Kaylee's marriage, I could tell Eddie about you. He'd disappear in a flash."

"Amy?" A nurse was holding open the door to the inside of the office.

"Hey, Marianne! How are you doing?" Amy was fond of the

woman, who was the first person her father hired in his private practice eight years earlier.

"Good to see you, Honey," she smiled. "Your father thinks you're going to ask him for money." She let the door to the waiting room close and led Amy down the hallway to Doctor Clear's office.

"I hadn't thought about that!" she said. "Should I ask him for ten or twenty?"

"Pssshh! Don't settle for less than fifty."

"Hey, Dad!" She entered the office and went around the desk to hug her father.

"What a surprise, Pumpkin," he said. Then he frowned, and touched an index finger to her cheek. "I thought we talked about the importance of sun screen."

"And Mother Nature reminded me you are right. I got caught on a cliff doing a police job." Her eyes got wide, she spoke louder, "I almost died, Dad. I fell off a cliff, but I landed on some ledge, and, and–"

Smiling, the doctor said, "Deep breath. Another one. Come on, another one."

Sheepishly she obeyed, then began to tell the story of her adventure in Arkansas. Finally she looked up and said, "Paul, I need you to tell Dad the rest."

"It's Paul. Great to see you, James." The doctor grinned to hear from the dyad who had turned up in Amy when she was a child, and who had become another member of the family. "The suspect shot us with a .22. He said he was shooting at a bear, but it's not like we've gained weight and grown a wookie suit. We were on one side of a ravine and he was on the other."

"I'm embarrassed, Daddy!" Amy added. "MeMaw was disappointed when that drug kingpin shot me a couple of years ago."

He patted his daughter on the shoulder, shaking his head. "Well, you walked in under your own steam, so it can't be too bad. Where did you get hurt?"

"Right thigh, posterior, lateral and medial. I think the bullet went through me." She unbuckled her belt and kicked off her slacks.

"Put your foot up on this," the doctor pushed a step-stool toward her, "let's take a look." He started with the outside of her right thigh, then ran his fingers under her leg to the other hole. It was his daughter he was examining so he didn't bother with latex gloves; he poked the angry red area and pronounced, "Exit wound. Probably some residual lead fragments. I've seen a million of them."

"James–Amy told an officer she was coming in to have her leg amputated. Got any whiskey?"

"We'll start with something a bit less radical," he laughed. "I'm going to flush that out and then slather it with antibiotic ointment. Wait here." He was shaking his head and snickering as he left to fetch some supplies from an examining room.

"Looks like we'll continue our bipedal existence," Paul said out loud.

"Dad laughed. I don't think he's angry."

"What? Were–you were worried he'd be mad?" She hung their head, but did not answer. "My guess, he's thrilled you're okay, and he thinks a cop having a wound this minor is humorous. I'm just saying."

"This won't take long," James Clear said when he returned, holding a kidney pan and some syringes. "Hold this pan with your right hand, I don't want to mess up my office." He used some gauze to lance the infected area, spreading an ugly odor in the room. He aimed a syringe without needle to wash and flush the exit wound with saline. A small red smear in the pan quickly was diluted to nothingness.

The doctor patted dry Amy's leg, and spread an ointment over the area. Then he used white tape to fasten gauze atop it. "Apply this three times a day," he said, handing a small tube to her. "I'm going to write you a script for antibiotics, and I want you to take them every six hours until they're all gone. Do not stop just because you're feeling better, take them all." He looked up at his daughter, then smiled and said, "You're going to be fine, but I'm glad you came to see me. That could have gotten unpleasant."

"It's Paul. You mean we could have had lead poisoning?" Amy groaned; James said, "Like I haven't heard that one before."

The three of them talked for a couple of minutes, until James said, "I've got three rooms of people in paper gowns wondering where I am, so you two better get going."

"Is Uncle Charlie here today?" Amy asked.

"No. Since Margie died, his heart's not in it. He only comes in a couple of times a week."

They coughed, the sound they made when they both tried to speak at once. Finally, Amy said "Tell him I asked after him. You'll tell him I love him, right?"

"Of course, Honey."

"Me too, James."

"Sure thing, son. Good to hear from you." He hugged his daughter and pushed her down the hall toward the exit.

Paul knocked at Christine's door at six o'clock. The woman threw it open and leaped at him, calling, "Paulette! Are you all right?" She was hugging and kissing him in Amy's body, then pushing herself arm's length away to look at them, then embracing again. Paul was moved by her affection, her relief that they were not dead, or even damaged. *I missed you, too,* he thought to her in mid-kiss.

She calmed down into a broad smile. Then she took their hand and said, "Amy, thanks for bringing my Paulette back. And are you okay?" Christine always knew which of them was leading, and always gave physical deference to Amy. Amy and Paul both appreciated the woman's ability to limit her amorous touching to Paul.

"Good to see you," Amy replied. "Feed me wine and I'll show you my bullet hole."

"Eewww," she said, laughing, leading them into her tidy kitchen.

Over dinner and wine Amy and Paul related their adventure searching for and capturing Hunter Stringfellow. At one point she said, "I know you and Paulette are the experts with guns and all, but a bear can't shoot anyone. Bears don't have thumbs. Uhh—do they?"

"I hope not!" Paul said. "They'd take over the planet."

"It's Amy. Really, he said he was shooting at a bear that we didn't know was behind us on the east face. I don't know if I believe him."

Paul added, "I sort of do."

"He could have killed you," Christine said, as if the thought was just now sinking in on her. "He shot you. You fell off the cliff, you could have died. You could have frozen to death." Her chin began to wobble. "No. I can't think of that. Life without Paulette, no." She leaned forward and put her head in their lap, wrapping her arms around their hips. "Do you have to do such dangerous stuff?"

Amy petted the woman's multi-length, multi-hued hair. "Not all the time," she cooed. "And the neat thing is that Paul and I are never alone, we always have each other. Between us, we figure out a way."

Paul added, "I told Amy we had to survive or else you would haunt us both forever. I'm your Paulette." He felt her smile, but she kept her face in their lap.

They had more wine. Finally Paul announced, "I'm hitting a wall. We haven't gotten a lot of sleep lately. I love you, Christine, but I'm going to be zonked out in a minute."

Amy shook her head and stood up to leave. But Christine, still sitting, grabbed her hand. "Please don't go," she said. "If Paulette wakes up during the night, I want to be there for her. Is that okay? Amy?"

She sat back down, surprised. "I know you're not making a pass at me. You want me to stay?"

She nodded, bashful. "I like being near Paulette. I like sleeping with her, it makes me feel safe. And you know, you look just like her."

"Can I borrow a nightgown?"

"Only if you show me the bullet hole."

They each washed up and prepared for bed. Amy felt odd, almost unfaithful, as if she were sneaking behind Paul's back to sleep with his girlfriend. Ordinarily she and Christine were as comfortable with each other as sisters, but with Paul asleep she felt physically shy with the woman. It puzzled her.

When they crawled into the bed, a mattress on the floor, Christine reached for a little rosewood box and prepared her sleeping potion, a pipe of marijuana. Receiving the demurral she expected when she offered it, Christine lit the bowl and inhaled deeply.

"This is strange," Amy said. "It's so unusual for Paul to do this. I'm not used to being alone."

"You're not alone," talking funny to keep the smoke in her lungs, Christine said, "I'm here."

"I mean in my head. Paul's been in me for sixteen years. I don't remember what it was like before he came to me. It feels like something's missing."

Christine nodded and took a second hit.

"Do you ever miss your voices?" Amy asked. Christine had a history of schizophrenia that was well controlled now by medication.

"I used to, sometimes," again talking in an odd way to keep a deep breath, "when I didn't have many friends, they kept me company. But my voices are bad. They don't like me. Since Paulette–" she exhaled a long thin plume of yellow smoke "–whew. But since Paulette and you have been with me, and I'm more careful about the medicine, they stay away. No, I don't miss them anymore."

They lay quietly for a moment.

"I'm sorry if I've made you uncomfortable, Amy. If you don't want to stay, you should go home."

Amy leaned over to kiss the woman on the cheek. "Paul's asleep, and I don't want to be alone either," she said. When Christine turned off the light, Amy rolled to her side, facing away from the woman. She felt Christine snuggle against her back. She thought to her, *Good night, Christine.*

"Good night, Amy," she whispered back. "If you talk to Paulette before I do, tell her I love her."

℘ 19 ℧

Amy arrived at the police station to find that Kowalski was not at the uniformed muster. When the captain was finished, she went to the duty officer and asked his whereabouts. "He called during muster," Shakira said, "and he told me to let you know. His wife was in a car wreck, he's gone to Touro Infirmary to be with her."

"Aw, crap," Amy muttered. To Paul she thought, *We'll do this anyway. I don't buy into that 'always have a partner' stuff.* She walked down the hall to go to the detective's section.

I guess, Paul thought back. *The pisser is, I think he's announced his decision. He's staying with Roxy.*

Out loud she cried, "I don't want to hear that name!" She clopped down the stairs with a silent frown. *Anyway, I'm over that,* she thought to Paul. *He had his chance and missed it. That door is closed.*

Dubious, Paul thought back, *Uh, okay. Now, where is that place where Skyler works?*

In the detectives' work room, Amy opened her file. She leafed through a few pages, looking for the contact information for Skyler Blunt's job, then sat down heavily. "Crap, crap, double crap," she muttered aloud, holding her temples. "I'm pissed."

Paul let her sit silently for a minute before he thought to her, *I'm sorry it didn't work. And you're entitled to feel sorry for yourself for a day or two. But you have to man up.*

The expression made Amy laugh. "I'm the only woman in the world who can man up, and it's because of you. Can't I have a good cry?"

Sure, Paul thought back, relieved that she was laughing. *But not here. We need to find you a different guy.*

As she went back to the file folder she thought, *Too bad Christine doesn't know any men.*

She printed out the MapQuest and went back to her sedan to drive to Westwego Tree And Stump.

It was a twenty-five minute drive from the station house to Fourth Street, across the river from New Orleans. Westwego Tree And Stump was in what originally had been a sprawling private home. As demographics and the economy changed, the area had turned commercial. What once had been a backyard with swings and a sandbox now was a mixture of broken concrete and weeds. There were four cherry picker trucks sitting out there, and as many flatbeds with built-in wood chippers. Two ten-wheeled pickup trucks were near the huge pile of firewood that was seasoning along the property line.

Amy parked her sedan on the street. A bell jingled when she opened the door into the erstwhile parlor. "Can I help you?" asked a middle aged woman at a desk.

"I have a nine o'clock appointment with Larry Proctor," Amy said.

The woman laughed. "He never gets here before ten. You're welcome to wait, though," and she pointed at some folding chairs against a wall. "Can I get you anything? Some coffee?"

"That's okay. Did Mister Proctor leave anything for me? I asked him for some specific documents."

"Oh, you're the one." A hand rose to cover her mouth, and she said, "Uh, I'm sorry. No, he, uh, he said he'd deal with you himself. What's going on?"

Paul was amused by the receptionist's blunt honesty. But before he could mention it to Amy, she replied, "He's helping us with our inquiries. It doesn't have anything to do with you or Westwego Tree and Twig."

"Stump," the woman corrected, "Westwego Tree and Stump." She swiveled in her chair to return to paperwork.

Amy took a chair. Fuming, she thought to Paul, *For every minute the son-of-a-bitch keeps me waiting, I'm going to slap him.* She heard him think back, *And I thought the fun part of being a detective was the boots and the shouting.*

She glanced through a worn issue of *Tree Services Magazine*, but the article on "Step By Step: A systems approach to climbing and safety" couldn't hold her attention. *Maybe I'll pull a fingernail for every five minutes he's late,* Amy thought, tossing the periodical back on the side table.

It was twenty past nine when the door's jingle bell rang. "Traffic on the Huey Long bridge was awful," he called to the receptionist.

"Good morning, Mister Proctor," the woman said, then mouthed, "The detective." She pointed to where Amy was sitting, arms crossed, foot tapping.

Proctor was a short, wiry man in his forties, a bald spot spreading in the salt and pepper on the back of his head. He was wearing khaki pants and a green polo shirt with a wood chipper company logo on the left breast. He turned to Amy and said, "Ah, we spoke yesterday." Then he stared at her coolly, and said, "I expected you would be older. Would you–"

Amy interrupted, "And I expected you would be on time." She stood and stared back at him, a dominance pissing contest. The receptionist busied herself at the computer keyboard, her face blushing in embarrassment for her boss. Procter blinked first and said, "You better come back to my office."

It was a utilitarian room: two metal desks, some filing cabinets, and some more folding chairs. A two-year-old calendar from 2023 was on the wall by his main desk, turned to a month that featured a bikini-clad blonde woman wielding a chain saw. The floor was wood, badly worn. Hard to believe this had been a master bedroom thirty years ago.

As he went behind his desk, Proctor said, "You have a warrant?"

Amy stood with her legs against the back of the desk, leaning forward with her hands spread on the man's desktop. "You have your insurance certificates?"

"My–my what? Hey, what division are you with?" Paul noticed fear in the man's face, the very response Amy was trying to provoke.

"I'm investigating a homicide and grand theft. Personally, I don't give a rat's ass if your workman's comp is current. But if you give me a hard time, I'll call Jefferson Parish Compliance and they'll spring a surprise inspection on you. Probably before lunch today." She smiled and stood up.

When Proctor failed to respond, Amy gently asked, "May I see your personnel records?"

"Oh, uh, yeah. Sure." There were beads of sweat on his forehead. Paul thought, *He must be way out of date.*

"They always are," she muttered.

"Sorry?" He handed her a clutch of manila files.

"Just talking to myself," Amy said. "Where can I examine these? I'll need a little privacy."

He looked around his sparsely furnished office. "How about that other desk? I have to preview a job site in Mimosa Park, so you'll have the room to yourself."

She reached out her hand and said, "Thank you for your cooperation, Mister Proctor. I'll give these to your receptionist when I'm done."

"I'd rather you left them on my desk. That's sensitive information, you know."

"That's why I want to give it to her, so she can say I returned everything. Oh, and one other thing? Please do not discuss my visit today with your staff. I'd like you to tell your girl to keep this to herself. We don't want Westwego Tree & Bush to be interfering with an open homicide investigation."

"Stump," Proctor said, "Westwego Tree and Stump." He stood with hands on his hips, defensively. Then he said, "I'll tell Lenore to keep mum."

Amy arranged herself at the second desk and didn't pay attention as the owner left. *Let's see what we got on Skyler Blunt,* she thought to Paul as she opened his file.

The file confirmed date of birth, forty three years earlier, in a boondock area of Plaquemines Parish. A faded post-it note said "Angola, armed robbery," fifteen years before his hire. Paul thought, *Post-it so they always know he's a felon, but they can throw it away and say they never knew about his record.*

Skyler was hired by Westwego Tree & Stump nine years earlier. There were a few write-ups for being late to work, one for a fight with a co-worker a few years earlier, and a commendation for being polite when he told an unreasonable customer to "stuff it where the sun don't shine." And one week ago he was docked sixty-five dollars for having damaged a piece of equipment–he brought back a grappling hook that was missing a fluke and told his supervisor he didn't know what happened. *The piece on the museum roof,* Amy thought. *If Proctor still has the broken grapple and the hook from the museum fits it, we've got a direct link between Blunt and the murder.*

"The date is right," he murmured aloud. "Two days after the break-in. What else is in here?"

Amy leafed through nine years of medical insurance paperwork and tax forms. Then she uncovered a faded yellow sheet, a faint carbon copy of a Workman's Compensation form. She and Paul each read it twice, then silently shouted at each other. Thirteen months into his employment at Westwego Tree & Stump, a rope wrapped around the ring finger of Skyler Blunt's left hand and severed the last knuckle. Louisiana Workers' Compensation paid for treatment, and Blunt was off work for three weeks. "That fits what Bella told us," Amy muttered aloud. "What a vain guy." She opened her notebook and wrote down some details.

The broken grappling hook, Paul thought. *We need it. How do we get it without the receptionist telling everyone?*

Amy considered that. A note? No, the office girl could open it. A note in a sealed envelope? No, then Proctor would have time to dispose of it. She took out one of her business cards and wrote "CALL ME!" on it, then opened desk drawers until she found envelopes. She wrote Proctor's name on the outside, then sealed it with spit and tape. She propped it up on his desk, leaning against a "World's Greatest Boss" statue.

Paul led as they prepared to leave. He shuffled the employee files so Blunt's was buried somewhere in the middle. At the front desk he said, "Mister Proctor didn't want these to be unattended while he's away." As they handed them over he said, "It is important that you do not tell anyone I was here."

The woman smiled in response. Amy led to say, "It's a serious infraction to interfere with a police investigation. Do yourself a favor–do not talk about this."

"Oh, sure, yeah," Lenore said absently. Amy heard Paul think, *She's going to tell everyone as soon as we're out the door.*

"Look at me!" Amy barked. When the receptionist did so, Amy said, "You could end up in a lot of trouble. If there is a leak, I know to look for you." Without waiting for a response, Amy turned and left.

Wasn't that a bit harsh? Paul thought.

The Louisiana morning was warm, with lots of sun burning through the ever-present haze. As they got to the car Amy thought back, *You're the one who said she was going to blab when we left.*

"Oh," Paul said as they climbed in, "I guess I did. Can I drive?"

"Be my guest," she said, and retreated to let him get them to Lafitte and Skyler Blunt.

Starting from Westwego on the west bank, the ride to Blunt's trailer palace was a much faster trip than her first visit there with Officer Kowalski. Their conversation about Christine and a concert they were going to attend on Saturday made it seem even faster. When Paul stopped the car in the rutted dirt driveway, he saw Blunt sitting in a kitchen chair near the front door, by a cluttered card table. He was running a cleaning rod through a rifle barrel. The Rottweiler got up and ran to the car, barking wildly.

Amy thought, *That dog wants to eat me.*

"Leave him to me," Paul said. When the dog was jumping up and down alongside the driver's door, Paul threw the door open and knocked the animal back. It shook its head as they got out of Amy's blue sedan, then lowered itself and growled. Paul made eye contact with the dog, and made several feints at running toward it, each time with arms spread to make them look even bigger. Still barking, the Rottweiler retreated to Blunt's side–no, behind Blunt's chair. To Amy he thought, *We just have to convince it that we're a bigger alpha dog than he is.*

As she walked toward Blunt, she saw him smile wryly and kick the Rottweiler, muttering, "Worthless bitch!"

"Good afternoon, Mister Blunt," Amy said, notebook in hand. "I appreciate you making the time to meet with me."

"So, what the fuck do you want?" He continued to clean the rifle.

"Some of the things you told me last time, I've found out they aren't true. I'd like to go over them again."

"Not true? Are you accusing me of lying?"

"You're the only person using the word 'accusing.'"

"'Lying' is the word I'm concerned about."

Amy leafed back in her notepad as she said, "Another word only you are using. Ah. Tell me again how you met Mackenzie Slaton."

He sat back with a frown. "I don't remember." He placed the rifle on the card table and folded his arms across his chest.

"Maybe this will jog your memory," Amy said, and began reading, "'I saved her dog. It was in traffic, I pulled over and grabbed it and she was there.'" She paused and looked at Blunt with raised eyebrows, inviting a response. "No?" She went on, "I asked you what kind of dog she had and you said it was a little chick's dog. Ring any bells?"

"Okay," he spat, looking left and right, "so I saved her fucking dog. So what?"

"So what? Mister Blunt, Mackenzie Slaton did not have a fucking dog. She was allergic to fucking dogs. So how did you meet her?"

He went back to the cleaning rod and the rifle. "I don't remember."

"I...don't...remember," she said dramatically as she wrote in her notebook. "Several people do remember, so, would you like to try again?"

Silently he dipped a cloth swab in cleaning fluid and put it on the tip of the cleaning rod.

"No? Okay, how's this: By some magical coincidence you–a tree surgeon with nine and a half fingers–are invited to a publicity dinner to announce a charity fashion show with a bevy of stunning anorexic women."

"What the fuck are you talking about?"

Amy grinned. "It's how the fuck you met Mackenzie Slaton. At a museum. A museum that's run by your brother-in-law."

"I don't know what you're going on about," pushing the cleaning rod in and out of the gun barrel.

"Declines...to...discuss," writing in the notebook. "How's this, then: How many grappling hooks have you lost or broken at Westwego Tree And Twig?"

"Stump," he muttered, "Westwego Tree And Stump. Probably

two a year. The boss is okay with it, what's your problem?"

"Me? I got no problems." She heard Paul snicker inside. "But I think you do. That rifle you're cleaning? Just touching it is more prison time for a convicted felon like you."

He lay the gun back down on the card table and closed his eyes.

"How's your new phone service?" she asked.

"Cheap rates, no roaming charges, and no long-term contracts."

"Really? I may need to change providers. Who is it?"

"M-Y-B Company," he growled, "Mind your business."

She shook her head. "Nope. That's an official police question, Skyler. Who's your phone company?"

"Get off my property," he hissed.

"You can answer me, or I can arrest you for illegal firearms possession."

"You think you can?" he said, standing.

His movement seemed to alert the Rottweiler, which suddenly barked. Paul took the lead to make a false start at the animal. The dog slipped sideways and fell against one of the table legs, knocking the rifle and a bottle of cleaning solution onto the ground.

"Fuck!" the man cried, scrambling for the gun. "You see what you've done?" he shouted at Amy, "This is your fault. Shit. Shit!" He righted the table and placed the rifle on it, then went for the bottle of cleaner. "Now I have to get more out of the house. Shit!" He turned abruptly and went into his trailer. The Rottweiler trailed after Blunt, but was left on the top step outside the door. There was no sign of the blue tick hound.

"That seems to be going well," Paul said aloud.

Yes, it does, Amy thought back. *Let's look around.* She walked around to the back of the trailer, ignoring the occasional loud bangs and clangs coming from inside. There was a charcoal grill emitting just the barest hint of black smoke. *You think he grilled his lunch?* Paul thought.

The grill was a red rectangle sitting on two cinder bricks. Amy knelt by it and gingerly lifted the lid. She smelled scorched wool, an odor she'd avoided for years after an accident with an iron and a pair of slacks. "Euuuw," she muttered. Then, "Does this look like it was a shirt to you?"

"And how!" Paul exclaimed. "And look–" pointing with their

left index finger, "–buttons." Three of them, slightly melted and misshapen from the charcoal heat, but with the unmistakable holes that buttons always have. "Pay dirt," he said out loud.

Amy realized a shadow was blocking her light. From her crouch she looked up and saw Blunt. "What did you have for lunch? It smells like–"

The lights went out when the flat of the shovel bashed against the left side of their head.

❦ 20 ❧

It all happened at once. Cold water everywhere woke them, the sun was as bright as a klieg light, and they both felt a monstrous headache. They heard someone nearby, grunting. Squinting into the sun, Amy saw Skyler Blunt throwing a shovel into a wheelbarrow. He was on dry land. She was not. "Hey!" she shouted, but the effort made her head vibrate with pain. A little less loud she added, "What's the deal?"

Blunt was smiling. He held up her pistol and her phone, then dropped them back into the wheelbarrow. "They'll probably find you in a hundred years."

Paul splashed their arms, but it wasn't water. Cement? Mud? "Where am I?" he yelled, and learned the same lesson Amy had.

"Bayou Des Oies. Sort of." He laughed. "There are too many bayou to name out here. Bye bye, Detective. And good riddance."

He's leaving us to die! Amy thought to Paul.

Paul responded, aloud, "I don't want to get killed again. Blunt! What's the–" he reached for their keys and touched bare skin "– Hey! Where are our pants?"

"My favorite kind of fuck," he grinned, "unconscious." He stood, gloating.

"You raped us?" Amy was not paying attention to the conversation; Paul heard her think, *What is this? We're in quicksand.*

"No, not at all," Blunt leered. "I just kept you warm for awhile."

"You fucker!" Paul raved, thrashing their arms in the muck, "You God damned asshole!"

We have to be calm, Amy thought. *I know how to get us out of this.*

Paul kept on waving their arms and thought back, *Aren't you mad? That guy raped us!*

We have to be calm, she thought again. *I'd rather live through this than die in righteous indignation. Stop struggling and let me lead.* A mouthful of mud underlined Amy's instructions.

Skyler Blunt turned when he heard a man's voice saying *The next time you see us it will be the last thing you ever see.*

There was no one behind him.

"That's weird," he muttered, "but I know she's a woman. Oh yeah!"

Get out of my sight, Paul thought to the man. *We've got work to do.*

"You have a nice day," Blunt called as he wheeled the barrow away from the bayou and out of sight.

"You trust me when we swim, right?" Amy asked. "Trust me on this." She leaned back to let themself float on the swampy mixture of sand and water. When the back of their head got wet Paul flinched, but Amy maintained control of their body. "Don't struggle, that makes it worse."

It was impossible to move rapidly in the suction and pressure of the quicksand. A few minutes passed before they were floating on their back, arms spread wide. Amy took deep breaths, trying to subdue her fear and adrenaline. "See?" she whispered aloud, "We're not going to drown. It's going to be okay."

Paul felt sheepish, to have been so panicky while Amy had been calm. "How do you know what to do?" he asked.

"The idea of quicksand used to scare me, there's lots of it in Louisiana. Dad was no help when I tried to talk to him about it. Don't you remember those books I got from the library? That's where I found out how to deal with this."

"I guess I was reading something else. How do we get to shore?"

"I'm going to paddle. It has to be real slow. It'll take awhile." She flicked their hands and their body rocked like it was on a waterbed.

Paul began to relax, giddiness at surviving replacing his fear. "Good thing it's warm. What with no pants and all. I hope the mosquitoes don't find us. Shit! I hope the gators don't find us."

"You worry about the 'skeeters. I'll deal with the gators." She flicked their hands again.

"How should we kill Skyler?" he asked.

"Why would I do that?" Flick. "I'd rather arrest him."

"He raped us. He put his dick inside us without permission. Doesn't that bother you?"

"I'm sure it does." Flick. "But I'd rather live through this and worry about that later."

"You seem so calm, and all I want to do is mangle the son-of-a-bitch. I'm a man. You know I don't like sex with men. You've only had a couple of boyfriends I could deal with."

Flick. "I remember. Cameron. Timmy. That loser a few years ago. You used to raise such a fuss!"

They heard a rustling noise behind them, from the dry land where Blunt had been. Slowly, Amy flicked her hands to turn their body, then lifted their head to look.

It was olive green. It was twelve feet long. It had tiny black eyes that stared back at them from the Cretaceous period. It was scaly. And it had dozens and dozens of dagger-like teeth. Paul whispered, "You said you'd deal with the 'gators. Deal! Deal!"

"This is like watching public TV," Amy said, fascinated. The reptile was surprisingly fast when it darted to its left, eyes always on its floating prey. It stared a long time, then ran to its right. Every now and then its gullet bulged, as if it were swallowing.

Fear returned to Paul, their pulse pounding in their ears. *He wants to eat us.*

"I believe you are right," she responded. "But he can't get to us while we're floating. He can't deal with the quicksand."

"How do you know?"

"We haven't been eaten yet."

"Oh shit! We can't just float here forever. He's just going to wait us out! Oh shit, oh fuck–"

Since they couldn't both speak at once, Amy thought to him, calmly, *He's beautiful. All those greens. And those bumps on his back. You know, gators are living fossils, they're prehistoric.* She felt safe from the beast for now, so she gave rein to her curiosity. *Have you ever tried to think to an animal?*

"We don't know anybody with a dog," still frightened, "No." Even so, he felt a smile on their face as Amy whispered, "Got nothing to lose."

Hey, big boy, she cooed, thinking directly to the alligator. It swung its head left and right, then stopped and continued staring. *You're such a pretty gator. And so big! It's a pleasure to see you.* The impassive black eyes blinked. *You're not hungry. It's warm, you want to go over there and splash in the water, don't you?* Again it looked up and down the bank of the bayou, settling on an area a hundred yards away, where a big cypress log was floating in free water. *You can get all wet and cool there. I won't hurt you, big boy. You'll be safe up there. You just head up there...*

It snapped its jaws twice, then darted to its left again, still focused on Amy's floating body.

Crap, she thought to Paul. *I guess he doesn't understand English.*

"It's hard to reason with a wild animal," he said. "What are we going to do? We're dead meat if we land where he's waiting."

She craned her neck to see more of the bayou shore, and the motion made their body rock on top of the quicksand. When a little lapped into their right ear, Paul reflexively shook their head, which increased their rocking. *Let me lead,* Amy thought softly. *I've kept you alive this long, trust me.* She felt him take a deep breath, and another, and barely nod their head.

She saw one section of shoreline that was cluttered with debris— sections of tree trunks, long branches, even some pickets that had been left behind as trash. "If I take us there," she said aloud, "we should have some cover when we land." She heard Paul think, *Okay. Waaahhhh.*

She flicked her hands to turn and aim down the swamp toward the protected landfall. Paul said, "If we had some sunscreen, this wouldn't be too bad." When she didn't reply, he added, "I hope we're peeling something fierce tomorrow. I don't want to end up as alligator shit."

Me neither, she thought. It took a good part of another hour to approach her target, and the gator scrambled in that direction only once.

When their head bumped the shoreline Paul said, "He's pretty far away. Let's make a run for it.*"*

Shhh, she thought back, *don't talk. No audio cues. Uh–I don't know if alligators have ears. And I don't know if I can outrun one.* She flicked her hands to turn sideways, still floating on her back, until she was close enough to grab a beached log. *Land ho!* she thought.

Paul thought, *What are we going to do? I hope you have a plan.*

Yes, me too. She took a deep breath, and hauled themself onto land. She was careful to keep the pile of wood between her and the reptile, about twenty-five feet away. She stood, dripping brown goo. Her shirt, her naked hips and legs, her hair, even her face, all the same brown of the bog she's been floating on for hours. The front of her body was encrusted with dried mud; the back was wet and slimy. *I wish I could take a shower before I deal with Mister Mesozoic over there.*

Yeah, well, I wish we could have a drink of water. Or beer. Yeah, beer would be good.

Slowly, Amy stepped backwards, away from the alligator, back–she hoped–toward Blunt's trailer, and maybe even her pants.

Abruptly the gator moved toward her, at a run, a gallop. When it registered on her that the animal was attacking she turned to run and fell over a tree stump. Paul and Amy could hear the gator feet hitting the ground, almost like a running horse. Paul grabbed one of the pickets, and a moment later pushed it at the animal's open mouth. It stopped for a few seconds, long enough to snap the fencepost into three pieces. Then it slowly crept toward them, body swaying from side to side with each step.

I don't think running will work, Amy thought as she stood up.

Paul picked up a long branch. It was heavier than he expected. *Like with the dog,* he thought back, *we have to convince it we're the bigger alpha croc.* He held their arms out and stood with their legs apart and bent, like a Sumo wrestler, trying to make themself seem larger to the animal. He waved the heavy branch overhead, and made roaring noises like a wild beast. As with Blunt's Rottweiler, he feinted runs at the gator. It stood still, body low to the ground, eyes riveted on Amy. It was a standoff until Paul made a mistake.

He laughed.

The alligator opened its jaws and lunged. Paul stepped aside but the animal's tail whacked them across the back, sending them sprawling. Before the gator could regroup, Paul rolled toward it and on top of it. He heard Amy scream as the gator spread its jaws again. Knowingly, Paul rested their left hand on the beast's nose and pushed its mouth shut. He continued to lean on it. *Nothing can open a gator's clamped jaws,* he thought to Amy, *but this is enough to keep it closed.*

He felt Amy's fear mutate into curiosity and wonder. *No kidding? Let me.* She moved their right hand to the gator's snout. She took control of their left hand and began to pet the animal's head. The scales were smooth in one direction, raggedy in the other. "Nice," she said. "Good boy."

Suddenly it thrashed side to side, its tail whipping as a counterweight. It bucked Amy off, then turned to face her as she sat on the ground. Once again it opened its jaws wide, a jaw spread three-and-a-half feet high. Paul had lost the branch he'd been carrying, but nothing was at hand as he looked around in panic. Between fear and exhaustion, they were immobile, helpless before the six-hundred-pound reptile.

They heard a sharp, loud noise, and then their ears stopped working. A small red spot appeared in the palate of the looming beast's mouth, then a second and third. Abruptly the animal fell backwards and landed about twenty feet away, its tail and hind legs slipping into the quicksand.

Paul silently called to Amy. She thought back, *Why can't I hear anything?*

A touch on her shoulder startled her into a fear response–she rolled to face the stimulus, hands balled into fists. She was looking at a Glock 9mm pistol. Behind it was Patrick Kowalski. She saw his mouth moving, but couldn't hear him. When she stood up, the officer holstered his weapon. Amy took two steps toward the man and fell against him. "Water. Please. Water," she whispered. Her head was spinning.

Amy felt Kowalski's arms around her and then under her, as he carried her back toward the trailer. She felt the vibrations in his chest that told her he was saying something, but her ears were still shut down. *Paul?* she thought. She heard him babble silently about a wet eagle. *Pat's here,* she thought to him, *We're going to be okay.*

You hang in there, buddy.

It took her a long time to figure out she was lying on a sofa, under a blanket punctuated by cigarette burn holes. Her head ached, her body felt feverish. When she smacked her lips, looking for water, she faintly heard Kowalski say, "Drink it slowly. The ambulance will be here soon." Greedily she sipped from the glass he held, until he pulled it away. "Slow," he said. She thought the man was whispering, but then it occurred to her that her hearing was returning slowly.

"What happened?" she gasped.

"I felt bad about bailing out on your interrogation. I knew you'd talk to Blunt without backup. As soon as I could get free, I came to help."

She sipped more water. When Paul thought, *Why are we burning up and freezing?* it made her cough. The officer pulled the water glass away and let Amy lie back on the couch.

"Where am I?"

"Blunt's trailer."

"He won't like that." She smiled a little, but the sudden pain in her dehydrated lips stopped her.

"He won't mind," Kowalski said, "he's hightailed it. His truck is gone, and your car is burning in a ditch."

"It's what?" she asked, but she was too exhausted to be angry. Paul thought something she couldn't comprehend, but she felt him rub their right arm with their left hand, 'his' hand.

"You rest. Alligator fritters for breakfast tomorrow."

"No. Wait." Amy took breaths after each word, she was so tired. "Back yard." Breathe. "Ashes." Breathe. "Buttons. In." Breathe "Charcoal grill." Several breaths. "Find them."

"I told you to rest," he said, smiling. "Forensics will look in the back. I'll look."

"My phone," she wheezed. "My–my gun." Breathe. "Wheelbarrow." A pause. "Pants."

"We'll take a vacuum and a rake to the place. Drink the water, now."

"You saved me. Thanks, Pat. You're–you're–" she coughed, and their mind felt like an old cartoon, irising out to black. Instead of Porky Pig, Paul thought he saw Albert the Alligator in the center.

℘ 21 ঽ

"Hey, coonass. When you and that monkey brother of yours leaving Illinois?"

Beau Sonier was in their room at a boarding house, laying out clothes for the next leg of his circus travel. He wasn't thrilled to hear Skyler Blunt's voice. "Day after tomorrow," he said, cell phone perched between cheek and shoulder as he placed some shirts in a valise. "You want we'll send you a postcard from Dayton?"

"Fuck that, I want money. You got that pistol I gave you to sell?"

"Non. Sold it two weeks ago. Got two hundred bucks for it."

"You get those rocks I sent you?"

He sighed. It was easy enough to handle Blunt, but it had to be done a particular way. He wasn't looking forward to the time it would take. "Yah, sure. Me and Darius, we unload that stuff already. How you want your money?"

"I'm coming to see you. I'm bringing more stuff for us to sell. I'll get my money then."

"Hey, what is this? More them pretty rocks?" He dropped some folded work shirts into the suitcase. "What will my cut be?"

"The usual, ten percent."

"Fuck that. Ten percent is fine for car parts, but this stuff is a little riskier."

"We'll work it out when I get there."

"Non, we work it out now. Otherwise, maybe I say don't come up here. I think twenty-five percent. You're talking shit with a jail term if I get caught."

"That's easy, you stupid cunt. Don't get caught."

"Twenty-five percent." He put some coveralls in the luggage.

"You're busting my balls. Twenty percent. I'm practically giving it away."

"Bullshit. If I know you, you didn't spend a penny on it. Twenty percent. Deal."

Blunt began, "I'll be up there in a couple of days. Will —"

"Tell me the percentage, Sky. I wanna hear it out of your mouth."

"Twenty percent. Mother fucker."

The call over, Sonier let the phone drop on the bed. There was a smile on his face, of having put one over on his increasingly difficult acquaintance in crime. Beau was sure he knew every crooked pawn shop and jeweler in eleven states. He'd get rid of more gems. Just wait 'til he told Darius about it!

✆ 22 ✇

When the nurse roused Amy for medication, other people were in the room with her. She heard "Detective," and turned her head to see Officer Kowalski; next to him was his wife Roxy, with her arm in a cast and sling. "Hey, Officer. Missus." She didn't have the energy to smile.

"Commander Ramirez sends his regards," Kowalski said. "He said he needs you back as soon as you stop peeling."

"I'm peeling? Peeling what?" She looked down and saw an IV pipe in the back of her hand, and a lumpy sheet thrown over her body. "Alligator?" she offered.

Brightly, the nurse said, "That's a nasty burn. I didn't know young women were sunbathing nude. Did you fall asleep?"

"I guess. I'm peeling?"

The nurse rubbed her arm with alcohol and injected another dose of her medication. "You're legs are a mess. I think you'll spend the rest of the summer in long pants."

Amy heard Paul think, *Oh, right. No pants. Blunt. He raped us.*

She shifted and pulled her elbows back, trying to sit up. The nurse put a hand on her shoulder, then pressed a button on the hospital bed control. She rolled an overbed table to Amy, and set her up with a styrofoam cup of water and a flexi-straw. "Don't tire her out," she admonished when she left the room.

"I wanted to make sure you were doing okay," Kowalski said, his arm around his wife. "Roxy is the reason I couldn't do the interrogation with you. She's going to be alright, but the car is totaled."

Roxy Kowalski smiled grimly. Amy looked at her uncomprehendingly. This is the woman who found her with her husband. The one person in the world who made her feel guilty about anything. *I want her to go away,* she thought to Paul.

After an awkward silence the officer went on. "Did they tell you your condition?" Amy shook her head slowly. "Too much sun, really. Sun poisoning, sun stroke, sun burn. Dehydrated like a hunk of jerky. They've been pumping GatorAde into you by IV since you were admitted. They tell me you'll feel human in three days."

She nodded.

Patrick sat on the side of the bed while his wife remained standing. "Can you tell me what happened? How did you end up wrestling an alligator?"

"Blunt. He knocked me out. With a shovel." She spoke in shallow bursts. "He threw me in. Quicksand. Gator turned up. Hours. And Blunt. Raped me."

Roxy blanched. It was as if Detective Clear suddenly became a real person to her, instead of a generic home-wrecking whore.

"We'll find him," the officer said. "And we got a hit yesterday. A pawn shop in Tulsa, Oklahoma got part of the Rothschild Jewels."

She closed her eyes and nodded. "Good." Then, "Did you find the buttons? My pants?"

"I guess they were your slacks we found. Forensics is looking at them." He stood up and took his wife's hand. "Look, I'll check on you tomorrow. I feel bad that I wasn't on patrol with you. I'm sorry."

Amy smiled and waved a hand dismissively. "Thanks," she whispered.

She was asleep before the Kowalskis had left the room.

✆ 23 ☙

At the front door of the Big Easy casino, Richardson waved an envelope at the bouncer. "I'm here to see Mr. Alphonse again." It was a hot, humid lunch hour, but somehow the bouncer looked cool and trim in his tuxedo.

"Here, I'll take it," the doorman said. Richardson swung his arm to hide the envelope behind his back. "No, no!" he said, "I have to talk to Mr. Alphonse about it."

The casino man pulled a walkie-talkie from an inside pocket and spoke a few words. When he replaced the device he said, "Mister Harry will be out for you." He started to fold his arms in front of his chest, but saw a client coming down the walk. "Good afternoon, Mister Rhee," the bouncer said, smiling as he held the door open. They exchanged nods. But when Richardson attempted to follow the customer in, the bouncer's arm came down to block him. "I told you, someone will come for you." He stood, feet apart and hands on hips, blocking the doorway.

Richardson paced up and down on the paved walk along the front of the building, always turning away so he wouldn't have to see the penguin-clad doorman staring at him.

After four or five laps, he heard someone say, "Mister Jake! Would you come with me?"

Richardson pivoted to see Mister Harry, chief goon for the casino owner. He was well over six feet tall, thick hair that Richardson envied, and a gleaming black tuxedo. His hand was out, beckoning.

Richardson's attempt at small talk was met with polite but short, non-committal answers. They walked through the several gaming areas, with their sparse lunch-hour attendance, then through a pocket door and down a hallway to Mister Alphonse's inner sanctum.

"I understand you wish to discuss something with me," the thin man said when Richardson and his guide entered.

Excitement washed over Richardson at being in the same room with Mister Alphonse, with the man's words directed to him. In Richardson's mind, Mister Alphonse was the reason the roulette wheels turned, the cards were dealt, and the dice were thrown; and this made Mister Alphonse an earth-bound god of gaming, of fun, of chance. Being near him was exciting.

"What a delight to see you, Mister Alphonse! You know, I was thinking–"

"I believe you wanted to discuss something. Do you have a check for me today?"

Too infatuated to realize he had been snubbed, Richardson presented the envelope. "I am short this month. That's what I want to talk to you about."

Mister Alphonse looked at the envelope in Richardson's hand as if it were soiled. He nodded to Mister Harry, who took it and opened it. The goon held the check up for Mister Alphonse to see.

"Our contract calls for three thousand dollars," the boss man said. "Indeed, this check is short." He stared at Richardson. "Now, what are we going to do about this?"

"I wanted to see you to tell you this," said Richardson, "so you know I'm acting in good faith. I am coming into some valuable property I hope to sell, so next month I can get back on schedule."

"Really?" Mister Alphonse sat on the edge of his desk. "If it is an inheritance, I am sorry for your loss. What kind of property? Perhaps we can, ooh, barter."

"Capital," the museum director said. "It is a large quantity of cut gems."

"Provenance?"

Richardson twisted his arms, showing open palms. "Ah, well..."

The owner picked up a manila file folder from his desk. He looked at a few loose pages in it, then said, "Would this so-called property perhaps be related to the events of July 23rd?" Richardson's silence spoke louder than words.

"We are both businessmen," Mister Alphonse said. "We take

certain risks in order to work toward rewards. Sales. Wealth." He let the file fall to the floor. "And as a businessman, you know that some risks just aren't worth–well, they're not worth the risk."

Richardson hung on every word. He loved the man's southern, not Cajun, accent. His intelligence. His viewpoints. And for Mister Alphonse to include him as an equal, as a fellow businessman, made him feel connected.

The casino owner stood up and walked to the chair where Richardson was half frightened, half elated, staring up at him open-mouthed. Then he shook his head, saying, "Mr. Jake, I will not exchange your debt for stolen jewels. Once you convert them into cash, I will be interested in you buying down your debt. You would be able to save quite a lot of interest that way."

Richardson nodded like a bobble-head doll. "However, we must get back to the check you brought today." He returned to his desk, leaning against the forward edge, with his arms folded in front of him. "Perhaps you have noticed on your monthly mortgage statement, it says 'partial payment not accepted.' I sympathize with the bank; their attitude is the correct one. People must live up to their obligations, fulfill their contracts. It's a matter of honor. Of reputation. Do you understand?"

Still nodding mindlessly, Richardson whispered, "Oh, yes. What you say, it makes perfect sense."

"Ah. Yes." He made a sign to Mister Harry, who came around to stand behind Richardson's chair. "Unlike the bank, I will accept your disappointing offering. But there are...consequences."

Alphonse Perez was an accomplished leader. Through various complicated interlocking stock deals and LLC pyramids, he was personally responsible for thirty-seven percent of the gambling profits in Orleans and St. Bernard Parishes. More, if one counted the enormous amounts he was able to skim off the top of his cash-heavy empire. He surrounded himself with loyal men, strong men, men whose muscles were greater than their intellects, men who derived pleasure from inflicting pain, but most of all, men he could control. It was helpful that his charisma—what else could one call such a wonderful gift?–worked on supplicants and debtors as well as his employees. It seemed the more someone owed him, the deeper their affection for him, their hunger to be with him. If only he could afford the pay cut, he thought, he'd be elected Governor in a landslide. And here was Mister Jake, Bradley Jacob Richardson, one of New Orleans' elite, ready to kiss the whip. He did not even try to hide the smile.

"Mister Harry will explain things to you." He looked up at his lackey, his myrmidon, his goon. "I think the side door."

"Very good, Mr. Alphonse," he said, understanding some code. He put a heavy hand on Richardson's shoulder, "If you'd be so kind, Mister Jake?"

Richardson was dizzy from the rare atmosphere of Mr. Alphonse's personal talk. To be the center of that man's attention was exhilarating. Erotic, almost. He walked where Mister Harry pushed him from behind, down the hallway, through the pocket door, and through the game rooms. When they were outside, he turned to his guide and said, "Weren't we supposed to use a side door?"

"We haven't gotten to it yet," the goon said. "Let's take a little walk."

Adjoining the casino was several acres of boggy land–not exactly swamp, but not exactly solid ground. After the rich rapture of being close to Mr. Alphonse, Richardson enjoyed a feeling of self-worth. It was a pretty day despite the heat, with sky as close to blue as it ever got in New Orleans.

When they reached a clump of trees, Mister Harry spun Richardson around and delivered a punch to his face. The pain matched the blood that spurted. Two kicks and Richardson was on the ground, dimly wondering what the loose things were in his mouth. A final blow caught him in the face, and the vision in his left eye suddenly was like a comic book drawing, stars and Saturns and little red and blue birds spinning in circles.

"Mister Alphonse prefers full payments," the goon said, rubbing his hands as if clearing them of dirt. "Do not forget that, Mister Jake." He tugged at the ends of his tuxedo bowtie and walked back to the Big Easy casino, whistling some old Mariah Carey song.

℘ 24 ♋

Amy and Paul dozed fitfully. A nurse would wake them for a pill, or they'd get tangled in the IV hose, or one of them would dream of some gaping reptilian maw. They exchanged short thoughts, each relieved the other was still there.

Amy jerked awake with an adrenalin-fueled burst of fear: she was not alone. It took a moment to realize Christine was lying next to her on the hospital bed, her arm over her shoulders. When the woman saw she was awake she said, "Paulette? Amy? I'm so glad to see you."

Looking at the woman's pretty face, crooked tooth, multi-length and multi-colored hair, Amy thought to Paul, *She's lovely. You're a lucky man.*

Despite their physical weakness, Paul took the lead. He squeezed Christine's hand and tried to smile. "I don't always. Look like this," he said.

The sound of their voice relieved her of worry. She smiled. "I know. And usually you're dressed better." She touched her Paulette's face, traced the scaly lips and peeling skin. "I brought you a Barq's and a candy bar."

"You brought me Christine," he replied.

The woman pulled up her legs and curled against them. "I was so worried," she said, talking to their left armpit. "I called you and some man answered and was swearing. So I called your partner. He told me what happened."

"Good for Kowalski." They were so weak, the most he could do was whisper. "Thank you. I'm going to be okay. I–I'm pretty sure."

"When they let you out, you can stay with me. I'll take care of you."

It hurt to smile, but inside, that's what Paul did. "Yes," he whispered. "Amy?" Sounding exactly the same, she echoed, "Yes."

As always, Christine knew who was speaking. "Did he hurt you? Or is this just from the sun?"

"He hit me with. A shovel. He said he. Raped me. Dumped me in. A bayou. Quicksand."

The woman shivered and pulled herself closer. "Raped you? And Paulette? Oh, no."

"I don't know. That he did. But he told. Me he did."

"You're so brave," the woman said, lower lip trembling. "You and Paulette. I'm so proud of you, but I worry."

Amy waved her hand. "You are a dear," she said. Then Paul added, "Love you."

"I love you, Paulette. You too, Amy. Can I stay until visiting hours end?"

"Sure. I'm so tired. But it's great. You being here. You're so. Good to me."

"Oh, you silly girl," Christine said, and kissed them on the cheek.

℘ 25 ℞

Doctor James Clear discharged his daughter the next day. "You don't need to be here anymore, but for God's sake, rest. No work. No sun. No nothing but liquids and sleep. You hear me?"

Amy was still in the hospital bed, but a nurse already had removed the IV from her hand. "Yes, Dad. Paul and I will be good. I'm staying with his girlfriend for a couple of days."

"Paul? You have a girlfriend?" He stopped writing, but still held his hand over his clipboard.

"I'm too tired to make a joke about it. Yeah. Christine."

"Uh–how does that work?"

Before Paul could answer, Amy interrupted, "Daddy, I swear I am not a lesbian."

A disoriented blink. "I never thought you were, Honey."

"It's Paul. Christine is a lesbian. She's schizophrenic and it's under control with medication so she's great. But it wasn't always. She remembers having voices. So she accepts Amy and me. She knows I'm a man, but she calls me Paulette."

The doctor put his hands on their shoulders and looked down at their face. "Well, that makes as much sense as you waking up inside Amy's head. Look, I'm sorry I asked. I love you, I love you both. I don't care what you're doing as long as you're careful and safe. And next time I ask, tell me to mind my own beeswax."

Amy said, "I was afraid you were going to scold Paul for two-timing me."

"Nope. Just for not making you use sunscreen." He retrieved his clipboard to sign the discharge order. Looking down again, "Feel better, Sweetie. Anything comes up, you call."

"I love you, Dad. Thanks."

When he was gone, Amy thought, *That was awkward.* She heard Paul think back, *I forgot, never say anything to a father that implies his daughter is having sex.*

"I have to tell Christine about this. She'll scream." Amy sat up slowly, fighting dizziness after two full days on their back. She swiveled themselves to get their feet on the vinyl flooring, and started to change into street clothes. When it occurred to her that she was admitted without pants, she fell back on the bed. *I'm never going to get out of here!* she cried silently.

Shortly after five o'clock Christine knocked at the open door, calling, "Paulette! Amy! I've come to rescue you!" When she saw them still in bed, she said, "What's wrong? Aren't you coming home with me? Why are you–"

"I don't have any pants!" Amy shouted. A moment later she said, calmly, "I don't have any pants."

"That's how I love my Paulette," Christine teased. "Look, they're going to put you in a wheelchair anyway. We'll just wrap a blanket around you and get you into my car." She knelt on the bed and leaned over to whisper, "You in my house with no pants. Yay, Paulette!"

"I wish I felt well enough to enjoy it," Paul whispered. "Amy's kind of cranky about it."

"Oh, okay. My jeans'll fit you at home, so it's going to be okay." She pulled at her lover, "Come on, you're a free woman. Let's go!"

Amy rang for the floor nurse, and a tall, thin porter arrived shortly with a wheelchair.

The porter stood at Amy's chair at the hospital entrance while Christine ran to her car and brought it to the curb. Amy absently, weakly, said "Thank you" to the porter and reached for change in a pocket to give him a tip. "Oh, damn it to hell," she muttered when she touched her skin. Clutching at the blanket around her midsection and legs, Amy feebly half stood, and swung themselves into the passenger seat. Christine stood by the car, smoothing the blanket and trying to make Paulette more comfortable, but Amy barked, softly, "It's okay. I'm in. Please, can we just go home?"

"I'm sorry, Amy," she said when she climbed behind the wheel;

uncanny, she always knew which one of them was speaking. "I'm just trying to help."

"I know you are," she replied, "but I feel like dog poop and all I want to do is cry and sleep."

"I'm about the same," Paul added. "We appreciate you looking after us, though. Maybe tomorrow we'll be able to play."

She kissed them on the side of the head and cranked the engine. "It's okay. I'm not worth a damn when I'm sick, either."

Silently, Amy told Paul, *I love your girlfriend, but I'm going to scream if she doesn't let me go to sleep. Doesn't she know I nearly died?*

She means well, you know that, he thought back. *But I understand.*

Christine prattled as she drove from the hospital in Uptown to her double in West End. Amy and Paul faded in and out for much of the drive, until Paul thought directly to the woman, *Can we stop? I need something to drink.*

"There's a Gas Buddy a few blocks up," she answered aloud, perfectly accepting of Paul's male voice having sounded in her head. Amy had not heard Paul's private conversation and responded out loud, "You are a mind reader. Gatorade? The lime flavor?"

"I know you love limeade," Christine said. "I'll get a bunch of 'em." She turned briefly to smile at her passenger, then went back to watching the road. When she stopped in the parking lot, Amy said, "I can't give you any money. No pants."

"My treat," Christine said brightly. She kissed Amy on the cheek and jumped out of the car and into the convenience store. Now that they weren't moving, Amy felt the air was hot, humid, and oppressive.

It was only a few minutes later that Christine woke them, pushing a cold green drink against their cheek. Without opening their eyes, Paul whispered, "Oh, that feels good." He unscrewed the cap and sipped cautiously. Between swallows, Amy said, "Is he still shooting?" For once, Christine was startled. "Who, Amy? Who's shooting?"

Amy pulled the bottle away from Paul's control and drank half the contents in two very long gulps; some of the sweet, sticky liquid dribbled across their cheek and down their chin, landing in the blanket over their legs.

Christine waited for Amy to catch her breath before starting the car. "Nobody's shooting."

"Good." She drained the rest of the Gatorade. "No more–" and she leaned against the passenger door, asleep.

As she drove on, Christine softly called her lover's name. "Everything okay?"

"Sshhh," he whispered. "Amy's asleep. Me too, in a minute. We are wiped out."

She thought a moment. "You're not decimated," she finally said, smiling, "you're desiccated." She was disappointed that her Paulette had fallen unconscious before hearing her clever wordplay.

Paul and Amy vaguely knew that Christine was helping them out of her car, and walking them to her double door. The blanket fell, leaving them naked from the waist down, and all Amy could think was that the cool air against her legs felt good. Christine guided them down the hallway to the bedroom, and then let them fall against the mattress on the floor. They bounced. The jolt woke Paul for a moment; weakly, he whispered, "Wheeeee," then fell back to sleep.

Frustrated, Christine tried to sound happy as she chattered non-stop to the sleeping dyad. At times she woke Paul or Amy for medication, and spoon-fed them soup or juice. They would comply limply, as alert and responsive as a one-hundred-and-nine-pound Raggedy Ann doll. After administering some pills at nine P.M. and rubbing cream on Amy's burnt and peeling legs and forehead, Christine turned her TV set on. She had wanted to show her love and her caring to her lover and their best friend. Instead, she was disappointed that neither Amy nor Paulette knew she was there. She tuned in a rerun of Big Bang Theory and rolled a joint.

Four twenty-two A.M. It wasn't a scream, exactly. It was more like a low bellow, a rasping, wordless vocalization that came from Amy and Paul's mouth. Instantly, everyone was awake. Aloud and silently, everyone was saying, "Are you all right? Is everything okay?"

Paul reached out their arms to touch Christine. "Whoa. Dream." Then, "Whoa."

"Was it good or bad?" she asked, rubbing her lover's shoulders.

"Good. Definitely good. Amy?"

"Good. Oh, yes." Silently she thought to Paul, *Did you dream what I dreamed?*

"Oh, one of those dreams," Christine laughed. "You must be getting better." She kissed Paul on the mouth, and rested her head on their chest. "Was I in it?"

"Wait," Amy said aloud. Christine heard nothing while Paul and Amy talked silently to each other.

I was back in my old body. And the woman was Christine, but you know how it is in a dream, I knew it was you. I got to make love to you.

That's uncanny, Amy replied. *We pretty much had the same dream. I was with Christine, but like you say, I knew it was you.* Awkwardly, Amy moved their right arm from Christine's body to pat their left hand, 'Paul's' hand. *And there was this penis.*

"Don't tease me," Christine finally said. "Tell me all about it. Was I in it?"

They coughed from both trying to speak at once. Finally, Paul said, "You sure were—boy, howdy!"

"You want to show me what happened?" Another kiss.

Amy spoke up. "In the dream I wasn't peeling and all full of ointments. Give me a few days, and I'm sure Paul will treat you to an instant replay."

Christine curled her toes and pressed against them. "So I was in your dream too?"

"Yes, you sure were."

"Oh, that means you love me, too. And it was a good dream?"

"Any dream where you, and Paul, and I are happy," she said, petting the woman's hair, "that has to be a good dream."

And just like that, all the resentment leaked out of Christine, replaced with feelings of love and relief and security with her Paulette and her best friend Amy.

Amy and Paul were silently planning their day when Christine's alarm clock went off. "Morning, Honeybunch," Paul said, shaking the woman gently. "Wakey, wakey."

Christine grunted back, rolling over and hugging them. "What time is it?"–it sounded like 'whtmsit,' muffled against their neck.

"Let's get naked and wet in the shower," he said. "Then you can rub zinc oxide all over me. What do you say?"

He was glad to see her smile. "We're feeling pretty good. Amy wants to change her locks and rent a car and check in at work." He rubbed her shoulders, enjoying the feel of her soft skin.

Christine looked worried. "Are you sure? I can stay with you. Amy?"

"You were a life-saver yesterday, and now my life is saved. Really, I have to find a car. New locks. A drivers' license. And–"

"Okay, you," she grinned, and kissed them on the cheek. "But promise me you'll call if you need anything. And I want to come over after work. I'll make dinner."

"Tell you what. Bring over a 12-pack of Dixie, a couple boxes of popsicles, and some more aloe vera. They will make my life complete." Paul added aloud, "As long as you're there to share them with."

"Paulette, I'm so glad you and Amy are feeling better." Christine climbed up off of the floor mattress. "And it's all because of Doctor Hodges' tender loving care." She grinned on her way to the shower.

When Christine was dry and getting dressed, Paul ogled her from where they lay on the floor bed. "You are such a babe!"

A smile broke across the woman's face, exposing the twisted front tooth that he adored, the one that mirrored Amy's. "Aren't you a sweet-talker!" She did a silly dance step and pretended to do a backwards strip tease, slowly pulling a pale yellow blouse over her head. He heard Amy think, *I'm glad you found her. She's fun. She's smart. She likes both of us.*

When she fastened the belt on her skirt Christine threw her arms in the air and said, "Ta-DAH!" Paul applauded. "I'm going to work now–" she knelt by the mattress and kissed her Paulette gingerly, trying to avoid the white ointment on their nose. "See you at your place around five. And look–" she stood up again and jabbed her finger into her palm, "If you need anything, you call me."

When Christine was gone, Amy said aloud, "She's a sweetheart, she really is, but remind me never to be sick around her. I thought she was going to suffocate me."

"Hey!" Paul rushed to his girlfriend's defense. "She loves us;

she wants to show us that."

Amy patted the back of their left hand. "I know she means well. Maybe her mom hovered when she was sick, but mine didn't. 'Your dad will give you a shot when he gets home, you'll be fine.' Honest, all I wanted to do was sleep."

"Yeah. I know. You remember what Chris the DJ said?"

"Who?"

"'Sometimes it's difficult to avoid the happiness of others.' Sometimes you put up with things you're not crazy about so the people you love can feel good. I think taking care of us was important to Christine."

"Who?"

"Christine."

"No – oh, never mind. I think I understand. But it's hard to be so Zen when you feel like armadillo squeezings."

They lay in silence for a few minutes. Finally, Paul whispered, "That was some dream."

"Ummmm."

"Did you ever figure out how to plan dreams?"

Amy laughed, remembering a conversation they had when she was fourteen years old. "No, never did."

"Me neither." He rubbed their right arm and then caressed their side.

"You're going to smear my ointment and make a mess," Amy grinned. "Wait a few days and you can have your way with me."

"Promises, promises. No boom today, there's always a boom tomorrow."

"Come into the bathroom with me; I'll show you my boobs."

"But I don't have any Mardi Gras beads to give you, little girl."

Amy sat up. "Enough. I have to Jill up and be a cop now. Where are those sweat pants?" She looked around and saw them on a chair. Gingerly, she put their legs into Christine's comically enormous sweats.

"Oh, wait."

"Hmmm?" Paul asked.

"No cell phone."

"Christine's got a wall phone in the kitchen. Are you hungry?"

"Christine's wall phone doesn't have all my contacts. Crap."

She looked up at the ceiling, then added, "Okay, deep breath. I know the number to the station. I'll call Kowalski, I'll get the numbers from him, okay, okay," nodding violently. "I'm ready." She took a legal pad from a shelf in Christine's bedroom, then walked to the kitchen and tossed it on the table.

"Hungry?" Paul asked again.

"I'm thinking our culprit has to be Skyler Blunt, and maybe, somehow, Richardson."

He thought to her, *Hungry!* It was not a question.

"Oh, go get yourself something, I'm busy. Stringfellow is a waste of time. He shot me, but we've got nothing on him for the museum job." She was making a note on the pad.

Paul placed their left hand, 'his' hand, around their throat. *Me hungry!* he bellowed inside, and shook their body. She laughed and stood up, and started opening cupboards. "Cheerios? Christine has soy milk in the refrigerator."

"Sounds better than the table leg. Gangway!" Paul took the lead to put together breakfast. As he spooned the little cereal "O"s into their mouth, he thought, *So, you think Stringfellow is off the hook?*

"For the museum, yes. But he still shot me, the booger."

Blunt?

"Well, duh!" She waved the spoon. "Needs money and has the skill to rappel. And if he's run off to Bloomington or wherever, he may have sold some of the jewels. I wish we could find the murder weapon." Another spoonful of cereal. "And he tried to kill me in that quicksand bayou."

"I can't figure out Richardson," Paul offered. "He's an oily guy."

Amy answered, "He didn't kill the guard or the model. I met him a minute after the murders and he was coming from the fashion show area. I don't think even Tarzan could rappel wearing an ascot."

"Yeah, but...all those calls to Blunt, and they're supposed to hate each other. Would he be in it for insurance fraud?"

Amy let out a low whistle. "Never considered that. Hmmm. Hmmm. Let me mull on that for awhile."

"More cereal?"

"You are a gluttonous pig. I've got a figure to maintain, so–NO!"

Amy rinsed the bowl and spoon in the sink, then went back to her legal pad. "First things first. Kowalski." She punched the station number into the wall phone, then asked for the officer.

"Pat Kowalski," she heard, "can I help you?"

"It's Amy," she said, glad to hear his voice. "Any news?"

"Hey, you sound great," he offered. "Feeling better?"

"Yes, thank you. Hero. I'm coming in to the station in a little while. Can we go over the museum investigation?"

"You're back already? That's great. Yeah, I'll be here."

"I'm just running errands today, I'll be back at work tomorrow," she said. "Do you think fleet services will let me check out an unmarked car? Or will I have to drive a cruiser?"

"Gascon's a good guy," Kowalski chuckled. "Bat your eyelashes and he'll probably come up with a civilian vehicle."

"Thanks for the advice. Look, get all the contact info we've got on this case so I can use it when I get in. I'll see you in a while."

I can't wait to get outside, Paul thought. *We've been indoors for, like, weeks now.*

"Three days," she said aloud. "Quicksand spa on Monday, today is Friday. Uh – isn't it?"

Sure, it's Friday. But what month?

Amy went to the mirror in the bathroom to apply another coat of the gooey white ointment that may have been limiting the peeling, but not the itching. As she smeared it on her face she asked, "Do you like Goth girls? I never had the right skin tone for it before, but I sure do now."

"Goth? Doesn't that come with tattoos and nipple piercings and lots of drugs?"

"Not on this woman," she said, screwing the cap back on the tube of zinc oxide. "There, that should scare the panhandlers. I'm calling a cab."

Later they were sitting on the wall along Christine's driveway. Amy was holding a plastic grocery bag weighted down with the ointments her father had prescribed. She and Paul had been going over the day's projects. "Blunt got my keys, too, and he knows where I live. I must change the door locks. You'll help?"

"Piece of cake."

When the taxi pulled up she told the cabbie to drive her home to the Carrollton section. Glancing in the rear-view mirror, the driver said, "Are you sure you're going to be okay? You're not going to die in my cab or nothing?"

"Oh, the cream. Bad sunburn, that's all. I promise I won't get it on your upholstery."

When they arrived, Amy asked the cabbie to wait. "I need to go to the police station on Rampart Street, but first I have to change clothes and pick up a few things." She heard Paul think, *We don't even have a wrist watch to offer the guy for collateral.*

Inside her house, Amy found her duplicate Optimo credit card and her mad money stash of seventy-five dollars. She changed into a long skirt and a clean green blouse, and quickly laced up a pair of beat-up sneakers. She was grateful that the cab was waiting for her.

Her first stop at work was the HR Department. "Good God, sister, what happened to you?" asked LaTanya Grimoire. "That white-face is not a pretty look on you, uh-uh."

Amy explained the sunburn, and her need for new credentials.

"If you're lucky, I've still got your picture in the computer. I'm not going to risk breaking my camera by taking a new photo. How can you go out in public like that?"

Paul felt Amy's anger swell. He took the lead to answer, "You do what you have to do. But next time you change hair styles, don't ask me what I think. Okay?"

"Touchy!" she smiled. "Give me an hour, I'll have your new ID."

"While we're at it," Amy added, "can I replace my pistol permit?"

"An hour fifteen, then."

As she walked the hall toward the fleet office she thought, *I damn near died in that bayou. Can't anyone give me a break?*

The cab driver didn't know any better. LaTanya should have.

Amy flopped down in a chair across from Marcus Gascon, the lieutenant who ran auto fleet requisition. The man smiled at her and said, "Are you feeling any better?"

"Oh, man, you are my new best friend!" she exclaimed. "Everyone's been giving me crap about looking like a zombie leper. I appreciate a kind word."

He nodded. "Kowalski told me what happened, that he found

you wrestling an alligator. I'm glad to see you back at work."

"Huh! Kowalski's the reason I'm not gator kibble. Did he tell you the perp torched my car? I want to sign out a car for a week or two. Something maybe that doesn't come with flashing blue lights?"

"Yeah, sure. We're not supposed to lend them out in place of a personal vehicle–" he looked up at her with a huge smile, "–but yours was destroyed in the line of duty. Everyone was worried about you, Detective." He hit the chit with a big rubber stamp, then initialed something and slid the paper in front of her. "Sign this and I'll get you the keys."

Her next stop was the armory. She let Paul lead to fill out a requisition for a replacement sidearm. "What do we have in a .40?" he asked Walter–the oldest officer in the building, but only a sergeant.

"I got nine millimeters out the ying-yang. Will that do?"

Paul as Amy reached up and tugged gently on the man's pony tail. "How do you get away with a headband and jeans every day?"

"The commander and me, we go 'way back. I saved his life once—we were in Desert Storm together."

"That explains a lot," Paul said as he took the standard issue 9mm Glock. To Amy he thought silently, *I can't come close to signing your name.* He heard her laugh while they juggled the pistol from right to left hand, leaving her free to sign the requisition.

Walking to the uniformed section, keys in hand, Amy heard Paul think, *Good. Transportation and a weapon. Now can we find Blunt and kill him?*

"Ummm, no. Tomorrow we can start looking for him, but we're not going to kill him. Do you hear me?" There was silence. She repeated, "Do you hear me?"

Nope. I will not be happy until we have that man's guts in our bare hands.

"Euwww. Why the rage?"

He raped us!

So he said, she thought back. She entered the patrolmen's bullpen and saw Kowalski at the far end of a long table, receipts and expense chits all around. "Hey, Hero!" she called.

The officer knocked his chair over getting up and rushed to her. "A sight for sore eyes," he smiled. He hugged her, but before he could lift her off the ground she yelled, "Ouch! Stop, stop! I hurt!"

"Oh, I'm sorry, I should have realized—"

"It's okay, Kowalski. And I'm glad to see you, too. Thanks again for saving my life."

They stood staring at each other, goofy smiles on their faces. Finally he said, "Uh, hate to say this, Detective, but you look like three-day-old shit. What's the junk on your face?"

"Yesterday I felt like crap. Today I don't. It'll take my face and my legs a few days to catch up. Can I sit down?"

He pulled a chair out and placed it in front of her, in the middle of the room. *This is the bad boy I had a crush on,* she thought to Paul. She sighed. *When he's not trying, he's a cutie.*

"So you're back at work already?" He dragged a chair for himself to face her.

"Tomorrow," she answered, sitting down. "Today is for running errands. I have to replace my driver's license, all that kind of thing. But what's the latest? Anything on Blunt? On Richardson?"

"I cleared it with Legal; yesterday we posted an APB on Blunt. No hit on him yet. No new jewelry sale. But here's a twist: the pistol that fired the shot that killed the museum guard? It turned up after a liquor store was held up in Springfield, Missouri."

"What do you know?" Amy responded. "After Jermaine's field trip to the range, and we got a match on the shell casing after all."

It was Paul who added, "Wait. If Blunt was our shooter—jacking a package store doesn't sound like him. I'll bet he sold the gun to the perp. Either he's got a world-class fence, or Blunt must be in Springfield—or he was."

"One more thing," the officer added. "Fort Smith made a courtesy call for you. They released that Stringfellow boy without charges."

"What?" Amy yelled, then closed her eyes and raised her shoulders, reacting to the burst of headache that came with her shout. Softly she went on, "He shot me. Why did they let him go?"

"When they contacted the park ranger—" He turned in his chair to slap the table top behind him until he found his clipboard "—Uh, Lafferry, Ranger Lafferry. He told them he had tranqued a brown bear two days after you picked up Stringfellow. He turned it over to state DNR, and they told him the bear had two fresh .22 wounds."

Paul said, "Hunter really was shooting at a bear?"

"He said he didn't see me," Amy added. "How did he not see me? Uh—this was before I changed my makeup to Lady Zinc Oxide." She shook her head, gently so as not to provoke another burst of head pain. "Well, pttthhhh. With dog crap on top. I don't think he's our perp, but he did shoot me. Look, I vaguely remember you telling me something about the buttons–"

"Oh, yeah, when I went to see you at Touro. Jermaine says they match the two we found at the museum. He couldn't do anything with the ashes, though."

Amy's jaw dropped. "The buttons match. He's our man."

"Still circumstantial," he shook his head, "but there's more; maybe it all adds up. We finally got the bank records we subpoenaed. Blunt is nearly broke, and Richardson has been writing a huge check every month to a casino."

"Casino? I asked him if he had a problem with gambling."

She heard the officer snicker. "Something about these criminals, you just can't trust anything they say."

"Paul–I mean, a colleague suggested Richardson might be in this for insurance fraud. Especially if he needs cash. Hmmm, I'm still working on this. I'm sure Blunt is the shooter, but I smell Richardson's *eau de oink*."

Kowalski jogged his chair closer. "Oh, of course, you haven't heard. Richardson is at Ochsner Baptist. Somebody beat the holy living shit out of him and left him near the river in Chalmette."

"No! Is he all right?"

"Well, he's going to be. But right now he's pretty far from all right. Broken nose, broken orbital, and some broken teeth. Somebody worked him over."

Amy felt sorry for Richardson for the pain he must be in, and the indignity of suffering a beating. She heard Paul think, *Bella will be glad;* then out loud, "Did he get kicked in the balls?"

"Uhh...just the eyeballs. I think."

"And I'm thinking we pay him a visit."

"I talked to the St. Bernard boys who interviewed him. Richardson says he doesn't know who did this or why."

"Where in Chalmette did they find him?"

The officer dragged a city map off the table behind him and dropped it on their laps. "About here," he pointed to a section near the Parish line, just outside New Orleans proper. "Anonymous phone call to 911."

She pushed his hand away to study the map. "And where exactly is that casino he's paying off?"

Pat leaned back for a file folder and leafed through some print-out. "Well, son of a bitch."

"Maybe he was late with a payment?"

Kowalski replied, "That would fit Alphonse Perez's MO. And Richardson's not talking, which tells me he damn well knows who did it. And why."

"Put it on our schedule for tomorrow." She heard Paul think, *Flowers and chocolate? Or just a card?*

"I recognize that smile," the officer said. "You're talking to yourself again, aren't you?"

It was Paul who said, "Guilty as charged. I see I can't fool a dedicated exemplar of law and order like yourself."

The officer went on, "I went to that tree place in Westwego and talked to the owner. For some reason he insisted on showing me his certificate of insurance. Anyway, he gave me the broken grappling hook Blunt turned in. Jermaine says the snapped fluke we found on the museum roof is a match."

Paul thought, *You were right. Blunt is the killer; he's the rope climber.* Amy said, "I hope we get a hit on the APB."

The officer leaned forward and said, "So what's next, Boss?"

She pushed herself and her chair back a few inches. "I'm back tomorrow. I want to talk to Richardson's wife," as she extended her right index finger; she added her middle finger with, "and let's bring some candy and flowers for Uncle Brad in the hospital;" and then a third finger, "and Blunt's daughter may know something. I can't imagine any of them out to kill me, but you want to ride shotgun on those?"

"Yeah. Let's not take any chances."

After a pause, Paul said, "How is Roxy's arm?" He heard Amy scream in their head.

"No change, the doc says it'll mend."

He heard more silent shouts but plowed on, "Did it make her

feel better to see us in a hospital bed?"

"Not 'us,' Detective, 'you.' And yes, I think so. She feels less threatened now."

Internally Amy elbowed Paul back. "Oh, God, Pat, I'm sorry," she sputtered. "I had no business asking–"

"You're pretty astute, Clear. They tell me women always see the emotional stuff than goes over a man's head."

Even as she heard Paul laugh inside, she said, "I'm starting to think it has more to do with age than with sex."

"Yep. I'm sure you twenty-somethings are older and wiser than a forty-year-old like me."

There was an awkward silence for a moment. Then Paul said, aloud, "Say goodnight, Gracie." He heard Amy and Kowalski say in unison, "Huh?"

"We've got so much to do," Paul said, standing up. "I need to copy phone numbers so I can set up those interviews for tomorrow."

The officer stood as well and said, "I'm glad you're doing so well. Let's wrap this up tomorrow, okay?"

Amy limped downstairs to the detectives' section to make copies of the case files. Silently, she shouted, *Paul Dominic Owens! There are times when I hate you, hate you, hate you!*

Did you say something? he thought back.

Which side of my head do I have to bang to shut you up?

"The inside," he said softly. "Will you just take a deep breath and tell me what I did that was so wrong?"

Why did you ask him about that woman? I don't want him to think I care about her. Or him.

"Oh."

Yes, 'oh'. Is that all you have to say?

I didn't realize that was bothering you, he thought contritely, *and I'm sorry. What I wanted to know was if she was better or worse after he took her to see us at Touro. He said she's better– mentally, I mean. If he gets less grief from her, he'll be less tense at work and will be more useful. But I didn't consider that asking him was going to hurt your pride.*

"Don't give me that 'foolish pride' crap. You crap. You, you crap-and-a-half." She was sitting at a long table, and laid their forehead down on it.

No, I was serious. We all have pride, and it was bad of me to hurt yours. I–just, I didn't do it on purpose. I'm sorry, Amy.

His apology calmed her down. "You used to call me by name all the time," she whispered. "You don't do that anymore. It was nice to hear you say it."

I probably don't say 'I love you' very much anymore, either–but I do. Amy.

"You must be Irish; you've got a way with words, I'll give you that." She lifted their head, a smile on their lips. "Just let me make copies of these files and make a few calls. Then Louisiana DMV, God help me."

Amy wrote out bullet points for the calls she planned to make, and reached for the phone. Paul said, "Aren't you going to talk to Hunter's folks?"

"God, no!" Amy said, shaking their head. "He was all angry daddy last time we talked. Besides, if Fort Smith police let him go, I'm sure Hunter's already called home." Instead she dialed RockWallUSA. There was no background noise when a mature voice answered. "Is this Bill?" she asked.

"Unfortunately," the voice answered. "Can I help you?"

Amy pulled her chair closer to the table as she introduced herself. "I want to let you know about Hunter Stringfellow. He spent a few days in jail in Arkansas, but they've let him out. You might–"

"I remember you," the gym owner said. "Hunter called me at home the day before yesterday and explained. He begged for his job back."

Paul raised their eyebrows. "Are you going to take him back?" he asked. Amy crossed fingers on their right hand.

"Yeah. I'm just an old softie. He's always been a good kid; this is the first time he ever went off the deep end. You told me he'd been arrested, but they released him without any charges. He's what, twenty-one? Yeah. He'll be back at work tomorrow. Thank God."

"Bill, that's great," Amy said. "He's impressed me, too. Tell him I said hello, and he really ought to get insurance for his, uh, his expeditions."

"I have no idea what that means," he said, "but I'll tell him."

As she put the handset in the phone cradle, she said, "That's so sweet. I told you Bill looked at Hunter like a surrogate son."

Paul observed, "I notice you didn't tell him that Stringfellow shot you."

She smiled. "There's such a thing as too much truth."

She dialed the next number on her cheat sheet.

"We haven't met," Amy began. "I'm the detective investigating the theft at the museum. I'm hoping you can help our inquiries."

"I don't know anything about it, except that Bradley has been distraught ever since it happened. And then that mugging yesterday. Surely you need to talk to my husband." Holly Richardson's voice was strong, and her accent unmistakably upper-class New Orleans.

"Actually, I'm trying to locate Skyler Blunt. When is the last time you saw your sister?"

There was a long pause. Amy heard a faint classical music radio station from Holly's side of the connection. The woman said, "Officer, I'm about to lead a development meeting for the wetlands protection council I lead. It's a twenty-minute PowerPoint presentation, and then I am going to ask two donors to write checks for a million dollars each. Can we talk another time?"

"It's Detective. How about tomorrow? Where will you be around ten?" Amy was writing notes to herself.

"Library board meeting at eleven. Can you meet me there?"

"The one on Rampart?" "Actually, it's on Loyola–" "Yes, that's not far from the police station," Amy agreed. "How about ten o'clock? Where will I find you?"

"I'll be in the board room upstairs. Just ask any of the librarians where it is." Then, away from the mouthpiece, "I understand, Lady Blanc. Just a minute. Yes–yes–yes, Miriam, just a minute." She returned her attention to Amy and said, "I really must go. We'll talk tomorrow. Goodbye."

"One down," Amy said aloud. Next she squandered some of NOPD's money by calling 411 and having them connect her to Ocshner Baptist Medical Center. Visiting hours be from eight A.M. to eight-thirty at night. "Two down."

She leafed through the Xeroxes she had made, then dialed Bella Blunt's phone number. At the prompt, she left the station's number and said she wanted to meet with the woman the next afternoon.

It was Paul who said, "I want to kill her daddy."

"There will be no daddy killing. I'm a detective, not an executioner."

"Speak for yourself." Then, "I don't understand. Why aren't you furious? He raped us!"

Concerned for some privacy, she thought back silently, *He said he did, but Touro couldn't find any evidence–*

Christ! Not after floating half naked in a swamp for five hours!

So, no evidence, Amy continued. *And I was unconscious, so it's not real to me.* She heard her thought and added, *Huh! What if–if he posted some video of it, that would make it real. Or if I miss my period. Otherwise, it's just some words from a known lying thief and asshole.*

She could feel how tense Paul had become, hearing her. "It makes me feel weak," Paul added, aloud. "Vulnerable. And angry." Then, silently, *Hell, I'm furious. I want to make him pay for violating us.*

"Okay, I hear you," and she patted the back of their left hand to comfort him. "I don't feel so violated because I don't believe he did anything. I'm pissed that he tried to kill me, but I survived so I'm getting over it."

"You are a fucking saint," Paul said aloud, their voice shaking with his rage. "I am not."

Her appointments for the next day lined up, if not locked down, Amy headed back to HR to collect her replacement ID and permit, and then to motor fleet to check out the brown coupe that would be her transportation for a while. Next stop was halfway to Christine's double by the New Basin Canal to replace her drivers' license, where a flash of her new NOPD ID turned what usually was a four-hour nightmare into a fifteen-minute dream. She made a dash to Iberville Bank to straighten out her credit cards and to make a withdrawal.

Finally she announced she was ready to buy new locks for her house. In the privacy of her loaner car, Paul said, "Let's go home. We need to take some measurements."

"What are you talking about?" she said, surprised. "A lock is a lock is a lock – right?"

"You're lucky to have a built-in house-husband to take care of these things. How thick is the door? The lock is how far from the edge? Do we want a dead-bolt? There are differences."

"Huh." She glanced at her watch. "Well, let's hurry. I'm getting worn out. I might need a nap before Christine comes over for our five o'clock feeding."

Paul led to drive home and parked the loaner outside her house. Amy lingered in the car to load her new pistol. "We're only going what, fifteen feet to our front door," Paul said. She replied, "Blunt has the keys to that lock and he knows where I live. And this time there's no cab driver standing watch. I want to be prepared."

Aaah, yeah, Paul thought. *If he's inside, can I shoot him? Please? Pretty please? I'll be your best friend!*

As she opened the car door she answered, "I can handle this one." She used Christine's old key to unlock the front door to their house, then threw it open and took a shooting crouch, holding the Glock with both hands. Systematically she went through all four rooms and both bathrooms. There was no sign of Skyler Blunt. "Damn!" Paul said. "It would have been so convenient if he'd been here."

It took another ten minutes to arrive at Freret Hardware to find a lock that would fit their front door. He was concerned about the length of the bolt, while Amy dithered over the color, going back and forth between polished brass and satin chrome. When she finally gave her approval, Paul forced open the package and had duplicates made of the key. "I want to give one to Christine tonight," he answered her question. "And I know you want Florence and your folks to have copies." He felt her shrug and added, "It'll be one less trip to the store."

Back at home, Amy asked, "What do you need to put in the lock? Screwdriver? Drill?"

"Beer," he said as he dragged her tool box out of the closet and opened it by the front door.

When Christine banged on the door, Amy woke up on the living room floor. "Wait–wait–Christine?" she called.

"It's me," the woman yelled back. "This wine won't drink itself, you know. Let me in!"

Paul jumped to the lead and stood up, turning the newly

installed deadbolt and opening the door. "How great to see you!" he exclaimed, arms wide. Christine's hands were full, but she pushed against her Paulette and let him wrap their arms around her. "You're in a better mood," she said to their chest, "I'm glad. Help me with this stuff." She stepped backwards and let Paulette take the shopping bag with dinner fixings. Once inside, Christine said, "What's that on your face?" She was peering at them.

"The ointment. And my nose, I hope," he said, then turned to a mirror on the wall, by the coat rack. There was a long black streak across one cheek. "What the hell?" Amy said. "What have you done to my face? My one and only face?"

"Me?" he answered, "I didn't–"

"Come here," Christine barked. Paul and Amy fell silent, and Amy meekly walked to the woman. She licked her thumb, then reached over and used it to flick at the mark. Once part of it was off their face, Christine examined it closely. "Grease pencil," she pronounced. "Paulette, why do you have grease pencil on your face?"

A smile slowly spread across their face. "I changed our door lock," Paul began. "I used a china marker to tell me where to use a chisel on the door jamb. I don't remember–" He heard Amy laugh inside and tell him, *I know.* When he fell silent, she continued aloud, "I was so tired after running around all day, I fell asleep on the floor after Paul finished with the lock–" she turned and pointed back at the front door "–and I must have landed on the marker. Wow, I was tired!"

"Happy ending," Christine chirped. "I hate it when you two fight. Sometimes you squabble like an old married couple, you know that? Let's open this wine and I'll make dinner," and she was walking toward the kitchen.

"We fight?" Amy said, trailing after her.

"Like an old married couple?" Paul went on.

"I brought some Chinese take-out. You know that place on South Broad that we like? Do you want the crawfish lo mein or the chicken and broccoli? Oh, and I brought ice cream."

"Like an old married couple?" he repeated.

"Only sometimes," she grinned. "So you had a nap. You and Amy feeling better?"

"Lots." And then Amy said, "I was so messed up from the sun, I know I treated you terribly when you took care of me. I'm sorry. I want you to know how much I appreciate Doctor Hodges' TLC."

"That's okay, Amy," she replied. Somehow, she always knew which one of them was speaking. "I'm no fun when I'm sick, either. But I had to make sure my Paulette was going to get better, and you're the sister I never had, so of course I took care of you, too."

Embarrassed, Amy shook their head and looked down. "When I'm sick, I just want to crawl into a hole until I get better." Then Paul took the lead and looked up with a weak smile, "We get cranky."

"Cranky, indeed," Christine said as she spooned lo mein onto two plates. "But you're better now, and that's what matters. Open that wine, will you?"

A few minutes later the women were sitting on Amy's worn-out living room sofa, their dinner plates–and the wine bottle–on the coffee table before it. "I'm having an argument with Paul," she began, hesitantly. "He wants to kill our perpetrator."

"What? No way! Paulette, is that true?"

"Yes it is," he said, while Amy continued to push their fork into the lo mein. "I don't understand why Amy doesn't want to, also."

"But, why? I mean, KILL him? As in dead?" Christine sat with her fork in mid-air.

"When we woke up in that quicksand bayou without our pants, Blunt said he raped us while we were unconscious. Yes, I want to kill him. Dead, even."

Christine put down her fork and folded her hands in her lap. "I–I'm torn," she announced. "It's wrong to go killing people, we all know that. But if I'd been older than seventeen when that boy–" she shivered at the memory of the high school *apres prom* that turned her against men, something she had confided to Paulette and Amy long before "–I might have wanted to kill him, too, instead of wasting a few years thinking I had done something wrong. But not KILL kill him. How–You really want to kill him?"

"Yes," he hissed.

It was Amy who said, "See what I mean?"

Christine reached her hand over to Amy's knee. "You can't let her do that. I don't know if I can, you know, be in love with a murderer. Even one as great as Paulette."

"Why is this so hard to understand?" Paul asked aloud. "He raped us. He violated us. He stuck his unwanted dick in our body. I think that's grounds for killing him."

Christine shook her head silently. After a moment Amy asked, "When your voices were bothering you, before you got the medication straight–did they ever make you do anything you didn't want to?"

"That depends. They made me unhappy. I didn't like that. But they didn't make me eat cookies or steal stuff or hurt people. Just me." She slurped up a noodle. "Are you worried that Paulette might–No! Paulette! You wouldn't do that to Amy, would you?"

"I think you misunderstand. It's Skyler Blunt I want to kill. Not Amy."

"I know that! But what that would do to her–she'd go to jail. And I'd only get to see you on alternate visiting Thursdays of months with an 'X' in them." Christine became agitated as she spoke, waving her hands in front of her, "So you'd ruin her life, you'd ruin my life, and I'm thinking you'd pretty much ruin your life." She closed her eyes, considering the possibility. In a moment she was wiping her running nose on her sleeve. "Paulette! Don't do this to me!"

He melted, like he did so often for this woman he loved. Paul dropped the fork and reached out to Christine, and she leaned her head against their chest and held her arms around their neck. He heard Amy think, *Your girlfriend agrees with me.*

"I know it's wrong," he whispered to Christine. As he began to rock against her, he went on, "And I'm probably not going to do anything more than think some nasty things to him when we catch him. But I want to–oh, maybe I just want to see him dead." To himself he thought, *No. I want to be the one that snuffs out his miserable life.* He realized with sadness that something had fallen between him and the separate woman whom he loved–he could never again discuss this with Christine; it would be his own personal lie forever.

"That's okay, I guess," she said, straightening up. "Sometimes you scare me, Paulette."

"Yeah, well, sometimes I scare myself. Hey, you got great stuff for dinner. Thank you."

After the bottle of wine was empty and they had made a significant dent in a second, Amy announced, "Even though tomorrow is Saturday, I'm going to work. I've got to hit the hay." Paul added, "Will you stay over? I've got something for you."

"Sure. Amy, is that okay?"

"Of course, you know that. I'm curious what he has for you."

Once they had washed and prepared for bed, Paul said, "Christine, this has your name written on it." He walked to Amy's dresser and picked up one of the spare house keys he had made. "This is for you. This is to my home. And my heart. And it's with Amy's blessing."

"Whew!" She picked up her purse and set to adding the key to her keyring. "I knew why you needed the old one back from me, but I felt–I don't know, kind of lost without it. I'll keep it safe, Paulette, you know I will."

Paul led as they got under the covers. He thought to Amy, *Are we ready to, uh, demonstrate that dream to her?*

I itch too much, I'm still peeling. Next time, okay?

❦ 26 ❧

Saturday was their first day without the gooey salve painting their face white and leaving the front of their legs sticky. True, they still had that peculiar orange glow of a nuclear radiation accident, and large slabs of dry, dead skin sloughed off constantly. And the itch. The itch was the worst part. The itch didn't care if skin was about to peel or already had done so. It didn't care if what was left of their epidermis was pink, orange, or scab. Oh, God, it itched!

"I have to cut all my fingernails off," Amy growled as they drove to the police station. "I may have to wear mittens." She was rubbing the heel of their right hand against her right thigh, trying to relieve the itch without ripping her pants or her skin.

"I think we look good with blonde eyebrows," Paul offered. "We're sun bleached like a California beach babe."

"Next time I'll settle for a tanning bed. Let's collect Kowalski and get to the library. I'm looking forward to talking with Mrs. Richardson."

The officer was waiting in the parking area when Amy pulled in to the police lot. She pressed the button that lowered the passenger window and said, "Climb in, cowboy."

"I think we should use a squad car," he said, pushing his cap back on his forehead. "It lets people know you're serious."

"I don't know, Pat, I'm–"

"I'll let you drive it."

"–I'm, I'm thinking that is an excellent idea." To Paul she thought, *My turn,* and he groaned aloud.

"Problem?" Kowalski asked as he opened Amy's car door.

"Only the itching. Everything else is okay. Where's your cruiser?"

"This way," and he walked ahead. "Who do we see first, the wife, the daughter, or Richardson?"

"The wife's sister," she corrected. "Daughter is later, across the river. And visiting hours for Richardson last until eight-thirty. I'm hoping one of them knows where Skyler Blunt is."

He handed the keys to Amy, and she unlocked the doors, crawling behind the wheel. *Please, please, please,* she heard Paul silently begging, *let me drive, please, oh please, ask him if we can use the siren, oh please please please!*

"What's so funny?"

"There is a part of me that loves driving a cop car. Can I turn on the siren?"

He laughed as he fastened the seat belt. "Sure, first red light we come to, turn it on and keep going."

She thought to Paul, *Happy? I'll let you do the siren, but I'm driving this time.* She started the engine and backed out of the parking bay. "If we can pinpoint Blunt, we can go collect him. And if he's in possession of any of the Rothschild jewels, so much the better."

"I wish we knew how Richardson fits into this," Kowalski replied. "He's such a creepy bastard, but we don't have anything linking him to the theft or the murders."

She was heading south on Rampart Street. The light ahead at Canal blinked from amber to red. "Siren?" Paul asked out loud. Kowalski pointed at a toggle switch on the dashboard. "Go for it, but slow down to make sure you can get through without creaming some civilian."

Paul grinned like a maniac when he flicked the switch. Without realizing it, Amy accelerated instead of taking the officer's advice. She roared across the nine lanes of Canal Street, missing an inbound streetcar with at least four inches to spare.

"Yeah, the siren does that to you. Uh, you can turn it off now." Paul felt like a child told to put away his candy, but he flipped the toggle switch. "What a rush!" he muttered.

A block later, Amy made a right on Tulane, then a left on Loyola in front of the main office of the New Orleans library system. She drove over the sidewalk and parked in the narrow end of the pie-shaped grass sward in the park surrounding the building.

"You got your notebook?" she asked as they got out of the squad car.

They adjusted their gear before walking around the corner to the library's entrance. Amy was wearing the baggiest pants she owned, with new pistol, baton, and cuffs hanging from her belt.

Patrons made no notice of Kowalski in uniform, but Amy, dressed as a civilian, saw that people were edging away from her. "Do I still look that bad?" she whispered to the officer.

"It's the gun," he hissed back.

Paul looked down to their hip. "This isn't church or the post office," he answered aloud. "This is the library, right?" He bunched up Amy's jacket and draped it over the holstered weapon. "They're so freaked out by a bad person with a gun, they don't realize the only thing that will save them is a good guy with one."

"Easy, Detective," he muttered. "They're just civilians."

At the checkout desk, Amy showed her badge and asked directions to the board room. The librarian pointed down a hallway and told her what floor to take the elevator to. "Thank you, Miss," she said, and started walking.

"What do we know about Mrs. Richardson?" Amy asked. Kowalski rattled off details and benchmarks–"Fifty-one years old, married in 2002. Son is age 22, in grad school at UC Berkeley. Daughter died in infancy. Sits on several organization boards, I don't remember how many, but they all seem to be legit and noble."

"Family?" Amy asked. She mashed the button for the third floor.

"Maiden name is Oswald. Her sister is married to Skyler Blunt; her brother is married and lives in Oregon. Parents are dead. Father was a dentist, successful, so the family was not exactly scrounging for meals."

"Local?"

"Well, Shreveport."

When the door opened on the top floor of the library, a distinguished-looking older black man was waiting for the elevator. He smiled at Amy and Kowalski. "Is there something I can help you with?" he asked.

"Can you point us to the board room?" she replied.

The man turned to the uniformed officer. "Why on earth do you need the board room?"

Amy tapped him on the shoulder. "I need the board room. We are meeting Holly Richardson on police business."

"She's done nothing wrong! I'll have you know my board is—"

Paul interrupted, "Never mind. We'll find it ourselves." They walked around the sputtering man and headed down a hallway. "If I were him," Paul hissed to Kowalski, "I'd be more concerned about how we parked."

A woman came out of a rest room, wiping her hands with a paper towel. Kowalski asked, "Board room up this way?" She looked down the hall and offered, "Make a left at the tee; it's the only door down that way." He tipped his cap and they walked on.

The door was standing open, so they entered. An earnest young man was seated at one end of the board table, writing notes or preparing for the upcoming meeting. At the other end was a well-dressed woman in her early fifties, wearing a grey-and-white tweed suit. She was leafing through the current issue of *Southern Lady Magazine*. Her hair was salt-and-pepper with a blonde streak, in a tidy swirl. There was an elaborate silver brooch on her jacket, below the tight string of pearls. Her most notable feature was the penetrating icy blue color of her eyes. "Mrs. Richardson?" Amy offered.

The woman looked up. "You must be the detective," she replied, and held out one arm to invite Amy to sit. Kowalski left an empty chair on her left, and Amy did the same on the right. They had to turn in their seats to look at one other.

After Amy introduced the officer, she asked, "When is the last time you spoke to your sister?"

She held her left hand against her chest and tapped her breastbone. "I think it was last week. She wanted to tell me about a sale at the place where she works."

"Has she said anything about her and Skyler leaving town?"

"I don't think she would," shaking her head. "Bella is in Marrero and I can't believe she'd leave her."

"Tell me about her husband."

"I am not fond of Skyler, but he is the father of my niece. Detective, I'm sure my sister regrets her marriage every day. He's a felon, he's rude, he's obnoxious—Bradley simply cannot stand him.

It's been a few years since we had a family Christmas or Easter together."

"In the weeks before the break-in and theft at the museum, Skyler and your husband were in constant phone contact."

Her jaw dropped. "I–I don't believe you! Bradley detests him! Your information–"

Kowalski interrupted, "We have the telephone records from Bellsouth. They were calling each other as often as four times a day."

Mouth open, the woman swiveled her head from Amy to the officer and back again. "You're sure of this?"

Amy nodded. "Any idea what they were talking about?"

"I'm still absorbing the information that they were talking at all. Really, Officer, they despise each other."

"Detective. I believe you, Mrs. Richardson. But hate or not, they were talking. A lot."

She heard Paul think, *I've got one.* She nodded, and it was Paul who asked, "What has your husband told you about the theft and murders at the museum?"

"He's been very upset. He's concerned about the insurance, about donor reactions, and about the ability of the museum to attract future exhibits."

"What can you tell me about your husband's gambling debts?"

"He doesn't have any gambling debts. Bradley has his issues, of course, but I don't believe gambling is one of them."

"For the last three months, he has been writing a check for $3000 to the Big Easy casino," Amy said. "Does he often keep secrets from his wife?"

"Two things, Detective," the woman said, turning in her chair to face Amy. "First, if he's successful at keeping secrets from me, I'd be the last person to know, wouldn't I? And second, Bradley and I have a relationship that may be different from what you think."

Amy raised an eyebrow but stayed silent. She thought to Kowalski, *Take notes!* The officer clicked his ballpoint pen, then peered at Amy.

"Bradley doted on our daughter. We were a very happy family– Laertes was three, and Ophelia was an adorable little girl. She was barely a year old when we found her–" the woman paused, swallowed, and swallowed again "–we found her in her crib." Amy and Kowalski remained silent.

"We were never the same," the woman continued, "Bradley never recovered. He became withdrawn and moved into a separate bedroom. We spent less time together. He still was a wonderful father to Laertes, but our marriage–we became more like brother and sister.

"Don't get me wrong, Detective, we are still very fond of one another. But we are not, uh, intimate, in any sense of the word. Bradley has his assistant, and I have my charity work."

Amy shook her head; softly, she said, "That's awful."

"No, dear, it's not awful. It's my life, and I rather like it."

"But to be married, and not close to your husband? I imagine that–"

The woman snorted but smiled. "How old are you, Detective?"

"Umm, I'm twenty-six." Amy felt her face turning red, and it wasn't from the sunburn.

"Yes. If you don't mind, I suggest that you withhold judgement when you are presented with something beyond your experience, and perhaps pay a little attention to those who are dealing with it. You might learn something."

"Yes, ma'am," Amy said, looking down.

"Now, is there anything else?"

Amy perked up. "So you don't know anything about your husband's debt to a casino. Is there anything you are aware of that could put him in need of money?"

"Just the medical expenses," the woman shook her head. "The museum provides excellent insurance, but we weren't prepared to meet the entire deductible at one time."

"How about you? Alcohol? Gambling? Anything that has put you in the control of other people?"

"I buy a lot of shoes," she smiled, "but I promise you, I can afford them."

Amy stood up and held out her business card. "I appreciate your time today, Mrs. Richardson. I plan on visiting your husband this afternoon, even though what happened to him was outside my jurisdiction. Please call me if you hear from your sister. Skyler Blunt is our main suspect in the theft and murder, and I am afraid

Crystal may be in danger. You'll call me?"

"Of course, Detective. I don't much care for Skyler, but I love my younger sister."

In the elevator on the way down to the ground floor, Kowalski asked, "You told me to take notes. How did you–"

"Ventriloquist, remember?"

"But Richardson didn't hear you."

"Hey, I'm good. I aim when I throw my voice."

He stared, hands on hips, until the elevator went 'ding' and opened into the lobby.

As they climbed back into the squad car, Amy asked the officer what he thought of the woman. "She seems, I don't know, respectable. Give her a few years and she'll be matronly."

"I mean, do you believe her?"

He thought for a moment while Paul put the car in gear and started down Loyola. "Yeah, I do. It has to be hard to talk about finding your kid dead, and it's got to be embarrassing to say your husband has gone gay on you. I think she was honest with us."

Amy shook their head and began, "I don't know. I'd hate to–" She heard Paul think to her, *What was Holly's advice?* After a moment, she went on, "Ah, what do I know about being married? I've never kept a boyfriend for more than five months. I guess her life is okay if she says it is."

"You're kidding!" Kowalski exclaimed. "Smart, good-looking woman like you, and you haven't had a long-term relationship?"

Amy argued with herself, then answered, "I've got issues. And permission denied, Officer."

They did not speak while Paul drove across the river and headed for Marrero on the Westbank Expressway. Finally Paul, silently, thought, *Maybe Christine knows a guy?* She thought back, *Only you. God, my life is zoned a disaster area.*

When we get rid of Kowalski, he returned, *let's you and me talk. You know I want you to be happy, right?*

"Yes," she muttered. Kowalski looked up but did not speak.

"It's going to be all right," Paul said, aloud.

"Of course, Detective. Why–"

"Yes," she repeated, "I believe you."

"Say what?" Kowalski asked, puzzled.

"Sorry, Pat, just talking to myself."

After a pause he said, "You really answer yourself?"

"Sure. Don't you?"

"Uh—no, I don't."

"You're missing half the fun, then."

Paul remembered the way to the small clapboard house where Bella Blunt lived with her boyfriend Darius and his brother Beau. He parked the cruiser at the curb by the walkway to the front door. *Thanks for letting me drive,* he thought to Amy, *It's all yours now.*

They stood in the little residential street. First she arranged the gear hanging on her belt; then she attacked an itch that had been tormenting her thigh since before they crossed the Huey P. Long bridge.

She noticed the officer watching with a half smile. "What? You can't believe how much it itches!"

"I know the itch. I had a broken leg once. Tell me when you're done."

She gave herself one more satisfying scrape of fingernails across her pants, then said, "Let's go before it starts up again."

Bella Blunt answered the door barefoot, wearing jeans and a yellow-and-red tie-dyed tee shirt. She nodded at Amy, then looked past her and asked, "Who's your friend?"

Amy made the introductions. Bella smiled broadly at Kowalski and, sounding like a '30s movie, said, "Charmed, I am sure."

The living room was as badly lit as she remembered, and the walls still were bare. There was a powerful odor of stale cigarette smoke and...and something else...

"Dog," Paul exclaimed.

"Yeah. I got Squidward with me." In a big heap next to the sofa was the Bluetick hound that seemed to like Amy when she first interviewed Skyler Blunt.

"Wait," Amy laughed, "I know who Squidward is. How did your dog get that for a name?"

"When we got him, dad said he was a Bluetick hound." She bent down and rubbed the dog's head, eliciting a short, happy "Wruff." "Squidward is blue." To the dog, in the kind of voice an adult might use with a child, "Yes, you're my Squidward. Aren't you? Aren't you?" She looked up at Amy and said, "Hey, I was, like, six years old. Give me some slack."

"Excuse me," Kowalski said, "What's a Squidward?"

Bella's jaw dropped in disbelief. Amy laughed and said, "Somebody's never been to Bikini Bottom. Look–" she turned to the officer, "–it's a cartoon thing. I'll explain it later."

"Anime?" he asked, hopefully.

It was Bella who answered, "Nope."

The women sat on the sofa, while the officer took a wing chair. It wasn't an ideal position, being opposite the couch, but just enough light came through the window drapes that he could see to write in his notebook.

"How long has he been here?" Amy asked. "Last time he licked my hand was in Lafitte."

"Oh, just this week. Mom called me Monday or Tuesday and told me to go get him. They had to leave town and there wasn't anyone to take care of him." She frowned. "Dad up to his old tricks, I expect."

The officer asked, "What about the other dog, that Rottweiler?"

"Spike. He's Daddy's dog. They took him with them. Squidward's always been my baby."

"Did your mom say where they went?"

Bella grabbed a package off the table and slid out a cigarette. "No, but it's so funny–" she lit it with a yellow Bic lighter and let out a long plume of blue smoke "–Not ten minutes later Darius called me and said my parents were staying with him and Beau in Dayton. They're going to do the circus thing with my honey."

Paul thought, *Either this is fantastic good luck, or we're being set up. This is too easy.*

"The reason I wanted to talk to you today is we need to find your father. How long is he going to be in Dayton? Where does the circus go next?" Amy leaned forward so she could rub her itching calf with the heel of one hand.

"Why do you need to find him? I spent years trying to lose him."

"Bella, he's a suspect in a double murder. I'm worried about your mother's safety."

She took a couple of puffs, clearly torn between a tatter of loyalty to the father she hated and a concern for the mother she didn't respect, but nonetheless loved. Finally she said, "Let me get the itinerary." When she left the room, Squidward raised his lazy head, looked around, and lay back down with a soft "Wruff."

Can you trust her? Paul thought. *Would you rat out your father?*

Amy replied silently, *No way. But I can't imagine my dad being a murderer, either.*

Bella returned with a handwritten letter on yellow paper. "Darius gave me their schedule when they went on the road in July." She leaved through the pages, laughing at something her boyfriend had written, then said, "The last show in Dayton is tomorrow's matinee. It takes them a couple of days to break down everything, then they're headed for Nashville. Opening day is next Thursday."

"Where does a little circus get to perform?" Paul asked. "I once saw Barnum & Bailey, but it was indoors at a sports arena."

"Tyke-Town Circus won't be in the Superdome unless they all buy tickets to a Saints' game." She sat back down on the sofa and tucked the letter part-way under a seat cushion. "They use fairgrounds a lot, big open areas where they can raise a tent. That's what Darius and Beau do. They specialize in rigging and steeple-jacking and that crazy stuff. I'm afraid he's going to fall. He doesn't get a net like the trapeze people do."

Amy thought to Paul, *You have any questions?* Bella wondered why she shook her head. "Pat? Anything else?"

"Yeah, actually." He closed his notebook and waved it as he spoke. "This conversation is part of a criminal investigation. I urge you not to say anything to anyone about it. It would be unfortunate if Skyler learned we were coming to see him and went on the lam. It would be unfortunate, Miss, because that would make you an accomplice after the fact. The law says an accomplice in a murder case is just as guilty as the person who pulled the trigger." He paused, but Bella held his gaze. Finally she reached forward and stubbed out what was left of her cigarette. Kowalski asked, "Do you understand what I just said?"

"Yeah," softly. A pause. Then, animated, "Darius and Beau have gone straight. It's not their fault that they became friends with my dad a million years ago. Darius is clean. Right?" She turned between Amy and the officer, looking for reassurance. "Right?"

Amy touched her on the back of the hand. "As far as we know, the Soniers are in the clear. We're looking for your father, and we want to protect your mother."

The woman nodded, "Okay. Yeah, thanks. I told you before, I worry about Mom."

Kowalski took the wheel for the drive back over the river to New Orleans proper. The Ochsner Baptist Medical Center was uptown in the Milan and Freret districts, not all that far from Amy's house.

"Tyke-Town Circus," the officer mused. "I have to wonder what kind of man works for an outfit with a name like that."

It was Paul who responded, "The kind of man who gets to slip it to Bella Blunt."

He heard Amy silently shout *Trash mouth!* while the officer did a double-take. "Just when I think I understand you," he said, "you do or say something that makes no sense."

Paul was grinning. "What doesn't make sense? Should I say knock boots? Do the horizontal bop? Make the beast with two backs?" Kowalski was laughing, but Paul went on, "Give her a beef injection? Hide the salami? Dip his wick? Get his ashes hauled?" Amy silently asked, *How do you know all this? Stop!* but she was laughing inside as hard as Kowalski. "Lay some pipe? Put his tool in the shed? Have a squeeze and a squirt? Scrub his scrotum? Or would you rather I just said 'have intimate relations'? Does it make sense now?" Paul was laughing along with Amy and the officer.

"Damn, Clear! You're one of the guys, you know that?"

Paul let Amy answer: "Thanks. I think." Then she thought to him, *You amaze me. You embarrass me, too.*

"It's all good," he whispered; silently he added, *Glad to bring some entertainment to your life.* He moved their left hand–'his' hand–and put it over the back of their right hand.

"Now what?" Amy asked. "How do we get an arrest warrant for Tennessee? And how do we get Blunt?"

"We talk to Legal on Monday." Kowalski flicked on the flashing overhead lights to pass a semi. "Then we can contact Nashville PD. And if you're feeling adventurous–" he turned his head for a moment to glance at her "–we go there to participate."

She heard Paul think, *Let's go! I want to shoot the bastard!*

"Oh, hush," she said softly; then, to the officer, "Have you done this before?"

"I've gone out of town to pick up prisoners, but never to hunt one down."

She thought about it. Amy gnawed on the side of her right thumb while she scratched a peeling itch on her leg with her other hand. *It'll be fun,* she heard Paul offer, *even if I don't get to shoot the bastard.*

I don't want to hear about you shooting anyone. I'll tell Christine and she'll give you what for. Paul laughed out loud.

"What's so funny?" Kowalski asked, then immediately added, "Oh, you're talking to yourself. Never mind."

"Yes, I was. Actually, that was myself talking to me."

He turned to look at her. After a long moment, he shook his head and returned his eyes to the road.

"After careful consideration between me and me, I think I'd like to go up there and help them find Blunt. Finish the job, you know? Otherwise, those cops nab him and I'll feel like it's not quite over. What do you say?"

He took a deep breath and said, "Got to clear it with the ball-and-chain." He glanced at her with a grin, but her sober face wiped it from his mouth. "Did I say something wrong?" he asked.

"Oh, Pat. No, it's okay. It doesn't matter. Part of me is glad you and Roxy are doing better." Amy switched to her left thumb. "You deserve to be happy."

And she heard Paul think, *So do you.*

She closed her eyes and turned, sightlessly, toward the passenger door window. She was missing the approach to the Huey Long Bridge and trying very, very hard not to let a tear leak out. Silently she thought, *Thanks. Sometimes I forget that you love me.* She rubbed her eyes with the back of her hand. *I love you, too. Paul.*

Kowalski parked his cruiser on the sidewalk near the front entrance of Ochsner Baptist, and turned on the overhead blinking blue lights. "Let's see what Doctor Richardson has to tell us."

In the hospital lobby, Amy headed for the gift shop. "My mom would kill me if I didn't bring something on a hospital visit." She spent a few minutes looking at cards, settling on the most neutral one she found. The front had a drawing of a sad basset hound with a thermometer in its mouth and an icepack on its head. Inside, the message was, "Doggone it, get better soon."

"I can't believe a dumb card is four bucks!" Paul muttered on the way out. Then Amy turned to the officer and ordered, "Give me one of your business cards." She slipped it and hers inside the envelope.

They stopped at the registration desk, and Kowalski asked the sister for Richardson's room. The young nurse looked it up, then smiled at him when she said, "Three-twelve. That's the third floor."

The elevator was enormous, suitable for two or even three gurneys at a time. Brushed stainless steel walls gleamed on all sides. Amy said, "I feel like I'm in a refrigerator showroom."

It wasn't just huge; the elevator was agonizingly slow. Kowalski had time to ask, "What exactly are we going to do?"

"Cheer him up. He's in the hospital and he's had the stuffing knocked out of him. I figure we can do a song and dance thing, like a vaudeville show." Amy did a faux dance step and twirl, pretending to hold a cane. "And find out what happened to him."

The orderly waiting on the third floor eyed Amy's dance pose suspiciously when the elevator door opened. "Ah," she said as she and the officer exited, "my adoring public."

The nurse's station was only a few steps away. One of the sisters asked the uniformed policeman if she could help. "Room three-twelve," he said, "Bradley Richardson?" She pointed the way.

The door was standing open. As they approached, Amy saw a tense and tight-lipped Holly Richardson in a chair against the side wall. She was wearing the same gray-and-white tweed jacket she sported at the library that morning. The same copy of *Southern Lady Magazine* was rolled up in her hand, but it had been crushed in her grip.

"Good afternoon, Mrs. Richardson," Amy said as they entered the room. Immediately she saw the source of Holly's tension: Lance, the assistant in the museum office, was sitting on the other side of the hospital bed, holding a cup of water while Bradley used a flexi-straw. She could hear the aide was speaking, but his voice was too soft for her to make out the words.

As for Bradley Richardson, he was unrecognizable on the bed;

he looked like the star of a horror movie about an avenging mummy. His broken nose and fractured eyesocket were swathed in white, while a mouth guard to protect what remained of his teeth distorted his cheeks and jawline. There was an IV tube into his left arm, and a green oxygen hose taped under what little showed of his nose.

The wife turned but did not speak or stand. Amy thrust the get well card out toward Bradley as she said, "Wow, what does the other guy look like?" Paul, always monitoring their peripheral vision, noticed the beginning of a smile on Holly's face.

Mostly undecipherable sounds came from Bradley. He shifted, as if trying to sit up. His assistant pressed the control that raised the head of the bed.

Amy sat on the side of the bed. "I was so sorry to hear this has happened," she said earnestly. "It was outside my jurisdiction; I'm not here to give you a hard time about it. Is there anything you need? Anything NOPD can do?"

More sounds came from the man, as well as a shaking of the head. Lance spoke up, "I don't think you should be disturbing Doctor Richardson. Really, this is most inappropriate."

Amy turned to him. "You're Lance, right?" He nodded. "Tell you what, Lance. I'd like you and Mrs. Richardson to give us five minutes with your boss."

He made eye contact with the wife, possibly for the first time in years. "I don't–I mean, this is so–"

Holly stood up and tossed her rumpled magazine under her chair. "Come on, Lance. I'll buy you a cup of coffee." While she waited for the man to reach the wife, Amy mouthed the words, "Thank you." Holly nodded and left with her rival.

Kowalski stood and leaned against the door so no one could accidentally disturb them.

"Really, Doctor Richardson, I am truly sorry this has happened." She stood by the bed now, hands clasped in front. "Is there anything my people can do?"

A grunt, a headshake.

"Can you tell me who did this?"

Another grunt.

"Why they did this?"

And another.

"Here's my theory," she began. "One of the lugs working for Alphonse Perez took you outside for a come-to-Jesus session." When he made more inarticulate sounds, she said, "How about one grunt for yes and two grunts for no? Let's try that. Did one of Perez's people beat you up?"

He closed his one exposed eye and grunted twice.

"Okay. Did you miss a payment?"

Another two.

She sighed. "You're saying grunt grunt, but I'm hearing 'yes.' We know you owe Perez money. He owns the worst cops money can buy, so you're going to have to pay up or live in pain. I'm sorry."

One grunt.

"There's a piece of news about the Rothschild jewels," she said, changing the subject. "Some loose pieces from them have turned up in a couple of pawn shops, and not around here. It may take some time, but we'll be able to find the people who sold them." When Richardson was silent, Amy went on. "I thought you'd be glad to hear that. I'm sure your insurance company will be."

One grunt.

"And we're going to ask for an arrest warrant for Skyler Blunt. Isn't that peachy?"

With a slurred but coherent voice through broken teeth Doctor Bradley Richardson said, "I want a lawyer."

Amy nodded, but it was Paul who said, "I'm sure your loving assistant or loyal wife–I'm sorry, your loyal assistant or loving wife—can arrange that." They nodded to Kowalski. "Thanks for your time, Doctor Richardson," Paul said over their shoulder. "We hope you're feeling better soon."

When they got back to the station house, Amy and Kowalski each wrote up their case notes. The officer showed her what form to use to request an arrest warrant, the right code phrases to use on it, and where to deposit it for action Monday morning. They'd need Commander Ramirez's permission to go to Nashville, but the officer thought the man was so anxious to close the case that he'd grant it. They would ask the Nashville police to let them lead the search. If the Tyke-Town Circus was starting on Thursday, they would drive up on Tuesday and go to the circus location on Wednesday, while the tent was being set up. "If we can find Bella's boyfriend, we can find Blunt," she said. Kowalski tapped a pencil against his lower lip, then suggested they ask for a bunch of plainclothes help, so their presence wouldn't alert their quarry.

"That's it," Amy exclaimed. "I have to go home. My legs itch like I fell in a mosquito nest. Time for a calamine lotion bath."

"See you Monday," he offered.

As Paul led to drive them home, he said "Can we see if Christine is available? She'd be happy to curry us. And we were going to act out that dream for her."

"Sure, why not? All I've got at home is half a bottle of wine and a TV set. Maybe she does know a man. Uh, present company excluded."

Paul pulled the loaner over to the curb and dialed his lover. When she answered he said, "How's my favorite Christine?"

"Paulette! It's good to hear you. Is the itching better? How's Amy?"

"I'm fine," Amy answered. Even over the phone, Christine could tell which one of them was speaking. Paul said, "If you don't have any plans, I was wondering if we could come over, or if you wanted to stay at our place?"

"Yes, yes, yesyesyes!" the woman shouted. "My place is a wreck. I haven't cleaned it up since you and Amy stayed here. How about I come by tonight." They heard her voice go off the phone mouthpiece as she must have turned her head, saying, "I've got a bottle of vodka here somewhere, and–there it is!" Her voice was back full strength. "I'll bring it. That'll make the itching stop."

"You are a sweetheart," Amy said, then Paul led to say "We'll get something together for dinner. We're still kind of tired and all. But we don't have that goo on us anymore."

"Good. I didn't want to tell you, but with that white stuff on your face, you looked like a Goth girl."

"Shall I dress up for you?"

"No! You just be my Paulette. You're all I want."

"See you soon, Christine."

"I love you Paulette."

He folded their phone and resumed the drive back to their

Carrollton house. After a few blocks, Amy said, "Some day she's going to decide that if you won't marry her, she's leaving."

"What? Christ, just shoot me now."

"I've been thinking about this. You really love her, don't you?"

Paul said, "We've been together four years and you aren't sure?"

"It's so weird. Because of you I've been with Christine nine times longer than I've ever been with a man. I wonder if I shouldn't just give up and become a lesbian. I mean, we make a great threesome."

"That would be convenient," he said. "But I don't like the idea of you giving up."

"Me neither." Paul parked at the curb, a few cars down from their front door. As they walked to the house Amy thought, *If I do give up, which one of us proposes to Christine?*

Paul stopped. They stood in the street, keys in hand. Out loud but softly he said, "Don't tease me. Please."

As soon as they were in the house, the new lock fastened behind them, Amy said, "Tonight. Let me lead. Okay?"

"Are–are you sure?" She didn't answer. Paul identified his emotion: "I can't believe it, I'm jealous."

"Never mind. I'm sorry. I don't know what came over me."

"Give me a minute. This is serious, so let me think. Are you really that lonely?"

They were looking in kitchen cabinets, pulling out cans and boxes for dinner. The conversation took a surreal turn. Amy said, "How can I be lonely? Yes, the kidney beans, there should be some Basmati. I mean, you're in here–" she pointed at their head "–with me all the time. Do we have onions? And you know I love Christine, she's my best friend. Uh, my best female friend. I miss–I miss–" and she stopped.

Paul laid the rice and onions on the counter, then wrapped their arms around their body to hug Amy. "What do you miss?"

She let their head drop to one shoulder. "I miss having someone to hug. Someone to hold me." Paul felt a drip down their face. "You've got Christine. Mom's got dad. My sister has Eddie. And Amy's got nobody."

He tightened their grip around themself. "I'm here. Amy's got

Paul. I know it's not the same, but you don't ever have to be alone."

Amy shook herself inside, then took a deep breath to keep her nose from dripping. Still, she left their arms around themself. She and Paul had been doing that since she was eleven, when he was the exciting grownup who suddenly came to live inside her head. He loved her, she knew he did.

"Do you think–" she started, then took another deep breath "– Do you think you can share her with me?"

"I already do. You two are best friends. She says you're the sister she never had."

"Yes. But when she knows I'm leading the way she touches me isn't like that. She always can tell. How does she do that?"

"Do you want her to do that? Does she turn you on?"

Amy thought while Paul rubbed their hands up and down their arms. "I guess not. I don't know. I love her, but she doesn't turn me on."

"So–what's the problem here?"

"I want someone I care about to do what you're doing. Somebody with a body."

For a moment he felt hurt, but he told himself she wasn't being cruel, only honest. He had the advantage of physical contact with Christine, a woman he loved, a woman his man-mind adored. She didn't, because Paul's only body–anymore–was Amy's. "And it would be okay if it was Christine?"

Oh, I don't know!" She stood, eyes downcast, not seeing the dinner fixings on the kitchen table or the floor that needed sweeping beneath it. "I think so. I–I–I don't know. I know her, and I trust her, and I'm tired of being so damn lonely."

Paul sat them down in one of the kitchen ladder-back chairs. He could feel Amy's confusion and sadness. It wasn't like her to feel sorry for herself–if anyone was a make-the-best-of-it person, it was Amy. Finally he said, "We can talk to her about it. I bet she'll understand."

"But I don't want to make things weird for you and her. Or for me and her, for that matter."

"We're all friends," Paul said. "We trust her. She trusts us."

Amy thought as they sat in the kitchen, Paul still holding their arms around themself, *Maybe I can just take the lead and we'll see what happens?*

"Umm–I don't think so," Paul objected. "She always knows which of us is leading, you know that."

"I'm going to try," she said aloud. "I don't know what's going to happen. I don't know what I want to happen. I just need someone to hold me tonight."

She slammed her fist down on a cutting board; the salt and pepper shakers tinkled against each other. "Just–just be ready in case I'm a coward and..." she trailed off. Paul waited for more, but Amy was silent. Finally he said, "What else for dinner?"

"Salad fixings are in the fridge. You want to take a nap? Suddenly I'm wiped out."

They stayed awake long enough for Amy to take the afternoon dose of medications. When they woke, fully dressed, lying on top of the duvet, Christine was sitting on the edge of the bed and reading aloud from a paperback novel. "She looked out over the green rolling pastureland that was her property and thought, 'I don't need his help. I'll just run this ranch myself.'"

Paul was touched–not by the content; as much as Amy enjoyed Debbie Macomber, he thought her books were potboiler stuff–but from her taking the time to read aloud to them. *That's a lot nicer than an alarm clock,* he thought to Amy. He felt her laugh, but then she became tense. He heard her think, *Now,* and he felt her retake control of their body.

She sat them up and rubbed Christine's shoulders and neck. "That's nice, you reading," she said, "but I have a better idea."

The woman turned to face them. "Sure, Amy. What?" She was smiling, happy to be with her surrogate sister, knowing her boyfriend Paulette was in there somewhere.

Amy let go of the woman. "How do you do that?" she shouted, "How do you always know which one of us is talking?"

Still smiling, she answered, "I don't know, I just do. How do you think into my head?"

Amy was silent, but her expression was one of defeat. "What's wrong, Amy? Paulette, is Amy okay?"

Amy fell back on the bed and covered their face with their hands. Paul thought to his lover, *She's upset. We talked earlier. She's*–he hesitated to reveal Amy's secret, but then went ahead–*she says she's lonely.*

"That's silly," Christine replied. "I'm here. You're always here." But Amy kept her face hidden, feeling doubly alone that Christine didn't understand why she felt that way. After a few moments, Christine said, "But if that's what you feel, Amy. Can I do anything?"

Amy moved their hands to expose their face, and reached toward the woman with their right hand. "Please don't laugh at me," she whispered. "Just hug me. Hold me."

Christine took Amy's hand and pulled her up to a sitting position, then put her arms around her friend. She petted Amy's hair and rocked slightly. Amy took a deep breath and exhaled for what seemed like a minute, relaxing just a little bit. She was holding Christine tightly. Paul's lover said, "What is it?"

Amy didn't speak, so Paul thought to Christine, *There are some things I can't do for Amy. I can't hug her like you're doing. She's feeling empty today.*

Christine nodded, and whispered to Amy, "I'm here. It's okay. You're not alone now. I'll be with you all night. It's okay."

After a minute Amy asked, "Will you kiss me? Please?" Christine planted several on the cheek that was near her mouth, but Amy said, "No. Like you kiss Paul. Please?"

"Oh, Amy!" she replied, and sat up and away. "I do that all the time when I'm kissing Paulette." She was smiling.

"But that's for Paul," Amy replied. "I need it for me."

Christine's eyes widened, as if she were just then understanding the depth of Amy's unhappiness. She hugged her, but did not offer the beseeched kiss. "I love you, Amy," she said. "But I'm in love with Paulette. Don't make me–I mean–I–I can't treat you like her. You're like my sister. You're different."

Paul thought to Amy, *I'm here. Christine's here. We love you. And I'm in love with you.*

Great, she thought back. *Then tell your girlfriend to kiss me!*

So Paul thought to Christine, *It's okay, you can kiss her.*

"No, it's not," Christine said, even as she hugged Amy tightly. "You're my lover. I want you. I'm faithful to you."

He thought, *Do you understand why I'm conflicted? Your fidelity is a gift, a wonderful gift. But I also want Amy to be happy.*

"I'm sorry, Paulette. I can't do that. I won't. Not even for Amy."

Listening to Christine's half of the conversation–she could not hear what Paul thought directly to the woman–she wondered how she had become so lonely. Was it Kowalski choosing his wife over her? Or what had Kowalski said about her limited boyfriend life that she now regretted having volunteered to him—was that what suddenly made her painfully aware of this hole in her life?

Amy turned her head to kiss Christine's cheek, then released her grasp on the woman. With a weak effort at a smile she said, "Thanks." She was drowning in disappointment.

Christine poked her index finger on Amy's nose and flicked it off. "Didn't anyone ever tell you not to thank someone for a hug?"

"Uh, no. Why not?"

"Well, when it's someone you don't know well, it might sound needy. Or low self-esteem. I guess it's different with us."

"I guess. Uh–I know this is a long shot, but do you know any men?"

"My brother, but he's married. Usually I stay away from boys." She reached up and stroked Amy's cheek. "I wish I could make you happy. I wish Paulette could. I'm sorry."

Amy grasped the hand on her cheek and held it against their face, then turned their head to kiss Christine's hand. "Yes."

Paul thought, *I'll lead. You can relax. Okay?* He felt Amy withdraw.

"Paulette!" Christine squealed, "Yay!"

"I promised I'd show you that dream we had," he said, nuzzling her ear.

"I don't know." Her hand was still on their face, in their hand. "I don't want to make Amy feel bad. You can show me later, okay?"

Amy thought to her, *Thank you for postponing that. It would be hard to endure the two of you getting it on right now.*

"That's what I figured," Christine said with a broad smile.

Aloud, Amy said, "The guys never understand that. I'm glad you do."

Eventually they went to the kitchen to fix dinner. The three of them in two bodies chopped onions, boiled water, measured rice, and made the salad. As they worked, Amy explained to Christine what had happened that day. "First, a woman we interviewed put me in my place because I said it was sad she and her husband weren't close. She said I should keep my mouth shut and listen to people who have been dealing with that kind of thing before I passed judgement." Amy took two glasses from a cabinet and slid a bottle of Chateau Bayou St John out of her collapsible counter-top wine organizer. Paul used their left hand to pick up the corkscrew from behind the breadbox.

"Then I said to Pat that I'd never kept a boyfriend more than five months and he laughed at me." The bottle opened, Amy poured a glass for Christine and a very full one for herself. "And then I decided I wanted to go to Nashville to be part of the apprehension team instead of sitting here and letting the Nashville crew get the credit. So I asked Pat if he wanted to do it with me. He said he had to check with his wife. It—it made me feel sad." With the wine glass in one hand, she stirred the pot of red beans and onions with the other. "And then he started to apologize for mentioning her. I told him it was alright, that he deserved to be happy, even though I think she deserves to spontaneously combust in an inexplicable burst of molten lava."

Christine said, "That was a nice thing to say. Especially since you don't believe it."

"And then Paul says to me that I deserve to be happy, too, and I damn near started crying."

She stood there, waving a gooey wooden spoon, "Suddenly I felt so isolated. You've got Paul. My mom and dad have each other. Kaylee's got Eddie. Pat even has that damn Roxy." She took the two steps to where Christine was watching the rice boil and kissed her on the cheek. "Everybody's got somebody. But all of a sudden I felt scared and empty because I don't have anyone. Nobody to hug and kiss me, or rub my feet, or anything physical."

"Amy?" Paul asked. She let him go on. "We learned to love each other pretty quick after I woke up in Amy. She was just a little kid, but she was smarter than me and she insisted that we become friends." The grin came from Amy. "But it pisses off both of us that we will never be able to kiss each other. We can't really hug. And making love is just a fantasy. We hate it."

"I never thought of that. How sad. Because, Amy, I have to tell you–Paulette is great in bed."

She smiled. "Sometime you'll have to tell me all about it. And don't leave out any of the good parts, you hear?"

During dinner Amy offered, "I'm leaving for Nashville on Tuesday. The plan is to stake out the circus grounds on Wednesday while they're finishing the setup for Thursday's opening." She spooned more beans onto her plate. "I'll be in charge of the Nashville undercover unit so we don't tip our hand with a lot of uniforms. If Blunt doesn't show up we'll just follow his friends to wherever they're staying and pick him up there."

Wide eyed, Christine asked, "Is it dangerous? I worry about Paulette and you."

Paul responded, "I'm convinced he's the murderer, and I'm guessing he's still got the pistol he took from Amy. But she's a good shot. Better than I am."

Amy said, "Yes. I out-shot you that first time you took me to the target range. And I nailed that drug creep when your arm was paralyzed."

"Stop!" Christine squinted at them. "I can tell which one of you is leading even when you're not talking. But Paulette, which arm is yours?"

He laughed. "Our agreement is that both arms are Amy's. But sometimes she lets me lead. She's right handed and I'm left handed. We caught a ricochet in our left arm which meant I couldn't even hold a gun. Amy shot the bastard."

"I only wounded him," Amy said, modestly.

"Yeah. Wounded him to death. All his blood leaked out because of you."

"So, Paulette, what do you do when Amy is doing this kind of thing? Are you a policeman, too?"

Amy laughed over their long-running disagreement. "No, I'm not," Paul said. "In fact, I hate cops. I'm scared of 'em. They make me feel guilty even when I haven't done anything wrong."

"So how do you two–you know, get along?"

"I'm not a policeman," Amy said, "I'm a detective. They're different."

"Yeah. Detectives solve problems," Paul jumped in. "They

don't look over your shoulder like a cop does, waiting for you to break some law you may never have heard of. Detectives come to a crime scene and try to figure out who the bad guy is."

Christine nodded, "Okay, I see the difference."

Paul went on, "So even though Amy is the one with the credentials and nobody on the force knows I exist, I do what I can to help. I think cops suck, but detectives rock."

"So you look out for each other. Good, I'm less worried. I know you'll take care of each other."

Amy held out their right hand and Paul held out their left. They touched Christine on her shoulders. "Yes," Amy said. "We take care of each other."

Christine spent the night, and Paul demonstrated the erotic dream he and Amy had while they were recuperating at Christine's house. When they were finished Amy said, "Can you hold me, Christine? I–I just need a little more."

"Of course, Amy!" Christine curled up alongside them, her left leg over theirs. She rubbed her shoulders, and planted a kiss on the cheek. "I love you. Paulette loves you. We both would be lost without you."

Amy muttered, "This has to be the weirdest damn thing in the world," but she was smiling.

"Only because I take my medication," Christine answered. "This is nothing compared to voices telling you the King of Nutopia wants you to wear everything in green."

❦ 27 ❦

"For God's sake, fly! We'll find the money somewhere," Commander Ramirez told Amy and Officer Kowalski on Monday at the police station on Rampart Street. "The mayor has been making my life miserable because we haven't closed the museum theft and murder. Now we've got an arrest warrant, and you're pretty sure you know where our perp is."

The detective and the uniformed officer were standing in the commander's wood-paneled inner office, while Ramirez sat at his cluttered desk. He was holding the requisition form for the warrant that he'd found in his mailbox twenty minutes earlier. "Can I ask," staring at Amy, "how sure are we that Blunt is in Nashville?"

"Pretty sure. Maybe eighty percent," she offered. "His daughter is living with a man that became Blunt's friend in prison. He's going to Nashville on his job, and he told the daughter that her mother and father were with him."

He drummed his fingers on his desktop. "What's the plan?"

"I'm about to call Davidson County PD in Nashville. Officer Kowalski and I want to lead a pack of their plainclothesmen to the place where the daughter's honey is part of a crew raising a circus tent."

Kowalski cleared his throat and Amy let him take over. "We expect to find Blunt on site. If not, we'll follow the boyfriend to wherever he's staying and we're bound to find him there." She nodded as he spoke.

"I've worked with you for years, Detective Clear, and you've never let me down. And Officer Kowalski, you know you are one of my inner circle." The commander paused, getting his thoughts in order. "As long as the Mayor is chewing on my ass, I'm willing to take a chance. Make your calls. Talk to Shanika about booking your flight to Nashville. Close this case!" He looked at one and then the other, then waved them out of his office.

It wasn't just unsolved murders that bothered the mayor so much; New Orleans's murder clearance rate, a pathetic 39 percent, made sure there was no shortage of them. No, hizonnor's concern was a perfect storm of the upcoming election and the reluctance of wealthy donors to support him as they had in the past because the mayor had bragged that bringing the international treasure, the Rothschild jewels, to New Orleans was his personal project–and they were stolen on his watch. And never mind the phone calls from the mayor's personal secretary; it was the visit from the mayor himself that made it clear to Ramirez how important this task was. And, since shit flows downhill, the commander let the mess drop on Clear and Kowalski. If anyone could solve this, it was them.

He sighed. Thirty years earlier, Chief Pennington escaped New Orleans to take over the police department in Atlanta. If this didn't work and the mayor fired him, Ramirez could always find another job. Maybe.

Amy and Kowalski went to the uniformed officer bullpen and found Shanika Jones at her dispatch station. "Who do we know in Nashville PD?" Amy asked. "Davidson County."

In a flash the woman had called up her electronic Rolodex. "County is unified under city police. Chief is Lamar Pardue. Press is–"

Kowalski interrupted, "CID or homicide."

"Well, then," a couple of computer clicks under her two-inch fingernails, "Homicide section, Captain Phillip Squires."

"You are a wizard, Shanika. Can you place the call and I'll take it out here. And Pat needs to talk to you about plane tickets." When the light for line three began to blink, Amy picked up asked for Captain Squires. It took three transfers before she was speaking to the Captain's yeoman, a sergeant named Bobby Young.

She introduced herself and explained she wanted help executing an arrest warrant in his jurisdiction. The sergeant said he didn't see any problem with that; he had manpower, and there had been fewer homicides in the city than the previous year. "Let me get the captain on the line for you. Can you hold on?"

It wasn't long before she heard a sharp, brusque voice say, "Squires. What?"

After she introduced herself, she explained that she and her uniformed partner wanted to exercise an arrest warrant in Nashville. "Sure," he said. "Knock yourself out."

"We'd like some help. Can you spare some plainclothes officers or detectives to work the location on Thursday?"

After a moment Squires answered, "Maybe three men. That's all you can have tomorrow."

Paul thought, *Wrong day.*

"Our perp will be there on Thursday. That's when we'll–"

"I don't know what I'll have available that day. Call me tomorrow," and he hung up.

She held the phone handset out to look at it, and practically handed it to Kowalski as he reported, "Shanika says NOPD has enough budget for us to ride in the baggage compartment tomorrow noon."

Amy related her call to the Nashville homicide section. "I wonder..." she began, "I wonder if he doesn't take a female seriously. You want to call him? Tell him I got disconnected and then I had to, I don't know, do my nails?"

The officer got Shanika to place the call again. He got as far as Sergeant Young, who told him the captain had told him to tell New Orleans he was serious about them calling tomorrow. "Tell me, did my detective do something wrong? Did she piss him off or something?"

"Uh–no. He's like that with everyone."

"Oh, great. Sarge, can you set this up so we don't have to bother the boss?"

In a low voice he heard, "Ask for me tomorrow."

When he hung up, Amy asked, "Was it me?"

"Nope. The sergeant says it's him. He's like that with everyone."

"When I am queen of the world, five years from now–oh, seven, tops–I won't have to put up with this crap." Looking at Kowalski, she mused, "I'll be hiring minions and sycophants. Let me hang on to your resume."

He turned to Shanika and asked, "What just happened?" but she was on the radio, arguing with an EMS dispatcher.

He followed Amy down the stairs to the detectives' section. "You'll be hiring onions? And sick elephants? What?"

"Just trying to make myself feel better after that captain was a jerk," she answered. "We have to make plans. Sit down." She motioned him to the detectives' bullpen table, and she sat next to him, in front of the computer. "We'll need copies of the pictures of Skyler–" she opened a jpeg and set it up to print six copies "–and those photos Bella gave us of the Sonier brothers. Is that one Darius or Beau? I can't believe anyone in 2025 has a mullet." She sent them to the printer as well.

Paul mused aloud, "I wish we had a photo of Skyler's wife."

Kowalski stood by the printer, waiting for everything to spool out. "At least we know what she looks like."

Paul answered, "And she can recognize us. And so can Skyler."

Amy pulled up the law enforcement version of MapQuest, which offered better resolution than the commercial website and easily allowed printing of satellite images. "I want to know every inch of the fairgrounds where the circus is going up," she said. "Blunt probably isn't familiar with it, so let's turn that to our advantage." She stared intently at the big screen monitor, chin in one hand with fingers tapping her jaw. The officer dropped the printout on the table as he sat back down.

"What the hell?" It was Paul. "A race track?"

Amy answered, "I'll bet they put the tent in the pit, in the center."

"There's a creek in that corner," Kowalski volunteered. "How much green cover is there? Could he hide there if he saw us?"

"Excellent question." Her face not six inches from the screen, she stared intently as she enlarged the aerial image. "Not a lot, but enough. And if he goes under that bridge," pointing, "we've lost him."

The officer grabbed a pad and began making notes. "Three men between the creek and the track. They're bound to use the two infield buildings and the bleachers so they don't have to haul in Port-a-lets, so we'll have to cover them." He wrote some more instructions to himself.

"We call tomorrow," she sat back, and held up an index

finger. "We fly up on Wednesday," a second finger extended, "we go on location on Thursday—" a third "—we arrest his ass, and we come home heroes," holding up her hand with all digits outspread.

Paul added, out loud, "And on Friday we fly the body back to New Orleans."

"How dangerous do you think he is?" the officer asked.

"He's got our old gun now," Paul went on, "and we're convinced he used the one that turned up at the liquor store hit on the guard. We expect the worst."

A blink. "'We', detective? 'Our' gun?"

Silently she swore at Paul for his constant use of the first person plural. "It's the royal we," she told Kowalski. "I'm practicing for when I—excuse me, when WE become Queen of the World."

"Too bad there aren't two of you," he smiled. "Then we'd only need another eight people on the stake-out." He showed her the rough diagram he'd drawn, with proposed assignments. "Since you and I know Blunt, we get to float."

"Great job, Pat. I was still an hour away from getting to that. Now all we have to do is convince *El Capitan Del Capitan* to give us eight men."

Patrick Kowalski felt an embarrassing wave of gratitude. Police officers are not known for handing out compliments, except as condolences to widows. Once again he thought he would walk through walls for Detective Amy Clear. "Yeah," he managed. "Uh, nine. Nine men."

"I'll check in with you tomorrow; we'll call Nashville again. For now, I want to see the fencing report." Amy turned back to the computer as the officer left. She plugged into the Automated Pawnshop System, and sorted on jewelry.

In an ideal world, every item purchased by every pawnshop and used store would be entered into a searchable database so police could look for things reported stolen. But here in the real world, not every jurisdiction uses the APS, nor is it mandatory in all the places that do use it. A crooked pawnshop owner can risk trying to fool the APS with incorrect serial numbers or descriptions that purposefully leave out distinguishing characteristics, although such deceptions are felonies. Build a better system and it leads to better criminals.

Amy scanned the database for loose gems and descriptions of broken settings and found three: a pair of loose emeralds, a pair of loose rubies, and one sapphire in a broken yellow metal setting.

The emeralds were listed eighteen days earlier at a pawnshop in Greenwood, Indiana, outside of Indianapolis. The entry characterized them as faceted and rectangular, and estimated each of them at one-third of an ounce. The shop paid $100 for each of the stones. *A third of an ounce?* Paul thought, *That's like, a package of Kool-Aid mix.* The customer's name in the database grid was "Cash." When she clicked on it, all the record indicated was "Cash Only."

"If these are from the Rothschild jewels," she sighed, "those itty-bitty green things are worth seven or eight thousand each." She printed out the records.

Paul moved the computer mouse to their left so he could click on the rubies that Amy had found in the database. "Faceted, teardrop, bright red, large but no weight." When he asked, Amy said, "That probably means they didn't register on the owner's scale. Five carats is huge, but it's less than one-tenth of an ounce. These guys are pawnbrokers, not jewelers." They were sold in Dayton, Ohio ten, eleven days ago. The store owner paid $250 for each of them. When Paul clicked on the customer field he said, "It's our old friend Cash Only."

"He gets around, doesn't he?" Amy mused aloud. "The museum brochure said the rubies were from India and in today's market they are priceless." Then she shouted, "Wait!" She reached out and dragged her purse to them, and began searching it for her notebook. "Here! I wrote down the circus itinerary Bella had in her boyfriend's letter. Three weeks ago the circus was in Indianapolis. Two weeks ago it was Dayton. Last week—when Skyler hooked up with them—they were in Bloomington, Illinois."

Paul said, "Let's check out that sapphire and setting piece."

Amy took back the mouse and looked at the last record she had flagged. "Blue gemstone in broken yellow metal setting, rectangle, faceted. Weight ¾ ounce."

"That's huge!" Paul cried.

"Part jewel, part metal. But if it's from the Rothschild exhibit, it's worth a lot more than $150." She pointed at the location,

Hudson, Illinois. "I'll bet that's up the road from Bloomington." She clicked on the customer field and once again saw "Cash Only."

She sat back to consider the circumstantial web. Silently she told Paul, *Three places where the circus has been. Three transactions that read like they could be parts of the museum loot. I'm thinking Blunt fronted some of the pieces to the Soniers, and I guess the pistol he used to kill the guard. And then he showed up in person with more of the jewels. He has to be my perp, has to be.*

"So when we find him," Paul said aloud, "he'll have more of the jewels on him or where he's staying. Oh, wait."

"Hmmm?"

"That makes Bella's boyfriend an accomplice."

Amy chuckled. "Nuh-uh, not if he's got a decent lawyer. We don't know that Beau and Darius knew about the murder."

She printed out the rest of the search results. Then Paul asked something that struck her as odd: "Can we bring a metal detector with us on the plane?"

"A metal detector?" laughing, "Why on earth?"

"Wonder Warthog killed the bank robber before he found out where the money was hidden."

"W-Wonder Warthog? I don't believe I've had the pleasure. What are you talking about?"

"If I kill Blunt before he tells us where he's hidden the Rothschild jewels, a metal detector will let us find the broken settings and the rest of the gems."

"Now, listen!" she barked, the laughter gone. Silently she went on, *There will be no killing. We are going to take him into custody and let a jury of twelve make that decision.*

"So you keep telling me," replied Paul, out loud.

If you kill him, she thought, *I won't like you. And Christine said she won't be able to love you anymore.* Amy collected her various printouts and sorted them into a portfolio.

"I'm counting on forgiveness being easier to get than permission."

She sat down and held her temples in both hands. Silently she thought to him, *If you murder him, I am the one who goes on trial. I am the one who goes to jail. It's my name that will be ruined. It's my mother and father and sister who will be ashamed of ever having known me. Do not do this to me!*

As she sat, Paul whispered aloud, "And if you go to jail, where am I? I promise, I promise, if I get to settle our score with Skyler Blunt, it will look justifiable."

"I thought I knew you," Amy whispered back. She thought the rest to him, *You really could kill someone out of anger and revenge?*

Paul decided it would be better not to answer her.

On Tuesday, Amy spoke to Sergeant Young in the homicide unit at Nashville PD. He promised ten plainclothes and one uniformed officer. The bad news, he said, was that Captain Squires would be the one in uniform. "How can I give orders if the Captain is there?" she asked. His answer: "You can't." They arranged to meet at the South Precinct division headquarters in Nashville Thursday morning at seven-thirty, and then they'd all arrive at the fairgrounds around nine.

ꕥ 28 ꕥ

Amy said, "But I feel naked without my gun." The TSA agent at Louis Armstrong International Airport explained that, law enforcement or not, she and Kowalski would have to pack their unloaded weapons in checked baggage, and declare them to the ticket agent. "Damn," Kowalski complained, "I wanted to avoid the baggage claim nightmare." Because they were sworn officers, the TSA man let them unload right there in front of God and everyone, and find minimally appropriate ways to secure their gear in what they had hoped would be their carry-on baggage. To satisfy security, both unloaded pistols went into Amy's bag, while the ammo went in the officer's. She heard Paul think, "Fair division. Two boxes of bullets weigh more than the two guns."

The two legs of the flight passed in an uncomfortable haze of narrow seats, limited recline clearance, and a stranger in the aisle seat for the first half. Kowalski attempted to nap. Amy tried to read her Kindle, but Paul didn't like the book and took to making silent rude comments about it. Finally she gave in, and they played twenty questions. Their favorite pastime for such situations was Rock Paper Scissors, but they had learned from experience that playing it where they could be seen made people very uncomfortable.

They had a layover in Atlanta to change planes. While they ate sandwiches at one of the outrageously overpriced restaurants in the secure area, Amy asked the officer about the next day's stakeout. "If their captain is there, how can I tell them what to do?"

"You can't. It's a bitch."

"Is it because I'm a woman? Is the captain some kind of troglodyte–"

"It's because you're an Officer III and he's a captain." He

smeared mustard on the top piece of bread and put his meal back together. "And not only does he outrank us, we're out of our jurisdiction and he's not."

"But we know what Blunt looks like!"

"You brought the pictures, right? The whole squad will know." When he saw how disappointed she looked, he said, "You can't win a pissing contest with someone who outranks you. Don't even try." He had no way of knowing it was Paul who stuck their tongue out.

They ate in silence for a while. Then Amy dropped what remained of her sandwich back on her plate and exclaimed, "What if he tells his people to do something stupid?"

"If that happens, my advice is to say 'yes, sir.' Detective, you have got to man up."

Paul thought to her, *That's why I want to kill the bastard. Gets the job done even if the captain is an idiot.*

Silently, Amy thought *Tch!* to him.

The flight from Atlanta to Nashville was on a smaller plane, and Amy and Kowalski had a row to themselves. He leafed through the issue of *Sports Illustrated* he'd picked up at a newsstand, while Amy and Paul went back to Twenty Questions. Just before the pilot announced the final approach to Nashville, Amy muttered, "That is so wrong! I thought you said it was mineral."

"Uh, Detective?"

"You cheated!" Then she opened her eyes. When she saw Kowalski she said, "Uh-oh."

"You're talking to yourself again, aren't you?"

"Give the man a prize!" she said, relieved. Then, silently, she thought to him, *Move along, nothing to see here.* He smiled broadly and shook his head, then went back to the article about why the Orioles didn't have a prayer in hell to win the pennant, even though their third baseman was the best hitter in both leagues.

Why do you do that? Paul asked silently. He wasn't being judgmental, just curious. Amy heard it the way he intended and thought to him, *It's fun. I've actually convinced him I throw my voice. It may come in handy sometime.* When Amy was a child, when Paul first turned up in her head, they both worried about being labeled as crazy and sent off to some institution. They agreed on a plan if that ever happened—she would say it was just a joke, there was no voice inside her, and Paul would refrain from speaking aloud until they were released. There never had been a need to implement that strategy. When Amy was in college she noticed how bizarre so many of her friends and fellow students were; since then she worried less and less about waking up one morning at the state mental hospital in Mandeville. Actually, Louisiana had sold the campus to a private company and moved the state mental health unit to Jackson, but Mandeville remains the local synonym for crazy. Their private running joke was that someday, when they had a couple million dollars to spare, they would endow a wing and make the hospital call it the Clear-Owens facility.

The NOPD budget allowed them to rent a tiny sub-sub compact, and to check in at a Hampton Inn by the airport. It wasn't too far from the South Precinct station where they were to meet with Captain Squires the next morning. Once they were set up in adjoining rooms, Kowalski said, "I'm going to take the car. An army buddy of mine lives over the river in Scottsboro. You'll be alright on your own, right?"

"Have a good time, Officer, but make sure you get plenty of sleep. Tomorrow is show time."

When he was gone, Amy sat heavily on one of the two queen-size beds in her room, arms folded across her chest. "He could have invited me," she muttered.

In a fake oriental sing-song Paul said, "Oh, you better off." Then, "He's going to swap lies with an army buddy, and my guess is the army buddy has a wife and some kids. Aside from the beer, it wouldn't be fun for us."

"Beer," she said. "Hey, let's get something other than Dixie." She stood up to head downstairs to the lounge.

"We don't have to drink Dixie at home," he said as they walked down the hall to the elevator bay. "Or Abita. There are some great microbrews. And the German ones."

She thought to him, *But you like the heavy ones and I like the sweet ones. We both can stand Dixie.*

Some other people were on the elevator when the door opened, so Paul thought silently to her, *I'm open to anything but Dunks or Stroh's. Or Olde English 800.*

I never heard of any of those.

Count your blessings. Pisswater, utter bilge.

They had two beers with dinner–Becks–and then bought a six-pack of Yazoo Sue at the Kwik-E-Mart across the street from the hotel. Amy turned the room TV on to CNN News, and Paul muted the commentary. "This is fun," Amy said. "It's nice to get out of town with you. The air smells different here."

"They have mountains here," he replied, then took another sip of Yazoo. "I grew up with mountains in West Virginia. Louisiana is some kind of flat, you know that?"

"Easier to go for a hike." It was her turn to tip the bottle. Whichever one of them was leading would get the most taste–and the most impact–from alcohol, so they alternated.

They went over the plans for the stakeout at the fairgrounds. Amy moaned again about being outranked by Captain Squires. Paul said he missed Christine.

"I do, too," she sighed. "When you met her and started going out, I went through disgust–" she opened another Sue and took a long gulp "–I mean, a woman touching me, ugh." She laughed at the memory. "Then I was jealous. I remember telling you to pack up your stuff and move in with her."

Paul took the bottle with their left hand for his drink. "I remember that. You made me realize I don't have any stuff. A couple of old pictures of my sister and my parents, that's it."

"Does Christine think I'm weird?" she asked, seriously.

"You don't think she's weird, do you?" Amy shook her head and took another sip. "She doesn't think I'm weird, so why would she think you are? You know, she tells me you and I look alike."

"I mean, you know, that–that thing I went through the other day, when I wanted her to hug me and kiss me."

"Felt good to me. And friends take care of each other. You were lonely or something, That's not a crime. And it's not weird."

Amy took another sip of Yazoo Sue. "She pissed me off that she wouldn't kiss me." And another one. "But then I thought, what a loyal girlfriend she is. You're a lucky man." And one more, a small leak onto their shirt dripping to the counterpane. "And if you're happy, that increase- increase- increases the odds that I'm going to be happy."

She turned on the bed so the flickering TV screen wouldn't

distract her. Paul took another swallow, and asked, "So, what's up with Kowalski?"

"Give me that beer!" and she drained it. Well, most of it; she wiped the spill off the side of their face with their sleeve. "He looks great, he's a great guy when he's not trying, and he's turned his future over to what's-her-witch. Roxy." She made a face. "I'm sure he'd like to sleep with me. But as much as I'd like him to, I've had my fill of being little Miss Homewrecker. No, he made his choice." Paul was silent, and after a few moments she muttered, "Bastard!"

"Blackguard!" Paul responded.

"Cad!"

"Scoundrel!"

"Rogue!"

"Scalawag!"

"Miscreant!"

They both laughed–Amy out loud, and Paul inside. Then he sat them up and said, "Rock Paper Scissors for who finishes the beer?"

"You're on!" Paul worked their left hand and Amy their right. When Amy won, he cried, "Two out of three!" She won the next one, too. "Just a sip for a parched old man?" he asked. Amy shook her head, grinning, and guzzled all but an inch of the brew. "Okay, some crumbs for you," and she let him lead to get the very last from the bottle.

He tossed it at the trash can and missed; it rolled across the floor and came to rest at the end of the hallway, against the door. "I'll get it later," he muttered. They both were buzzed.

"Remember that dream?" Paul said.

"And what dream would that be?" she responded, even though she knew exactly what he was talking about.

"The dirty one. You know–" he held their right thumb and index finger in a circle, then poked their left index finger through it a few times "–that one."

"Oh, that one," she teased. "I think so. Vaguely. What about it, big boy?"

"It's a romantic evening in a hotel out of town, we've put away a lot of beer and we're feeling fine, and it's just you and me and these two beds..."

A big smile spread across their face. She unbuttoned their shirt, saying, "There's something so sexy about a man who's invisible."

"Hah! If I were invisible, could I do this?" and he slid their hands under their shirt and rubbed their arms, their breasts through the bra, their shoulders.

"Ummm. Remember when mom caught us doing this and she told me it was perfectly normal to masturbate?"

He was trying to unhook the bra. "You were what, fifteen? You think she's figured it out yet?"

Amy leaned forward so Paul, using their arms, could unfasten the piece of clothing. "She doesn't want to know. Dad either." She lay back to let Paul seduce her. "Remind me about this dream," she said.

ॐ 29 ॐ

A thumping on the locked communicator door woke Amy at five forty-five in the morning. "Get your butt in gear, Detective," she heard the officer shout. "Breakfast downstairs in thirty minutes."

She stretched, then rubbed their face. Paul said aloud, "Hot damn! I've been waiting for today."

"Why's that?" Alone in the hotel room, she shed her underwear and headed for the shower.

"We get to deliver justice, swift and sure, to Amy Enemy Number One."

She groaned, either from his comment or from the cold water on their hand. "Promise me you won't kill anyone unless they are about to kill me."

"Boil in oil, stew in lye," he replied.

When she got the temperature right she stepped under the stream. *I don't get these tiny bars of soap,* she thought, wrestling to unwrap something smaller than a credit card. *When the soap at home gets this small I throw it out.* She managed to work up some lather on their body.

When they were dry, Amy strapped on her thigh holsters for her pistol, her baton, her handcuffs, and her badge case. Because she didn't even own a uniform, she had brought a deep blue man's tailored shirt, and a blue maxi-skirt, mid-calf length, with lots of pleats. She thought it was ugly, but it hid all the hardware she had to conceal as a detective. She glanced at their watch, then turned off the lights and walked to the elevator bay.

Does it bother you when I wear a skirt? she thought to him.

Nah. Once you finally taught me how to sit in one, I realized they're great. If I ever get a man's body again, I'll wear kilts.

Can you order them online? she snickered.

Kilts? I guess.

That's not what I meant. She entered the elevator and nodded at the three or four people already on it. Surrounded by outsiders, all Paul could do was sputter inside, much to Amy's amusement.

Kowalski was seated at a small table in the hotel's informal dining area, with the remains of a fried egg breakfast. "Good morning, Officer," she called to him. "Did you have a good time with your Army buddy?" She took a seat.

"Sure enough. And his wife's a good cook. I'm glad I don't have little kids, though." Amy smiled when she heard Paul think, *What did I tell you?*

She wanted to go over strategy with Kowalski. "I'm concerned about this captain's symptoms of megalojerkism. How do I get him to do what I want?"

"Depends," he answered, stealing a forkful of hash browns from her plate. "What is it you want him to do?"

It wasn't until he asked that she realized she didn't know. "Uh, gee, uh–" she was making sounds while her brain turned "–I guess, let me decide how to handle any situation that comes up."

Kowalski appeared to think about it for a moment, and offered, "With this sort of thing the captain may have more experience than you or me. And flattery is a known tactic. Maybe just brief him on Blunt, and the Soniers. I plan on keeping my eyes open and learning."

Her disappointment was so severe that Paul could feel it. *I wouldn't have a clue what to do,* he thought to her. When Amy remained silent it was Paul who said aloud, "Yeah, I guess you're right."

"Are you okay, Clear?"

Amy responded, "Yes, I think so. Why?"

"I don't know, you just didn't sound like yourself."

"Where are we going?" changing the subject, "The Southern precinct or something?"

"I programmed it into my phone GPS. Whenever you're ready, Detective."

Amy gulped down the last of her coffee, hearing Paul think,

What? No chicory? What kind of benighted hellhole excuse for a burg are we in?

"What's so funny?" Kowalski asked as they headed for their rental car.

"Just amusing myself. If I was home, I'd have a lot more coffee with chicory in me by now. Do you ever drink so much you're vibrating?"

"You think that's funny? I quit doing Red Bull because of that. Then I transferred off the night shift."

Amy rehearsed her presentation while Kowalski handled the short drive. The car's digital clock read seven-twenty-five when he parked in front of the South Precinct on Harding Place. It was a single-story red brick complex with odd round rooflines, squeezed between train tracks and a creek in the midst of an industrial area. Kowalski whistled and commented, "Looks better than our dump." Paul sniffed, "Looks like a middle school." They sat another moment, until Amy slapped her thighs and said, "Show time, partner. Let's break a leg." She retrieved her briefcase from the tiny trunk, and they entered through the huge glass doors.

A yeoman was waiting for them with temporary ID badges, and led them down a hallway to a brightly-lit conference room. Two men were in uniform–the captain's yeoman, Sergeant Bobby Young, and the elaborately dressed Captain Phillip Squires.

"Good morning, Captain," Amy and Kowalski both said. The man nodded but did not rise from his chair. "Officer," he nodded to Kowalski, and "Detective."

The captain was a big man, even seated. He looked to be in his fifties, with retreating grey hair and a partial comb-over. Three hundred pounds was packed into his dark blue uniform. He had a wide, beefy face, with jowls and two or maybe three chins that disappeared into his shirt collar without benefit of a neck. He wore wire-rim spectacles and had a brushy moustache.

He motioned down the table to where nine men were seated in street clothes, looking like drifters and down-and-outers. "This is my undercover team. We want to get moving, so, Officer, can you tell us what we're up against?"

Kowalski answered, "I'd prefer to let Detective Clear do the briefing; she's the project leader."

"Really? What jurisdiction are you from?" he said, archly.

"New Orleans PD and Orleans Parish. We're consolidated, like you are here with the county."

"And they let girls lead murder investigations? Well, well, I'm only a country cop, what do I know."

She heard Paul think, *He's trying to push your buttons. Don't give him the satisfaction. Don't let him get to you.*

"I expect you have a great deal more experience than I do with this kind of stakeout," she began. She hid the way her hands were shaking by busying herself with her briefcase, pulling out files. "We have an arrest warrant for this man–" she handed a photo to the Captain, and gave the rest to one of the plainclothesmen to pass around the table. "Skyler Blunt. Forty-three years old. He spent several years at Angola for armed robbery in his twenties. For the last nine years he's worked with a tree service, and he is expert at rappelling and rope work. The warrant," for the first time she looked at the Captain head on, "is for two murders committed while stealing almost thirty-four million dollars' worth of jewels from a museum exhibit, the Rothschild jewels. He's also charged with the assault and attempted murder of a law enforcement officer."

"Go on," Squires said impassively.

"Blunt is here with his wife, who is not a party to his criminal activity. However, we believe they are staying with two prison associates, Darius and Beau Sonier." She gave the first copy to the Captain, then again handed the rest of the photos to the nearby undercover man. "They are low-level fences. We don't think they were involved in the murders or robbery, although they have sold some of the stolen gems. We know from Skyler Blunt's daughter that he is staying with these two men. They are in Nashville as part of the crew that is setting up the Tyke-Town Circus in the fairgrounds. They are tent wranglers. It is possible that they have put Blunt to work because of his expertise with ropes, but that is a guess. We do not know for a fact that Blunt will be in the fairgrounds during the circus setup. If he does not appear, our thought is to follow the Sonier brothers to wherever they are staying and apprehend Blunt there."

The Captain turned his head to Kowalski and prompted, "Officer?"

"Detective Clear's presentation is accurate and comprehensive, Sir." Amy thought to Paul, *He doesn't trust me!* She heard Paul think back, *Doesn't look like it. Don't get mad, just prove him wrong.*

"One last thing," Squires said as he stood up. At six-foot-five he was an imposing figure. "Is your man armed? Is he dangerous?"

Paul took the lead. "He has a stolen pistol. If I were him, I'd be packing it." Then Amy continued, "He's not a berserker; he's not going to hold up a liquor store or shoot at random people." She thought for a moment and finished, "He'll be a bear when we corner him. He's not a 'It's a fair cop' kind of guy."

"Thank you, Detective," and he made a hand motion to Sergeant Young. The officer removed the lens cover from a projector and then leaned toward the wall to flick a light switch. "This is the fairgrounds," Squires said to the room. "We're there every year for the fair and the NASCAR races, so we know every square inch of the place. Here's how I want it to go down." For such a heavy man, he was quick and light standing up.

They were looking at a line drawing of the fairgrounds, but Amy recognized it after having studied the satellite imagery of it. "Mason, Hernandez, Bennett, and Strait, you'll be at the creek. Hernandez, you're the leader. One man at each bridge so this man can't leave the fairgrounds–" the Captain tapped the projected drawing, "–the other two work it up and down, up and down. Keep in radio contact with Young.

"This is set-up day for the circus, so we don't expect the public to be an issue. Concessions probably won't be open, but the bathrooms in the two buildings and the bleachers–" again pointing to the objects of his instructions "–we'll keep an eye on them. Francis, you and, uh, where the fuck is Roberts? God, find him and when we're done you make him clean those toilets with his wife's best underwear. Also grab Anderson and Washington; tell them to dress down and keep a watch on those doors."

"That leaves us," motioning to Amy and Kowalski, "and MacPherson here." A man in a nondescript coat tipped his felt hat. "We float. We stay in touch with Bobby Young. You two–" he turned to Amy and the officer "–let's get you radios on our frequencies, and then let's get moving."

****

Silently they followed the captain down a long hallway. Three turns later they were in the communications room. The captain told his man what he wanted and left.

Kowalski exchanged chit-chat with the comm man while Amy silently complained to Paul. *If I catch Blunt single-handedly he'll say it was luck,* she pouted. Paul thought back, *Let him. What matters is getting Blunt. And Commander Ramirez will know the truth.*

You just don't know what it's like to be considered incompetent because you're a woman, her lower lip sticking out.

Guilty, he thought back. *Hey, your opening was terrific. Telling him you were counting on him, that was good. I'm telling you, flattery is underrated.*

The lip retracted and a smile started. "You think so?" she whispered.

"Come on, Detective," Kowalski called. "Quit talking to yourself and watch how their radios work." He handed her the unit the comm officer had prepared. "See, the microphone is this clear tube. No one will know you're wired unless they look real close."

They made their way to the lobby where they found Sergeant Young. "You did pretty well," he said to Amy. "Some outsiders leave here in tears."

"Does he have a problem with women in command?"

"Ah," he smiled, "you noticed."

She heard Paul think, *Hold your tongue. Wait for him.*

After a silence, Young added, "There are ways he's an old fart. But he's a brilliant tactician. We'll get your man, don't worry. C'mon," and he led them to the rear parking lot.

Everyone piled into an unmarked Econoline van for the ride to the state fairgrounds. Amy grabbed Kowalski to make him sit between her and the captain. It was eight-forty on a pretty summer day that promised to be clear and temperate.

Smiling vacantly, she thought to Paul, *He set it up pretty much the way I wanted to.*

Good, he thought back. *It shows you have good instincts. If he's got some tiny ego that has to take all the credit, let him. You and I know better.*

How do you do that? How are you always so sure what to do? She was working at ignoring the idle chatter to her right. She felt Paul smile inside as he answered, *Ah, you forget I'm seventy-one years old. I've had plenty of time to do things wrong. And second, I guess a lot. Sound as if you know what you're doing and the people around you assume you do. I think that's what most people do.*

"Detective, the captain wants to–oh, will you quit talking to yourself for a minute?" Amy blinked and turned to Kowalski. "The captain wants to know how you think we should approach Blunt when we spot him."

"By surprise and from behind," the words came out of her mouth before she had a chance to think them. "He'll recognize me and the officer; we had dealings with him during the investigation." Paul added, aloud, "He's already killed two people, so there's nothing to stop him from doing it again if he feels trapped." Amy grabbed the lead back and said, "Wait. I still think he's not a danger to bystanders."

They heard the captain mutter, "Fuck. I need two more men." He pushed the send button on his comm unit. "Sergeant, find Lundgren and Diaz. Tell them to dress down and meet us at the fairgrounds." He turned back to Kowalski and Amy. "Since he knows you two, you get to be the center. Me and MacPherson and the two guys on their way will work the compass points so one of us is behind the perp when you spot him. That way we can get him from behind, like you suggest."

Amy's mouth fell open. She thought to Kowalski, *I don't hate him anymore.*

The officer spun his head to face her, "What?"

"Ventriloquist," she whispered. In her head she heard Paul doing a "Go Amy!" song.

The driver passed the main entrance, then turned down a side street that led to a back parking lot, behind the grandstand and some support buildings. Squires told the creek crew to get moving, and the rest of them stood in a bunch by the van. "Francis, get your men out to cover the latrines. You know the drill." The plainclothesman nodded, then pushed his three men in different directions; they would enter the active area of the fairgrounds individually so a wary quarry might not sense a stakeout.

"I'm north," the captain said, then told the remaining undercover officer, "You take south." He flicked the comm button and barked, "Bobby, tell Lundgren he's east and Diaz he's west. They're on their way, right?" Amy couldn't hear the sergeant's reply, but Squires' next "Right!" told her the additional manpower was on its way.

"You two stay together, no matter what," the captain told Amy and Kowalski. "If one of you takes a leak, the other goes with him. Or her. Keep moving; we'll keep a visual on you. Let the sergeant know when you spot him; he'll get the rest of us in position." He paused. "Any questions?"

"Sounds like a great plan," Amy offered. "Pat?" The officer shrugged, "Thanks, Captain."

Squires turned toward the top of the fairgrounds, the north end, and headed toward the racetrack.

"Let's go," Amy said, and led Kowalski to the nearest likely gap between the work buildings.

They came around the side of the bleachers and took in the ground-level view of what had just been satellite pictures and Nashville police drawings before. The racetrack was a half-mile concrete oval, wide enough that had it been a city street it could be striped for six lanes. A smaller oval was connected to the west leg of the big track, and about a third of the large infield was paved.

A half-dozen separate canvas tent sections were spread out across the grass and gravel portion of the infield; long lumps indicated tent poles lying beneath them. Two dozen roustabouts were most of the way through the task of hammering enormous stakes about ten feet beyond the edge of the canvas, ten feet apart. Three men were at each stake, each wielding ten-pound sledge hammers, teaming up in choreography worthy of Alvin Ailey or Martha Graham. A John Deere skid steer was parked at the edge of the infield.

Amy pointed and said, "Let's see if the Soniers are there." The two went in that direction, while Amy kept scanning the fairgrounds. "A hundred and some-odd acres is just a number when you read it," she said as they walked. "This place is huge." At the north end, beyond the track and the scoreboard, she saw big trucks and more men preparing a temporary foundation. To the east, between the big oval and the creek, other trucks were setting down the rides; she could make out a Ferris wheel, and maybe the sorriest excuse ever for a roller coaster.

The infield was full of the motion and noise of the circus version of gandy dancers. Another group of men was scurrying to and from one of the semi-trucks parked on the track, carrying or dragging more tent poles toward the places they would be needed. A few men held clipboards and seemed to be the foremen; anytime a stevedore approached them, they pointed somewhere and sent them off to another task.

"Do you see the Soniers?" Amy asked. She and Kowalski both were scanning the workers, on the lookout for Bella's boyfriend and his brother.

The officer snickered and said, "Mullets are still in with the circus folk. Nah, I don't see either of them yet."

They walked around the track to make sure they saw all of the tent workers. A cheer went up when the last stake was driven, and the crew gathered at the place that would be the entrance to the completed tent. The foreman jogged over to give instructions for the new tasks that would follow.

Someone cranked up the skid steer and positioned it at the opening. After some stevedores arranged the canvas, the driver lifted the pallet hauler attachment up a full seven feet. One of the foremen pointed at half a dozen workers, who went under the lifted canvas and began the project of lifting and installing the edge poles that would hold up the wall of the completed tent. Within a few minutes the entire front of the tent was upright.

As they walked on the near side of the oval, where the not-yet-raised back of the tent still lay on the ground, Amy poked Kowalski. "The guy leaning against the wall–the one smoking. Is that one of them?"

Pat took a monocular from his shirt pocket and held it to his right eye, twisting the outer ring to focus. "Might be one of them," he said, and passed the device to Amy.

"Bingo!" she said. "I don't remember if that's Beau or Darius, but it's one of them."

Kowalski pressed his comm unit button. "Sergeant, we've spotted one of the secondary targets. Tan workshirt, blue jeans, smoking a cigarette, leaning against the wall of the latrine building." Sergeant Young said something that Amy couldn't hear, and Kowalski went on, "No, don't apprehend him now, that would tip our hand. Can you keep an eye on him? Yeah–yeah–right. Thanks."

Paul thought to Amy, *The other one must be nearby. Good.*

"Peachy," she said.

The officer smiled and said, "You ought to introduce me to that other you. She seems to keep you amused."

If he only knew!

"Umm–I don't think that would be a good idea. But I'll pass on the, uh, worthwhile things the other me says."

"The captain told us to float," Kowalski said. "Let's check out what's happening over there."

As they walked toward the Ferris wheel, Paul blurted out loud, "That's an elephant!" She thought back to him, *So that's what they call it.* In the distance, the animal had its trunk wrapped around a piece of roller coaster track and was holding it up while two roustabouts on ladders bolted it in place. Riding the beast was what looked like a dark-skinned child in a bright red shirt. He or she was shouting encouragement to the elephant, praising it and instructing it in a heavily accented sing-song voice.

Parts for several rides were spread out – bumper cars, rotating teacups, and old-fashioned flying horses, a carousel. A dozen men were busy with pegs and sledge hammers, with ladders, with pneumatic wrenches, and–in the case of one grizzled roustabout–an open can of beer. He was standing shirtless in the shade cast by a truck, with sweat glistening on his lean and heavily tattooed torso.

"Do you see Blunt?" Amy asked, trying to scan the workers. She saw Hernandez, walking along the creek behind the workers, and she spotted a very young man she took to be one of the people the captain summoned from the car—was that Lundgren? Kowalski reported the same thing she found–"No Skyler."

Amy turned to look back at the track. The entire tent wall was up. The driver of the John Deere drove into the tent; they could see the sunken roof being poked up by stevedores with poles inside. The whine of the diesel motor strained, and they saw the center of the roof rise slowly. There was a group shout when the forty-foot king pole was dropped into place. Amy heard Paul think, *How do they do that so fast? Have we even been here an hour?*

Amy nodded, then heeded the officer when he said, "They're putting up a smaller tent over there," pointing north. When she looked, she saw Captain Squires beyond the workers, his blue-and-gold-trimmed uniform standing out even at that distance.

When a man in mime makeup nearly ran them over on an enormous unicycle, Amy thought maybe a day had passed and the circus had begun. Two men walked on stilts, not bothering with their comic costume pants that would hide the wooden helpers. A woman dressed like a gypsy was talking with her hands to one of the roustabouts, who was laughing heartily; when she turned, Amy saw it was the bearded lady. "Looks like the sideshow is rehearsing," she said, enjoying the lunacy, the incongruity, the spectacle of it all. A very tall man walked to and from, juggling four balls and a banana. "Can you do that?" she asked aloud. She heard Kowalski in her ears, and Paul in her head, both say, "No." Amy laughed and said, "The circus. That definitely will be my next job."

They encountered yet another tent that had been blocked from their view earlier. "Holy shit!" Kowalski shouted as he took off his cap and began to fan it in front of his face. "What is that smell?" As if on cue they heard a ferocious roar, then another one. Twenty feet away, in a miserable small cage, was a stunning white Bengal tiger. Another cage harbored two zebras, and by itself, watching carefully from a third, was a kangaroo.

"Let's go look!" Amy exclaimed, grabbing Kowalski's sleeve like a child dragging her daddy. Standing in front of the tiger, with only bars and a few feet of fetid air between them, she marveled, "I want to pet him." It looked like a silver tabby cat on steroids, weighing four hundred pounds. She heard Paul laugh, but not him thinking to the huge cat. *Hey, Tony the Tiger, you are a handsome fellow!* The animal looked left and right, then stared back at Amy and Kowalski.

I'm having a conversation with Fluffy, he thought to Amy, then went back to complimenting the tiger, mind to mind. After a minute, the beast backed away from the bars. Paul continued to chat at it, but it lowered itself to the concrete floor and placed an enormous paw over its face. *Well, he's no fun,* he thought to Amy, about the time the jungle cat whimpered.

"Naughty boy," she said to Paul, out loud. Kowalski said, "I'm all for the wonders of nature and everything, but I'm afraid my 9 millimeter wouldn't make a dent on that thing."

She nodded, "You're right. Let's get back to work."

They strolled around the first tent they had spotted, the one being set up as the side show. It was odd to see people in street clothes instead of their performing costumes as they swallowed a sword, or spit fire, or threw knives at a plywood target, always landing just outside the outline of a woman. And among them all were the roustabouts, shouting orders and telling dirty jokes as they erected the tents. It was a temperate, sunny day, with a brilliant blue sky that set off the few white wisps of clouds. Paul said out loud, "What a great day!"

"And indeed it is," Amy added, "a great day to find Skyler Blunt. Let's head back to the infield. Maybe he's shown up."

The six shorter shafts had been raised in a geometric pattern around the king pole. The roustabouts had a lot more work ahead to make the structure stable and safe for two weeks of paying customers, but from where the NOLA officer and detective stood, the Big Top was up!

They saw two men climbing ropes that were attached to the parts of the center poles that stuck out above the tent fabric. One was making sure the adjoining pieces of canvas were laced together tightly with the weatherproofing strip in place; the other was bouncing his bare feet off the tent as he moved sideways, checking on the vulnerable corners of the structure. Paul thought, *Looks like a vertical trampoline. Neat.*

"Something Bella said when we interviewed her," Amy said to the officer. "She worries about Darius because his work is dangerous and there's no net. Let me have your monocular."

She turned the ring until she could see the mullet flying behind the bouncing man. "Come on, turn around, come on..." she muttered. Finally the worker did turn, to shout something to someone on the ground. "That's one of them!" she said, and aimed the optical device at the other tent climber. He seemed to be struggling with some stubborn rope loops. She couldn't hear him, but one didn't have to be a lip reader to know what the man was saying. When the ropes at last obeyed him he looked up. "Yes! That's the one who we saw smoking before."

Kowalski pushed his comm button. "Sergeant Young? Yeah, we found both of the secondary targets. They're the ones that are working on top of the tent." He laughed at something the Nashville officer said, and went on, "Me? Not for a million dollars. I don't even clean my own rain gutters."

While Pat dealt with the communications officer, Amy turned to scan the faces of all the workers, looking for Skyler Blunt. She thought she could spot the undercover man working the west side of the fairgrounds, but there were so many average-looking men in average clothes, looking nonchalant or smoking cigarettes or at least pretending to do something on their cell phones, she couldn't be sure if they were local undercover or just hangers-on. Quietly she said to the officer, "Their men do a better job of looking like wallpaper than our undercover squad." He nodded. "This captain may be a jerk, but he knows his stuff."

They were walking around one of the closed concession stands when Amy heard a woman shout, "Detective!" Startled and surprised, she made herself turn toward the voice. About thirty feet away, pushing through stevedores, was a frantic Crystal Blunt.

It took Amy a moment to recognize the woman. Crystal flung her arms around her and said, "Thank God!"

The woman's dress was a distinctive orange. "Pat, your jacket," Amy called, and the officer draped his blue police coat over Crystal. He heard Amy throw her voice, *I don't want Skyler to spot her with us. Let's get her out of here.* Kowalski started talking into his comm unit.

Amy began walking her to the south of the grandstand, looking for a walkway to the area where the Econoline was parked. "What are you doing here?" Amy asked.

"Skyler is here, he let me go to the ladies' room and I saw you." She was clutching Amy's arm. "Please help me."

Amy made out the purple bruise on the left side of her face, under heavy makeup, "He hit you again, didn't he?" The woman bit her lower lip, then nodded. "I want to see Bella," she said, pleading. "I want to go home. I don't want to run again."

Kowalski asked, "Ma'am, what is your husband wearing?"

"Oh, that ratty red plaid shirt with a vest and jeans. He's got–"

A nondescript-looking man in a camel-colored jacket met them and interrupted, saying, "I'm Officer Diaz; Sergeant Young said you need some help?" His voice had just the slightest trace of a Hispanic accent.

Amy walked him a few steps away from the distraught woman and said, "This is the wife of our perp. Hide her. I don't want the guy finding her, and I don't want her in the way." Diaz nodded and began to walk back toward Crystal, but Amy added, "One other thing. She knows we're here for her husband, but she may not realize we think he's killed two people. Be careful what you say in front of her."

Diaz's nod was more vigorous, and he returned to Blunt's wife and Kowalski. The officer was saying, "–keep you safe. This detective will look after you. Will you do that for me?"

The Nashville detective put his hand on her upper arm to lead her away. "Is there anything you need?" he asked her, "Can I get you some coffee or a Coke? What do..." and his voice faded away with distance.

"Red plaid shirt, a vest, and blue jeans," Kowalski said to his comm set; then to Amy, "Let's start looking."

As they walked around the infield a few times, Amy told him, "Did you see that bruise? He hit her again. I hope she's finally had it with him."

"She can testify against him if she wants to," he offered.

"Hey, most women think wife-beaters are scum of the earth. What I don't understand is why they sometimes make exceptions for their wife-beater."

She heard Paul think, *The fact that some women do is way more important than whether or not you understand it.*

"Oh, shut up!" she barked aloud. "There's no reason–" and she stopped. Still walking, she turned to an amused Kowalski and said, "I said that out loud, didn't I?" He grinned and nodded. "I really am talking to myself," she went on.

"I do that, too, but I don't remember the last time I had an argument with myself."

"Yes, well. I'll try to behave, but I don't make any promises." She thought to Paul, *Why did you make me do that?*

Silently, *I wasn't trying to provoke you. Maybe we can talk about it later?*

What's wrong with now?

Kowalski grabbed her arm. "Red plaid shirt. Vest. And that dog! Shit!" With his other hand he activated his comm link, calling, "Sarge! Perp spotted. Infield, near the north side of the tent. He's got a Rottweiler; it's a nasty piece of work." They tried to hurry in an unobtrusive way, working their way closer. "We'll be on him in a minute. Alert everyone!"

"We'll confront him, and Hernandez or whoever can grab him from behind," Amy said, trying to convince herself that it would go smoothly. Paul said, "Fucker thinks he killed us; maybe we can scare him that we're a ghost." She glanced around and saw the compass point plainclothesmen and even Captain Squires, alerted by the sergeant, closing around them. The net was being cast.

When Skyler Blunt noticed them, he dropped the leash from his gloved hands and let Spike charge them. Kowalski, wary after his first run-in with the dog, already had his hand on his mace. He stepped back and decoyed the animal into running past him; they both turned and the officer loosed the spray on it. Immediately Spike began to bay and howl in pain. They watched the dog rub its face on the ground, trying to get the corrosive capsicum out of its eyes and its sensitive nose.

And while their attention was fastened on Spike, Skyler Blunt ran up behind Kowalski. He threw his left arm across the officer's chest, and grabbed his service pistol from his hip holster.

Before Kowalski could respond, Blunt jammed the pistol into the side of the officer's neck. "Don't do anything heroic, copper," he muttered. He glanced behind and saw two of the undercover men coming toward him, guns drawn. "Get back!" he shouted. "Everyone get back or the cop gets it!"

Amy reached under her skirt to unholster her sidearm. Deliberately she racked the slide, a sound known to instill fear in any sane criminal. To Blunt she said, "No."

She stood eight feet in front of Kowalski, pistol aimed at Blunt's bobbing head. The stevedores and roustabouts ran for safety.

"What the fuck are you doing here? You're dead."

"Maybe I am," Amy answered. "Maybe I'm just your guilty conscience. Or maybe I'm the angel of death come to take you away. 'And you will know My name is the Lord when I lay My vengeance upon thee.'" She heard Paul shouting silently, *Shoot him! Shoot him!* Behind her foe Amy saw the captain and four other men, all closing in with drawn weapons.

She said, "So, are we going to stand here all day or what?"

"I won't wait that long," he said coldly. "Put down your gun or your chaperone here gets it." Then, louder, "All of you, drop your guns or I'll shoot him."

Amy thought to the officer, *I won't let him hurt you. When you get a chance, drop down so I can take him.* His expression did not change, since she had taught him to believe that she was a ventriloquist who could aim when she threw her voice. Then out loud in a calm, even voice, she said, "Shoot him. Then I'll shoot you."

It seemed to Paul that Skyler Blunt was beginning to wonder if he hadn't made a mistake. He saw the man's eyes darting left and right, seeking cover or a way out. His vest-covered back was exposed to the lawmen behind him, but they held their fire lest they shoot through the perpetrator and kill their brother in uniform. *Move to our left,* Paul thought to Amy, *then no one will be behind him when we finally get a shot off.* She nodded and took a few steps.

Round in the chamber? she thought to Kowalski. *Wave your hand if yes.* Slowly the officer spread the fingers on his left hand and waggled them. To Paul she thought, *Damn. That means Blunt has a live weapon. Damn!*

"This doesn't have to end bad," she offered. "The guard you killed was private sector, not law enforcement. And I don't think you pushed Mackenzie. You're going to do time, but it won't be forever." She stared at him, then added, "But if you shoot Kowalski you'll end up on a gurney in Angola with a priest holding your hand."

In the midst of this, the Romanian animal trainer slowly walked from the half-erected animal tent, with its tiger and zebras and kangaroo, toward Spike. Nicolae was in his late sixties, his hair a light gray over his weather-beaten complexion. He walked with an air of dignity, limping slightly; he was holding a yellow plastic bucket full of water mixed with baking soda. He ignored the standoff between Amy and Blunt, and seemed not to see the clot of Nashville undercover agents with drawn guns. When he reached the panting, whimpering Rottweiler, he dropped to his knees and began whispering in the animal's ear. He pulled a saturated cloth out of the bucket and slowly wiped the dog's face, talking and cooing non-stop. Spike gradually calmed down, seemingly grateful for the attention of the old man.

"Nu la spre un cîine," Nicolae muttered, refreshing the cloth and rubbing more firmly; it meant 'not even to a dog.' *"Ei cred că sunt animale"*–'And they think you are the animal.' The armed confrontation was unimportant to him; only the suffering animal mattered.

"I'll shoot him! Don't think I won't!" Blunt shouted. "And it'll be your fault!"

She shook her head, still aiming her pistol at him. "No. If you pull the trigger, it'll be your fault. But I'll take all the credit for shooting you a second later."

There was movement in the corner of her eye, so she risked a quick glance to the left. Still a distance away, Darius and Beau Sonier were walking toward the face-off. She poked her comm unit button and said, "Secondary targets approaching, someone get them."

Amy and Blunt stared at each other for a long time. She heard Paul think, *I want to pound that motherfucker into dust.*

"What's it going to be, Skyler?" she called. "You can die here. Or you can take your chances with a jury. Pick one."

"You'll never find the jewels," he taunted.

Amy laughed, but kept both hands on her gun. "So what? They're insured. And they won't do you any good in a coffin. Come on, big guy. Live or die? Which is it?"

One of the plainclothesmen, ten or twelve feet behind Blunt, coughed. Suddenly Sergeant Young's voice was in her ear, saying, "MacPherson did that to pressure your perp. Let him know it's not just you he's dealing with."

"If I put down the gun, you won't shoot me anyway?"

A smile spread across her face. "I might. But if you shoot my officer, I definitely will." She adjusted her shooting stance to add some urgency to her words.

They stared at each other for a long moment. Amy was worried for Kowalski, but she was not afraid of Blunt. He had tried to kill her in the quicksand swamp and failed, and the battle adrenalin working on her now filled her with confidence that he could not harm her. "This is getting old," she said. "Don't you have to pee? Standing here in the sun all this time, isn't your bladder about to burst?" She heard Paul laughing inside. "You don't want to wet your pants in front of all these people. Put down the gun, let my officer go, and you can take a leak."

The staring continued. Behind her, two of Captain Squires' men quietly took the Sonier brothers into custody.

She shrugged. "As long as we're out here enjoying this lovely day, tell me about Bradley Richardson."

Blunt laughed heartily. "That pompous fagacite. It was all his idea, you know."

"How so?"

"He's got a gambling jones, and he's broke. He called me out of the blue with a plan for me to steal the jewelry so we could sell it."

She heard Paul think, *Him telling us this in front of all these people will make our lives easier,* and then he said out loud, "We know he's writing a huge check every month to some casino."

"That's it," Blunt snickered. "I heard they beat him up over it. I think he likes it. Fucking queen."

"Diaz," she called to a nearby plainclothesman. "Can you get me some water, please? I'm thirsty." Then she addressed Blunt again: "So how's that working out? My sources say you've made about five hundred dollars so far." She shook her head. "Just the pieces you pawned were probably worth fifty thousand. Huh! Not much rate of return. You'd do better with an honest job. Oh, Diaz, would you unscrew the cap? Thanks!" She took the water bottle in her left hand, still holding a bead on Blunt with the pistol in her right hand. "Oh, that's good!" she enthused. She took another long drink. "Want some, Skyler? Here–" and she tossed the open bottle halfway to him. It lay on its side, contents draining onto the paved section of the infield pit. "Awww," she said, in mock sorrow.

Paul thought, *You're having fun winding him up, aren't you?*

Her smile got broader. *You mean it shows?*

Her adversary laughed, "We got a lot more than that. Some pawnshops are more, uh, cooperative than others."

"Anything else I should know about your brother-in-law?"

"Put down your gun. All of you!"

Another smile. "I guess I'll have to ask him myself. Look, Skyler, this is not a negotiation. Put down your weapon, or die here. There are ten men with guns trained on you. And I think the one with the sniper rifle, his trigger finger is getting kind of itchy. If you know what I mean."

She heard Paul think, *Did I miss something at the station house? What sniper?*

Smiling, she though back, *The only sniper is the one Blunt now thinks is aiming at him.*

Still holding Kowalski, Blunt slowly raised his right hand, in a tan cotton glove. Everyone could see him rotate the gun until he was holding the barrel. He crouched, and reached forward, and laid the weapon down.

Kowalski elbowed Blunt to make him release his grip, then ducked and rolled out of the way. Before Amy realized it, Paul took their pistol into their left hand, 'his' hand, and put three hollow point slugs in Blunt's chest.

"Paul!" she screamed out loud, "No!"

The detectives nearest to her ran to Amy; Diaz gently took the gun out of her left hand. Amy's anger at Paul was explosive; she used her right hand to slap her left hand, 'his' hand, again and again. She was crying. *How could you do that?* she yelled silently at him, *I hate you! I hate you!*

He tried to hug himself, but Amy had tightened all her muscles to keep him from controlling any part of their body. All he could do was think to her, *He has another–*

Shut up! she shouted silently, *Don't you talk to me! I hate you! You made me kill him!*

Listen to me, he has–

"No!" she moaned, out loud, and let herself drop to the ground, sitting cross-legged under her maxi-skirt, and leaning against Diaz's leg.

When the Rottweiler roused itself, the animal trainer Nicolae whispered in Gypsy to it. Spike stood up slowly and walked to its master. It sniffed at Skyler's still body, and whimpered, and settled down with its huge head resting on the man's shoulder. A long pink tongue licked the side of Blunt's face once. No, twice.

Diaz crouched by Amy and put his hand on her shoulder. "Be brave, Detective. It is always hard to take a life."

Some of the men clustered around Blunt and Spike. MacPherson put his fingers on the man's neck, then shook his head. "Ice wagon," he said into his comm unit. Unable to make herself move, Amy watched MacPherson pull the gloves off Blunt. As she expected, his left hand was missing the last part of its ring finger. When the plainclothesman stood up, a short, sawed-off piece of dowel fell from the glove. It registered on Paul that was the reason Blunt's finger looked strange on the museum surveillance video.

In his bright blue Captain's uniform with its gold trim, Captain Phillip Squires walked to where Amy sat. She had a close-up view of the mud on his shoes and the cuffs of his trousers, earned by patrolling the north section of the fairgrounds. "Get up, Detective," he said coldly. "And for God's sake, stop that fucking crying."

She took a deep breath. She wiped her sleeve across her face, then stood up.

"I've heard miserable things about New Orleans," he said, "but I didn't know it included shooting disarmed suspects."

Her voice was strained from the effort to keep Paul at bay. "I–I–I don't know what to say."

"Save it for a lawyer." He motioned to one of his plainclothesmen. "Detective, I am arresting you for the murder of What's-His-Face over there."

"With all due respect, Captain–"

"And you shut your fucking mouth," he hurled at Kowalski. "You're lucky to be alive, the way that–that–that *detective* was provoking your perp."

"She got him to lay down the weapon," the officer said. "Detective Clear saved my life today."

"And then she took the life of that scum. Permission denied, Officer. Get out of my face."

Kowalski put his arms around the handcuffed Amy. "Thank you, Detective. That was great work." Meanwhile, Amy continued to struggle against Paul's efforts to speak.

Don't freak out, Kowalski, the officer heard a man's voice in his head. *Ventriloquist. Blunt has another gun.*

He leaned back and stared at Amy, his face a question mark. "What?" she said; she could not hear when Paul thought to someone else.

"B-B-Blunt has another gun?" he asked slowly.

Her eyes got big as she replied, "He does? How do you know?"

Because I just told him, Paul thought to her. *He put down Kowalski's, but he still has yours.*

"Captain!" she shouted, but the retreating officer dismissed her with a wave of his arm. "MacPherson! See if he's got another gun." At that Squires changed direction, now heading for where Blunt lay.

The plainclothesman patted down Blunt's sides, careful to avoid Spike. Nothing. "'Scuse me, pup," he said, and started to turn the body by lifting at the shoulder and hip. Spike growled, but didn't move. "What's that?" one of the men asked.

Squires bent down and reached under Skyler Blunt's warm corpse, under the vest he had worn. When he stood up he was holding a blued nine-millimeter pistol in a leather 'small-of-the-back' holster. "I'll be fucked and fried," he muttered.

✆ 30 ☙

Freed from the handcuffs, Amy held her arm around the distraught Crystal Blunt. The woman wept non-stop, sometimes yielding to sobs. The dozen undercover men in the Econoline with them were subdued; the satisfaction of a successful stakeout was restrained in the face of the widow's grief. She thought to Paul, *How long before we get to the precinct and I can get the matron to take over? I'll never get that eye shadow out of this shirt.*

Am I forgiven?

She laughed inside but tried to retain a somber, compassionate face for the new widow. *You told me you'd only shoot him if it looked justifiable. I should have believed you.*

Kowalski, again sitting between her and the Captain, asked, "Okay, you're a world class ventriloquist. But how do you make your voice sound like a man's?"

"Don't know what to tell you, Pat. Just be glad that I can."

"So why didn't you tell me earlier about the other gun?"

She was leaning toward Crystal, patting her hand. It was Paul who said, from the corner of their mouth, "We did. At the station when we were looking at the satellite pictures of the fairgrounds. And then on our way here this morning."

He searched his memory. "So why didn't it register on me?"

Amy turned to him and answered, "It didn't register on me, either."

Her words were puzzling, but the officer was euphoric over being alive, at having survived being held hostage by an armed murderer, and his mind raced on. "Next time, say you really mean it or something."

"Sure thing, Pat. Next time I'll do that."

When everyone alit from the Econoline, two matrons were waiting to look after Crystal Blunt. Amy pulled one aside and said, "When you can, ask her if she knows anything about the jewels he stole. Or if he ever said anything about killing anyone."

The matrons led Crystal Blunt away, much to Amy's relief. "I'm going to call the commander." Kowalski stood by her.

"Yes, Commander Ramirez," she said into her phone. "Success. Tell the mayor you've closed the museum murders, and half the theft." Pat watched her listening to a response. "No, sir. Perpetrator is dead. Yes–yes, he put up a struggle. He took Kowalski hostage. No, he's fine. Do you want to talk to him?" Amy looked up at him as she heard her commander's response. "Yes, sir, I'll tell him. I'm sure he'll–yes sir, he'll be glad to hear that. Commander, the perp implicated the museum director in the theft, and I expect to hear more in a few minutes when we talk to the perp's fences. Can you order an arrest warrant for Bradley Richardson? Theft and conspiracy. Great, we can pick him up during the week–he's in a bed at Ochsner Baptist. And Commander? Okay, Johnny. The thing is, uh, thanks. The captain here is brilliant, but he's a jerk. You've been an Amy booster since I was eleven. Thanks, okay?" A big smile. "Yes, sir. Monday. Bright and early."

"What did he say?" the officer asked.

She folded her phone and returned it to the case under her skirt. "He said he owes you two weekends' furlough." Amy tried to control her smile as she added, "And he said something I didn't understand, something about talking to you about a stripe when we get back." In fact, she understood exactly what it meant, but she added innocently, "What's that all about?"

"Fuck a duck!" His mouth fell open, and his eyes popped wide. "A stripe! That's–" and it began to sink in on him: a promotion, a pay raise, maybe better control over what shifts he worked. He stared at her, then suddenly put his arms around her and lifted her into the air. "I don't believe it! He really said that? That's fucking awesome!" He did a little dance while Amy laughed at his excitement.

"We were afraid we'd lose our job," Paul said. Immediately Amy tacked on, "I mean, I was. Commander Ramirez told me to call him by his first name, so I guess I'm still employed."

"And not under arrest," the officer said. He wound down his dance and set Amy back onto her feet. "Detective, it's been a pleasure."

"The best part was you not getting hurt," she said. When Paul sensed she was thinking about kissing him, he shouted at her, *Look! A squirrel! Don't do it, please?* Even so, she leaned to the officer and planted one on his cheek.

"Diaz said they'd have the Soniers ready for us," she said, changing the subject. Walking into the building again, she said, "I want any testimony and evidence they have about Blunt. And I hope for Bella's sake they don't know anything about the murders."

"We'll never know if he pushed that model," he observed.

"Doesn't matter. A death in the commission of a felony is murder. You know, I'm kind of sorry Blunt's dead. I'd have enjoyed getting his butt convicted. But Ramirez said the mayor will be glad we saved the parish the cost of a trial."

Sergeant Young was waiting in the hall by two interview rooms, their doors closed. Amy volunteered, "You did a great job as comm point man. Thank you for your help." For the first time Kowalski noted that her professional praise seemed to matter to other officers, too. "You're very kind," Young said, looking at his feet. Then, "Uh, which one you want first?"

"I'll take Darius. Pat, you want Beau?" She thought to him, so Young couldn't hear, *I don't care about them fencing the jewels. Only if they knew about the murders.*

Amy found Darius Sonier in a wooden chair, at a large rectangular table. The interview room was a neutral gray, brightly lit with overhead fluorescents. Bella Blunt's lover was not under arrest and was not handcuffed or shackled to his seat, but he was sitting calmly, waiting for whatever would happen next. He was a broad-chested man, wearing a gray, two-pocket work shirt. At the ripe old age of thirty-four, Darius was the brother with the mullet–slightly receding, but plenty of healthy black hair on top, and hanging down to his shoulders. Suddenly nervous, he played with his work gloves that were on the table.

"Hello, Darius," she offered as she sat at the other side of the table. "My name is Detective Amy Clear. I know Bella, and I'm glad to meet you."

"How you know ma Bella?" he asked in a thick Cajun accent.

"I interviewed her a couple of times after the museum theft. I understand you and Beau were associates of Skyler Blunt. My only interest today is in wrapping up the state of Louisiana's case against Skyler. I have heard that you and Beau sometimes fenced things like auto parts, but that's not why I'm talking to you today. You get me?"

"Tell me the truth?" he asked, unbelieving.

She nodded, eyes closed, hands holding her temples. "Yes, Darius. Today I want to know about Blunt. Did he give you things to sell while the circus was traveling?"

"Ya, he do that for sure. First, he make me and Beau take a gun. Beau say 'non,' but Skyler, he say he take Bella back, so we take it."

She heard Paul think, *Ah! The gun he shot the guard with.* Amy asked, "Did he say how he got that gun?"

Darius laughed, a charming look on his broad mouth, with many a white tooth visible. "You do this, you sell stuff for people, you don't ask how it came to them. Don't you know nothing?"

"I know more now," she smiled back. "What happened to it?"

He seemed to replay some memories. "Springfield. Beau sold it to one of the carny ride men. We get two hundred fifty dollars. Beau, he tell Sky we get two hundred."

"Do you know what that man did with it?" His only answer was a shrug.

"What about jewelry? Did you sell any gems for Blunt?"

"We don't know how they come to him, but Skyler, he FedEx petit gems to us, he knows where we be at. Beau and me, we sell pretty green things, and some rubies."

"What about the money, Darius?"

"Beau, he one smart fella, you know? He get twenty percent cut from Skyler. When he an the missus come to Dayton, Beau give him his share. Sky brung more, too."

"Really? Skyler and Crystal, they stayed with you and your brother?"

"Yah. Lots of circus folk, we stay by a boarding house. They take a room there."

"You think the rest of his, uh, stuff is there?"

Another shrug. "You ask him."

It took Amy aback. Paul said, "It's a little late for that."

The man's jaw dropped, and he crossed himself. "Non! *Defan* Skyler. Tch, his missus, that a shame."

"Darius, did Skyler ever talk to you about a theft he did at the NOLA art museum?"

Shaking his head, the brother said, "Non, but I guessed. It's like I say, you don't ask. He got bunch of jewelry, yah?"

"Anything else?"

"I hear him laugh to Beau about some in-law he got, he don't like. I didn't hear the story, though."

Amy stood up. "Thanks for your cooperation, Darius. You've been a big help. As far as New Orleans is concerned, you're free to go. But I can't speak for the Nashville officers. Someone will be in for you in a little while, okay?"

The look of disbelief returned to his face. "For true? You tell me the truth?"

She nodded. "When you talk to Bella, say hello for me," and she left the room.

Kowalski was in the hallway, waiting on her. "Get anything interesting?" he asked.

"I learned that a fence doesn't ask questions about what he's given to sell. How about you?"

"Nothing unexpected," he glanced at his notes, "but when I told him Blunt was dead he said he was sorry and glad. Seems Blunt had been getting less, uh, reality based in the last year or so. He'd call at three in the morning; he'd demand they take loot that was outside their usual contacts. He turned into a bit of an asshole."

"Did he know about the murders?"

"He said no. But Blunt told him that Richardson was the reason for the theft."

"Our sources agree. I'm glad I asked Ramirez for the arrest warrant; we'll be visiting the good doctor again when we get home." She thought to Paul, *Good guess. You were the one who suggested insurance fraud.*

They were silent for a moment, until Paul said aloud, "I hope Crystal and Holly still get along. They're both losing husbands; maybe they'll end up living together."

They walked up the hallway, trying to remember where Sergeant Young's office was. "We need to say thank you to Squires," Kowalski said. "You may hate his guts, but it's still something we have to do. Etiquette."

Amy kept turning her head as they walked, looking for Sergeant Young's name plate next to a door. "I want Diaz or MacPherson to come with us in the morning to the boarding house. It would be nice to salvage some of the Rothschild jewels."

She heard Paul think, *I guess Wonder Warthog struck again.*

"What?" out loud; then silently, *Oh, him again. I guess so. What did people call him? Wonder? Mister Hog?*

Aloud, Paul answered, "The hog of steel."

"Give it a rest, detective," Kowalski laughed. "We'll go back to the hotel and you can have a whole Chautauqua with yourself."

"You're a pretty good sport, Kowalski. I like that in a flatfoot."

"Sure thing, shamus."

✄ 31 ✄

Officer MacPherson drove the squad car to the boarding house where so many of the circus folk stayed, and where it was hoped the late Skyler Blunt had secreted the bulk of the Rothschild jewels that he had stolen from the Orleans Parish Art Museum.

The place on Bransford Avenue near the fairgrounds was a rural relic that had been overgrown by urban sprawl. In an area of one-third-acre lots, Ma Hull's Rooming House sat on an oddly-shaped five acres. The guest house was a sprawling, single-story building that showed many additions in different architectural styles and paint colors. Also on the property was a modest, rustic house where Ma and Pa stayed to get away from the nagging of transient lodgers, and for Pa to putter in his primitive workshop. Visitors parked their cars or RVs on the east pasture that last saw a cow flop around 1979, and last saw a blade of grass shortly thereafter. To Amy it looked like the kind of leftover establishment that deserved historical monument status. "It's so out of place, I like it," she said to the sergeant as he parked on the street.

"With all due respect, Detective," he said, "you don't live around here. It might look cool in Franklin or Lebanon, but here in Nashville it's just an eyesore." He flashed a smile to show his opinion wasn't meant to be personal. "We're trying to class up the town. Twenty-first century and all, you know?"

They stood outside the car for a moment, each rearranging their gear. Only Kowalski had the advantage of wearing a uniform, with exposed weapons. MacPherson was wearing the same oversize jacket from the day before, all the better to hide the sidearm in his shoulder rig. Amy slid one of her thigh holsters to move her pistol butt away from a patch that hadn't yet recovered from her adventure in bayou quicksand. She gave it a final, unladylike scratch, and let her dirty blue skirt fall back in place.

The front door opened onto a large parlor, with worn burgundy carpet, wood paneled walls, and thick, old draperies that probably matched the carpet at one time. Two women were sitting in a swaybacked sofa, talking quietly. Behind a folding card table sat Ma Hull herself, in a flowered dress of yellow and red. Her sunken cheeks indicated she hadn't installed her false teeth yet, but it was barely nine-fifteen.

"Your jurisdiction, Mac," Amy said, holding her arm out for MacPherson to walk ahead. The plainclothesman said, "Good morning, Ma. It's been a few weeks since I made it to Sunday supper. You doing okay? Is Pa feeling any better?"

"Angus MacPherson, as I live and breathe," she said, with a somewhat frightening, toothless smile. "The mister is doing better, bless your heart for asking. You know, this Sunday I was going to whip up a batch of those boiled garlic potatoes you like so much."

"Wouldn't miss it for the world, Ma, you write my name down in ink." The woman reached across the card table and pinched the detective's cheek.

"Look, Ma, Sunday will be for fun, but today I'm here for work. This is Detective Clear and Officer Kowalski. They're here all the way from New Orleans. We need –"

He was interrupted by a shout from one of the women on the sofa. "Amy!" cried Crystal Blunt. "I didn't expect you so early." When the woman sitting with her turned to face them, they saw she was the bearded lady from the circus sideshow. Crystal stood up; without makeup, the big bruise on the side of her face was a ghastly yellowish green. Amy and Kowalski came to her couch, while MacPherson explained to his friend Ma Hull why the New Orleans police were there.

Crystal hugged Amy uncomfortably, still weeping. Finally she straightened, and taking Amy by the hand, said, "This is Madame Orloff. She let me stay with her last night. I just couldn't bear to be by myself after–after–well, you know." Madame took Crystal's other hand and petted it. With a thick southern accent the woman said, "It's going to be alright, Honey." Turning her gaze to Amy, she added, "Hey, Honey! You can call me Orly." Amy thought the voice clashed with the gypsy clothing, and she thought as much to Paul. He returned, *Just a costume, like the other sideshow people are wearing. I have to say, the beard looks real to me.*

Amy and Pat dragged wing chairs closer to the couch, then sat and let the women talk about Crystal's grief and Madame Orloff's ministrations–including, as it turned out, a bottle of 190 proof Everclear. When Amy felt she had been as solicitous as the situation required, she asked the widow, "When Skyler and you came here, did he bring any unusual luggage?"

The sad woman frowned. "You mean the jewels, don't you?" It wasn't so much a question as an indication of defeat. "Yeah, he brought them. They're in our room."

She coaxed Paul into handling the next step. "We're sorry to intrude on your loss," he said, "but the jewels are part of a criminal case. We have to insist that you turn them over to us."

She nodded sadly–everything she did was sadly, even breathing and blinking–and said, "Madame, would you come with me? I'm afraid to go in there alone again."

"Why, sure enough," the bearded lady said and stood up. While she waited for Crystal to work up the will to get up from the sagging sofa, Orly stroked her moustache and beard, grooming them with her fingers.

At the door to the room she had shared with her husband, Crystal Blunt stopped. Chin quivering and hands shaking, she turned the knob and pushed it open. Her weeping resumed.

"No haints," the Madame said, and stepped past the widow and entered the room. She pulled open the drapes on the two windows, exposing the gloom to the sanitizing power of sunlight. "I'll help you pack, Crystal. You'll never have to come in here again. Where's your valise?"

Amy put her hand on Crystal's shoulder and ushered the woman into the room. "We'd like to secure the contraband," Paul said. Immediately he thought to Amy, *I've always wanted to say that.*

"Yeah. Okay." Crystal opened the closet and pointed to a gym bag on the floor. Kowalski leaned in to pick it up. "Uh-oh," he said, carrying it into the room, "It doesn't weigh much."

"The museum info sheet said there were eight thousand karats of gems in the Rothschild jewels," Amy dredged from memory, "plus gold and platinum and silver settings. What is that in American? Six pounds, maybe?"

"Can we see?" asked Madame Orloff.

Kowalski dropped the poke in the middle of the carpet in a pool of sunlight, and everyone sat on the floor around it. He unzipped the bag and slowly overturned it.

A flashing rainbow of diamonds, rubies, emeralds, sapphires, and pearls spilled to the carpet. Pieces of metal settings were attached to some of them, and a few larger sections of the original tiaras or necklaces plopped out. The range of colors, with the sunbeams bouncing through the facets, was spectacular. Madame Orloff let out a low, sustained, "Wow," and even MacPherson's eyes popped at the sight.

For a minute everyone stared at what looked like the riches of the Orient, the wealth of Ali Baba. "This is like in a fairy tale," Paul whispered. "Hassan like!" Kowalski, then Crystal, and finally everyone reached in to examine stones, to hold them up to the light, to rest them on the backs of fingers to imagine them in personal jewelry. Even Crystal Blunt was smiling.

Madame Orloff timidly asked, "What's going to happen to these?"

"They belong to the Rothschild family," Amy replied, "so they go back to France." The officer added, "The insurance company will be thrilled. The original jewelry is destroyed, but at least the gems are back."

Paul thought to Amy, *Everyone here is either poor or living on a cop's salary. I'm thinking the next question we hear is–*

"Can we keep some? Souvenirs?" Madame Orloff voiced the question Paul had anticipated. Everyone turned to Amy.

She closed her eyes and took a deep breath. "No," she said. "We can play with them for a minute, but they come back to New Orleans with Officer Kowalski and myself."

Orly took out her cell phone and handed it to Crystal. "Take my picture!" she said, She lay prone, with her arms encircling the pile of gems and her hirsute chin resting in their midst. "My father will roll on the floor when he sees this."

When the smiling widow gave the phone back, Amy said, "Fun

time is over. Let's make sure we get everything back in the bag."
She was surprised when Paul took the lead to add, "Taking even one
of these puppies would be a screaming felony. Make sure you didn't
get one stuck in your shoes or anything." When he finished she
thought to him, *Thanks. You are an awesome bad cop, you know
that?*

Not so bad that I'd take one. A pause. *Actually, I might have
when I had my own body.* Another pause. *It's just as well you didn't
know me back in the day.*

"Madame Orloff," she said, "that looks like an emerald in your
beard. It's a charming look, but–" she pointed "–into the bag." The
woman appeared embarrassed as she combed her beard with her
fingers, loosening the emerald and then a small ruby. "I am so
sorry," she said, and Amy chose to believe her.

MacPherson got to his knees and walked that way to Amy. He
spoke in her ear to keep his words private. "This is not the way we
collect evidence up here." He sat back on his haunches.

"Skyler Blunt is dead, after confessing in front of a lot of
people. This isn't evidence, it's stolen property that has to be
returned to the rightful owner."

"An inventory?" he asked, embarrassed to be criticizing her in
public.

"You're probably right," she said. "Pat, when we get back to
the hotel, should we process this like evidence?"

"Hell no!" he said, surprised. "This goes straight to the safe."

She turned back to the Nashville detective. "Like I say, you're
probably right. I've been consulting for the police in New Orleans
for five years, but believe it or not, this is the very first case I've
handled since I was sworn in." She saw MacPherson try to hide a
look of surprise. "My commander talked me into it." He blinked.
"It's complicated," she finished.

When Amy stood up, a small diamond and a small emerald
were revealed where her feet had been. "See what I mean?" she
addressed the group. Carefully she picked the gems up and dropped
them into the bag, and she waited until everyone else was standing.
There were no more outlying jewels.

Amy moved to Crystal and put her hand on the new widow's
arm. "I'm glad you were ready to escape the abuse, but I am so

sorry that it turned out like this." Crystal Blunt smiled weakly and nodded, then leaned forward and gave Amy a quick hug. "Yeah," is all she said.

"Pat, let's get out of the way so Orly can help Crystal pack. MacPherson?" Kowalski picked up the gym bag with its millions of dollars' worth of cut stones, and the Nashville plainclothesman led them out of the room.

For both legs of their flight back to New Orleans, the gym bag sat in Amy's lap, at least one arm through the handles. They picked up the checked bags with their weapons from the carousel at Armstrong International, then drove back to the station in Amy's fleet loaner. It was a surprised Sergeant Robicheaux who was roused from a nap—no, "Just resting my eyes a minute, Officer. Detective. What can I do for you?"

"I've got something for the evidence locker," Amy smiled.

Robicheaux pulled a form off a stack and slipped it onto a clipboard. "What you got, hey?"

She unzipped the bag.

The sergeant's face blanched, and his mouth fell open to display nicotine-stained teeth. He finally was able to say, "These things ain't real, are they?"

Paul snickered and said, "We'll find out for sure on Monday, but, yeah. They're real. Is there room in the safe, or should we take them home with us for the weekend?"

"Safe? Uh–I make room in the safe, I guarantee."

"Detective, maybe we should count them first."

"You're welcome to, Officer, but I am going home. If I don't change clothes my skin will walk off without me."

Pat said, "You heard the boss." Robicheaux wrote "whole bunch of jewels and such" on the evidence voucher and retreated into his evidence room to put the bag into the safe, beyond harm, if not his own temptation.

As they walked to the parking area, Amy mused, "What if Blunt swapped the jewels? What if ours are fake and the real ones are–where? On his property in Lafitte?"

Paul thought to Amy, *Damn you, Wonder Warthog!* She did not laugh.

Kowalski answered, "Like you said, we'll find out Monday. I

hear Jermaine is no slouch with gem identification."

Paul thought to Amy, *Can we go? I want to call Christine, tell her all about it.* When she smiled, Kowalski said, "You're doing it again!" Amy smiled even wider and nodded, "A-yup."

"Enjoy tomorrow off; we've earned it. See you Monday."

"You too, Pat." Amy walked off to her loaner and let Paul lead to drive home.

In the car they had the privacy to talk out loud to each other. Paul asked again, "Am I forgiven?"

"Yes. I forgive you for shooting Blunt. He was trying to sucker us and he'd have done a lot of damage. Including to me. Ugh."

"Let's hang out with Christine tomorrow. It'll be fun to tell her what happened in Nashville."

"Laundry first." She thought a moment and said, "Ramirez is going to suspend me on Monday."

"Why? We're heroes." He made a right turn on Magazine.

"It's standard. Any police shooting, you get desk duty or you're suspended with pay until the Public Integrity Unit clears you."

"Sounds like a reward to me. Extra vacation time."

They drove in silence for a few blocks, until Amy asked, "Did you have a good time?"

Paul laughed. "The best! The circus was fun, you were totally awesome dealing with Blunt, no good guys got hurt, and I got to kill Blunt. Yeah, I'd say I had a good time."

"I didn't," Amy said. There was a long pause before she went on, "It was satisfying to finish the job. Getting yelled at by Squires was painful–he never did apologize, he just said I wasn't under arrest anymore."

"I know there's more. What?"

"I got shot. I fell off a cliff. I had my head bashed in, maybe got raped, and damn near turned into gator kibble. And then the standoff with Blunt. I wasn't scared, I was sure I would take him, but I can't say it was fun. It was more like a root canal–you know you need to do it, but it's not something you enjoy."

Paul parked near the front of their house. The sky already was violet and the street lights shone on empty sidewalks. Amy took the lead. She locked up the car, then wheeled her suitcase to the door. Once they were inside, she threw the new deadbolt Paul had installed and dropped onto her sofa. "I never want to leave here again."

"Can we still use the bathroom?" Paul asked. She nodded and smiled.

"I don't want to be a cop," she said out loud. "It's too much work. It's not a good fit for my sense of humor. And Christine's right, it's dangerous."

Paul patted their right hand, 'Amy's' hand, with their left. "You know I hate cops. I'm scared of them. But what's next?"

"The problem-solving part is okay," she mused. "I don't know." She sat awhile. "I just don't know."

She got up and walked to the kitchen to pour themself a glass of wine. "Not too old," she said, mouth puckered from the oxidized taste. She drained it and refilled the glass, saying, "Your turn." Paul led for his share of serviceable, if outdated, alcohol.

"How's this?" Paul asked. "Clear, Hodges, and Owens, Private Investigators." Her silence told him she was not taken with the suggestion. But before he could offer another idea, to become groupies for SpongeBob SquarePants, Amy said, "That is brilliant. Do you think Christine would go for it?"

"I'll ask her."

"Ooh, and I love your name in the title. We can come up with all these great stories to explain why you're never there to meet clients."

Laughing, he took their phone from the case under their dirty blue skirt and pressed the button for his lover's number.

❦ Afterword ❧

James Mayer de Rothschild (Jakob Mayer Rothschild) was one of the five sons of Mayer Amschel Rothschild. His father tasked James Mayer with creating the French branch of the Rothschild banking empire. He did so in 1817, becoming an important financier of the French ruling monarchs.

In the year 1826 King Louis XVIII refused to allow at court James Mayer de Rothschild's wife, Betty Salmon, because the woman was Jewish. In response, Rothschild ceased to do any business with the Bourbons. When Louis-Philippe brought the House of Orleans to the throne in 1830, Rothschild rescued the nation with a series of loans and other financial arrangements.

However, the "Rothschild jewels" featured in this novel are imaginary.

Coming soon from Amy and Paul:
The Strawberry Birthmark!

She could hear Ryan washing up behind the closed bathroom door. Amy lay on his king-size bed, naked, but with the sheet pulled up to her chin. "What are the possibilities?" she whispered. "He's Ryan. Or he's Jeffrey. Yow."

Paul thought to her, *If he's Ryan, great— no change, you've got a great boyfriend, have a good time.*

"And?"

He sighed and whispered, "If he turns out to be Jeffrey, you've still got a great boyfriend. You still can have a good time."

Amy pumped her legs under the covers. "If he's Jeffrey, my bedmate might be a killer."

"Wouldn't be the first time. But—" he turned it over in his mind "—maybe he just took advantage of a peculiar situation. Maybe he found his brother dead and for whatever reason decided exchanging identities would be a good thing."

"What? What's a good thing?" Ryan turned the bathroom light out as he walked into the bedroom, a towel around his midsection. He was smiling. Then, "Are you cold?"

"What?" She looked down and realized she was shaking under the drawn sheet. "Oh. I guess so." She snaked her right arm out from under the covers and patted his side of the mattress. "Come to bed, big boy."

"Let me get the lights."

"No," and she leaned over to snatch the towel away. "I want to see every bit of the glorious you." She heard Paul think, *No birthmark.*

Laughing, he fell on the bed and moved against her. Despite herself, Amy smiled and opened her arms for the man–whatever his name was.

During a lull she had a chance to look carefully at the man. Well muscled, with just the tiniest bit of belly fat; a small five-pointed star tattoo on the back of his left shoulder; and a long, thin purple scar on the left side of his abdomen. A shiver of excitement ran through her, a sense of danger that did not frighten her.

"What happened?" she asked, pointing at the scar.

"Appendix. Turned out I didn't need it." He poked at the side of her right thigh, just above the knee. "What about you?"

"Souvenir from a murder suspect." She leapt on top of him, rubbing his chest. "And you know what? He wasn't even the killer."

He laughed and kissed her. "What did the real killer do to you?"

"He tried to do a lot, but Paul and I shot him dead."

He stopped caressing her. Slackjawed, he was looking up at her.

"He was trying to kill me," she offered, apologetically.

Ryan struggled to sit up, pushing Amy to the side. "It's a little weird," he said, "knowing that you killed someone."

"I guess this isn't a good time to tell you I killed more than one person as a police detective."

"Really?" He stared at her. "How do you sleep?"

She teased, "On a good night with you I don't." But she saw he was stuck in a serious frame of mind. "I'm not a murderer," she began. "What I did was with the force of law. And they were trying to kill me." His expression didn't change. "And every time it happened I went on leave and did some soul searching. I don't know about you, but killing a person is not something I ever did lightly. Or for a personal motive."

He reached out and embraced her. "Please," he said, "forgive my curiosity. My morbid curiosity."

Amy felt reassured in his hug. "So what's it like for you? Did you ever kill anyone?" She heard Paul think, *An honest answer would be nice.*

She felt him shake his head, but he said nothing. Breaking his embrace, she said brightly, "I've got an idea. Let's be happy." She looked around. "There's all this skin, and I don't see anyone but you and me–"

He got the hint.

Later, before exhaustion engulfed a happy and tired Amy, Paul thought to her, *It doesn't bother you that Ryan is really Jeffrey?*

We don't know that. But—No, I guess not. He's still a fun guy. She yawned. *And he likes me.*

Tomorrow, let's call Walter to find out more about Jeffrey's suicide.

Umm... Sure...

Amy? Sleep had claimed her; there was no response. Paul turned their head and was looking at the man's unconscious face. *At least he's smiling,* he thought to himself. *As long as he's good to Amy and can tolerate me, it's okay.* But part of him felt it wasn't okay at all. If only to protect his dyad, the owner of the body he inhabited, Paul felt he had to know for sure who this man was. It was awhile before he joined Amy in sleep.

They were hurried in the morning; the appointment at the lawyer's office in the Central Business District was nine o'clock. Amy hugged Lucas and wished him luck, then kissed Ryan. "I've got stuff to do today. Can I come out tomorrow?"

"Right. Paul's girlfriend. I'll call and let you know how things go with the lawyer. Tomorrow we can all go to dinner."

Amy rubbed his smooth, shaved face, and kissed him again. Then, "It's Paul. Don't let the lawyer cheat you."

They sat in Amy's old yellow Benz and watched Ryan and Lucas drive off for their appointment. "Call Walter," Paul said aloud.

"No. I don't care if he's Jeffrey."

Her reply was so unexpected that he stammered, "Wh—wh—what?"

"I like him. He likes me. I don't feel like I'm in danger. I don't care what his birth certificate says."

"There's a part of me that likes to know things. Like people's names. It makes me feel more in control. Please, can we check out the guy for my sake?"

Amy started the car—she had gotten used to the glow plug ritual the diesel engine required— "Is this your new way of trying to make me stop sleeping with a man?"

Cold! he thought back. *No, I just close my inside eyes and think of Christine, I'm good. I wish he'd shave at night, though.*

A smile. "Agreed. But now I have that fresh-faced, red-cheek look."

"Sergeant Francks?"

"Umm, I'm thinking Doc Jermaine."

She waited until she was home before she called her old NOPD station house and asked for Doctor Tallant. "I need some information," she told him.

"My goodness, Miss Clear. This is an unexpected pleasure. What can I do for you?"

Amy gave him the date of Jeffrey's suicide from the newspaper article she had found online. "Was there an autopsy?"

"Let me look," he said as he opened the search box on the police database on his computer. He repeated the date from 2027 as he keyed it in. "What's the name again?"

"Doublet. Spelled like double t."

She heard his snicker. "I know how New Orleans names work, Miss. Let me—Ah, yes. Looks like the autopsy was done by a fraud and a charlatan named Jermaine Tallant."

"Oh, I hear he's pretty good," she teased. "Photos?"

"My God, Miss Clear, have you taken up some new and disturbing hobby?"

"No, sir. Just the same old and disturbing hobby, looking for criminals." The medical examiner had no way of knowing it was Paul who spoke. "Can I stop by and get some copies? Maybe look at the report?"

"Hmm. If you were to sit at my office computer, I could probably spend a few minutes looking out the window. We have rules about using Police resources, but if nobody notices—well, then it didn't happen, did it?"

Amy smiled. "What can I bring you?" she asked. "A beignet? Muffuletta? Cheap stogie?" Jermaine had been her favorite colleague at NOPD: intelligent, desiccated sense of humor, eager to teach receptive ears, and full of courtly respect.

"I'm running low on eye of newt," he said. "See if Rouse has gotten any in lately."